The Day of Small Things

O. Douglas

Must Have Books
503 Deerfield Place
Victoria, BC
V9B 6G5
Canada

ISBN 9781773239897

Copyright 2023 – Must Have Books

Who hath despised the day of small things?

ZECHARIAH, iv. 10.

TO ALICE
WITH LOVE

Chapter I

Every neighbourhood should have a Great Lady.'

JANE AUSTEN.

Mrs. Heggie had a cold which, she felt, might easily go into bronchitis if she were not careful, and the day was wet, one of those dripping October days when it is really too close for a fire, but miserably cheerless without one, a day when polished furniture looks smeared, and everything feels sticky to the touch.

Mrs. Heggie stood in the window of the drawing-room in Knebworth, Kirkmeikle, and looked out at fallen leaves on which the steady rain pattered, at the red tiles of the houses clinging to the brae face beneath her, at the grey sea with the grey sky resting on it.

Surely, she thought, it was a very long afternoon; only half-past three now, and it seemed half a day since luncheon.

A pile of books lay on a table and she took up one which had an attractive paper cover, but after reading half a dozen pages without getting an inkling what the story was about she gave it up in despair, and wondering ruefully why every one nowadays was so clever, she lifted a newly launched illustrated magazine for women. After looking through the recipes, she began a story with a promising title, but before she could get interested in it she had lost it, and it was too much trouble to track the rest of it to its hiding-place among advertisements of tinned fruits, the latest electric cleaners, and cures for all ills that flesh is heir to--*Epilepsy and its Treatment*; *My Life was made a Burden with Superfluous Hair*; *Healthy Legs for All.*

Answers to correspondents on the subject of health next caught her eye, and she read several. Some were interesting: the delicate child with the cough (how stupid not to advise the mother to give it cod-liver oil, *not* emulsion but the old-fashioned pure oil!): the lady of thirty-two whose circulation was so bad that her fingers went dead; and the husband afflicted with nightmares. Odd to write to a paper about one's ailments!... This woman sounded rather like herself: inclined to be stout; sixty years of age; acidity; throbbing in the head.... What did they say to the poor body? *Advised to seek at once the advice of a qualified medical man.*

Mrs. Heggie moved uneasily in her chair. She was not sure that she felt quite well. Certainly she did have some odd sensations at times, especially if she had eaten unwisely. Pork, for instance.... Of course, a little indigestion was nothing: but *was* it indigestion? 'A qualified medical man.' In her case that was Dr. Kilgour. She wished he was not so terribly bracing. He would come in like a blast of east wind, and before she knew where she was, blow her off to a Nursing Home for an operation.

Well----. Mrs. Heggie braced herself up. It was best to face the worst. Almost every one sooner or later had an operation. And wasn't there a Nursing Home just started in Langtoun? Somebody had spoken of it--yes, Mrs. Stark. She had said in her definite way, 'My dear, I *enjoyed* my illness. I simply wouldn't have dared to be ill in my own house--I can see the faces of my domestics!--but in this Home I was made to feel important; a victor. It's a doctor's widow that runs it--a Mrs. Pirrie, and she is both kind and capable; superintends everything herself. The cooking and service leave nothing to be desired. A perfect bed, good home-made food, a fresh rose on your breakfast-tray--what more could you ask? Oh, I assure you, I stayed on much longer than was necessary simply because I was happy.'

It had certainly sounded attractive as described by Mrs. Stark. Convalescence in the Langtoun Home (supposing you were spared to convalescence) might be rather pleasant. Friends coming in with flowers and gossip, nurses always about, nice chats with the doctor's widow. Certainly much more lively than sitting alone in Knebworth with a cold!... If only some one would come to call, but she could think of no one who was likely to pay her a visit. Joan was locked into her room writing poetry. Not that Joan was much use as a conversationalist; she scorned to talk of people, and her mother cared to talk of nothing else. It was unfortunate, Mrs. Heggie couldn't help thinking, that Joan was so circumscribed. It was possible, surely, to care for poetry and art and yet enjoy a comfortable gossip. There was Nicole Rutherfurd. She was cultured enough, and yet who was more delightful to tell things to? Her air of breathless interest was most inspiring, and then she was so willing to laugh! Mrs. Heggie smiled to herself remembering that laugh, and thought what a blessing it was that the Rutherfurds would soon be back at the Harbour House. That very morning, in Mitchell the baker's, she had seen Agnes Martin, the Rutherfurds' cook, who had said they were expected directly....

Another hour till tea! If only some one would come in, even a collector would be better than nothing.

She went again to the window. The rain still slanted down; a long spray of creeper had been dislodged and hung down in a disreputable way; the chrysanthemums that yesterday had stood up so gallantly were battered and spoiled; the leaves were all over the lawn and----What was that stopping at the gate? The baker's cart most likely, or a van from Langtoun. Peering through the rain-dimmed pane, Mrs. Heggie was surprised and excited to see that it was a car, out of which was stepping a lady in a blue leather coat. A visitor!

Mrs. Heggie moved as swiftly as her bulk would allow, to the bell.

'Bella,' she said breathlessly when the parlour-maid appeared, 'a motor has stopped. Bring tea in about a quarter of an hour and see that everything is very nice. Hot toast

5

and the best silver.... There's the bell.'

All expectation, Mrs. Heggie seated herself in a high chair, and presently 'Mrs. Jameson' was announced, and following her name came a woman of about five-and-thirty, with alert grey eyes under a becoming blue hat.

'Oh,' said her hostess, 'Mrs. *Jameson*! And on *such* a day!'

As an oasis to a traveller in the desert so was this visitor to Mrs. Heggie. A newcomer to the district, the purchaser of Windywalls--here was new country to explore! She beamed and repeated, 'On *such* a day!' as she drew forward a chair.

But the visitor would not be pitied.

'Oh,' she said, 'it looks worse than it is, and it's the best sort of day to find people in. I was sorry to miss you when you called at Windywalls.'

'Not at all,' said Mrs. Heggie, wondering how long Mrs. Jameson had been a widow. With her gay colours and cheerful voice she was strikingly unlike anything of the kind. Widows as she knew them were subdued things, black or grey or purple; by their demeanour reminding the world of what they had lost. She herself had never got beyond a little grey or white in her hat, although her James had been gone fully ten years.... Still, this was a comparatively young woman, times were changing, and it did not do to be narrow-minded.... 'And how do you think you're going to like this part of the world? Perhaps you have some connection with it?'

Mrs. Jameson, smiling pleasantly, shook her head.

'No. I heard by chance of Windywalls, and when I saw it I liked it, and here I am.'

There were a hundred questions on the tip of Mrs. Heggie's tongue. It was almost more than she could do to bite them back and merely remark, 'Indeed! Perhaps you play golf?'

'I play, but I'm not much good. No, I didn't come for the sake of golf. I came because I like the country, and quiet, and a garden, and a sight of the sea.'

'Oh,' said Mrs. Heggie, and added brightly, 'and pleasant neighbours. With me it's always more the people than the place.'

The visitor nodded. 'Neighbours certainly count,' she admitted, 'tell me about the people here. I know no one, for I always seem to be out of reach when callers come, and yours is the first call I've returned. I'd be grateful if you'd put me wise about the neighbourhood?'

Mrs. Heggie sat forward in her chair, her broad face beaming, all gloomy fears were banished; here was a task that her soul loved.

'Tell you about the people? Certainly I will, but--I hardly know where to begin.'

'Mayn't we begin where we are? What a pretty house this is! Do you live alone?'

'With my daughter Joan.' She looked deprecatingly at her visitor as she continued: 'It seems absurd with me for a mother, but Joan writes poetry. Yes, she's had one little volume published, and people who know say it's good, but I'm no judge. The only one I could understand Joan said was poor. Her father, too, was so unlike anything of the kind. He liked what you might call the practical side of life, and I doubt if he knew a line of poetry, but you never really know what a family's going to take to. There's my son George out in China---- But I mustn't wander away. We were to talk of our neighbours.... Haven't you met *any one*? Not even the minister?'

'Not even the minister. Ought I to have made a point of seeing him first?... I dare say I might have seen callers if I hadn't been so keen to get things on in the garden before the winter's upon us. I'm afraid I didn't encourage the servants to come and look for me.'

Mrs. Jameson leant back in her chair and smiled at her hostess, who opened surprised blue eyes as she asked, 'But didn't you *want* to see callers? I'd have thought you would have been so interested.... Have your nearest neighbours called, the Erskines of Queensbarns? They have? They've made a fine place of Queensbarns, and of course they've heaps of money to keep it up. There are two girls, and they entertain a lot and go to London and the Riviera and all that. I remember the Erskines as quite plain people in Langtoun--I forget whether it was linoleum or jute--but they not only know how to make money but how to spend it, and nobody worries that Mr. Erskine's father began at the foot of the ladder--why should they?... Then the Fentons, Sir Robert and Lady Fenton.... They have called too? They are one of the real old families, there have always been Fentons at Balgowrie. The present people are very pleasant, I believe; quite young and given over to pleasure. If they're not in London dancing at night-clubs, they're at Le Touquet or the Lido or one of those places. I constantly see their names in the papers, and pictures of them in *The Tatler*.... Eh well, they're young and idle, and Lady Fenton is pretty in the new way.'

Esmé Jameson raised enquiring eyebrows, and Mrs. Heggie explained.

'No hair to speak of, and long thin legs, and an unlikely complexion--*you* know. I suppose it's the way I was brought up, but it fairly frightens me to see people given over entirely to frivolity, never giving a thought to their latter end. Joan says I'm so middle-class. I am, of course. It says in the Bible, *Not many great, not many noble*, so it looks as if Heaven was to be more or less middle-class, and that's a little disappointing too.--Oh, here comes tea! Nearer the window, I think, Bella, away from the fire.... We need all the light we can get this dark day, and the fire is almost oppressive, don't you think so, Mrs. Jameson?... Now, are you quite comfortable there? I'm so glad to have a visitor; it's more than I expected--neither sugar nor cream?--for the Bucklers next door are in Edinburgh, and the people in Ravenscraig have influenza in the house, and the Lamberts--the minister's people--have chicken-pox, and the Harbour House is still shut up, and...'

Mrs. Jameson held out a protesting hand. 'Oh, but you're going much too fast. Do, please, stop and explain as you go along who is who.'

Mrs. Heggie laughed comfortably. 'To be sure they're only names to you. Well--now, do help yourself--the Bucklers live in the next house, Lucknow. There are three houses you would notice, on the hill, Lucknow, Knebworth, and Ravenscraig. Mr. Buckler is a retired Indian Civilian, and very nice neighbours they are. They had some money left them not long ago, and are very comfortable. A son and daughter just grown up. They go to Switzerland for winter sports.'

'That sounds very pleasant.'

'Quite. On the other side is Ravenscraig. It belongs to a Miss Symington--now Mrs. Samuel Innes. That was a very odd thing.'

Mrs. Heggie stopped and looked thoughtfully into the fire, and Esmé Jameson studying the tightly corseted figure sitting on the edge of a high chair, wondered at the impression of steepness that she gave.

'Yes, if any one appeared to be intended by Providence for a spinster it was she. An angular eight-and-forty with long skirts, and buttoning boots, without conversation, and as dull as ditch-water, that was Miss Symington.'

'Sounds pretty hopeless.'

'Hopeless! If you had seen her--. Till one day she suddenly appeared a changed woman. The stretched-back hair loosened and waved, the ugly clothes replaced by soft pretty things; and not only herself but the whole house transformed. For all the world it was like nothing so much as the fairy-tale where the godmother turns the pumpkin into a coach and the kitchen-maid into a princess!'

'*Dear* me,' said Mrs. Jameson, 'and who waved the wand?'

Her hostess nodded her head mysteriously.

'Miss Nicole,' she said. 'But of course you don't know who she is either. It's a long story,' she added happily.

'Tell me.'

And Mrs. Heggie told.

'Three years ago at this very time we heard that the Harbour House had been taken. You've been down to the Harbour? Then you would notice a house standing broadside on?'

'Oh,' Esmé Jameson laid down her cup. '*That* house, with the pointed roof and the crow-step gables and the nine windows looking on to the sea? A lamb of a house. I wondered who was lucky enough to live there.'

'That's it. Not exactly a house for ordinary people. Most of us would object to being so near the sea, and the fishy smell, and living cheek-by-jowl with the poor folk-- villas suit us better. But the Harbour House has always belonged to gentlefolk. Mrs. Swinton, who used to live in it, was connected with all the old Fife families. I didn't know her. She didn't call when he built Knebworth and came to live in Kirkmeikle, indeed she called on no one in the place, she was a lonely, proud old woman, and there were few to mourn her when she died.... When I heard the house had been taken by Lady Jane Rutherfurd I expected it would be the same thing, only more so, but we were neighbours in a way, so I risked a snub and called. I got no one in, and I thought probably a card would be left in return and that would be all I would ever know about the Harbour House, but a few days later I was sitting here alone, Joan was out somewhere, and who should arrive but Lady Jane Rutherfurd and her daughter Nicole.'

There was an impressive pause, and Mrs. Jameson felt she was sipping her tea in a sacramental way, then Mrs. Heggie continued: 'Before that Kirkmeikle had been the dullest little place. I really sometimes wondered if I could stand it: just Miss Symington and the Bucklers, the Lamberts, and Dr. Kilgour and his sister, none of them what you might call given to hospitality. I used sometimes to say to Joan we could hardly have chosen a *less* sociable place to settle in. She didn't care; a fountain-pen and an armful of books satisfy her, but I do like a little society.'

'But round about Kirkmeikle there are people,' Mrs. Jameson reminded her.

'Yes, oh yes, but it wouldn't occur to them to call on us. Not that we're not perfectly respectable people. My father was a doctor, and my husband was a linen manufacturer who left me very comfortably provided for, but then, you see, I'm middle-class inside me, and that seems to be about the worst thing you can be in these days. Joan flings the word at me when I venture remarks about her friends' new ways, or the books she reads. I think Joan is what you call Bohemian, or at least would like to be, and my middle-classness stands in the way.'

Mrs. Heggie stopped to sigh, and Esmé Jameson had a vision of a gathering of Bright Young People with, in their midst, sitting steeply, the large figure of her hostess, white frilling framing her rosy face, her child-like blue eyes looking out on life surprised and puzzled.

'It's like this,' Mrs. Heggie went on, 'if you're to stand out in a district and make people aware of you, it's not enough to be comfortably off and willing to entertain. You've either got to be spectacularly rich, or else out-of-the-way clever and amusing. People like the Fentons, for instance, have no use for me. I can imagine them saying, "Mrs. Heggie, who is she? Lives in a villa in Kirkmeikle? Oh"--and that's enough of me.... Oh, you needn't think I mind. I quite understand their attitude, but it made it all the more wonderful when Lady Jane came and made a friend of me. Yes, that's what she did, and not only of me but of almost every one in the place. She drew us all together, she and Miss Nicole, and...'

'But, but...' Mrs. Jameson was obviously puzzled. 'Why is Lady Jane here at all? The Rutherfurds are Border people, and...'

'Oh, I know--' this was Mrs. Heggie's story and she could brook no interference, 'but Rutherfurd had to be sold--Glasgow people called Jackson bought it--and Lady Jane and her daughter and niece took the Harbour House. Of course in a way it was a terrible comedown, and no one could have blamed them if they had kept theirselves to theirselves, and simply never looked at any of us; indeed it was no more than we expected.'

Mrs. Heggie held out her hand for the visitor's cup, filled it, indicated the cake, and proceeded.

'It isn't, you know, as if the Rutherfurds weren't the real thing. Lady Jane's father was the Earl of Elleston and her mother was a duke's daughter; her husband's people were in Rutherfurd long before Flodden--or was it Bannockburn? I'm awfully unsure about dates--yet Lady Jane sits and talks to me as if I were her kin.'

'Quite,' said Mrs. Jameson, remembering with an inward spasm of laughter the lines:

'There never was a king like Solomon
Not since the world began;
Yet Solomon talked to a butterfly
As a man would talk to a man...'

'And this Miss Nicole,' she said, 'is she young and beautiful?'

'Seven-and-twenty,' said Mrs. Heggie promptly; 'she told me so herself. *I* think she is lovely. I've seen better features, more regular anyway, but there's such a sparkle about her, such a--I don't know the right word to describe her, but she seems to light up a room: that sort of person.'

'I see. And the niece, is she also very attractive?'

'Oh, she's quite nice. She doesn't live any longer at the Harbour House. She married young Mr. Jackson and reigns at Rutherfurd in Lady Jane's place.'

There was a note of resentment in the speaker's voice that made Mrs. Jameson say:

'That was surely bad management. It would have been much more suitable if Miss Nicole had gone back to Rutherfurd.'

Mrs. Heggie nodded. 'So we all thought, but Providence has His own ways of managing, and it was Barbara Burt that was the chosen one.... But I'm told she makes an excellent wife, and now there's an heir, so I dare say it's all for the best.'

In spite of her acquiescence in the ruling of Providence Mrs. Heggie looked profoundly dissatisfied, and presently she said:

'I'm very sure if Andrew Jackson had only seen Miss Nicole first he would never have looked at her cousin, but he and Miss Burt were as good as engaged before he ever set eyes on her. Anyway, I don't believe Miss Nicole would have taken him.... There was a young man living in Kirkmeikle when the Rutherfurds came--Simon Beckett; you may have heard of him? He died in the Everest Expedition. Well, of course I don't know and I would never think of asking, but he was never away from the Harbour House that first winter. I didn't see the Rutherfurds after the news came of his death, they were just going away for some months. When they came back Miss Nicole was as gay as ever, but I just sometimes wonder...'

The door opened and she turned her head.

'Oh, Joan! Mrs. Jameson, this is my daughter.' Then, brightly, 'Wasn't it good of Mrs. Jameson, Joan, to come out this stormy day to cheer us up?'

Joan shook hands gravely, not committing herself to any opinion about the visitor's goodness. She was a sallow-faced creature with a rather unkempt-looking shingled head. It was difficult to understand why such a fresh-faced mother should have produced such a dingy daughter. Taking the cup of tea handed to her, she sat down and began to eat bread and butter, while her mother tried with her eyes to remind her that there was such a thing as social obligations.

'Joan,' she said at last, 'you know that Mrs. Jameson has taken Windywalls? I've been telling her all about her new neighbours.'

'You would enjoy doing that,' said Joan dryly.

'I certainly have enjoyed hearing,' Mrs. Jameson broke in. 'It seems to me that I've been guided to a really interesting neighbourhood.'

Interesting?' Joan's voice expressed amazement.

'Well--isn't the lady who suddenly transformed both herself and her house rather unusual? And the inhabitants of the Harbour House?'

'Oh, the Rutherfurds! You'll be tired of hearing of the Rutherfurds before long. But it's not their fault that the world is full of snobs.'

Mrs. Heggie protested. 'It's not snobbishness, Joan, that makes every one like Lady Jane and her daughter.'

'Isn't it?' Joan took another bit of bread and butter.

'It's just that we can't help it,' her mother went on. 'There's something in Lady Jane's sweet, sad face and her gentle ways.... I'm sure Mrs. Jameson will feel the same.'

'I'm sure I shall--if I ever get to know them. Did you say they are away just now?'

'Expected home any day,' Mrs. Heggie said with great satisfaction. 'And time too; they've been away three months.'

'Kirkmeikle,' said Joan, 'will live again.'

'No, but really,' Esmé Jameson was leaning forward in her chair, 'do they make so much difference to the place, these Rutherfurds?'

Joan nodded. 'Absurd as it sounds, they do. And not only to my mother and the other villa-dwellers, but to the shop people and the cottagers.'

11

'I told you,' Mrs. Heggie broke in, 'I told you that before they came we were a dull, detached little community, and the Rutherfurds seemed to link us all together in some strange way. They showed us to each other in a new light so that we all became better friends. And they do things, take on responsibilities that no one else would dream of--You know, Joan, little Alastair Symington--. The nephew, Mrs. Jameson, of Miss Symington who transformed herself and her house and married at forty-eight. I don't believe she ever cared for the child, she couldn't have, when she was willing to give him up. When she was going to be married and it was obvious that she felt him in the way, what d'you suppose happened? Lady Jane took the boy, adopted him legally, I suppose, but I never ask questions. You see, she lost both her sons in the War, so her heart is soft to wee boys. Alastair was a white-faced, suppressed little fellow, always dressed in too large overcoats, and now you would hardly know him for the same boy. And they adore him, Lady Jane and Miss Nicole.'

Mrs. Jameson laughed. 'I don't blame them. There is something terribly appealing about a little boy in a too large overcoat.... Well, I must go. I've greatly enjoyed my first call. Will you please come soon to Windywalls and let me show you all I've been doing. You will tell me if you think it's improved--or spoiled?'

'But I've never been inside the house at Windywalls,' said Mrs. Heggie. 'The Drysdales didn't call on us when we built this house. And, indeed, I don't think I'd have summoned up courage to call on you, if it hadn't been that knowing the Rutherfurds sort of gave me self-confidence--Yes, Joan, it's quite true, you needn't laugh.'

'Then,' said Esmé Jameson, 'I'm already one of the people who have reason to be grateful to the Rutherfurds. But do let's fix a day now for you to come so that I shan't miss you. It's particularly pleasant to me to have a place to ask people to; I've been out in Kenya, and wandering about looking for some place to settle for years.... But if I don't go now you'll never ask me back.'

'Indeed,' Mrs. Heggie assured her, 'I've been more than glad of your company. I don't know how it is, but I seem to need people. Sitting here alone this afternoon with the rain falling I'd begun to feel quite ill; I actually had thought myself into a pain and saw myself taken off to a Nursing Home! And you just put me right.... Now, when you come into Kirkmeikle there's always a welcome here. Lunch at 1.15, tea at 4.30. You'll remember that?'

She patted her visitor's hand, remembering that she was a widow and young and alone. 'Good-bye, and may you find happiness in your new home. Better button up your coat before you leave the room. I'd come out to see you off but I've got a touch of cold on my chest.'

Joan came in from speeding the parting guest, and stood with her back to the fire watching the servant removing the tea-things.

'You've had a happy afternoon, Mother,' she said.

'Oh well, Joan,' Mrs. Heggie's tone was rather apologetic, 'it's a pleasure to me to talk, you know that, and I like that Mrs. Jameson, she's a good listener and an interesting woman, don't you think?'

'She's certainly no fool,' said Joan.

'I wonder what her husband was and how long she's been a widow. She seems to have no family. English, do you think? I make a point of never asking questions, but----'

Joan looked at her mother, and her face was lightened by her infrequent and rather surprisingly pleasant smile.

'But--you'll find out everything in time, won't you, Mother?'

Chapter II

'It is more in our power than is commonly believed to soften ills.... Strictly speaking there is but one real evil--I mean acute pain. All other complaints are considerably diminished by time....'

LADY MARY WORTLEY MONTAGU.

When Rutherfurd was put up for sale and Lady Jane Rutherfurd, with her daughter Nicole and her niece Barbara Burt, had to seek another home, the Harbour House in the Fife village of Kirkmeikle had seemed a heaven-sent refuge.

Away from the Borders, so that they would not be worried hearing of the doings of strangers in their old home, small enough for their means and large enough for their needs, a dignified old house with high-pointed roof and crow-step gables; with its front door to a narrow street, a little secret garden behind, and nine small-paned windows looking out to the sea. Sitting in the long drawing-room at high tide it was as if they were surrounded by water. Nicole said it smelt salt and fresh and, she might have added, fishy. Certainly not a house for everybody. To many the large bleak villas at the top of the Brae--Knebworth, Lucknow, Ravenscraig--would have seemed much more desirable, but the Rutherfurds being what they were, found in the Harbour House a habitation after their own hearts, a house to love.

Three years had passed since that October afternoon when Lady Jane had first seen her new home. Barbara had gone to Edinburgh to travel back with her, and Nicole, helped by Nature, had staged the scene. The tide was out, and beyond the low wall that bounded the road before the house, hard, ribbed sand lay white in the half-light, a very new moon hung bashfully in a clear sky, and the mast of a sailing ship stood up black beyond the Harbour.

The hall had glowed with welcome. A great bowl of red berries stood on a Jacobean chest; sporting prints that had come from the gun-room at Rutherfurd hung on the walls; the clock, the chairs, the half-circular table were all old friends. And when Lady Jane had entered the drawing-room she had cried out with pleasure. The curtains had not been drawn, for Nicole liked the contrast between the chill world of sea and gathering dusk outside and the comfort within. The firelight fell on the old, comfortable chairs, the cabinet of china, the row of pictured children's faces over the mantelshelf--Ronnie, with his serious eyes and beautiful mouth; Archie, blue-eyed and obstinate; Nicole, bright-tinted, a firefly of a creature; and Barbara, their cousin. The tea-table stood before the sofa, with the familiar green dragon china on the Queen Anne tray; Lady Jane's own writing-table was placed where the light of the window should fall on it--It was not Rutherfurd, but it was home.

Three years ago! Nicole was thinking of those years as she sat in her favourite window-seat, looking out to the sea.

Feeling a hand on her shoulder, without turning, she put her own hand up and held it.

'Mums--I didn't hear you come in. Sit beside me for a minute and look. It's just as it was the first time you saw it--a baby moon, a tall mast in the Harbour, the sea, and the lights beginning to blink. Can you beat it? And away over there somewhere is Edinburgh, with its high, mysterious "lands," and the bugles sounding from the Castle Rock, and the wynds through which Queen Mary rode to sing French songs in Holyrood. Isn't it wonderful? To come back to it after three months in England and-- oh, but I forgot, you're English, poor darling!'

Nicole put back her head and smiled provokingly up at her mother who merely said:

'Yes, it's hard to have to labour under that disadvantage! But come and have tea now. You know you hate it in the least cold.' She gave a glance at the table. 'I wonder if Effie has everything here to-day?'

'I should think so,' said Nicole. 'She has tiptoed about for the last quarter of an hour, breathing heavily, and surveying the results of her labours with her head on one side, and then darting downstairs for something she's forgotten--a painstaking child.'

'Yes, Mrs. Martin tells me that both Effie and Jessie have the makings of good servants. I'm glad, but I confess I miss Christina and Beenie.'

Nicole sank into a low chair opposite her mother, remarking, 'Oh, so do I. It takes me so long to get used to strange faces. Don't you think, Mums, slaves must have been a great comfort? Slaves can't tell you that they are wanted at home--like Beenie, or that their "lawd" has now got a house and can marry--like Christina. You could really settle down comfortably with slaves! Has Effie forgotten milk after all? Just give me the merest dab of cream.'

'I'm afraid poor Beenie will have to stay at home now indefinitely,' Lady Jane said, leaning forward to lower the flame under the kettle. 'Mrs. Martin heard from her that her mother will never be able for much again, and there are six in the house to cook and wash for.'

Nicole nodded. 'It is hard for Beenie, especially when she compares her lot with Christina's. You saw Jean Douglas's letter this morning? I left it on your table. Yes, here it is. She's been to see Christina.'

Nicole leant forward to get the light of the fire to read by. 'This is what she says: "I climbed up to Shielgreen yesterday--heavenly it was, golden bracken and flaming trees under a pale-blue October sky--and found Christina most comfortably tucked away in a fold of the hills. Her cottage, as she proudly pointed out, was not only two 'ends,' but a garret, and I explored every inch of it.

'"Christina does credit to whoever trained her. Such a shining little house for any young husband to come home to in the gloaming! Christina, neat in a jumper suit and a shingled head"--That's something new, Mums--"was singing as she ironed 'Elick's' shirts. I saw traces here and there of what she had learned at the Harbour House--the glass of berries and red leaves on the dresser, a window open and unobscured by geraniums in pots, old brass candlesticks polished lovingly. The presents you gave her were pointed out, and your photographs hang prominently on the wall. She insisted on stopping her ironing and making tea for me in what she described as 'ma granny's Britannia-metal teapot!' and produced excellent home-made scones and butter and honey, also a cake from the baker's cart, which she kept wrapped in a cheese-cloth in the meal-kist! She came out to show me the garden all ready for next spring, and she told me she had some bowls of bulbs put away in the dark, for she 'aye liked to watch Miss Nicole's bulbs.' I mustn't forget her message to The Bat. 'Tell Maister Alastair that I've got a burn at the door, and a pool and a flat stane where I can scrape ma pots, and get silver sand to scrub ma table white.'--

'"I said 'I needn't ask if you are happy,' and she said in her soft Tweeddale voice, 'Ay, mem, I'm happy. Elick's a guid man to me, an' I'm rale content.'... That isn't bad for five miles from a station and ten from a picture-house!"'

Nicole drank her tea hurriedly and passed in her cup.

'Boiling hot, please, Mums. I let the last get cold.... That's good hearing about Christina.'

'Excellent hearing. "Elick" is to be envied.... Shielgreen used to be our favourite picnic place--you remember, Nikky?'

'Of course I remember. Once Archie lost a gold sovereign he had been given, and we all helped to search. I must have been very small, for the bracken nearly met over my head. More than twenty years ago! My word, how old we are, Mums!'

But Lady Jane was not listening. Her thoughts had flown far from the Harbour House. It was an August day in the south country, and she saw a long vista of rushy park and wild thorn-trees, the heather flowering, and Lammerlaw hanging like an amethyst in the pale heavens. She heard children's voices, and towards her came her husband's tall form in his old tweeds, Ronnie and Archie at his heels....

15

She came back from the past, which seemed almost more real than the present, to reply to her daughter's question as to what she had been doing all afternoon.

'Oh,' she said, 'I was putting things away, and going over my clothes with Harris. We shall have quite a lot for Mrs. Lambert's Jumble Sale, I can see.'

'Have you anything suitable for old Betsy? I thought the shawl she was wearing this afternoon most inadequate--washed-in and skimpy.'

'You've been to see Betsy?'

'Not only Betsy,' said Nicole. 'I've seen almost the whole population of Kirkmeikle since luncheon. First, I put my head round Mrs. Brodie's door. She said, "Mercy! what a fricht!" but showed no other emotion on beholding me. Two of her nine are now working in the "Roperee," six are at school, and the "wee horse" was a train when I saw him, shunting up and down on the flagged path and giving painfully realistic squeals. He is four, and his mother is looking forward to getting him away to school and off her hands in another year.'

'Is the "wee horse" four? It seems only yesterday that he was jumping like a hooked trout in his mother's arms, and she said to him, "Ay, I ken ye're a wee horse."'

'I remember,' said Nicole, and continued: 'Dr. Kilgour bounded down an outside stair in the Watery Wynd and proceeded to tell me tersely his opinion of the household he had just left. He also told me his age, as he always does, and that of his sister. He's a young and vigorous seventy, I'll say that for him. He went down the Brae like the east wind, his voice trailing behind him. I *think* he was making enquiries about you.'

'Very unlikely,' said Lady Jane. 'What other people did you meet?'

'Well, I was exchanging the time of day with "Roabert" in the bakeshop when who should darken the door but Mrs. Heggie! That good lady is larger than human, but I do think she is glad we are back at the Harbour House. She gave me such a welcome, and poured out streams of news. How she gleans it all from such barren soil I know not. She didn't want "Roabert" to hear, so it was said in a hissing whisper which left both Roabert and me unenlightened. Then I met the Bucklers walking about with two dogs. Mr. Buckler said it had been the most wretched summer on record--did you notice that?--and they are thinking of going to Tenerife for the winter to get a little sunshine; so that's that. I saw, too, the people who have taken Ravenscraig; unemployed-looking people, the man delicate, the woman robust, with a fixed grin. Rather painful people.'

'Did you see the Lamberts?'

'For a second. The children have grown both up and out, and perhaps it was their increased size that made their parents both look shrunken, or I may have forgotten how small and thin they always were: I think their zeal eats them up. I asked them and Mrs. Heggie and her daughter to lunch on Friday; was that right?'

'Quite right. I'll enjoy seeing them again. But, tell me, how is my friend Betsy?'

16

'More crabbed than ever. I knocked at the door before I opened it and went in saying, "Well, Betsy," trying to be very bright and genial.'

'"It's you," she flung at me over her shoulder, not troubling to look round. I got myself into her line of vision, and she said, "You're a great stranger."'

'I pointed out that we had been away for three months and had only just got home, and that here I was at once on her doorstep. She thawed a little then and asked for you, and if we had been at Rutherfurd. I told her that we had, and she said, "Are thae Jacksons aye there yet?" I reminded her that Barbara was now Mrs. Jackson, and that she had a son and heir, but all she would say was "Tets," and mutter under her breath. She was interested, though, to hear of Christina being settled at Shielgreen. When I told her of Jean Douglas's letter this morning with the description of the burn at the door, and the flat stone at the pool for scraping pots, her poor face got pitifully eager. She said, "Eh, I hope the lassie kens hoo weel-aff she is. What wud I no gie to get awa' frae that nesty jumblin' sea that's aye stare starin' at me when I gang to the winday, and see the lang fields o' Tweedside, and the canny sheep, an' the burns rinnin' an' singin', an' each wee hoose wi' a gairden--nane o' yer ootside stairs."...I was sorry for the poor old body, Mother. It's a terrible thing, heart-hunger. Go and see her, won't you? You are the only one who can really comfort her.'

'We'll comfort each other,' said Lady Jane.

Nicole looked up quickly, crying, 'Mother, aren't you happy then to come back?'

Lady Jane smiled at her daughter. 'Well--very content anyway, darling. Happy is too--too rich a word for me now. I had my day of happiness and, thank God, I realised I was having it. But it's you, Nikky----'

Nicole sprang up from the stool on which she had been crouching by the fire, and sat down on the arm of her mother's chair.

'You needn't give a thought to me,' she said. 'I'm absurdly pleased with life. Of course things are different now, but once you accept that fact it's all right. To you and to me this is the day of small things--. Who said that? Some one in the Bible, wasn't it? And the small things keep you going wonderfully: the kindness of friends; the fact of being needed; nice meals; books; interesting plays; the funny people in the world; the sea and the space and the wind--not very small, are they, after all?'

She put her arm round her mother's shoulders.

'It is lovely to have you to myself again, after sitting for months in other people's rooms. True, they were very charming rooms--though not to compare with this sea-chamber! Don't you always connect this room with tea? A room where it is always afternoon. Some rooms are quite obviously of the morning and breakfast, and others speak of lit candles and port----'

'It is a dear room,' Lady Jane said, 'I looked forward to being in it again with you. Let's read Trollope aloud this winter.'

17

'Shall we? That reminds me there's a box of books from *The Times*. I do hope there will be something in it that will appeal to Mr. Lambert, and Dr. Kilgour wants the latest famous trial. That man positively steeps himself in crime...'

Chapter III

'And still that sweet half-solemn look,
When some past thought is clinging:
As when one shuts a serious book
To hear the thrushes singing.'

AUSTIN DOBSON.

Esmé Jameson felt that she had been fortunate in securing the property of Windywalls, for the house was not too large, thoroughly well built and comfortable, with a southern exposure and a wide view over rich pasture-lands to the sea. Her friends had told her she was foolish to saddle herself with even a small property in these troublous times, but she had wanted a place of her own, and now she had it.

She was sometimes surprised at her own interest, even excitement, over her purchase. She had often felt old and tired among the throng on board ship or in big hotels, young things, many of them, mad to taste all they could in life. She thought her apathy must be due to the background of sorrow and suffering which she could not forget. For three years her husband had lain ill, and she could not yet think without almost intolerable pain of that long-drawn-out losing battle. And when he knew that he had lost, that life was over for him, still Death would not come. He lay waiting, his body a wreck, his mind terribly clear.... When first they had met he had been so young and keen and ambitious; life had been bursting with promise that July day in 1914 when they were married, but it had held only for him an interrupted honeymoon, a few months' training, six months' fighting in France--a broken body and years of suffering.

If only, Esmé thought sadly, if only he could have been with her now, outside on this delectable autumn morning, looking across the fields and the woods and the red-tiled cottages to the sea. What fun to have gone together to the stables--Archie had had a passion for horses, and the hunting here was good; to have pottered together over the new car, to have planned for the garden. They had never done anything together. If, she thought, they had even had six months together before catastrophe overtook them, time to do little things, time to arrange their wedding-presents, to feel themselves householders; but there had been nothing but bewilderment, anxiety, pain. Nothing more? Yes, Archie's unquenchable laughter, his patience, and her own efforts to help him keep the banner of courage flying to the end....

She walked down the flagged path between the hedges of lavender--how delicious that would be when summer came--and on the lawn she found the old gardener gazing discontentedly at the turf.

Esmé hardly knew what to make of this servitor of hers. John Grierson was a legacy from the former owner of Windywalls who had asked as a special favour that he might be allowed to stay on in his cottage and potter about in the garden so long as he felt able, but Esmé felt that the old man regarded her as an interloper. He certainly had no manners, and treated his new mistress as a thing of no account. He listened with a small sour smile to her suggestions and made no attempt to carry them out.

It was provoking, but Esmé was good-natured and inclined to be more amused than angry at the old man's perversity. On the few occasions when she had insisted on her own way he had remarked threateningly:

'Aweel, I'll juist gan' awa',' but nothing further had happened.

'Good-morning, John!' she said. 'Isn't this a glorious morning?'

John made an abortive attempt to touch his hat, and without looking at his mistress, said: 'There's naething wrang wi' the mornin' but there's a heap wrang wi' this green. It's a fair hert-break. I look efter it like a seeck bairn, but there's nae gratitude in't. Ay, an' it's juist the same wi' that plot doon by the tennis-ground. I plant it oot every year wi' calcelarys an' ither braw flooers, an' I come in the dark wi' a lantern an' pick oot the slugs--could mortal man dae mair?--but they juist dee on me.'

'Oh well,' Esmé said, 'I don't care greatly for that plot, anyway. It might be as well to do away with it. I like masses of flowers, not neat little ordered rows.... And this turf looks to me very good. A bit mossy, perhaps. Don't people put sand on in winter?'

John in response merely muttered under his breath, and Esmé asked the whereabouts of the under-gardener, David by name.

'Hoo should I ken? Undaein' some o' ma wark, I wadna wonder! They think they ken better nor me, him and Tam, me that's been at it near seventy years! The impidence o' thae young folk! I dinna need to work; I've ma pension frae ma auld maister; I juist stay on for an obligement to ye, but if I'm driven to leave this garden that I've wrocht in a' ma days, an' young David an' Tam get a free hand, I quaiston what'll happen....'

He shook his head sadly, took another look at the turf, and hobbled away.

His mistress looked after him rather ruefully. It was the old antagonism between age and the younger generation. How long would David stand his carping? It would be better for every one if the old man would make up his mind to 'gan' awa',' yet it would be hateful to see him leave....

But good days are not so plentiful in October that one can afford to waste them on small worries. It had been a night of wind and rain, but now the clear shining had come and the whole landscape lay in a radiance of pale sunlight; the air seemed washed; beech-hedges framed in gold the rich black of an early ploughed field; a robin, very young and impudent, perched on the sun-dial, chirped the beginnings of a song in an assured way. This was a morning when it was impossible to repine. There would come days of sweeping rain and wind, days of bitter frost and snow, when sad thoughts would not be inappropriate; this day was made for cheerful work. Esmé, thankful that she had a job in hand, went off to a neglected corner of the garden, where, helped by the maligned David, she was planning a rock-garden. It was absorbing work, and after luncheon she went back to it, and was blissfully grubbing among mud and large stones when a servant came out to tell her that callers had arrived and were now in the drawing-room.

It was not welcome news, and as Esmé straightened her back and became aware of the state of her hands and her boots, she wondered resentfully why people liked to ruin fine days for their neighbours by inflicting visits on them. Deciding that she could do nothing towards making herself presentable except wash her hands, she went into the cloak-room off the hall, glancing as she passed at the cards which lay on the table.

Lady Jane Rutherfurd! The Harbour House people! She smiled as she remembered Mrs. Heggie's infatuation. Now she would see for herself.

They were standing, Lady Jane and her daughter, in the big bow-window that looked out on the lawn and the sun-dial. They turned as their hostess came in holding out a rather damp hand and apologising for muddy boots and gardening clothes, and she, after a quick glance, told herself that Mrs. Heggie had been romancing; this Nicole was a very ordinary looking girl.

'How you must dislike us,' Lady Jane said. 'I don't know anything more exasperating than to be dragged from gardening to see visitors!'

'What were you doing?' Nicole asked, frankly curious. 'We have only a back-yard, where we live--oh I know, Mums, you've done wonders with it, but it's still a back-yard--and I've almost forgotten the delights of gardening.'

'Well,' said Esmé, 'I was really only making mud-pies. It's a corner of the garden that seems to have been considered little more than a rubbish-heap, and I've a notion to try and make a rock-garden. The under-gardener is interested in it and does most of the work; I was only "plowterin' aboot," as old John says scornfully, but I love it. It's great fun to acquire a garden of one's own. I've tremendous plans for next spring.... You see, over there hidden by those trees'--they were all in the window now, looking out--'there's a little stream that winds, and I'm going to make that part a spring garden. The banks will be masses of forget-me-nots--just think how lovely the blue will look through the drooping branches of cherry blossom! and in the grass there will be clumps of polyanthus, yellow and orange and terra-cotta; and David says that under the beech-trees wild hyacinths come out by the thousand.... Oh, and before that, of course, there are snowdrops, and then the daffys, so we'll go on from January.'

'And the lilac and laburnums,' said Nicole, 'and best of all the red and white hawthorn, and the copper beeches.... There's no end to the beauty. What fun you'll have!' She smiled at her hostess, her face radiant, and Esmé Jameson, as she smiled back, owned to herself that, after all, Mrs. Heggie had been right; there was something amazingly likeable about this Nicole. Her eyes looked so frankly into yours, there was such a gaiety and sparkle in her glance, as well as kindness; and never, she thought, had she seen anything more lovely than the way the girl's head was set on her shoulders.

'It is good of you to come and see me,' Esmé said. 'I heard of you from Mrs. Heggie.'

Nicole grinned broadly. 'Dear Mrs. Heggie--. Tell me, did she say that my mother had a sweet, sad face and that I was full of charm? Yes, I can see she did. Don't you *loathe* people who are full of charm? You feel them oozing charm all the time until you long to hit them.... But we know you too through Mrs. Heggie, so we are quits. We heard all about your visit. You pleased her very much.'

'Did I? She made a wet afternoon pass very pleasantly for me--Lady Jane, do sit down and try to be comfortable.' Mrs. Jameson looked discontentedly round. 'Somehow, I don't feel that I could ever like this room. Of course, at present it smells of paint, and needs firing and living in, but I don't think it could ever be a really kind room. These large windows are so unfriendly, somehow, and that gleaming floor, and that mantelpiece.... I like the book room so much better--library is too fine a name for my modest collection; I've been having my meals there--pigging it, rather, but it *is* so comfortable.'

'Yes,' Lady Jane said, 'books are so companionable that they make a solitary meal seem like a pleasant party. I love eating in a library.'

'Come and do it now,' Esmé cried. 'I can't bear this bleak room. I don't feel acquainted with it at all, and tea will be ready in the book room.'

But Lady Jane shook her head, while Nicole explained that they were invited to tea at Queensbarns.

'Have you met the Erskines yet?' she asked. 'What with rockeries and one thing and another you've had no time, I expect. They're very friendly people, fond of getting up things and entertaining their friends. The Fentons, of course, are almost nearer neighbours, but they are a lot away--very sociable, though, when they are at home.... You are having the experience we had three years ago: it's rather fun, I think, meeting new people.'

Esmé laughed. 'I think so too.' She turned to Lady Jane. 'It means a good deal to me that people should be kind. I'm a solitary woman--. My husband died after a long illness, from wounds received in the War. I stayed with a brother in Kenya for a time, but I've always wanted a place to settle down in and now I've got it. If people are nice to me I shall be grateful, but I feel it won't be very amusing for them to come here. I dare say I shall have a certain number of people staying with me, but I'm afraid I've got rather to like living alone.'

21

'Ah!' said Nicole, 'that grows on one,' while Lady Jane said in her grave way: 'Thank you for telling us about yourself. Nicole and I are solitary too, and, like you, don't mind it much. We are fortunate in having a small boy to help us along. We have just had to let him go off to school and are missing him horribly. But we look forward to the Christmas holidays--. Now, Nicole, we must be off. We are keeping Mrs. Jameson from her tea--so much needed and so well earned after an afternoon in the garden. You will come and see us soon, won't you? The first wet day, perhaps?'

'Yes, please,' Nicole urged. 'The first wet day we shall be in and have a particularly good fire and nice tea ready for you--. You know where to find us? You turn round the corner at "Roabert" Mitchell's shop and straight down the Brae to the foot. D'you drive yourself? Be careful, then, not to imitate the Gadarene swine....'

Esmé Jameson watched her visitors depart in their small car, and then went back into the drawing-room. The room hardly seemed so bleak now, there lingered in it something of the personality of the women who had just left it. Lady Jane's gentle friendliness remained in the mind like the fragrance of a flower, Esmé thought. And Nicole? There was a tiny green-edged handkerchief lying on the chair she had sat in; it smelt faintly of geranium, the scent of the leaf when you crush it in your fingers. She had been dressed in green, Esmé remembered, and there came back to her the echo of the girl's gay laugh, her soft quick way of speaking, a certain way her eyes had of taking you into her confidence.

'I might be Mrs. Heggie,' she told herself.

It would certainly be amusing to go the first wet day to the Harbour House.

Chapter IV

'Girl, there were girls like you in Ilion....'

HUMBERT WOLFE.

They had expected to miss the small Alastair from the Harbour House, but they were hardly prepared for the very large hole his going to school made in their daily life. Alastair had lived most of his short life in Kirkmeikle, having been sent home from Canada when his father died, to his aunt, Miss Symington of the villa Ravenscraig. She had given him a home somewhat grudgingly, and the child had led a dreary existence until Simon Beckett took rooms next door, and Nicole Rutherfurd came to the Harbour House. They had both taken an instant liking to the lonely, small boy in the too large overcoat whom they christened The Bat, and had tried to make things gayer for him.

22

When Miss Symington surprised every one--herself most of all--by marrying Mr. Samuel Innes, a widower with two schoolgirl daughters, it was obvious that she regarded Alastair as an encumbrance, and when Lady Jane, urged on by Nicole, proposed that they should take the boy and bring him up, she, though amazed at such an offer, gladly accepted it.

Since then, for Alastair, the desert places had blossomed like a rose. His nurse (known as Gentle Annie, owing to her partiality for a song of that name) went with him to the Harbour House, and when she left--very reluctantly, though she was going to 'better' herself--a cheerful young governess took her place and tried to guide The Bat's unwilling feet along the thorny track of knowledge.

He had still the same Puck-like face and concerned blue eyes, but he had grown tall and his legs were brown and firm. He was not, perhaps, such a virtuous child as he had been while an inmate of Ravenscraig, though Nicole declared that he was much too virtuous for her liking. Because of his gentleness they had been a little afraid of how he would get on at school. But Barnabas, a young cousin of Nicole's, and a great friend of Alastair's, was at the same school, and he seemed to have settled down without trouble. Rather dirty, oddly spelt letters arrived at intervals at the Harbour House containing such items of news as: 'I am quite hapy.' 'A boy gave me a founting pen it won't write but it was kynd off him....'

A few days after their call at Windywalls Nicole and her mother sat at breakfast in their dining-room with its white panelled walls, striped silk curtains, and Hepplewhite chairs. There was something particularly fresh about morning in the Harbour House, a tang in the salt air, a feeling of life and activity from the Harbour; fishwives passing with their creels, cheerily gossiping; fishermen working with their nets.

'Posty!' said Nicole, as that worthy passed the window. 'Dr. Kilgour was telling me yesterday that this postman's predecessor was a great character. He was old and lame and amazingly casual. He would sit on the Green Brae with his letters laid round him, and read all the postcards; then he would begin his rounds, shouting at one door: "Mistress Speedy, yer gude-dochter's comin' tae see ye the morn's mornin'," and at another, "Mrs. Johnston frae Langtoun'll be here to tea this afternoon. See ye bake." One day he announced to Dr. Kilgour, "There's a caird to ye from Nice" (which he pronounced to rhyme with mice), "an' there was a letter but it blawed intil the sea." As Dr. Kilgour was expecting an important letter he didn't think it was as good a joke as Posty did. But wasn't it amusing?'

Lady Jane smiled and said, 'Almost too amusing. I'm glad we don't live in his day.... Here comes Effie with our budget. What a lot! And I was congratulating myself on having got out of debt with a lot of people--Yes, there's one from The Bat. His writing hasn't begun to improve yet....'

Nicole glanced over her share of the letters, and leaving her mother still engrossed, took Alastair's dog, Spider, for a run. Spider was a cross between a wire-haired terrier

23

and a Sealyham, with a black patch over one eye and the disposition of an angel.

It was a bright morning, but earlier there had been an ominously red sky, and Nicole distrusted the brightness.

'It will be pouring by luncheon,' she prophesied, 'so we'll gather sunbeams while we may....' Spider evidently agreed and scurried out of the front door as if escaping from jail. It was an anxious business taking Spider for a walk; for he had a trick of squatting in the middle of the road when he saw a motor approaching, which turned his owner's heart to water. Nicole's own private conviction had been that he was a surprisingly stupid dog, but this morning when she lost sight of him, and after calling and whistling wildly, turned round to find him standing with a distinct smile on his face so close to her heels that she had failed to notice him, she began to wonder if he were not more knave than fool.

At luncheon Lady Jane was rather silent, and her daughter asked if she were still thinking about her morning's letters.

Lady Jane was peeling a pear, and she waited till Effie had left the room before she said:

'I had a letter from Blanchie this morning. She is terribly worried, poor dear, about Althea.'

'That's the Gort girl?'

'Yes, her only sister's child. I don't think you ever met Sybil and Freddie Gort? It was a miserable business. Freddie was a likeable creature to meet but he made a wretched husband, and Sybil wasn't without blame either. They were divorced, and this poor child, Althea, lived between the couple, not much wanted, I fear, by either. When her mother died last year Blanchie took her to live with her and brought her out--you remember she wanted you to go up for the coming-out dance?--and really gave her every chance. I was so pleased about it, for Blanchie has had rather a lonely life since James died, and Althea might have been such an interest to her, but the child seems to have got into rather a bad set and got entangled with some undesirable--Blanchie isn't very coherent....'

Lady Jane held out several scrawled sheets to her daughter who seemed rather callous over the tale of woe. She took them, remarking:

'"*Written from bed*," I see it's headed. As St. Paul might say, *Written from Rome*. Bed always was a very present help in time of trouble to poor Aunt Blanchie. It's amazing what a defence sheets and blankets are to some people against fortune's slings and arrows.'

Nicole puzzled over the letter for a minute, then looked up at her mother and shook her head.

'So far as I can make out, the wretched Althea does what she pleases, frequents night-clubs and comes in at any old hour, while Aunt Blanchie lies in bed and weeps. What a situation! Of course she never was fit to look after a girl. Providence knew that and sent her only boys.'

'You see what she suggests?'

Nicole took up the letter and read aloud:

'"My one hope, dear Jane, is in you. The idea came to me suddenly in the night: an *inspiration*, I am sure. Will you take Althea to live with you for a little? She would be away from temptation and surrounded by your wonderful influence. I always say that *no one* does me so much good to be with, and dear Nicole would be such a splendid example for Althea----" Mummie, she *is* a fool. What a preposterous suggestion!'

'We might think it over!' her mother said mildly.

'*Mother!* You don't mean to say that you would entertain even for a moment the thought of having that girl here? Why--why she would simply shatter us. Have you any notion what the girl of to-day is like? With a mild Victorian creature like me for a daughter you've been shielded from the worst.... What would a girl like Althea do here? A restless creature, probably never happy except when amusing herself, caged in the Harbour House! And what would we *say* to her? There was a girl at Bice's last month; just out, frightfully attractive to look at, but to speak to--Nothing interested her, not plays nor pictures nor books. She said she didn't mind games, but the only thing that really amused her was to wriggle her body in time to the latest tune. I thought I could talk to any one, but I was beaten that time.'

'Althea doesn't sound uninteresting,' Lady Jane said meekly, 'but she may be exactly what you describe. Only--she hasn't had much of a chance, has she? I can't think that either Sybil's friends or Freddie's were very improving; however--. It's really for poor Blanchie's sake. Naturally she feels responsible, and it would be such a pity to let the child ruin her life by marrying some undesirable if it can possibly be prevented. And with The Bat at school--and you did say, darling, you wished you had more work----'

'This wouldn't be work, this would be martyrdom,' Nicole said bitterly.

The discussion continued in the drawing-room until Nicole, exasperated, cried: 'Mums, you really are a provoking woman! You pretend to be convinced by my unanswerable arguments, but you always return to the attack--I can't think why you want the creature here....'

About three-thirty Mrs. Jameson appeared, announcing as she entered 'You said the first wet day, and here I am.'

Lady Jane gave her a kind greeting, while Nicole remarked: 'You are particularly welcome, because at the moment there are strained relations between my mother and myself.'

'Yes,' said Lady Jane, 'we've been quarrelling for about two hours.... Is that where you like to sit, Mrs. Jameson? Won't you be cold so far from the fire? No?'

'I love a window-seat--and you have three, all looking to the sea: what riches! Do please go on with your work, Lady Jane.'

'Then take off your coat and look as if you were going to stay for a while--It's for the seat of a chair. Yes, it is rather a good design.' Lady Jane chose a thread of silk and asked: 'Have you done any more to your rock-garden?'

Esmé Jameson laughed. 'It would hardly know itself under the name. At present it is nothing but a mud-puddle with some stones in it. I shall have to give it up till spring--' She looked round the quiet, pleasant room full of treasures out of other days, and made a discontented face. 'How this room makes me hate my own drawing-room. All your things seem to mean something; mine look so accidental, somehow. I expect I haven't caught the knack yet of making things look homelike. You see, although I'm thirty-five, this is the first time I've tried my hand at home-making.'

Lady Jane nodded. 'You have lived abroad....'

'Yes--for about nine years. I married in July 1914. That in itself explains a lot.'

There was silence for a minute, then Lady Jane said: 'I think you said you had a long time of nursing.'

'Nearly three years. We were married in July, and we had got a little house in Westminster that we meant to furnish by degrees, just as we picked things up. We were always finding treasures and storing them up, even on our honeymoon we were looking out for old brass and lacquer and having it sent back... but that all came to an end on August 4th. After that my husband was in camp training, and I lived in rooms as near as I could get to him, and in six months he was in France. In 1916 I got him home, broken.... I was in Nairobi with my brother for some years--then he married and I travelled about, longing yet dreading to come back. At last I was driven back by my desire to have a house, a place to dig myself into. I found Windywalls--and that's all about me.'

'I think,' said Lady Jane, 'this is favourable soil. When we were pulled up from our home in the Borders we came here and quickly struck root--We are fortunate, Nicole and I, to have each other.'

'Fortunate!' said Nicole darkly.

Dr. Kilgour walked in with Effie and the tea.

He was a man of nearly seventy, with white hair, a high-coloured face, and a manner as brusque as the prevailing wind of his native place.

On being introduced to the stranger he said:

'Windywalls? So you're the new tenant! It'll take you all your time to fill Mrs. Drysdale's shoes.'

'So Grierson the gardener seems to think,' Esmé said ruefully.

26

'Old Grierson's staying on with you? I dare say it would kill him to leave, though he must hate to see strangers about the place. He's about the last living example of that loyalty to a family that used to be so common. Not that he ever let the Drysdales know he adored them, but to the world outside he boasted late and early. I remember meeting him when Pat the youngest Drysdale joined up. "Ye canna keep them back," he said, and the pride and grief in his eyes was almost too much for me. I saw a lot of him at that time, his wife had a long illness and I was in and out of the house. When she was getting better she knitted constantly for lonely soldiers whose names she had been given, and every fortnight they sent away a parcel. She told me "We pit in socks and comforters, and cigarettes and sweeties, an' Fawther there pits in a cheery word aboot killin' Germans."

'"Fawther" was one of the few bright spots in the War. He was, or pretended to be, enormously confident. The first thing he pinned his faith to was "The Rooshians." Thousands, he told me, were on their way through Scotland to France. A cousin of a man he knew saw them knocking the snow off their boots as they passed through Galashiels in August. The Rooshians were going to finish the War almost at once. Then it was the Ghurkas: "thae wee fellays wi' the crooked knives," they were the men to tackle the Germans. Russia, the road-roller, was the next prop. "When they get gaun," he said, "I quaiston what'll happen." But Russia broke in his hand. His sole remaining prop was the Drysdale boys. He bore Norman's death, but when Pat the baby went, it was too much for him. "We'll win through yet," I said, trying to cheer him, and I felt as a country we had reached our lowest, when he answered: "*Faigs, I doot it.*"'

'Oh,' said Esmé, 'I'm glad you told me that. I thought he was merely a cantankerous old man. I'll be more patient with him now.'

'A great fellow old "John Grumblie." Let him go his own way. He's worked in that garden, boy and man, for nearly sixty years, and it can't be long now before he goes to give in his account. I think myself he'll get an abundant entrance.'

All the time when speaking, Dr. Kilgour was devouring, rapidly, scones, sandwiches, cake, and draining several cups of tea, and he now sprang to his feet and announced his departure.

'Just like the beggars--eat and go. Good-bye, Mrs. Jameson, hope you'll like Fife-- Miss Nicole, I've got a job for you.... I'll tell you again. Good-bye, Lady Jane, and thanks for my good tea----' He disappeared out of the door, still speaking, and in a second they heard the front door slam behind him.

Lady Jane poured some boiling water from the kettle into the teapot and said placidly: 'A country doctor has a busy life,' while Nicole remarked:

'I know no one who gives me such an impression of the shortness of time. When I meet him tearing about the wynds, or far out on the country roads, he shouts, "There are twelve hours in the day."... He is terribly conscientious about his panel patients, and all the poor folk, but somewhat short with the leisured classes. Can you wonder?

His one great desire is to work at the book he is writing on the town and district--he is exceedingly learned--and very rarely does he get a few hours off in the evening. No sooner does he sit comfortably down by the fire with his books round him than he is called up. His sister says he always begins by saying flatly, "*I won't go,*" but in a little while she sees him drawing his old boots from their hidy-hole. He sometimes says, "If I go, it'll be simple colic: if I don't go it'll be appendicitis.'"

'Still, it must be lovely to be busy,' Esmé Jameson said, looking into the fire. 'I envy him more than I pity.'

'But,' said Nicole, 'you must be a contented person or you wouldn't contemplate settling down in this quiet neighbourhood. Most of your evenings you'll be alone, except when the Fentons have their house full, or the Erskines are feeling lively. Every day you'll do more or less the same thing.'

'Ah, but I love a routine. It doesn't bore me to do the same thing at the same time every day. And I like to fiddle in the house and play myself in the garden and read by the fire at nights, but that is only pleasing myself. I'd love to help a little.'

'It's not so easy to help,' said Nicole. 'One is apt to do more harm than good. So long as one takes a hand with the local things, and gives what one can----'

'And,' said Lady Jane in her gentle voice, 'does any bit of work that comes to one's hand.'

Nicole nodded her head at the guest. 'That remark's aimed at me,' she said. 'My mother wants me to take on a bit of work.... Let's put it to Mrs. Jameson, and get her advice--Would you like to take a young girl of nineteen to pay you a long visit, a spoiled, very modern girl who will hate the country...?'

Lady Jane demurred at this, but her daughter insisted. 'She's sure to. Why, she only knows cities--London and Paris--Monte Carlo.'

'I wouldn't like it much,' Esmé Jameson confessed, 'but I'm not very good with young girls; they make me feel shy, they are so confident--most of them. But you'--she turned to Nicole--'you are young enough to cope with the modern minx.'

'But why should I? Why should we spoil things for ourselves by bringing a strange girl into the house? She will never come with my goodwill....'

Lady Jane smiled at her daughter.

'You sound very firm, Nikky, but I've a hope that you'll be like Dr. Kilgour and the man in the Bible who "afterwards repented...."'

Chapter V

'Only one youth and the bright life was shrouded:
Only one morning, and the day was clouded....'

ALICE MEYNELL.

When Mrs. Heggie came to luncheon at the Harbour House, Mrs. Martin, the cook, took extra pains, for, if one may so put it, Mrs. Heggie was worth the feeding. Her excitement over a new dish, her appreciation of good cooking, was highly encouraging to any cook. All the appointments of the table interested her, and she kept up a running fire of comments and compliments.

Nicole often said that it would be a much more interesting world if there were more people in it like Mrs. Heggie, and certainly she gave spice to Kirkmeikle society. Mr. and Mrs. Lambert, the only other guests, seemed almost like phantoms against her broad beaming exuberance. Mr. Lambert was the small shy minister of Kirkmeikle, a man widely read and deeply learned, much better fitted for a professor's chair than for his present job. He had no small talk, and it was torture for him to visit pastorally his flock; he could not remember the numbers and ages of the different families; it was absolutely impossible for him to make facetious remarks; he had never been known to relate an anecdote, and what conversation he had was impeded by a stammer.

It was a painful sight to see the small figure of the minister sunk sadly in a chair, while a decent man and his wife rubbed hands, damp with nervousness, on their garments, and tried vainly to think of something to say beyond, 'Ay, it's cauld the nicht,' or 'Rale mild for the time o' year.'

It was different, they acknowledged, in time of trouble. Then Mr. Lambert came as one having authority, and his people were glad of him.

Mrs. Lambert was a fragile slip of a creature with a face like a wood-anemone, but she had a high heart and worked like a Trojan to help her husband. And when the door was shut on the outside world the two were blissfully happy, with their books and their music, and their small daughters, Bessie and Aillie.

Lady Jane was one of the few people to whom Mr. Lambert found anything to say, and on this occasion she so inspired him that he conversed quite volubly all through luncheon on seventeenth-century poetry.

Mrs. Heggie was heartily sick of him, but directly they had moved to the drawing-room, he looked at his watch, muttering to himself like the White Rabbit, shook hands with his hostess, and incontinently departed, without either his wife or his umbrella.

29

Then Mrs. Heggie got her chance. 'I know,' she said, 'that it's not the thing to stay long at a lunch-party, but if you aren't going out at once, Lady Jane, I would like to stay for a little and hear the news.'

'Of course you must stay--As a matter of fact I'm not going out at all and shall be very glad of your company this rather dreary afternoon.... Mrs. Lambert, can't you stay a little? It's so long since we saw you.'

Mrs. Lambert said, 'I'd like to stay. It seems always a long three months that you are away, though the holiday month comes in to shorten it. Yes, we had a very nice time. We were in Ayrshire--Ballantrae--quite lovely and a complete change.'

'And the children?'

'Well, thank you. Bessie has gone to school and Aillie's feeling terribly left out. We have had to give her a satchel and a lesson-book, and she pretends all morning that she is doing lessons----'

Mrs. Heggie gave an impatient lurch forward in her chair, and with an expectant smile on her face, said: 'And *now* I'd like to hear about the baby at Rutherfurd.'

'The baby,' said Lady Jane, 'is a dear. Nikky, you might get the snapshots Barbara sent.'

'Andrew Rutherfurd Jackson--there he is,' Nicole said, handing the photograph of a very young, very solemn infant to the beaming Mrs. Heggie. 'Yes, he's a fine fellow, but three months is not the most interesting age. He merely eats and sleeps and gurgles and is very virtuous. His nurse says there never was a better baby.'

'And Miss Bar--Mrs. Jackson, isn't she very proud of her son?'

'Very, and over-anxious--. I wouldn't have believed that Barbara would have been like that. Constantly running up to the nursery and fussing over him, going pale if he seemed to cry without reason. She is so proud of him, so thankful for him, that she can't smile about him. I verily believe poor Babs has had an anxious pain ever since he was born. It's not all fun having a beautiful little son.'

Mrs. Heggie shook her head in profound understanding.

'The first,' she said, 'is always an anxiety. When there's half a dozen you take things easier.'

Nicole laughed. 'You're thinking of Victorian families, dear Mrs. Heggie. In these later days children are few and precious.'

Lady Jane objected. 'Not more precious, Nikky, than each of the six or eight or ten of the Victorian days.... But it's quite true what you say, Mrs. Heggie, numbers bring with them a certain placidity. I was one of nine myself, and I have a picture in my mind of my mother, still quite young and very pretty, with her whole brood tumbling about her at a birthday picnic or some such celebration. Accidents constantly occurred, for there were five wild boys, and I remember the composed way she received cuts and bruises, and even broken bones: plenty of petting for the injured one, remedies at once applied, but always a twinkle of amusement behind the sympathy, which kept us from being too sorry for ourselves.'

Mrs. Heggie listened almost reverently, remarking with a sigh, 'Yours must have been a beautiful family circle, Lady Jane.'

'Oh, we were a happy, riotous lot. Looking back I can see so many pictures: my mother telling us stories on winter evenings, with the light of the fire glinting on the gold of her hair and her sparkling ear-rings, my father standing back in the shadow watching her, the boys roasting chestnuts while they listened. And hot summer days when we took tea by the lily-pond, and my mother allowed herself to be taken on a tour of inspection round our different gardens which my father used to say reminded him of the parable of the sower of the seed, they seemed to give so little return for the care bestowed and the pocket-money spent on them. I wish all mothers would fill their children's minds with pictures. They may be quite happy at school and in the holidays, but they ought to have more to remember than long days in nursery or schoolroom; being pulled up about their manners; or dressed up for evenings at parties or pantomimes. They want intimate pleasures. Parents must give themselves if they want to mean anything to their children.'

Mrs. Heggie, as she listened, thought of Joan and wondered if she had failed somewhere in bringing her up. She doubted if Joan had any pretty mind pictures of her childhood, though she felt she had honestly done her best as a mother. Perhaps she had not known how to tell stories well, at least the children had not cared much to listen; the boys had either been taking things to pieces--they were mechanically inclined--or playing violent games with other boys; and Joan even as a child had been slightly scornful of her mother's efforts. Mrs. Heggie supposed it must be different with children in the higher walk of life: middle-classness was at fault again.

She listened now, humbly, for she felt very much aware of her own shortcomings, to a story Mrs. Lambert was telling about Bessie noticing few men in church and remarking to her mother: 'I suppose religion is only for ladies and children.'

'How sweet!' she said, then eagerly to Nicole, 'How is Mrs. Jackson, senior? I expect she's frightfully pleased about the baby?'

'Pleased!' said Nicole. 'That's a feeble word to describe Mrs. Jackson's state of proud bliss. You would think no one had ever been a grandmother before. We were all there for the christening, and it was more amusing than any play to see her manoeuvring to get the baby to herself. She began at once to call him Andrew, and she addresses him as if he were about her own age, makes long speeches to him and supplies the answers herself. It has given her a wonderful new interest in life. First it was perambulators--she raked through all the Glasgow shops for the very latest model, had it done up in the shade she thought most suitable, embroidered a fine cover, and that was that. Then the christening cloak, the silver quaich, and mugs and spoons; the mass of small woolly garments--she must have been a boon to bazaars! And this winter, I expect, she will roam happily through the toyshops, purchasing gigantic plush animals and jumping-jacks and balls for that poor solemn infant who doesn't know his right hand from his left.'

'Is that so?' said Mrs. Heggie, awed.

'Nicole exaggerates,' Lady Jane put in, 'but it is a little like that. Barbara looked rather despairingly at the things that were crowding up the nursery, for Mrs. Jackson doesn't stop at toys and woollies, she goes on to furniture. She saw and admired a set of nursery furniture, white wood painted with characters from nursery rhymes, and that arrived and looked quite out of place among the other things. It would have been delightful for a nursery in a bright new flat, but at Rutherfurd--But it makes her happy, and Barbara has the sense to appreciate the good intention.'

'Yes, indeed,' Mrs. Heggie agreed, 'she has need to value the kind interest, for the years take away those that care most, and young Mrs. Jackson hasn't a mother of her own--though I'm sure you've been more than a mother to her, Lady Jane.... I remember so well how I missed my mother when my third was born. I just lay and cried, remembering the fuss she had made over the other two and the way she had sat at the fire with the new baby on her lap and said, "My, but you're bonnie."'

Mrs. Heggie wiped away a tear at the recollection, and Nicole tried to imagine her friend as young, and perhaps, slim. It was difficult to see her except as trimly upholstered in shining black; but her eyes must have been the same when she was a child, round and innocent and wondering.

Mrs. Heggie was enjoying herself immensely, and hoped Mrs. Lambert would not make a move to go for some time. She broke again into speech.

'Mrs. Jackson's a delightful person. I never forget how much I enjoyed meeting her when she stayed here. I wish I could see more of her. She gave me some fine recipes. I've tried them all, and we have them regularly. Will she be paying you another visit soon, do you think?'

Lady Jane looked vague, and Nicole said: 'I'm going to visit Mrs. Jackson in Glasgow some day: she has got a wonderful new villa called "The Borders," built from her own plans, at least she told the architect what she wanted and saw that he gave it her. I quite long to see it, though I know I'd hate to live in it.'

'If old houses were only easier to work,' said Mrs. Lambert.

'Some are easy,' said Nicole. 'I know some old houses which have had electric light and central heating put in and all sorts of labour-saving devices, and they aren't spoiled at all.'

'But they'll very likely be burned down,' Mrs. Heggie predicted cheerfully. 'Haven't you noticed it in the papers time and again? With great loss of life too. That's my great fear about old houses. Now Windywalls is a nice sort of house, neither too old nor too new, just settled and comfortable looking--Have you managed to call yet,

Lady Jane?'

'Yes, we called, and Mrs. Jameson came to see us yesterday. Such a nice woman.'

Mrs. Heggie leant forward. 'Did you hear how long she has been a widow? She hasn't a *vestige* of mourning.'

'Her husband died of wounds,' Nicole said. 'I don't quite know when. She was only married in 1914.... I do hope Mrs. Jameson will like being here. She is prepared to be pleased, and that is the chief thing. I wonder if having seen a lot of the world makes it easier to settle down, or the reverse! Having seen nothing, you want to see nothing; having seen much, perhaps you want to see all.'

'Well,' said Mrs. Heggie, 'Kirkmeikle and the neighbourhood *is* very quiet. I often wonder how you stand it, Miss Nicole?'

'Oh, I like it. But we shall have to try and see more company this winter, for we are to have a girl staying with us. No, not a relative exactly: a connection--a what, Mums?'

Lady Jane laid down her embroidery frame to calculate.

'My sister-in-law's niece,' she said. 'She is very young, not quite nineteen, so we must try and amuse her as best we can. Her name is Althea Gort.'

'Oh yes,' said Mrs. Heggie. Gort. The name seemed vaguely familiar. She must have seen it in the papers. 'That will be nice for you, Miss Nicole.... And how is little Alastair?'

'Oh, very flourishing. He evidently likes school. We shall have a swaggering young man coming home at Christmas. I feel we've lost our little boy already.'

'When I think of him,' said Mrs. Heggie, noting with disgust that Mrs. Lambert was preparing to depart, 'the queer wee fellow he was with his big overcoat and his wee white face! My heart was sore for him many a time. Do you ever see Mrs. Innes now?'

And even as she said it the door opened and Effie announced 'Mrs. Innes.'

(Mrs. Heggie, recounting to an inattentive daughter the events of the afternoon, said: 'For all the world, Joan, it was like a scene in a play. Just as I said "D'you ever hear from Mrs. Innes?" in she walked. As large as life with a Persian-lamb coat and ospreys in her hat! You could have knocked me down with a feather, and I'm sure it was as big a surprise to Lady Jane, but she got up, quite kind, you know, but rather stately and, "Mrs. Innes," she said, "how kind of you to call!" or something like that.')

Mrs. Innes, once Miss Janet Symington of Ravenscraig, explained that she had had to come to Kirkmeikle for the afternoon in order to see about something the tenants wanted. 'A house,' she said rather fretfully, 'is a great nuisance. Tenants are never satisfied, something is always breaking; and if you let to a delicate, idle man it's the limit, for he has nothing to do but find flaws and write to the owner.'

Nicole laughed. 'That is annoying. I shouldn't answer if I were you. Let him go and find a plumber himself.'

'And let me in for paying great bills! No, indeed. I like to look into things myself and give my own orders. I'm a practical woman, as my husband often tells me.'

'How is Mr. Innes?' Nicole asked.

'Oh, he's all right except for a touch of rheumatism. He's a very busy man and much sought after for public meetings. I'm sure you must often see his name in *The Scotsman*. He's interested in all good work.'

'And the girls?' Nicole asked. 'It must be cheerful for you having two grown-up girls at home.'

'But they're not at home,' said their stepmother resentfully. 'Girls are so independent nowadays. The elder one, Agnes, insisted on learning typing and shorthand, and has got a very good post in London as a secretary, and Jessie persuaded her father to let her go in for singing, and she is studying in London too. It isn't as if they *needed* to do anything; they've a good home and a most indulgent father, and I'm sure I'd be pleased enough to take them about, but they had the impudence to tell me that Edinburgh was a back number. Yes! What girls are coming to I don't know. Said they couldn't stand the people that came about the house--their father's friends, mind you, and mine!... We try to keep an eye on them as well as we can. We go to London for a week every little while to see them in their flat, and urge them to let us meet their friends, but----' Mrs. Innes shook her head, and Nicole, much interested, asked what the friends were like.

'Oh well--they're not the class of people they've been used to meet in Edinburgh. They're not solid, if you know what I mean. Journalists and actors and artists--those kind of people. Not people Samuel has anything in common with. No church connection, you know. I live in dread of hearing that Agnes has got engaged to one of them. That would be a blow to her father, for he's still hoping she'll settle in Edinburgh.' Mrs. Innes dropped her voice and Mrs. Heggie leant forward, her eyes round with interest. 'A very good offer; a nice Edinburgh family; the right age and a presentable fellow; a W.S.'

'What could be nicer,' said Mrs. Heggie with obvious sincerity.

'And how's Alastair?' Mrs. Innes asked. 'I dare say you'll be glad enough to get him away to school.'

'Hardly that,' Lady Jane said gently. 'We're both living on the thought of the Christmas holidays. But he sounds happy, and that is all that matters. We sent him to Evelyn's because I have a small nephew there, a friend of his, and that made it easier for him.'

'Samuel was hearing that that is a very expensive school he's gone to. D'you not think it's a pity to bring him up like that? He'll have to work for his living, remember.'

Lady Jane looked thoughtfully at her visitor for a second or two without speaking, then rose to say good-bye to Mrs. Lambert and the reluctant Mrs. Heggie.

'Are you both going? I had hoped you would stay for tea.... Well, it's very pleasant to be back again. Thank you for coming.'

After a few minutes Mrs. Innes also rose to go, refusing tea, and Nicole went with her downstairs.

They stood together at the open door, looking out in silence.

Mrs. Innes gave a short laugh.

'It seems odd to be back again--and yet very natural too. Mrs. Heggie and Mrs. Lambert and everything just the same. And the leaves falling.... That's how I always think of Kirkmeikle. It gives me a queer feeling somehow....' She seemed to give herself a little shake. 'Well, I must go if I'm to catch that train. My husband wants me to go out with him to-night to something or other. He's meeting me at the Waverley, and we'll have our dinner at the hotel Grill.'

'I'm glad,' said Nicole, 'to see you looking so well and happy.'

'Yes,' Mrs. Innes said in her matter-of-fact voice. 'Taking everything into consideration, I think I was wise to marry Samuel.... How d'you like my coat? Yes, a birthday present from my man! Well--good-bye.'

Nicole stood in the hall when the door shut behind her visitor. Kirkmeikle in October with the leaves falling! That was how she thought of it too.... It was in an autumn gale that she had first met Simon Beckett; he and The Bat on the rocks watching the waves!

Three years ago! Three long years ago....

She went back to her mother in the drawing-room.

Chapter VI

'...all the men and women merely players.'

AS YOU LIKE IT.

Nicole made no effort to stage-manage Althea Gort's first sight of the Harbour House, as she had so carefully done for her mother. She cared little what the girl thought of the house and its inhabitants, in fact she harboured a secret ashamed hope that she would hate it at sight and leave at the first opportunity.

Nicole meant to do her best for Althea, she was their guest and as such must have every consideration. She had herself seen to it that the white upper chamber looking across the sea had been made to look as attractive as possible. But she was honestly puzzled as to what they were to do with the girl. She was eighteen, or was it nineteen? Almost a decade younger than herself. At that age her life had been overshadowed by the War, but this child probably lived for pleasure. Lights, crowds, dance-music, magic of heat and sound, cocktails, lipstick, clothes constantly renewed--those probably made up the sum of her enjoyment. What would she do with the decorous round of the Harbour House? Of course they must get other boys and girls to play with her--Nicole smiled to find herself forced into the position of maiden aunt! The Erskines were considered Bright Young People in Kirkmeikle, though probably they would fall far short in this London girl's eyes. They were older than Althea, more her own age, she remembered. Lady Fenton would play with her; she liked to go about with very young girls and be kittenish; and, anyway, she concluded, if Althea were bored she didn't need to stay.

The visitor was expected in the late afternoon.

'Much the nicest time,' Lady Jane said. 'She will get tea and go to her room till dinner, and probably she will go early to bed and we can all begin and make friends in the morning light.'

Nicole looked doubtful. 'I don't know about the morning light being conducive to friendship. You're such an optimist, Mums--But I hope it will be all right. As you say, the worst will be over when we get the greetings said. *How* I hate strangers coming!' She leant down to pat Spider's nose. 'So do you, I know. All right, old man, we'll go for a run along the sands.... Must I meet her, Mums? Won't Harris do? I'll tell you what, I'll order a closed car and send Harris.'

'Oh no, darling. Go yourself in the little car, it would be so much more friendly! The luggage can be sent down later. The child will feel strange perhaps....'

'*Perhaps*,' Nicole broke in. 'My dear, nothing shakes the composure of the girl of to-day....'

There was only one passenger from the train that could be the expected guest, and Nicole went up to a tall young girl with a fur coat over her arm and a dressing-bag at her feet, and said: 'I expect you're Althea? I'm Nicole Rutherfurd.... A porter will bring down your luggage if you'll see if it's all there, and I have my small car here.

'This is Spider.' Nicole made the introduction when they left the station and found that small black-and-white gentleman occupying the driver's seat. 'Get down, silly. Jump in, will you, Althea, and put that rug round you. I expect you find it pretty cold here. Now then... we've only a very short way to go. What sort of journey had you? Oh... good.'

Lady Jane was waiting in the hall to kiss and welcome her guest, and they went at once upstairs for tea.

Nicole took stock of the girl as she made tea and her mother made conversation, and was amused to find that she was almost exactly as she had pictured her. Very tall, as so many girls are now, she had long slim legs, a small pointed face with very dark blue eyes; a golden-brown curl on each cheek, a string of pearls, ear-rings, a good deal of make-up. She spoke in a quick, almost breathless, way, and her voice was pleasant. She had taken off her tweed coat, and sat in a fawn jumper suit, in a chintz chair with 'lugs,' her legs stretched out before her, answering Lady Jane's questions.

'And your Aunt Blanchie, how is she?'

'Oh, Blanchie's all right. She's only gone to bed for safety.' She gave a small mirthless laugh. 'She does hate so to be upset, poor dear. I expect she's up to-day and preparing to go off to Egypt now that she's got me shunted.'

Nicole laughed. 'I shouldn't at all wonder. Will you have your tea there, or sit in at the table? Anyway, make a meal of your tea as we say in our hearty country way.... This is your first visit to Scotland, isn't it? No, I'm not going to ask you what you think of it.'

'You would have some time in Edinburgh to-day?' said Lady Jane. 'I envy you seeing it for the first time.... Do take jam with your muffin.'

'Shall I? Thanks.... I spent the morning sight-seeing. The friend I travelled with wanted to see the Memorial. It's pretty good, I thought.'

'It's wonderful,' said Nicole. 'The bed-rock coming through the floor.... And the cold blue windows seem to me so right, all of a piece with the cold grey city and the cold blue Firth.'

Althea turned to look out of the window. 'Is that,' she asked, 'the Firth of Forth I'm looking at now?'

Lady Jane shook her head. 'No, that is the real sea.'

'Oh, the Atlantic?'

'No, the North Sea.'

Althea took another muffin. 'I don't think I knew there was a North Sea,' she announced calmly. 'Where does it go to?'

'To "Norraway ower the faem,"' said Nicole. 'Did you ever hear of the king who sat in Dunfermline town drinking the blood-red wine?'

"Fraid not. What else did he do besides drink?'

'He sent Sir Patrick Spens over the sea with other Scots lords.... Yes, seas are very confusing. I remember, coming home from India the Captain asked another girl and myself what sea we were navigating at the moment. I guessed the Persian Gulf, and my friend said confidently, "The Baltic."'

37

'How amusing!' said Althea, and Nicole retired behind the teapot.

Lady Jane took up the burden of the conversation. She had a way, when things were at all difficult, of talking gently on, not waiting for an answer, not seeming to expect interest, and Nicole enjoyed her tea in grateful silence, merely throwing in a response now and then.

Althea ate very fast for about ten minutes, drank three cups of tea in quick succession, and then, not waiting to be offered cigarettes, she produced her own case and a very long holder, and changing from the big arm-chair into Lady Jane's own low chair, she lay back in great ease.

Effie removed the tea-things, and Lady Jane sat down near a light with her embroidery. Nicole knelt on a window-seat, watching the tide creep in.

'Wouldn't you like to see your room now?' she said presently.

Althea did not trouble to turn her head. 'I'm all right, thanks. When d'you dine?'

'Seven-thirty.'

She turned her wrist to the light. 'Half-past five now. I needn't stir for an age. I think I'll have a sleep! This fire's so jolly warm.'

'*Do*,' said Nicole, politely urgent, and settled herself by the writing-table to answer letters. As she addressed an envelope she told herself, with rather grim amusement, that so long as the visitor stayed she would probably be a better correspondent than ever she had been. Writing letters and doing embroidery seemed the only way of occupying the time while these long shapely legs were stretched before the fire, and this insolent child lay and blew smoke rings. Impossible to settle down to read with such a disturbing element in the house. Already the peaceful atmosphere was gone. Even her mother had a dispossessed air as she sat pulling the thread through the stuff pensively, like a queen in exile.

Nicole began to reply to an invitation from Vera Erskine.

'Althea Gort has just arrived,' she wrote, 'and I am sure she will love to go with me to dine with you on Friday. I'm afraid she will find this quiet place rather dull....' She glanced across at the little made-up face in the firelight, and added, 'though we shall do our best to amuse her.'

She wondered if Vera and Althea would get on well together. Vera was a hearty creature, very keen on hunting, proficient at all games, a tireless dancer, and ready always to be amused and interested. Well, that was *something*, anyway, for Althea to do, and they were lunching the next day at Knebworth--Mrs. Heggie and Althea, that would be diverting! and going to tea at Windywalls on Thursday. Quite a giddy whirl! But Althea was hardly the sort of girl to be interested in strangers, and she probably hadn't the manners to hide her boredom. Well, it couldn't be helped. Her mother had brought the girl here. On her head was the success or failure of the plan.

She took up another sheet of paper and began a letter to Jean Douglas, one of the Rutherfurds' oldest friends on the Borders, and interested in everything that happened to Nicole and her mother. At the moment she was shut up at her home, Kingshouse, with a husband suffering from sciatica, and letters were doubly welcome.

'Althea Gort came this afternoon. She has the longest legs and the shortest skirts on record, and is *very* pretty. At present she is sound asleep in Mother's own chair. I've only known her for an hour, but already I see why poor Blanchie gave it up and went to bed. I can well imagine that this young woman loose in London would be a terror. Happily she can't do much in Kirkmeikle, and even Langtoun offers little scope. But what are we to do with her? Obviously she regards us, more or less, as her jailers, and is as resentful as she can be at being sent here.... Mother refuses to meet my eyes, and sits at her embroidery looking like Queen Mary in Lochleven!... All the same, Mistress Jean, it's not really amusing, for I can see Althea will play havoc with our peace. It sounds horribly selfish to say so, and to grudge hospitality to a girl who hasn't got a home. When you think of it she has never had a chance to be a normal nice girl. Both her parents outside the pale: unwanted: knocked about from one relative to another, she was bound to develop a protective shell. I expect that is why she has such casual manners and an air of not caring a fig for any one. She feels herself up against the world, poor babe! At present, as I say, she is definitely hostile to us, but perhaps Mother's disarming gentleness and simplicity will soften her. I expect she's afraid I'll come the elder sister or the maiden aunt over her. She makes me feel at once very young and quite old!...'

It was very quiet in the pretty room: you could hear the ripple of the water on the sand outside, and the far-away cry of a sea-bird. Nicole wrote, her mother stitched and stitched, while her thoughts wove other patterns. Althea, broad awake--her dose had been little more than a pretence--watched the scene through half-shut eyes.

* * * * *

Later, she came down to dinner such a bizarre figure that Effie, who was young and unsophisticated, forgot all she had been taught about never appearing to look at any one, nor listening to the conversation, and frankly stared. The question which interested her was, would that brilliant red come off when the young lady drank, or was it water-proof, wine-proof, and coffee-proof? She had been helping Harris to unpack for Miss Gort, and never had she seen such clothes, so many aids to the toilet. She felt vaguely elated to be in the same house as such a strange and beautiful lady.

When they returned to the drawing-room, Althea went to the piano, and without being asked, sat down and began to play scraps of one thing and another, from Chopin to the songs from the latest revue. Lady Jane and her daughter had perforce to listen: there was no chance of reading or talking.

After Nicole had gone up with their guest to see that she had everything she wanted, she came back to the drawing-room and looked reproachfully at her mother.

'Aren't you ashamed of yourself, Mums? You have need to be. Talk about ruining a home!...'

'It won't be so bad when we get to know her,' Lady Jane pleaded.

'It'll be worse,' said Nicole, 'much worse.'

Chapter VII

'She knew what she knew, like a sound dogmatist:
She did not know what she did not know--like a sound agnostic.'

G. K. CHESTERTON.

Nicole's letter, written from the Harbour House on the night of the arrival of Althea Gort to her friend Jean Douglas, made that lady laugh as she read it.

Mrs. Douglas was frankly middle-aged, but very slim and straight and well-dressed. She wore her grey hair rolled back in a fashion of her own from her small, high-coloured face: her exceedingly bright blue eyes kindled very easily to anger, but they were just as liable to sparkle with laughter, or to melt with sympathy: what no one ever saw in them was a spark of malice.

'What's amusing you?' asked her husband. He was a large man with a round red face, an overwhelming admiration for his sprightly wife which he did his best to conceal, and a trick of taking sciatica which exasperated the said wife beyond measure. A good husband when well and able to be out of doors most of the time, she admitted that, but cooped up in the house he was a nuisance, for he hated cards, read nothing but newspapers and *The Field*, and did nothing but groan and mope. At present he was recovering from a bout and was in a complaisant mood.

His wife answered his question obliquely.

'Really,' she said, 'Lady Jane is almost too much of an angel.'

'What's she done now?'

'Done? She's gone and asked for an indefinite visit a girl who is a niece of her sister-in-law--no relation at all of her own, evidently a brat of a thing, and poor Nicole has got to entertain her as best she can. Of course I quite see Lady Jane's point. Alastair, who was Nicole's care, has gone to school: there isn't much to do in that quiet place, so she provides Nicole with an occupation, and at the same time helps her sister-in-law out of a difficulty. I dare say it will work out all right, but the picture Nicole draws of her mother and herself dispossessed by this young cuckoo is rather funny.'

Colonel Douglas puffed at his pipe. 'Who did you say the girl was?'

'Oh, you know all about her. Freddie Gort's girl.'

'Oh--Lord, yes. Poor little soul, she can't have had much of an upbringing.'

'That, of course, was Jane Rutherfurd's reason for bringing her. As I've said before, she's an angel that woman. She can't bear every one not to get a chance. She may make something of this Gort girl. She can't be more than eighteen or nineteen.... I knew her mother, a heartless, lovely minx. The sister Blanche, Lady Elliston, Jane's sister-in-law, is quite harmless, if silly. This girl could inherit nothing good from her father except a pleasant manner, which she seems to have avoided, if Nicole's first impressions are right.'

Tom Douglas grunted agreement.... 'I knew Freddie Gort in India. In 1902, it would be. Good man at polo: danced well too, and a first-class shot. I remember....' He went on for quite a long time with his reminiscences, while his wife looked over the rest of her letters.

When she had finished she said in a brisk voice:

'Well, are you going to venture out to-day?'

'Why not? The sun's shining.'

'But the ground is very damp.'

'Well, I'm not going to roll on it, am I? A walk'll do me a lot of good.'

'Put on goloshes,' said his wife, without, however, the smallest hope of seeing her suggestion adopted.

'Good Lord! Aren't my boots thick enough? I wonder you don't want me to put a plaid round my shoulders and carry a hot-water bag.'

'Oh, very well. But don't ask me to condole with you if you get another chill.'

Tom Douglas's face got apoplectic. 'How often have I told you that I never take chills? Sciatica's a thing any one might have. The strongest suffer from it--From the way you speak one would think it was a sign of weakness.'

'Whatever it is it makes you disgustingly cross and morose to live with, so in self-defence I ask you to be careful. You don't really think you've been a pleasant companion for the last fortnight, do you?'

'I thought women liked to nurse,' her husband grumbled. 'The only poem I ever learned was something about ministering angels. "*When pain and anguish wring the brow...*"'

He looked so like a large sulky boy as he stood there, that his wife could only laugh and, catching the lapels of his old tweed coat, kiss his aggrieved red face.

'You are an old silly, aren't you? Go away out, then, as long as the sun shines, but don't stand talking to Daniel in the stable-yard. I'll come out and look for you if you are too long. Alison Lockhart's coming to luncheon.'

'Thought she was in Italy somewhere.'

'She is only just back. She rang up last night and asked if she might come to-day. She says she's coming to get all the news of the countryside!'

'There's none,' said Colonel Douglas briefly. 'Well. I'll be back in lots of time. I'm just going to take a look round. When you've been shut up in the house as long as I have there's a lot wants seeing to....'

Kingshouse was looking rather beautiful that pale, windy, autumn day. It stood on the banks of Tweed, a plain Georgian house, with wide lawns sloping up to a beech-wood which, in early spring, was a drift of snowdrops. Inside were comfortable rooms, well lighted, well warmed, full of solid Victorian furniture; for Jean Douglas clung to the Victorian age, insisting that in it she found all the virtues. The round table that stood in her own sitting-room held Jane Austen and Trollope and Hardy as the daily bread of her reading: Douglas and Foulis's box supplied what she wanted of the literature of the day, but as she found little to admire in the modern novel, she confined herself chiefly to biography and travel. Once she said to Nicole about a much-praised and widely read modern masterpiece: 'I've read it, and in a way I've enjoyed it, but I couldn't let it lie on my table. I'd have hated to see it near my Bible.'

She was very good friends with herself, and never minded being alone, but she was keenly interested in her neighbours. A childless woman, she grudged no trouble where it was a question of giving children pleasure. The Kingshouse Christmas party had been a landmark to the young Rutherfurds, and to many others. She found something to be amused at in almost every situation in which she found herself, indeed, even on the most solemn occasions there was apt to be a suppressed twinkle in her eyes.

The twinkle was there this morning as she watched from the window her husband set off for his walk. He had started as if to go to the garden, but she suspected he would branch off to the stable-yard and pass the time of day with Daniel. Daniel had been coachman to the Douglases for many years, and now, when motors had taken the place of horses, he was a sort of adviser-in-general to the whole household. No one quite knew what his job was supposed to be, he did a bit of everybody else's: his own private opinion was that he held the whole place together. He was now sixty-five, and fifty of those years had been spent at Kingshouse. He could not imagine life away from that quiet place beside the Water of Tweed. Unmarried, he lived alone in a cottage, which he kept as neat and trig as any on the place. He was great friends with Mrs. Fraser, the cook (Mrs. only by courtesy), had been so for thirty years, but it went no further than friendship. He appreciated her as a cook, admired her as a woman, but distrusted her as a wife. He had gone his own way so long that the thought of being tied was insupportable.

Servants stayed long at Kingshouse, indeed they were seldom removed except by marriage or death. Mrs. Douglas's own maid had become something of a tyrant, if an affectionate and loyal one. Her mistress often said she trembled before Ellen, and not without reason. The whole household was an immense amusement to Alison Lockhart, the expected luncheon guest. On her return from her frequent wanderings she always reported herself first at Kingshouse.

'How refreshing,' she remarked when the servants had left the room, 'to come back here, where time stands still. Change and decay are everywhere--I found a perfect battalion of grey hairs this morning, and a front tooth is showing signs of having done with me--but you and Tom never get a bit older, two fresh young folk.... Lawson opens the door for me as he has done frequently for the past thirty years-- what a blessing not to see a different face every time you go to a friend's house! Mrs. Fraser goes on making the same delicious pastry and cakes that she made when I was a child...'

'This cake is specially made for you,' Jean Douglas pointed out, 'so you must have a bit with your coffee. Yes, I know it will spoil the flavour of the coffee, but better that than you should hurt Mrs. Fraser's feelings.'

Miss Lockhart laughed: 'Well--a tiny bit. I know it of old: it's my favourite cake.... Tell me, how is Ellen? Is she as masterful as ever?'

'Worse. I wanted to put on a new dress which has just arrived, that you might pronounce on it, but she wouldn't hear of it and forced me into this. Declares the new one must be kept for a party!'

'It's absurd, Jean,' her husband put in. 'Put your foot down once and for all. Say to her...' He paused.

'Yes?' said his wife pleasantly.

'Well, just say you will put on what you please, not what she pleases, and--what are you laughing at, Jean?'

'Did you see Daniel this morning?'

'Yes, but what's that got...'

'Did you find that he had done what you told him about the bridge?'

Tom Douglas's red face got a shade deeper as he looked steadily into his coffee-cup.

'Well,' he said, 'he hasn't done *quite* what I suggested...'

'Suggested,' remarked his wife, 'is good.'

'But,' he finished with dignity, 'I'm not sure that he hasn't improved on my idea.'

'Handsomely said.' Mrs. Douglas turned to her guest. 'Alison, do tell us something new and interesting to keep Tom and me from wrangling.'

Miss Lockhart ate the candy-sugar in her spoon (though she did not take it in her coffee, she liked some to sup) and said: 'Something new and interesting? My dear, you ask too much. I roam the world in search of amusement with no success, and come back to find it by Tweedside. Tell me what's been happening to every one. Remember, I've heard no news for months.'

Jean Douglas nibbled a salted almond. 'D'you mean to say,' she asked, 'that you didn't notice us in the picture Press? Tilly Kilpatrick was very much in evidence at Games and Gatherings--you know, reading left to right. Tom and I inadvertently got in once, but they put "In this group appear..." so the public were left to guess which was which of the disreputable-looking crew. Tom was also once mentioned as "the genial host," which pleased him very much.'

'It did not,' said that affronted gentleman. 'I'd like to know who writes that trash.' No one enlightened him, and presently he went off to his study leaving the women to their talk.

'And of course you heard about Barbara Jackson's baby? Oh yes, a boy. Andrew Rutherfurd Jackson. All things are added unto that girl.... I mean to go and call there this afternoon. I think Barbara feels that I only go when Lady Jane and Nicole are there.'

'I'd better go too, perhaps. I haven't been for ages. To tell the truth I never cared for Barbara. Have the Rutherfurds been back lately?'

'At the end of September. They were all there for the christening. Mr. and Mrs. Jackson from Glasgow in great form. I will say this, Barbara behaves very nicely to her mother-in-law, and it can't always be easy. Nor is it easy for Mrs. Jackson, she must see many things that she doesn't approve of. Several times I know, she was biting back remarks that would have given offence; she looked at me as much as to say: "You and I know what we think--but not a word!" I always did like that little woman. I asked her if she liked being back in Glasgow, and she said in that curiously soft Glasgow voice of hers: "Uch, it's all right. Father and I get on fine: he has his business and I've got my house, and we've lots of people coming about, but, d'ye know, we miss our county friends--ucha, we do." I can't speak like her, but Nicole has her to perfection. They are great friends, Mrs. Jackson and Nicole.'

'How is Nikky?'

'Happy, I think. She has accepted things. I was rather worried about her for a long time after they left Rutherfurd. She looked radiant at Barbara's wedding, but when she came back with her mother in the autumn there was a change in her that I can't explain.'

'You don't suppose she had banked on marrying young Jackson and getting back Rutherfurd?'

Mrs. Douglas shook her head. 'Oh no. At the wedding she was the gayest thing possible: not making-believe either. Whether something happened...'

44

'Didn't you ask her mother?'

'I did not: nor would you, my dear. Jane Rutherfurd is gentleness itself, but she can put people in their place in a way I've never seen equalled. I never risk a snub. Anyway, it was no business of mine, and Nicole seems to have got over it--if there was anything to get over. I had a letter from her this morning. They've got a girl Althea Gort visiting them. You know, Sybil Gort's girl.'

'Bless me!' Alison Lockhart twisted her mouth. She was a plain woman with a fascinating mouth. 'What is the idea of that? She's not a relation, is she?'

'A connection by marriage.'

'Of course. Sybil's sister married Jane's brother. Poor Sybil's dead. She was a pretty creature, but in horsey circles she would have been described as "a confirmed bolter"--I wonder what the daughter is like!'

'And how she will enjoy Kirkmeikle in November! One hardly knows who to pity most.... It seems her aunt--Lady Elliston, you know--isn't well enough to look after her, and asked Lady Jane, as a great favour, to take her for a little. I wonder what the girl will make of the Harbour House.'

'If she has any sense she'll love it and realise that to be taken in there is the best thing that ever happened to her. I don't believe in many people, but I do believe in Jane Rutherfurd.... By the way, I hear John Dalrymple's back.'

'Yes.' Jean Douglas poised the spoon on the top of her coffee-cup and considered it.

'Well?'

'Well what?'

'Oh, don't be absurd. You know quite well he's been devoted to Nicole since she was a child. I can't think why they haven't been married for years. Everybody thought after the War he'd settle down at Newby. You remember he got quite a lot done to the house, and was so much at Rutherfurd that we expected an announcement any day, instead of which off he went abroad and the place was shut up. I expect that was Nicole's fault. Well, that's about eight years ago, a lot of water's run under Tweed Bridge since then and Nicole's all that older and wiser. Let's hope they'll settle it up soon. Have they met, do you know?'

Jean Douglas put the spoon back in her saucer and said: 'Not yet, but Nicole and her mother are coming to Rutherfurd for Christmas. Alison, do be careful what you say to Nikky, what you say to any one. I'm *terribly* set on this marriage coming off. But if Barbara begins to manage or...'

'Oh. I know her heavy footed way! My dear, I'll be dumb. I'm just as keen as you are to see a Rutherfurd back on Tweedside.... Is John as imperturbable as ever? He's good-looking in a sulky way, and Nicole is the heaven-sent mate for him. A firefly of a creature needs a drab husband as a background!'

Chapter VIII

'...so genteel and so easy!... always something to say to everybody. That *is my idea of good breeding'.*

JANE AUSTEN.

Nicole introduced Althea to Kirkmeikle society with a sort of amused trepidation.

Althea had sighed resignedly when told that she had been invited to lunch at Knebworth.

'Need we go?' she asked languidly.

'Oh, there's no *need* about it, but invitations mean more in Kirkmeikle than in London, and Mrs. Heggie wants to be very kind.'

Althea seemed unimpressed, and when Nicole routed her out of an arm-chair to dress, she asked peevishly what she was supposed to put on.

Nicole laughed as she followed the girl into her room. The white chamber smelling of salt air and linen in lavender had suffered a change. The toilet-table was covered with a multitude of bottles and boxes; powder was spilt about; a box of paints and a sketch-book, some embroidery silk, bundles of patterns, two paper-backed French novels and a box of chocolates without its lid lay heaped in confusion on the writing-table. The wardrobe door refused to shut, and slippers and shoes tumbled about everywhere. The room, Nicole knew, was thoroughly tidied every morning, but in five minutes Althea would wreck any room.

Nicole suggested a coat and skirt or a jumper suit. 'You have so many nice things,' she said, 'and nobody dresses in Kirkmeikle: not to call dressing: we are decently covered, that is all you can say.'

When Althea emerged from her room she was the last word in smartness, and heavily made up.

'She wants me to protest,' Nicole told herself, so she said: 'I was taught that it was rude to make personal remarks, but I can't help congratulating you on your appearance. You can't think how thrilled Mrs. Heggie will be that you have taken trouble to dress for her.'

'I expect,' said Althea hopefully, 'that she'll feel she's got the World, the Flesh, and the Devil at the table to-day.'

'Very likely,' said Nicole. 'All she knows of the world is culled from the books she reads. She is a somewhat shocked follower of some of our more outspoken novelists. She is so believing, poor dear, that it's a shame to deceive her, but I sometimes feel inclined to try how far her credulity goes.'

The only other guests, Mrs. Jameson and Mrs. Lambert, were already in the Knebworth drawing-room when Nicole, in demure grey, and the exotic-looking Althea were shown in.

Mrs. Heggie had been looking forward to welcome what she described to herself as 'a bright young girl,' and when she met the cold eyes of Althea and realised the scarlet lips, she recoiled like a rabbit from a snake. The Rutherfurds had been a surprise to her in their simplicity and friendliness; this was what she had always expected the aristocracy to look like--cold, painted, proud.

She found nothing better to say than 'Well, well,' but, recovering herself, she introduced Joan, and the two stood looking at each other, surely the most oddly assorted couple one could see on a day's journey.

Nicole, while appearing absorbed in what Mrs. Lambert was saying to her, listened with amusement to the conversation.

'This is your first visit to Kirkmeikle?'

'My first visit to Scotland.'

'Oh.... You live in London?'

'Sometimes, when I'm not abroad.'

'Er... Do you... do you *do* anything? I mean, are you going in for anything?'

Althea raised her eyebrows enquiringly.

'I mean--are you keen on Art or Music or...'

'No.' Althea's eyes were roaming round the Knebworth drawing-room, noting the 'quaint' windows, and the 'artistic' door-knobs.

'Oh--Are you fond of the Drama?'

The girl let her eyes rest negligently on Joan as she said: 'I like a good crook play, and I don't mind a revue if it goes fast enough. If you mean do I like Shakespeare and highbrow stuff, I don't.'

She turned away her head as if, so far as she was concerned, the conversation was closed.

Joan was rendered dumb: never had she felt so snubbed, so put in her place, and when she turned and met an understanding gleam in Nicole's eyes she felt more warmly to that young woman than ever she had done.

Nicole came over and began to talk to her about a book of poems that had just been

47

published.

'You haven't seen it? Oh, may I send it to you? I bought several copies--it's only a tiny book. I met the girl who wrote it, Meta Strong, when I was away; we were staying at the same house and we made friends. I was so interested to find she knew your book. She may be coming later to stay at the Harbour House, and I hope you will come and meet her.'

She had soothed Joan's ruffled feelings before luncheon was announced. She told herself she wasn't going to have Mrs. Heggie's party spoiled by this unmannerly child, for it was a very high effort in the way of a party. Mrs. Heggie had taken infinite pains to please her guests. Her menu was carefully thought out. Every detail of the table was as perfect as she could make it. Bella, the parlour-maid, had been drilled and admonished until she hardly knew what she was doing! the cook was rendered nervous and unsure of herself.

Mrs. Heggie would have told you that she was very 'knacky' about a table, and to-day she had surpassed all previous efforts. Everything was pale yellow: the table-mats, the napkins, the glasses, the candlesticks, the candles. Instead of flowers a large silver dish stood in the middle of the table filled with artificial fruit. She had seen the same thing in a friend's house, and thought it very *chic*. Her breast, as she took her place at the table, swelled with satisfaction. Nobody else in Kirkmeikle, and not even in Langtoun, she felt sure, had such a colour scheme. Instinctively her eyes turned to Nicole and met her smile of congratulations. Mrs. Jameson, unfolding her napkin, was saying how charming the table looked, to which her hostess replied with a deprecatory murmur.

Joan envied her mother chatting so happily with Mrs. Jameson and Nicole. She, poor soul, laboured in conversation with Mrs. Lambert and the London girl. Mrs. Lambert was willing and anxious to do her best, but though she liked Joan's poetry, she cherished a nervous fear of the author of it, who was known to despise more or less everybody in Kirkmeikle, and wasn't likely to make an exception of the minister's little, shy, shabby wife, and the mere sight of Althea filled her gentle heart with horror. She had seen pictures of people like her in magazines, but had hoped to be spared meeting one in the flesh. The perfection of the clothes appalled her no less than the painted face and the cold, unfriendly eyes.

Still, she had accepted this invitation, now that she was here she must do her best to talk. Joan had evidently come to an end of her conversation, so she threw herself into the breach and asked in a small choked voice if the fruit in the middle dish was real.

'Wax,' said Joan, 'or china or something.'

'They are wonderfully natural,' went on Mrs. Lambert, and all three gazed solemnly at the dish.

'I prefer flowers myself,' Joan said with finality.

'But in winter,' began Mrs. Lambert, 'flowers are so difficult to get in Kirkmeikle.'

She raised her voice and, greatly daring, addressed the tall girl. 'I'm told that in London the flower shops are most beautiful. Indeed, the best of everything seems to go to London.'

'Don't you know London?' Althea asked.

'No, I've never been out of Scotland. But we've promised ourselves a week in London some day and we're saving up for it.'

Althea stared at the small transparent face that was like a wood-anemone, and said: 'I hope you'll think it's worth the trouble when you go. It's a pity to look forward to things, they generally turn out duds.'

'But it's fun to look forward,' Mrs. Lambert insisted. 'I'm not sure that the looking forward and looking back aren't the happiest bits; one isn't really *fearfully* happy at the moment of doing.'

'Is one ever really happy?' said Joan in her hungry voice.

'Yes,' Mrs. Lambert said, with surprising decision.

'You mean you are?' said Althea.

Mrs. Lambert nodded.

'I wonder why?' said Althea, and turned to help herself to a dish that was being offered.

'Why...' Mrs. Lambert was beginning, when she stopped. Why should she tell her tale of happiness to listeners who could never understand? So instead of telling she laughed and said: 'Certainly not because I've got the things that are generally regarded as essential to happiness.' She felt quite bold now, unafraid, though she was seeing herself as these others saw her, a little wisp of a woman with a shabby little husband who stuttered, and two rather plain little girls; a grey manse in a garden and a very small salary. 'We've got no money, we wear our clothes to the bitter end, we get few holidays, and never travel, but we refuse to be considered miserable. I suppose it's a sort of contrariness.' She stopped, found the table listening, and blushed.

Nicole was smiling at her, and the lady at Mrs. Heggie's right hand, whom she had not met before, turned to her saying: 'I'm very much interested to hear you say that. I'd like to see some statistics about happiness. But it's really temperament, don't you think? If you're born with a jealous, striving spirit, you'll be miserable till the day you die; whereas if you are contented, all other things will be added unto you.'

'That's true,' said Mrs. Heggie, 'I've noticed it myself.'

'Then you think,' said Nicole, 'that when the fairies come to our christening we shouldn't desire brains, beauty, wealth, but simply content?'

'Isn't there such a thing as divine discontent?' Joan said loftily and evidently feeling that that was what she suffered from. 'If every one was content, nothing would get done.'

'Well, that's true too,' said her mother. 'Telephones and wireless, and now this television. I'm told we'll be able to see people's faces when they're telephoning.'

Nicole groaned. 'What a horrible idea. Imagine seeing the stricken faces of people who don't want to come and have no excuse when you ask them to a party!'

Mrs. Jameson, refusing to be side-tracked, went back to her subject and said: 'Content is not laziness. Content is having a--what is it?--"a heart at leisure from itself"; where does that quotation come from? And a mind at ease from petty worries to do great things.'

Mrs. Heggie, while keeping a watchful eye on Bella, smiled kindly at her guest and said: 'You must be very contented yourself, Mrs. Jameson, to live happily alone at Windywalls.'

Esmé Jameson seemed to be about to say something, then, meeting Nicole's glance, she merely laughed, and Joan said peevishly:

'I can't understand what makes us stay in this dreary seaside village through a long winter, when we might be somewhere basking in sunshine. I'd like to go to Persia and Arabia.'

'I expect you've been reading Gertrude Bell's *Letters*' Nicole said.

Joan nodded. 'What a super-woman! I'd rather have had a day of her life than my whole existence.'

'Dear me,' said her mother, 'how you young people talk! Do you want to go to Persia, Miss Gort?'

'Not particularly,' said that damsel. 'It's hot and dirty, and I hate flies.'

'Bokhara's the place I want to go to,' Nicole said, 'but I'm afraid I've a morbid liking for Kirkmeikle in winter.'

'Indeed, it's not bad,' said Mrs. Heggie. 'Mrs. Lambert, if you don't like coffee, could they get you a cup of tea?'

'Does the rock-garden progress?' Nicole asked Esmé Jameson, who shook her head.

'Stuck till spring,' she said. 'I'm looking forward to seeing you to-morrow, you and Miss Gort.'

She looked at the girl, who was sitting over her coffee, her elbows on the table, a cigarette in its long holder in her mouth, and looked away again, without meeting Nicole's eyes.

* * * * *

Though Lady Jane did not care much to go out to meals, she enjoyed hearing about

50

them, and looked up from her embroidery with a welcoming smile as her daughter came in.

'Where is Althea?' she asked.

'Gone upstairs. I expect she'll lie on her bed and smoke till tea-time. I'm afraid she was badly bored; she had the appearance of despising her company.'

'Poor child!' said Lady Jane. 'Was it a nice luncheon?'

'All yellow,' said Nicole. 'Yes, everything. I do wish you could have seen it. It was very effective, and Mrs. Heggie was so proud. The food was yellow too.'

'Nonsense, Nikky.'

'But yes. Listen. Little yellow dishes with some sort of fish soufflé; cutlets-- yellowish; potatoes done in browny-yellow balls, *you* know; mashed turnips, *very* yellow; a creamy-yellow pudding, and oranges filled with jelly; African plums, bananas, oranges--all yellow. I felt the guests should all have got themselves up to match.... Mrs. Jameson was there, very neat in tweeds. Mrs. Lambert, dear soul, in her old fawn things, I as you see me, and that absurd child dressed like a circus! But I think Mrs. Heggie was rather flattered than otherwise; she felt she had been dressed for. What Joan thought I dare not think. Althea was frankly rude to her.... How long are we to stand it, Mums?'

Her mother drew her needle with its silk thread in and out several times before she looked up at her daughter.

'It's early days to talk like that, Nikky. Be patient with the silly child.'

'But I don't see why we should be. No, Mums, you needn't look at me with these calmly disapproving eyes. In this case we are not our brother's keeper. It's that lazy Blanchie, who has deserted her post and thrust us into the position of jailers, who is responsible.... You talk about "poor child," and she may be young in years but she's got all the wisdom of the serpent in that sleek little head of hers. In three days I've only found one good thing about her! She's fond of Spider.'

'Having said that, let's leave the subject,' Lady Jane suggested.... 'While you were on pleasure bent I went to see old Betsy. I know her much frailer since summer. And she's getting gentle, which is a bad sign. At least, perhaps "gentle" is hardly the word, less pugnacious anyhow.'

'Was she up?'

'Oh yes: sitting by the fire with her back turned to the window, and the sea which she dislikes so sincerely. We had a long talk about Rutherfurd. She says merely to hear the names of the places is like a drink of water to her. It is rather terrible that her spirit should still be so keen when her body is so frail: she is almost quite helpless now. She wraps her poor twisted hands in her shawl....'

Nicole nodded. 'I know. She looks the merest little crumpled wisp, but when she lifts these wrinkled eyelids her eyes are like a hawk's, so light and keen. I *wish* she didn't feel so much--Talking about helplessness, you remember I told you about a man I met at the Erskines called Walkinshaw? They've a place, Kinogle, which has been let for some time. Well, it seems his mother has got that dreadful arthritis and can hardly move. Mrs. Erskine was telling me about her. Quite a young woman--the son isn't more than six-and-twenty--she is shut off from everything. I'm told she's rather glad of visitors, so we might go one day, don't you think? She won't see us if she doesn't feel able, but I think she might like a visit from you, Mother. Yours is a consoling presence so to speak.... What? No, I'm not mocking: it's the truth.'

Chapter IX

'Although my life is left so dim,
The morning crowns the mountain-rim;
Joy is not gone from summer skies
Nor innocence from children's eyes.'

ALICE MEYNELL.

As Esmé Jameson dressed for the Erskines' dinner-party she reflected thankfully that Nicole Rutherfurd was to be there. That would be one known face, and a friendly one at that. She had not yet met the Erskines, as she had been in Edinburgh when they made their call, and they had been out when she returned it. There were two daughters, she knew, Vera and Tibbie, for Miss Rutherfurd had said she hoped they would make friends with the girl who had come to stay at the Harbour House, Althea Gort. Odd little thing that was, with her lovely, impassive face and unfriendly manners! A changeling at the hearth of Lady Jane and her daughter.

Esmé looked at herself in the glass. She was looking well, she thought: her face was rounder and she had a healthy colour. The life at Windywalls suited her. She had been a grey-faced, nervous creature, but the east winds of Fife were reviving, not to speak of work in the garden and wordy wrangles with old John Grierson. It was delightful to have a house of one's own, to order the sort of meals that agreed with one, to go to bed when one felt sleepy, in short, to have no one to consider but oneself. And the house was ceasing to be merely a house, with a certain number of rooms, each filled with so many articles of furniture, it was becoming a home, acquiring an individuality of its own.

This room, now. She looked round the airy, pleasant bedroom with its wide window looking over the fields to the sea. There was the bed she had always wanted, with its slender fluted mahogany pillars and little valance of chintz. The petticoated dressing-table had glass on the top, and under the skirt of muslin were drawers to tidy things away in, for she did not like a littered table. She had found a really lovely old Persian carpet, with colours as gentle as those of Hassan's treasured rug. The room was empty except for some chairs, a wardrobe that occupied the whole length of one wall, and an old walnut table at the bedside, with a shaded electric light, a stand of books, and a small case of brown leather which held the photograph of a young man in uniform.

In the years of her husband's illness her sleep had necessarily been broken, but after, when there was nothing to disturb her, her thoughts had kept her awake. The bitterness of her pity for Archie--If he had died in battle she felt that she would have had nothing but pride and thankfulness in her heart. Pity was wasted on those boys who, knowing only 'the singing season,' leapt into the great adventure of war, and, in spite of discomfort and misery and often black horror, laughed their way through, and died, in the April of their days, willing sacrifices, their hearts high within them. But Archie----

The War had crashed into their honeymoon, sweeping away all their plans and hopes, but that had mattered little. Archie had gone without a second's hesitation, as she would have wished. She would have thought his love for her a poor thing had it not made him love honour more. But those long years of helplessness and pain.... There were two things she would never forget. Once when she had looked at the clock at his bedside and said 'It's slow,' he had replied 'I keep it slow,' and in answer to her enquiring glance, 'It's nice to know that it's a little further on than it seems.'

She had laughed and turned away that he might not see the smarting tears in her eyes. Archie who had used to complain that time went so fast!...

Another time he had wakened from a sleep with a happy cry of '*Esmé*.' She was beside him in a second, and there would always remain with her the look in his eyes as he said: 'I must have been dreaming, I thought I was well again and we were going out for a ride.... I'm sorry to be such an idiot----'

So, for long, her nights had been a torment. She had often felt she hated her bed. All the more wonderful now, she found it, to think with pleasure of bed--to undress slowly, luxuriously, to read some pleasant book for half an hour or so, click out the light, turn over on her right side, her mind full of homely things, details of housekeeping, of garden-making, of half-remembered sayings... and know nothing until she awoke to morning light. After her weary years she could not get used to the wonder of it; she never ceased to be grateful. That alone would have made her love her life at Windywalls, but there were many other pleasant features. She liked the quiet regularity of it, the few simple junketings: presently there would be hunting.

She had hardly expected that she would so soon make friends, but in these last weeks, since the day she called on Mrs. Heggie, events had moved rapidly. That lady felt already quite an old friend, and the Rutherfurds--she smiled as she remembered the vague distrust roused in her by Mrs. Heggie's enthusiasm. But the mother and daughter had been so unaffectedly friendly that she could not but be grateful. She liked them: they were candid and simple, and though they were appreciative of the good points of the people they lived among, they had much too acute a sense of humour not to be amused by the human comedy that goes on everywhere.

She had asked Nicole what the Erskines were like, at whose house they were to dine that evening.

'I think you'll like them,' Nicole had said. 'They're so truly hospitable, almost as relentlessly so as Mrs. Heggie. Queensbarns was knocked down and rebuilt by Mr. Erskine's father, a manufacturer of sorts. It's like a very much overgrown villa, with heaps of bow-windows; and it's absolutely crammed full of things.'

'Furniture?'

'Furniture, yes, and pictures, great gilt things, seascapes mostly, rugs, ornaments of all descriptions, mostly Eastern, for the present owner of Queensbarns has something to do with India--jute, perhaps. Anyway, there are carved tables covered with brass animals, great bowls and jars with dragons walking round them; armies of elephants carrying things on their backs--you simply can't move for them. It would be a terrible house to have brain-fever in! They have a plethora of everything. You'd hardly think, would you, that you could tire of flowers? Well, I never feel as if I want to see a flower again after I've been to Queensbarns. Not only are the rooms kept filled by careful gardeners, but conservatories abound everywhere--you constantly find yourself looking into one.'

Esmé had nodded, remarking, 'I know that sort of house.'

'Mr. Erskine,' Nicole continued, 'is rather a boastful little gentleman. His conversation chiefly consists of relating episodes in which he got the better of some one. All "I said this" and "I said that"--somewhat monotonous. Also he loves titles and sprinkles his conversation with references to such of his friends as have been ennobled. They are very rich, and take a house in London for the season, and entertain a lot, and go down very well. Scots people do, don't you think, as a rule? An aunt of mine got to know them and told them about us when we took the Harbour House, and they were very hospitable and kind.'

'What sort of age is Mrs. Erskine--forty-ish?'

'Um--fifty-ish, I should say, but very gay and sprightly. She told me the other day that she felt perfectly at home with the young generation, and when I asked if some one was a nice girl she replied, "A topping kid." Yes, poor lamb, it's a pity, but that is how she talks. She is quite good-looking: buxom, I think, is the word. Her skin is very tight-fitting, her eyes are like agates, hard and bright, and her clothes are the very latest from Paris----'

'And the girls?'

'Haven't you met the girls either? Vera's about five-and-twenty, and Tibbie a year less. Nice, jolly, sensible girls. My cousin, Barbara, before she married, saw a lot of them. They're keen on everything, and they work as well--run Guides and get up things for the Nursing. I've helped them several times with small plays, and tournaments, and such like, and found them very easy to work with. They've always lots of people staying with them, and it's a cheerful house to visit.'

But as Esmé Jameson gathered up her cloak and bag and prepared to sally forth she told herself that she would be glad to be safely back in her own room. She felt shy of going among strangers.

It was amusing, though, to see how correct Nicole's description of Queensbarns had been.

A flight of steps led up to the massive door which was flanked on either side by a heraldic animal in bronze. In the inner hall was a figure of Buddha and some large copper kettles from Tibet. The hall itself, though large, seemed overcrowded: the tiled floor was covered thickly with rugs, the walls with trophies of the chase; there were numbers of tables strewed about, some with papers and magazines, others bearing ornaments. There was the same plethora about the servants: a butler and two footmen showed her in, and two maids took her cloak, and pointed to such an array of hairpins, powder, hand-glasses, and brushes and combs that it seemed as if a whole chorus were expected.

The drawing-room blazed with lights; the atmosphere was heavy with flowers; two fires sparkled, and there seemed to be more sofas and arm-chairs than had ever before been brought together except in a furniture show-room, but the whole effect was rather cheerful and inspiriting.

Mr. and Mrs. Erskine welcomed their new neighbour with great kindness, the daughters came forward with ready smiles; introductions were made and dinner was announced.

Mrs. Jameson was taken in by the host, Nicole was on his left hand, and Althea went in with a tall, dark young man. She was looking amazingly pretty in a rose-red dress. Very little dress, Esmé noted, and a great deal of Althea. Nicole made a striking contrast. She wore a long golden dress with long, tight gold sleeves, and made Esmé think of Verona. So might Juliet have looked as she lured her 'tassel-gentle' to come again.

Esmé enjoyed her dinner: it was long but good, and, as Nicole had warned her, her host's style of conversation called for no exertion on his partner's side. In the intervals of watching the other people she made interested eyes, murmuring at intervals, 'Of course,' 'Oh, that was excellent!' 'Now that is interesting,' and Mr. Erskine thought, and afterwards said, that Mrs. Jameson was a really intelligent woman. The man on her other side was the dark young man, but she got no chance of speaking more than a word to him, Althea kept his attention throughout.

In the drawing-room, some settled down to bridge, while the girls turned on the gramophone and danced. Esmé watched them happily for a time, and presently some one said her name, and she found Althea's dinner-partner beside her.

'We were introduced,' he said, 'but probably you've forgotten. My name's Charles Walkinshaw.... I'm frightfully interested to hear that you've come to live at Windywalls, for Pat Drysdale was my greatest friend, and I spent most of my holidays there.'

Esmé looked with interest at the young man. He was tall and very well made, and his face, though plain, was pleasant to look at. He had a short enquiring nose, and freckles, and a wide mouth, which at the moment was extended in a friendly grin.

'If you're a friend of the Drysdales,' she said, 'probably you regard me as a supplanter, as old John Grierson does.'

'Oh, rather not. By Jove, no--. I know that Mrs. Drysdale was jolly grateful to you for taking the place off her hands and being so decent about everything. She told me so herself.--Old John Grumblie doesn't mean any harm, he only feels a bit sore at all the changes. My word, he was the terror of our lives when we were small! Used to chase us with a dog-whip. Of course we did rile him a bit.... Though he called the Drysdales every name he could think of, and black-guarded them up and down the place, he couldn't see the sun shine for them really, I always knew that. But he didn't extend his affection to me--I was always a *budmash*, with jail as my probable end.'

'Then you and I are in the same condemnation,' said Esmé. 'That's cheering.... Living so much at Windywalls you will know this part of the country very well?'

The young man grinned. 'You couldn't be expected to know, of course,' he said, 'but this is my part of the country. Our home, Kinogle, is only six miles from this. But my father had a job in India for some years while I was at school, and that is why I went to Windywalls for holidays.'

'I see. I have a lot to learn yet about the neighbourhood. This is my first meeting with the Erskines: and I've still a lot of calls to return.'

'My mother hasn't called on you. She can't go out much; she's got that beastly sort of rheumatism that cripples you----'

'Oh, I am sorry,' Esmé said. 'How dreadful for her.'

'She did suggest,' went on the young man, 'that I should go over and explain to you, but I thought I'd wait till I met you somewhere; I'm not much of a hand at paying calls.'

'Oh, what does that matter.... Tell me, has she tried everything?--but I expect she has.'

'Everything, I think, and at this moment it's what they call arrested. She's not getting any worse. But she can only sit in a wheeled chair, she can't turn her head.... She's very cheerful, though. I believe she feels it most for my father and me.'

'Haven't you sisters or brothers?'

'No. I've got to do the best I can myself.'

'Do you think,' said Esmé, 'that I might go and see your mother?'

'I wish you would. It's pretty dull for her, you know, to sit in one place all the time.... My father and I take in all the news. We are learning to take notice, for she asks about everything. She likes to hear what we have for dinner, and if there is a new dish she asks the cook to try it. She will ask me to-night what every one wore--. It's rather like one of those difficult games you have to play if you stay with highbrows.'

'How will you describe the dresses to-night?' Esmé asked.

Charles Walkinshaw wrinkled his brows in perplexity. 'That's what I've been wondering.... Vera and Tibbie, I'll say, wore something scanty, with tucks.... That sounds rather snappy, I think. Yours is lace, isn't it? Black lace; that's easy. I like Miss Rutherfurd's dress, that long, plain gold thing.'

'Miss Gort's is pretty too, don't you think?'

'Yes.' His eyes were fixed on the rose-red figure--as they had been most of the evening.

Mrs. Jameson changed the subject by asking if her companion meant to spend much time in Fife.

'Well, I've only been back a few months. When I finished with Oxford I went on a long tour--round the world more or less. My father wanted me to do that. I hope to get into Parliament some day, and it's as well to know something of India, and our Colonies, and all that.'

'Indeed, it is--. And have you a constituency?'

'Well, I've one in view, near home. The present man means to retire soon, and it seems likely they may try me as a candidate.'

'Unionist, of course?'

'Why "of course"?'

'Oh, I don't know--. You aren't Labour, are you?'

Charles Walkinshaw looked at his companion with his straight glance. 'I'd be Labour to-morrow,' he said, 'if I thought they could do more to help things, but from what I see--I don't pretend, mind you, to see very clear or very far--our crowd, the Unionist Party, though they sometimes seem absolute stick-in-the-muds, do most in the end. And we've got a leader in Baldwin who has no axe to grind. It seems to me his great strength lies in the fact that the sooner he stops being Prime Minister the better he'll be pleased. He doesn't want anything we can give him. He's doing this job, because it seems at the moment to be his job and nobody else's, and he'll be mighty thankful when he can pay it down. It's something to have a leader like that, a bit of Old England.'

'With a dash of the Celt,' Esmé reminded him. 'You haven't mentioned that he's a poet.'

'I suppose he is, in a way,' the young man said thoughtfully. 'Well, he needs every quality he has for the job in hand.... Things are pretty rotten round here. Of course you won't have seen many of the places----'

'I've only been to Langtoun.'

'It's all right; prosperous place, but those mining towns--They are putting up a plucky fight, I can tell you. They have hardly been getting a living wage for some time, and now that some of the pits are closed, and thousands idle... it doesn't bear thinking of.'

'But isn't it largely their own fault? These idiotic strikes! They've pulled down their house with their own hands.'

'That's true in a way, and it's a great sop to our consciences when we're eating and drinking and dancing to think "Well, if they are starving it's not our fault; they went on strike, they ruined their pits and lost their market--" but all the same...'

'Come and dance,' Tibbie Erskine cried, running up to Charles. 'Mrs. Jameson, I think they want you to play bridge--do you mind? Here comes Dad to fetch you....'

As Esmé walked across the room to join the others she saw Althea look over her shoulder at Charles Walkinshaw.

Chapter X

'The expulsive power of a new affection.'

THOMAS CHALMERS.

Lady Jane lived her quiet life in the Harbour House with an air of great content. She seemed always to be happily occupied; writing letters for hours together, visiting the people about the doors--Mrs. Brodie with her brood of nine ('no' that mony if ye say it quick eneuch'), Betsy Curie, homesick for the Borders--talking in her gentle, kindly way to the fishwives and sailors; working at her embroidery, thinking long thoughts; so the days went on. She was the one who looked on, and as such saw most of the game.

Her daughter looked over her shoulder one afternoon and said, 'Mums, what *are* you reading?'

Lady Jane laid down the book. 'Mrs. Heggie kindly brought it for me to read. It's--a pleasant book.'

Nicole made a face. 'My dear, I've read it.... It's just like having a long talk with a housemaid. Oh, I admit that's better than having a talk with a scavenger or a barmaid, but I can't say I enjoyed it. *Must* you finish it?'

'I think I'd better, and then I can look intelligent when Mrs. Heggie recalls an episode.... Is Althea feeling better?'

'Yes, she's coming down to tea.'

'Poor child, she must have got a chill.'

Nicole nodded.

The night before she had been wakened by movements in the next room, and had risen and knocked at Althea's door. She found the girl sitting up in bed looking the picture of misery. She felt sick, she said, sick and shivering and miserable. Her disgusted, resentful face amused Nicole, but she was touched by the frail feeling of the shoulder that she put her hand on, and by the knowledge that tears were not far distant.

'Where's your dressing-gown?' she asked practically, and retrieving it from under the bed she wrapped it round the girl. 'I'll heat you a bag in a few minutes, and get you some hot water--you've got a chill, I expect. D'you feel very bad?--That's a silly question that doesn't need an answer: I'll be back in a minute or two.'

She had stayed with her for an hour, and when she seemed better had tucked her up warmly, and had even dared to lay her cheek for a second against the tousled head on the pillow. She seemed to need a comforter so badly.

True, Althea had been as aloof as ever when Nicole had gone in on her way to her bath to ask how she felt; but Nicole did not mind it, remembering a lonely girl in tears.

'Do you think Althea is getting reconciled to Kirkmeikle?' Lady Jane asked presently.

'It would be hard to say. I don't see why she shouldn't be quite happy, though, of course it must be terribly quiet after the sort of life she had in London. And then, if she's miserable thinking about the man--Did you ever hear who he was?'

'No, but Blanchie seemed to think that if Althea were removed from his immediate neighbourhood he wouldn't be likely to take the trouble to follow her--that sort of person.'

'I see; and poor little Althea probably realised that too. If she cared at all it was pretty hard lines.... I don't think he writes, at least I've noticed how eagerly she looks over her letters and then listlessly lays them down as if she couldn't be bothered opening them.'

'But surely she must realise that a man so casual isn't worth thinking about,' Lady Jane said.

'I've no doubt she does, but such realising isn't a bit pleasant, and at nineteen one hasn't much philosophy. We want, and expect to get what we want or we feel defrauded. Poor defrauded Althea! I'm really beginning to feel some slight warmth towards her.... I hope she is going to be friends with Vera and Tibbie. They're the sort of people who would do her good; open-air and sensible, full of vitality, and older a bit, which is all to the good. And there are always lots of people at Queensbarns. That young Walkinshaw I told you about--we've never called on Lady Walkinshaw yet; let's go to-morrow as ever was--seemed to get on very well with Althea when we met him there at dinner. I was just thinking what a suitable match that would be. He seems the most thoroughly satisfactory sort of young man, such an honest, good sort, and I'm told he's devoted to his mother. If a man is kind to his mother and fond of animals I don't ask much more: those are the fundamentals, so to speak.'

Lady Jane smiled as she asked: 'But would it be good for the young man to care for Althea?'

'Yes, there's the rub. If Althea's mind is full of this man--and if she had any constancy it must be--it would be very mean to encourage Charles Walkinshaw to come here.... But carelessness kills affection very quickly, and if the creature can't even cross the Forth Bridge to seek his lady, she won't care long. I wonder what Althea is like when she is happy? She doesn't soften much to us, does she? Or do you suppose that is her natural manner? No wonder Aunt Blanchie went to Egypt!'

'I've seen her,' said Lady Jane, 'talking quite happily to children on the sands, and Spider always wants to go out with her. Sometimes it seems to me that she would like to make friends and then she remembers and draws back.'

Nicole looked at her mother with indignation in her eyes.

'That's all very well, but she's nothing to remember against us. She may have the right to feel peeved with Blanchie, who, heaven knows, is a selfish old thing, but we are innocent. Mind you, Mums, I like her better than I thought possible at first. There's something rather interesting about that little, still, painted face; tragic, too, when you think of the age of the thing: and last night when she was seedy and looked so lonely it came over me that she'd never really had a mother...'

A hand on the door-knob stopped Nicole's eloquence and sent her to the window to make remarks about the weather, and Althea came listlessly into the room. Her face seemed smaller than ever, and she had not troubled to make up.

Lady Jane rose to kiss her and ask if she felt better, while Nicole rolled in the most comfortable chair and remarked that tea would soon be in.

'I expect,' she added, 'that you got a chill on the golf course yesterday, in the east wind.'

Althea looked at the fire and said: 'Does it matter where one gets a chill? The main point is that it's there.'

Nicole laughed. 'True, O King! But there is a certain satisfaction in tracing a cold to its source, at least it's a satisfaction to the people who have warned you that the wind is in the east and that a warm coat is indicated. It gives them a chance of saying--"What did I tell you!"'

'I suppose so,' said Althea. She shivered a little, and held out her hands to the blaze.

'I often wonder,' said Lady Jane, 'what it must be like to have a really bad illness, when one bad night leaves one feeling a wreck--Althea, dear, bed is the most comfortable place when one is seedy. I'm so afraid you get more cold down here.'

'Mother thinks,' said Nicole, 'that with the sea just outside there are bound to be draughts; but it's a very thick old house, and the windows fit. See what you feel like after tea, Althea; but it might be a good plan to go back to bed for dinner.'

It would certainly, Nicole felt, be much pleasanter for her mother and herself if the child did go back to her own room. To have a limp, speechless creature lying in a chair was most mournful. It was a relief when the bustle of Effie preparing tea began; and as they were sitting down to it Mr. Charles Walkinshaw was announced.

He came in reminding Nicole that she had said he might call, and on being assured that he was welcome, he shook hands with Althea, and sat down beside Lady Jane with an air of relief.

'Yes, thanks, both sugar and milk.... It's years since I was in this room. D'you mind if I stare a good deal? You see, my mother used to come here a lot and she'll be most fearfully interested to know what it looks like now.'

'I think your mother isn't strong?' Lady Jane said in her soft grave tones.

'She's almost a complete invalid; that is, she can't get about for rheumatism, but she insists that she is really quite well, and that it's a fine healthy complaint.'

'I suppose you've tried everything?'

'I think so; and it doesn't seem to matter much about the climate or anything, so when my father came back from India we came home, to Kinogle. Mother's so happy about it that I believe it's doing her good. She was so sick of hotels and hydropathics and foreign cures. And here she can keep house, and take an interest in the gardens; and anyway, we're together now, the three of us.'

'Oh,' said Nicole, 'how happy your mother must be to have you with her. It must have been dreadful to be alone and helpless.'

'Fortunately she's got an absolute jewel of a maid who understands that she doesn't like to be made to feel helpless.... How do you like being here, Lady Jane?'

'We love it. You know the house well?'

'I used to come here often, with Mrs. Swinton's grandson, Bob. He was older than me, an awful good sort: he was killed, you know, when he was nineteen. We used to

61

fish for podleys out there from the rocks and climb about the ships in the harbour. Mrs. Swinton was a grim old lady.'

'What did the house look like then, do you remember?' Nicole asked.

Charles looked round. 'Much as it does now, I think. You've made it seem lighter, somehow, but is the furniture not the same?'

'It isn't,' said Nicole, 'but I'm glad we've kept the same atmosphere. Tell your mother that.--I only wish she could come and see it for herself.'

'But won't you come and see my mother?' He looked at Lady Jane. 'She likes to see people. If you'd fix a day and come to lunch, you and your daughter and--Miss Gort.'

For the first time since he had come into the room he let his glance linger on that young woman, who smiled patiently when her name was mentioned.

'Althea,' Lady Jane explained, 'has just come downstairs. She's got a slight chill and feels rather shaky.--Aren't you going to eat anything, dear?'

Charles Walkinshaw leapt to his feet and proceeded to carry to the arm-chair hot scones and plum-cake, and was obviously discouraged to have them waved away.

'What you want, Althea,' said Nicole, 'is plain bread and marmalade. That's the best thing when one has no appetite. Effie will bring some grape-fruit marmalade: it has such a clean taste.'

Nicole spread the bread and cut it into delicate fingers. Charles set it before Althea on a small table, and presently he found himself in the chair next her, eating large quantities of food, and talking away to her, proud when he managed to make her smile.

'You must come again soon,' Lady Jane said, when he got up to go.

'I'll come as often as you'll have me,' said Charles. He was standing looking down at the embroidery Lady Jane had taken up. 'Is that easy? I wonder if my mother couldn't do something like that?'

'She might.... Does she knit at all?'

'Sometimes, not very much. But she can write letters.... I'll have a lot of news to give her to-day. And you will come to lunch, won't you--all of you?'

It was at Althea he looked last, and Nicole said to herself: 'He's finished, that young man. If he admired her in insolent health he can't stand for a moment against that little white face....'

Chapter XI

'I, too, have been young,' said the Moor Wife, 'and that's no disease.'

HANS ANDERSEN.

An invitation to luncheon at Kinogle followed quick on Charles Walkinshaw's visit, and the Harbour House party greatly enjoyed the occasion. They found a delightful old house, an interesting host in Sir James Walkinshaw, and a hostess who fascinated them.

They had expected to find an invalid much wrapped in fleecy shawls, wearing, at best, a look of suffering patiently borne, so it was something of a shock to find, seated in her wheeled chair at the luncheon table, a lady in a fur-trimmed velvet coat which exactly matched the blue of her eyes, a lady with golden hair turning silver, brushed back from a smooth white forehead; a lady with gleaming pearls and a gay laugh. After luncheon, which was a delightful meal with good food and good talk, they were shown over the house, which was old enough to be interesting, and contained heirlooms of value. It was a dry mild day, and when Sir James suggested that they might care to see what was outside, Lady Jane said she would like a walk. Althea followed with Charles, but Nicole said she would go back to Lady Walkinshaw. She found her in her own sitting-room, a south-looking room with several windows, cheerful with flowers, and cages of birds, and a bright fire. Nicole noticed the latest thing in gramophones, and a wireless cabinet, and her hostess said, observing her glance: 'Yes, it's wonderful what can be done to keep one in touch. Haven't I much to be thankful for?'

'You are a great surprise to me,' Nicole confessed.

Lady Walkinshaw laughed. 'Did you think I'd wear a grey shawl and huddle over the fire? That's the picture that jumps to one's mind when one hears of rheumatism.... I am absolutely helpless, you know, I can't even turn my head, but I can use my hands. I'm glad they are not disfigured and I can still wear my rings.'

'You are lovely,' Nicole said, with obvious sincerity.

'Oh, my dear.... I want to look decent as long as I can for the sake of my husband and Charles, they are so unbelievably good to me. And in a way I do enjoy life, and I'm tremendously fortunate to have my own home and a husband who has more or less finished his life-work and can now enjoy his garden and looking after the place, and a son who can be with us a lot. I have his future to look forward to.... And people are a great interest. I do hope you and your mother will come and see me when you can, and tell me what you do and what you read....'

'Why, of course. It will be a great thing for Mother to have your friendship. She's happy in Kirkmeikle, but she's away from all her friends and it's lonely a bit for her.'

'Not for you?'

'Oh, it's different for me, I can be friends with any one.'

'And it's nice that you have a girl friend with you, Miss Gort.'

'Althea. Yes, she's come to us here while her aunt is in Egypt.... It's rather difficult for her; she doesn't understand people like Mrs. Heggie.'

'Mrs. Heggie?'

'You don't know the Kirkmeikle people?' Nicole laughed. 'That's a pity, for you would enjoy knowing Mrs. Heggie. She is large and stout with the roundest, kindest blue eyes, and she wears "matrons' hats"--high and trimmed, you've seen them advertised?--sitting right on the top of her head. (I always wondered who wore those things till I met Mrs. Heggie.) Her great ambition is to know and be able to entertain a great many people, and she finds herself hindered in it by what she calls her "middle-classness." I don't know what she means by that, but she is the most innocent and likeable of women--Her daughter is a poet!'

Lady Walkinshaw's 'Really?' was frankly sceptical.

'Yes, really. It's odd, for to speak to she's very ordinary and rather dull, but there must be a soaring spirit in her, for her poetry has the true magic. It's not I who say so, remember, it's the harsh critics. I'll tell you what, I'll send you her little book.'

'Do; and tell me when you find something really interesting to read: a solid book that I can bury myself in for preference. Ah, here come the others. Sit by me here, Lady Jane....'

* * * * *

It seemed to Nicole that time galloped that winter. It was Hallowe'en, it was the end of November, it was Christmas all in a flash.

Alastair wrote: 'I am coming home on the 18th, three of us. Don't let Nikky come to meet us becos I want to cross the Forth bridge by mself. Ronny Macdermid is going to Aberdeen.'

In spite of this command Nicole went to Edinburgh to meet The Bat, and as she waited on the platform, she saw emerge from a carriage two dazed-looking small boys, who explained that Ronnie M'Diarmid has left them at Carstairs to continue his journey to Aberdeen.

Parents claimed the other boy, and Nicole took Alastair into the station hotel for a wash and a meal before going on. This was great excitement, and he talked all the way home in the train. Nicole decided that school agreed with him: he looked well, and he was taller and broader. He would always be a plain child, with his sandy hair and pale blue eyes, but there was something oddly attractive about the impish face, and Nicole's eyes were soft as she looked at him. To have a little boy come home for Christmas, how good it was! A little boy who would put his hand in hers and scramble with her round the Harbour, and stamp across the links, and sit importantly beside her in the car: a little boy to tell stories to in the firelight, to scrub at bath-time, to tuck up at night. And Alastair was dear not only for himself, but because he had been Simon Beckett's playmate and friend. Simon had said: 'Look after The Bat,' when he went away--Simon, she thought, would have been glad to see him growing a big strong boy: manly, too, but still with much of the baby softness in his queer little face.

'Is Spider waiting up for me?' he wanted to know.

'I expect so--and Mums, and Althea. You don't know Althea yet; she's a girl who's staying with us.'

'What size of girl?' Alastair asked suspiciously.

'A large size: about nineteen.'

He gave a relieved sigh. 'Oh, that's all right. I was 'fraid she might be a girl who needed to be played with--a little girl.'

'Wouldn't you like a little girl to play with?'

'No,' said The Bat, briefly, and added: 'Ronnie M'Diarmid wouldn't go into a carriage with a lady--we went in a Men's Only. He calls ladies hags.'

'What a low, rude boy Ronnie must be! I hope you never talk about ladies as hags.'

'I don't talk about them at all.... Ronnie won't get to Aberdeen till about eleven, but he thinks he's got enough money to take his dinner.... We had lunch in the train: it was three-and-six each, not counting the lemonade. We gave sixpence to the waiter, and I bought a paper and some chocolate, so I've only got'--he proceeded to count coppers carefully--'I've only got ninepence left. Ninepence isn't much to buy Christmas presents with.'

'Not very much, but you must be due some pocket-money. I haven't given you any for an age. Your sixpence a week's been mounting up. We'll go into Langtoun with The Worm, shall we, one day quite soon and make a tour of the shops--But we're not having Christmas at the Harbour House this year: we're all going to Rutherfurd. Is that all right?'

'Ye-e-s, Rutherfurd's fine. Kirkmeikle's jolly too, though. Remember last Christmas when Vera Erskine was a witch with a broomstick?'

'D'you like always doing the same thing at the same time every year?'

Alastair nodded. 'I don't like things different: but I expect Rutherfurd'll be all right. Can the baby walk yet? I expect he'd like to see me set off fireworks.'

'He's not six months old yet,' Nicole said. 'Later, I've no doubt Andrew Rutherfurd Jackson will take an intelligent interest in anything you do to entertain him.'

'I've got a lot of fireworks,' Alastair went on; 'I swapped the microscope Mrs. Heggie gave me for them. It wouldn't work anyway. We sat in the luggage-van to-day and talked to the guard. There was a parrot in a cage.... I didn't know a parrot could be luggage. It was a very nice parrot, grey and pink, and it swore. The guard said p'raps a sailor was taking it home to his mother for Christmas. I don't expect she'd mind though it swore....'

* * * * *

It was a busy week in the Harbour House. They were due to arrive at Rutherfurd on Christmas Eve, and before that all presents had to be got ready and dispatched by post to friends at a distance, and conveyed by hand to all within reach.

Althea took but a languid interest in the proceedings, said she hated Christmas anyway, and saw no reason for loading people up with rubbish on the 25th of December. She had been two months at the Harbour House and had become part of the household, but they seemed to know her very little better than the evening she came. She was, as Nicole said, perfectly docile, went where she was invited, played golf and badminton, and danced when there was an opportunity. She seemed to get on well with the Erskine girls, who admired her greatly for her very difference. Her stillness interested them, and when she did trouble to talk they hung on her words.

'Sometimes,' Tibbie told Nicole, 'we seem to have really made friends with her, I mean we feel quite easy and intimate, then suddenly, for no reason, she goes about a hundred miles away. What does she do to her eyes? She hoods them like a falcon does--not that I ever saw a falcon.'

'I think,' said Nicole, 'it was the falcon that was hooded, but it doesn't matter anyway, I know what you mean. Althea has a trick of making a frozen face.'

'But she's a darling,' said Tibbie. 'I could look at her all day: her lovely hands and ankles and slim legs, and her *dear* little face. I don't mind though she does make me look red and thick and clumsy in comparison. And isn't poor old Charles absolutely hopeless about her? I simply don't dare to rag him about it, I'm sure he'd think it sacrilege. But as for Althea, nobody knows what she thinks. She never babbles like other girls. It's rather unnatural when you come to think of it.'

Nicole ruffled up Tibbie's always-ruffled locks as she said: 'You're not unnatural anyway, Tibbie girl. Althea has had such a different upbringing, and it's made her reserved--I don't mind confessing that I dreaded her coming, and when I saw her I felt my worst fears were confirmed. She looked so hopelessly wrong in the Harbour House, one felt she had only come because she couldn't help it--her aunt was ill and had to go to Egypt--and that she didn't like the look of Kirkmeikle or anybody in it; but now I'm bound to admit we would miss her. She is interesting both in her stillness and her few moments of expansion, and as you say she's a joy to look at, especially now that she doesn't put so much stuff on her face.... You and Vera have done a lot for her; it's good for her to be with you....'

Before the Rutherfurds left, Esmé Jameson came over to spend an afternoon.

'I don't like to think you're going away,' she said.

'No,' said Lady Jane, 'I wish we weren't to be away your first Christmas in a new place.'

'But the Erskines want you to go to Queensbarns,' Nicole said.

'Yes, they've very kindly asked me, but they'll have a crowd, and I feel I'll be better at home.... I wish I could fall asleep now and wake when the New Year has got well started.'

Nicole laughed. 'And so say all of us! If it weren't for The Bat.... If you've got a child in the house it's quite different: you're a child again in spite of yourself. Why, when I fill Alastair's stocking I wish *I* were a nine-year-old with a stocking! Yes, I do. And I'm old enough, in all conscience.'

'How old are you?' asked Althea, crouching, as was her favourite habit, on a stool before the fire, a cigarette in one hand, the other supporting her little smooth head.

'Twenty-seven. I could be Alastair's mother: it's a solemn thought.'

Althea looked into the fire. 'What's the good of being young?' she asked. 'Quite old people are the happiest. Fat Mrs. Heggie is always beaming, so are the parent Erskines. Dr. Kilgour looks as if he enjoyed life....' She turned round and looked at Lady Jane. 'You don't beam, but you look contented--serene. Nicole----'

'Yes, what of Nicole?' Lady Jane's hand was suspended over her embroidery as she waited for an answer, her eyes watchful.

'Nicole's very bright,' Althea said demurely.

Lady Jane's needle remained in the air for a minute, while Mrs. Jameson broke a silence by remarking:

'It has always puzzled me why youth should be considered such a very happy time. It's like the month of April: at best it's perfect, but as April is often "uncertain glory," so is the happiness of youth.'

'It's a pity to expect much,' said Althea. 'I believe the Erskine girls are perfectly happy. They fill their days full with Guides and games, and country things here, and in London they enjoy balls and theatres and shops. They'll marry people exactly like themselves and go on being perfectly pleased.'

'And,' said Nicole, 'when the bright day is over I don't believe they'll even fear bad dreams. It's an excellent thing to take life lightly.'

'Excellent,' agreed Esmé Jameson. 'And it's a comfortable thought that most people do take it lightly.... Alastair, what are you so busy with?'

The Bat was stretched on the floor on a sheet of brown paper on which was a pot of paste and a brush, scissors, pasteboard, and a collection of pictures cut from magazines. He lifted a flushed face and explained that he was making calendars. 'You cut out a picture that you liked and pasted it on a square of cardboard, then you pasted on a small calendar, made two holes and put a ribbon through to hang it up with.'

'I see. They ought to be very nice.'

'Yes,' Alastair agreed rather doubtfully, 'they *ought* to be nice, but my hands get sticky, and the pictures go on crooked, and the white gets all smudged.' He sighed. 'I don't know how shops can sell calendars so cheap when they're so hard to make.'

'How many have you made?' Nicole asked.

'Only two, and they haven't got ribbons.'

'Well, wash your hands now and I'll help you after tea. You wanted to make four, didn't you?'

'Yes. Would Aunt Bice like a Madonna or a Sealyham? I thought that rabbit one would be nice... I don't know what else.'

'We'll choose good ones--Wash now, sonnie, you're stickying everything, and here comes Effie. Althea, take an end of this paper, will you, and we'll put it in the corner in the meantime.... What a sticky mess! I'm afraid The Bat wouldn't make much of a living as a calendar maker.'

Esmé Jameson said: 'I like boys, but they scare me. D'you find him easy to keep amused?'

'Alastair,' said Lady Jane, 'needs no amusing. I've never heard him say "What'll I do now?" The days are far too short for all he wants to put into them. Although he likes other boys he is quite happy alone. And of course he knows all the sailors and fishermen about the Harbour, so he doesn't entirely lack male society--' Lady Jane looked over at Althea and smiled as she added: 'I'm rich this Christmas with Althea as well as the small Alastair.'

The girl, Esmé noticed, did not return the smile, but looked gravely at Lady Jane, as if weighing her words.

Nicole said, 'You aren't to be quite alone this Christmas, are you, Mrs. Jameson?'

'I think so. But there are worse things than being alone. And after all, Christmas is only a day to get through like other days.'

* * * * *

'A day to get through like other days!' The words rang in Nicole's head as she and Althea went up the outside stair in the Watery Wynd to visit old Betsy Curle. Was Mrs. Jameson just getting through her days? If so, she pitied her. She had not asked for confidences, and Esmé Jameson had not offered them beyond telling them that she was a widow and alone, but to know that was to know enough....

To Betsy Curle, too, Christmas was only a day to get through. She sat in her little kitchen, unable now to 'do' for herself, dependent on others for everything, but still looking out on life with the same keen, unsparing eyes, still commenting on what she saw with the same caustic tongue.

'Here I am,' Nicole announced, laying the basket she carried on one chair and pulling another close to her friend. 'And how are you?' And as she spoke she said to herself--'I'm just like "Fawther" with his cheery word!'

'Here ye are,' said Betsy, 'an' what's brocht ye noo? Ye hevna lookit near me for guid kens hoo lang.'

'When you had my mother to visit you you didn't need me. And I've brought some one to see you--This is Miss Althea Gort.'

'An' whae's she?' said Betsy, peering suspiciously at the girl.

Nicole smiled at Althea as she said: 'I told you the last time I was here. Miss Gort comes from London and is paying us a visit. She has never been in Scotland before.'

Old Betsy sniffed. 'It's a peety she's seein' this pairt o't first....'

'We're all going to Rutherfurd for Christmas, Betsy. I expect Mother told you.'

'Ay. Winter or simmer it's the bonniest bit on earth. I dinna like when ye gang awa'. I feel nearer hame when her leddyship's within ca'. I hope ye'll come back safe--he gangs awa' at an ill time that ne'er comes back again.'

'There's not much danger about the journey to Rutherfurd,' said Nicole. 'See, now, what I've brought you.'

'They say the wife's aye welcome that comes wi' a crookit oxter, but I'd raither hae a sicht o' you and yer mither than a present.'

'Betsy, you're getting positively complimentary. This will never do--. We'll be back just after New Year, almost in time to first-foot you.... Dr. Kilgour loves to look in and see you--I believe you give him material for his book, and the neighbours enjoy looking in on you: and Mrs. Dodds keeps you comfortable, doesn't she?'

'Oh ay--comfortable eneuch: I'm no complainin'. But it's weary wark to sit and be done for, me that was sae blythe tae dae mysel.' She fixed her eyes on Althea. 'Ye're a bonnie crater, ye'll mak mony a yin sigh at their supper. But it'll a' come tae an end, mind that; beauty's juist a flower that time'll pu'.'

'But sweet while it lasts, Betsy,' Nicole pleaded.

'Puir bit things!' said the old woman.

Chapter XII

'E'en so swimmingly appears,
Through one's after-supper musings,
Some lost lady of old years....'

ROBERT BROWNING.

Mrs. Andrew Jackson was an excellent housewife, and when visitors were expected at Rutherfurd, always saw to it herself that bedrooms were warm and welcoming, that flowers adorned the dressing-tables, and that nothing was lacking in the way of writing materials and pillow books.

On the afternoon that the Harbour House contingent was expected she was going through the rooms prepared for them. Nicole had got her old room, looking out on the long lawn and away to the Lammerlaw, and Alastair was in the small room next door. Althea, as a stranger, had a more impressive chamber, while Lady Jane was to occupy the bedroom that had always been hers, with the sitting-room next door.

Barbara stood thoughtfully looking round these friendly rooms bright with afternoon sunlight. Three Christmases ago they had been settling down in the Harbour House, with Rutherfurd and the old days left behind. How wretched it had been to leave the old place, wretched for her, and thrice wretched for her aunt and Nicole, but they, strangely, had made no fuss, had said nothing. She, with less excuse, had been more vocal. She confessed to herself that she had not behaved very well about the change of fortune: she had grumbled at the Harbour House, so near a neighbour to the sea and the Harbour and to queer, fish-smelling little houses; she had grumbled about the people in Kirkmeikle; she had grumbled at the dullness--and then, suddenly, her grumbling had ceased. She went to visit the Jacksons at Rutherfurd and came back engaged to the only son.

And now was she content? she asked herself.

She had reason to be, she knew that. Andrew was always good-humoured and accommodating; she had things all her own way. Mrs. Andrew Jackson was quite a personage in the district. People said of her, 'One of the old Rutherfurds: yes, wasn't it a delightful arrangement? Very rich and an only son. The old people were rather--rather, but they had the good sense to go back to Glasgow, and the son is charming. Of course his wife has done a lot for him....'

Now that the boy had come her cup did seem full, but there were still moments when she remembered that she had intended to marry Andrew before Andrew had thought of marrying her, moments when she remembered his face the first time he met Nicole, when she had knelt on the fender-stool and talked nonsense about the picture above the mantelshelf--Elizabeth of Bohemia, *The Queen of Hearts*, Nicole called

70

her.... Andrew had been loyal to her, but would he have been loyal had Nicole given him the slightest encouragement to be anything else? She had not, Barbara knew that; she was too straight. Besides, all Nicole's thoughts were then with Simon Beckett, she probably never even noticed that Andrew hung on her words and followed her with his eyes.

And now she, Barbara, had everything--Rutherfurd, and Andy, and Andy's son; and Nicole had nothing. She could afford, she felt, to be sorry for Nicole, and yet it was not pity she felt for her cousin; it was, oddly enough, envy. Ridiculous: but so it was. Nicole had something--what it was Barbara could not put into words--that seemed to tip the balance in her favour, to weigh more than all Barbara's possessions.

If only she could feel that Nicole envied her Andy and Rutherfurd and the baby, how kind she would try to be to her, entertain for her, see that she met eligible men.

Others wanted to do that too. Lady Jane's relations were constantly begging her to go to London and elsewhere and have a good time with them, but Nicole would not. She stayed there in that little salt-sea house, actually seeming to enjoy the society of people like Mrs. Heggie and the like; didn't seem to want anything better. Why, she and her mother, free as they were, might have had a particularly varied life. Winter somewhere in the sun, spring in London, Scotland for the summer and autumn, London again in November. Instead, they had tied themselves up with a child who had no claim on them: the boy was all right, but he had relations of his own to look after him: it was quixotic and silly to take on the responsibility of a strange child....

As Barbara mused she straightened an ornament here, a bowl of flowers there, smoothed the satin-soft sheets, and when she turned to go, her step went almost unconsciously towards where her thoughts were always turning, the nursery of her son.

They would see a difference in him. He was already growing out of the dresses Lady Jane had made him. For barely five months his intelligence was amazing. There was no doubt he knew her, and he had a special chuckle to greet his father. How Andy adored his boy! It sometimes stabbed her heart to think by what a frail thread they held their child; a treasure in an earthen vessel.... But that was absurd. Why, children in slums, with everything against them, grew up, and her little son would have every care that love and money could give him. He could be a country boy, and would ride and fish and shoot, grow up strong and clear-eyed. Eton would be his school as it had been the school of all the Rutherfurds: so she told herself, forgetting that her boy was not all Rutherfurd but had both Burt and Jackson in his making....

At luncheon she and Andrew had discussed arrangements.

'I *hope* it will go well,' Barbara had said, doubt in her tone, 'anyway it's a real attempt at a family gathering. But I must say I rather resent the outsiders.'

'Meaning The Bat?' said Andy.

'Well, he has no slightest claim on any of us. Why can't he spend Christmas with that aunt of his?'

'He's a nice little chap.'

'Oh, I know that.... And this girl! Was there ever any one like Aunt Jane and Nicole for collecting people?'

'Succourers of many,' her husband quoted, but he did not go on to say what was in his mind, that Barbara would have found the world a sorry place if the Rutherfurds had not 'collected' her and given her a home and affection.

'The girl will be a nuisance,' Barbara went on. 'A boy plays about outside and hangs round with the keepers, but a girl is always sitting about, gasping to be entertained. I wonder how Nicole gets on with her. I gathered she wasn't too pleased about her coming. When you think of it, it is hard on Nicole, who, after all, is getting on, to have a young girl always round.'

Andrew Jackson looked up quickly.

'That's nonsense, surely. Nicole is the youngest thing ever.'

'Twenty-seven.'

'Well, that's very young; but no matter how long she lived Nicole and age would still be apart.'

Barbara gave a little laugh. 'Like Cleopatra, I suppose, and Mary of Scots. Nicole would be flattered to hear you--' She buttered a bit of toast and said, 'It'll be interesting to hear what Aunt Jane thinks of our improvements.'

'You can't expect her to be pleased. I know I'd hate it if I went back to my own house and found people had been mucking about with it.'

'But it's our house, not her house, and we've improved it immensely. Mr. Hibbert-Whitson has wonderful taste.'

Andy shook his head. 'Interlopers, that's what I feel we are. You, perhaps, have some claim to be here, but when Elizabeth of Bohemia looks at me enquiringly I feel like getting behind the screen. Perhaps the small Andrew will be able to face up to her--' He gave a little rueful laugh. 'I'm going up to the nursery now. Coming?'

Late in the afternoon, back to their old house came Lady Jane and Nicole, unwilling guests in a way, for it would have been easier and pleasanter to remain in the Harbour House, and yet in spite of themselves glad to be back, almost welcoming the pain of remembrance. To Lady Jane it brought back Christmases when Ronnie and Archie had come home from school and Johnson, the butler, had welcomed them with just that same mixture of dignity and fatherly affection. Archie had known nothing but the joy of being back, was exuberant in his greetings, darting here and there, seeing that everything was as he had left it, full of talk and laughter; Ronnie quieter, less expansive, not so able or so willing to show what he was feeling. Ronnie's grey eyes, Archie's blue eyes; boyish faces; rough tweed arms round her neck--the thought of them broke her heart. But Alastair was standing there, a little shy and strange: she put her hand on his shoulder, and he looked up in her face with eyes that were oddly like Archie's....

'Not in the least tired, dear,' she said in answer to Barbara. 'Johnson, it's good to see you again. How is your wife?'

'Poorly, m'lady.'

'The old trouble, is it? I'm sorry.'

'If your ladyship could spare time----?'

'Why, of course, Johnson. I'm coming in first thing--Why, Barbara, I never saw the house look so well.... You've changed something.'

Barbara put her arm through her aunt's.

'D'you like it, Aunt Jane? Andy was afraid you might be hurt; but I knew you wouldn't mind. You remember it was really rather unworkable, and Mr. Hibbert-Whitson has done it very cleverly. Perhaps you've forgotten, but here----'

Barbara was about to enlarge on the alterations, but Nicole broke in with: 'Mr. Hibbert-Whitson? That's the man who did up Kinogle for the Walkinshaws. He has a genius for making old houses comfortable. But you didn't let him loose in the drawing-room, did you, Babs?'

'No,' said Andrew, before his wife could reply.

Nicole gave a quick sigh of relief, while Barbara, half-laughing, half-angry, mimicked her husband's No. 'No. Because why? *He* wouldn't let me.... And Mr. Hibbert-Whitson said it was the chance of his life.... He has such perfect taste and he adored the room.'

'Then why did he want to spoil it?' Andy asked.

'Oh, he wouldn't have spoiled it,' Nicole said mildly. 'He might even have improved it--as he has done the hall. It's quite charming, Barbara--but to touch the drawing-room seems like profanation.' She turned quickly to Althea, who was standing leaning against a table watching and listening. 'I told you about it, Althea; it has a picture of the Queen of Hearts--may we see it now, Barbara?'

But Lady Jane demurred. 'Not now, Nikky. Barbara is going to show us our rooms.... Such a cavalcade, my dear--. Andrew's parents haven't arrived yet?'

'We expect them in time for dinner; they are motoring from Glasgow. The more the merrier.... Nicole, you're having your old room with Alastair next you. You know your way, Aunt Jane, I'll show Althea where she is, and then come and see if you are quite comfortable....'

Chapter XIII

'Here's a health and here's a heartbreak, for it's hame, my dear, no more. '

NEIL MUNRO.

Mrs. Jackson, the elder, often remarked to her husband in the seclusion of their brand-new villa, The Borders, 'There's no doubt living with in-laws is a strain.'

But one night during the Christmas visit, as the couple went to bed in the cheerful yellow room which Mrs. Jackson had furnished for herself when she reigned at Rutherfurd, and which Andrew insisted should remain unchanged, and always himself alluded to as 'Mother's room,' Mrs. Jackson said:

'D'you know, Father, I never thought to feel so free and happy in this house as I've felt this visit. Barbara's real pleasant and agreeable, and wee Andrew's a treat.'

'He's a nice wee boy,' said Mr. Jackson, who was not in the habit of making unguarded statements.

His wife sighed her profound agreement, and went on. 'I must say it's a great satisfaction to see Andy so happily settled. I'll never cease to regret that it wasn't Nicole--he once said to me that she never would have looked at him, but I don't believe it; she's the sense to see what a good fellow Andy is, and, anyway, he might have asked her--but Barbara does very well. She's a good housekeeper and she keeps her end up with the country, and I never saw a more careful mother. She's bound up in that wee fellow, and that's where the two of us can meet on common ground, so to speak. In the nursery she forgets that I'm a very common body--who wouldn't be here but for your money, Father--and just thinks of me as a fellow-worshipper and the baby's grandmother. It would be a joke if wee Andrew turned out a complete Jackson.'

Mr. Jackson stood with his collar in his hand, an unwilling smile twisting for a moment his lips, then his face settled back to its usual gloom as he said:

'Not much chance of that, Mamma; more likely to be all Rutherfurd, and high and mighty at that.'

Mrs. Jackson, a tight little figure in a purple satin underskirt and fur-trimmed slippers, was plaiting her hair briskly into pigtails, and she paused to say over her shoulder:

'Don't you believe it. He's the living image of Andy when he was the same age. D'ye think I don't mind what my own wee baby was like? I've got a photo in the album at home that I'd let you see--It's laughable. I can't see a trace of his mother in him. His nails are yours, Father, and there's something about his eyes that reminds me of my own mother.... Well, he's had his first Christmas, the laddie! I hope he'll see many a one and make a good laird of Rutherfurd.'

Mr. Jackson tapped his front teeth thoughtfully with the nail of his front finger and said: 'I'll have to keep things going. I'm well content to work and let who likes be country gentlemen.... But it would do no harm to give Andrew's boy a business training; it would come in handy for him managing this place.'

'So it would. But there's time enough to think of that.... Isn't she a queer girl, that Althea?'

'She's thin,' said Mr. Jackson cautiously.

'Thin! And as long as a flag-staff--a poor-looking creature. I can't make out right who she is, either; or what she is staying with the Rutherfurds for. Barbara says the mother was Lady Sybil Gort. I've a kind of notion I've seen that name in the papers, but in what connection I don't know. You get nothing out of the girl herself, she's a silent piece. To me she's got a disreputable look. Her lips were a fair disgrace to-night--I can't see her pretty myself but she's very like the pictures in magazines, and Nicole says she only needs knowing.... I don't think Miss Althea would think it worth while to let me get acquainted with her, and I'm sure I'm not sorry. My life's full enough without bothering about hoity-toity misses.'

'That's so,' said Mr. Jackson, 'you've about as many engagements as I have.'

'That's with you, Father, being concerned in so many public things. They ask me to do things out of compliment to you. I've opened two things this winter already. I can't say I did it well but I got through. I'll never make a public speaker! too gaspy and awful apt to get my sentences upside down; but uch! what does it matter? I don't believe anybody listens, and anyway, my clothes are all right. They can't say I don't trouble to dress for them.'

And suddenly, without warning, Mrs. Jackson dropped on her knees and began to say her prayers, while her husband climbed sadly into bed.

* * * * *

Further along the passage Nicole was sitting by her mother's bedroom fire. Lady Jane was reading a devotional book, while her daughter fed the fire with fir-cones, which Alastair had brought in and begged them to use.

Presently she said: 'Mrs. Jackson's more precious than ever, don't you think, Mums? She's much more important than she used to be, and presides, she tells me, at meetings and opens bazaars. How I should love to see her! The effort is evidently colossal, but the satisfied feeling afterwards makes up. She gave me a vivid description of how she opened her first bazaar. She said, "I had it all written out, but I lost my notes and I just told them that. I said 'I made a speech but I've mislaid it at the moment, so you'll excuse me if I merely remark that I've much pleasure in being here and the Sale is now open----'" How glad they must have been of her after the ordinary glib opener with her ordered little phrases.'

'Indeed, yes. Mrs. Jackson would make any Sale go: I can just picture her going round each stall and adding purchase to purchase and casting notes from her purse in all directions.... Going back to Glasgow has been a great success, don't you think?'

'Oh, great. You see the dear soul from her experience at Rutherfurd gained a certain amount of aplomb, so to speak, and back in Glasgow she will have the status of a county lady. She told me so herself with great amusement.... And then being a grandmother pleases her enormously. She points out to me rather impishly that the baby has Andy's nose, old Mr. Jackson's nails, and her smile: never a hint, you will notice, of Barbara! All the same I think they get on quite well together and Barbara does little things to please her, like using the silver she and Mr. Jackson gave her, and pretends not to see the things that offend her: and of course she enjoys her enthusiasm over the baby.'

Lady Jane looked over the top of her book at her daughter, as she said:

'Alison Lockhart said to me yesterday that Barbara and Andy were very popular in the place: they take such a good hand with things. And Alison doesn't say smooth things from choice.'

Nicole laughed. 'She certainly does not. She hasn't that fascinating twisted mouth for nothing, but she is an antiseptic person, and what she says of Babs is of value for she never liked her, nor did her justice. Yes--things have worked out wonderfully, Mums, but...'

'But?'

'Oh, nothing, but it's a queer old world when all's said and done.... The Bat's very happy here, anyway. It's funny to see him doing all the things we used to do, finding them out for himself--damming the burn, and making forts and defending them. Old Clay's grandson, Tam, is his henchman. I like to see them tearing about.... And presently the small Andrew will be the spirit of youth in the place.... Mums, I don't like Rutherfurd any more. I wish we need never come back.'

'Why, darling, I thought you rather liked being back, that you had got used to the changes. You have been so brave all through----'

With the tears wet on her face Nicole laughed. 'Not in the least brave. Babs says she envies me my faculty of taking things lightly--that's more like it, but somehow, to-night, when we were all sitting so decorously in the drawing-room with the Queen of Hearts looking down at us, I longed for the fairy flute to blow "*Everything in its proper place!*" What a scurry there would have been! I'm not sure that Andy wouldn't have remained just where he was, and John Dalrymple--they're rather like each other, those two. And Alison Lockhart would have remained seated on that brocade sofa watching everything with her bright hard gaze: Mrs. Jackson would have accompanied her husband back to Pollokshields: Althea would find herself in a night-club, poor babe! And Barbara...? I don't know.'

'And you, Nikky?'

The girl gave a sob.

'Not here, Mother. I don't like Rutherfurd any more. I never want to see it again. The trail of Mr. Hibbert-Whitson is over it all. The place is more beautiful than ever, but it's not our Rutherfurd. We're like ghosts, Mums, you and I, and it's sad to be a ghost.... No, Barbara is no real blood-kin to us, she's all Burt... it comes out more every day. I feel closer to Althea, that cold young cynic, and anyway, I wish we were all back at the Harbour House.'

There was silence for a moment, then Lady Jane said: 'I understand your feeling about Rutherfurd, but it doesn't extend to old friends, I hope--to Jean Douglas and Alison Lockhart--to John Dalrymple? You love the countryside as much as ever, don't you?'

Nicole considered. 'I expect at heart I do, but it hurts to be here--Only three more days, Mums!'

* * * * *

Barbara sat before the glass in her own room. It was a beautiful room, for Barbara's taste was good--and it was a satisfied face that looked back at her from the mirror as she brushed her hair.

Andrew was in his dressing-room, she could hear him moving about, knew the meaning of every sound: splash of water, he was washing his teeth--a soft whistling, he was brushing his hair.

'Andy,' she called.

He appeared in the doorway, brushes in hand. 'Yes?'

'Oh, I only wanted to talk about things.... It's been very successful, don't you think, our Christmas house-party?'

Andy sat down on the arm of a chair as he said: 'I've enjoyed it for one, and Mother's in great form. I don't think I ever saw her so interested in outside things. She used to be rather apt to shirk things and hide behind my father, but now she tells me she's in the full glare of publicity and appears to glory in it.'

'How nice!' Barbara said absently. She had not called Andrew in to discuss with him his mother. 'Didn't the dinner go well to-night? Nicole can be very entertaining when she chooses; she was positively *fey* to-night, and in that green and silver dress--John Dalrymple couldn't take his eyes off her. Andy, I do wish Nicole would marry him.'

'Why?'

'Why? Andy, you really are absurd. Because it would be a most suitable marriage in every way. Newby is such a lovely place, and the Rutherfurds and Dalrymples have always been friends. John Dalrymple has been in love with Nicole almost since she was a child. He asked her on her nineteenth birthday.... What? No, she didn't tell me, but I know. He's been abroad ever since, and now he means to settle at home.

Wouldn't it be splendid if the engagement came off here and now? What a delightful finish to our Christmas party.'

'Dalrymple's a good fellow,' Andrew said, 'if Nicole cares for him----'

'Why shouldn't she care for him? I do hope Aunt Jane will get her to see things sensibly. Nicole's been far too much made of all her life, she's had things too easy.'

Andrew got up and, standing with a hair brush in either hand in the doorway of his dressing-room, he said: 'It doesn't seem to me that Nicole's had things specially easy, all the other way--I'd be jolly glad to see her get some happiness now, but I'd like to be sure that she felt it was happiness, that she didn't do it to oblige...'

There was a pause, then Barbara said:

'What touching faith men have in a pretty girl's motives!'

She laughed, but her eyes in the glass were sombre.

Chapter XIV

'Here's the garden she walked across
...Such a short while since....'

ROBERT BROWNING.

Barbara felt that she was giving her guests a very full and gay week, with two dances, two dinner-parties, several tea-parties, and--a village concert.

It was Althea's first experience of this type of entertainment, and she was amazed at the fuss and preparation it seemed to require: to see Barbara and Nicole spend hours superintending the putting up of a stage in the village hall, devising means of lighting it, and dragging down curtains from the house to decorate it. And the performance itself: the wooden seats, the smell of paraffin lamps: the (to her) complete badness of every item in the programme...!

But to Mrs. Jackson, senior, it was an occasion of infinite importance. When the party from Rutherfurd filed in to take their places in the front row of benches (softened by cushions borrowed from the church pews) she felt proudly satisfied that the Big House was doing itself justice. She herself was an impressive sight in black and gold, heavily jewelled; she believed, she said, in giving people something to look at: Lady Jane, although so meek, always looked somebody: Barbara was quite the laird's lady--these were the diamond and pearl ear-rings that Andy had given her on Christmas morning: what had he paid for them, Mrs. Jackson wondered!

78

Nicole, gay in rose-colour, was nodding to many friends, and Althea was looking pretty, but bored--what was she bored for, the monkey?

Father was bored too, she could see that by the way he was tapping his teeth with his nail, but how well he looked in his new dinner-jacket. She was glad she had advised him to try a different tailor. Andy had a nice kind way with everybody, and the people he spoke to seemed to like him--as well they might, thought his mother.

There was Mrs. Douglas! Mrs. Jackson stood up and waved her friend to the front. 'Come away, Mrs. Douglas, and sit beside me. Have you not been able to persuade the Colonel to accompany you?'

'No,' said Mrs. Douglas, smiling greetings round before she sat down. 'Tom draws the line at a village concert. The seats are too narrow for one thing; and he hates music.'

Althea looked up from the typed sheet of paper that was the programme, and asked:

'Shall we have *music* to-night?'

Jean Douglas laughed. 'Improbable, I should think.... Who are the performers? Oh, they're not bad, and anyway, they're old friends!'

The evening wore on. A robust and cheerful young woman in a tight pink dress sang of tears and partings; a stalwart young man bellowed defiance at his foes; a tiny boy played Scots airs on his fiddle and the greater part of the audience stamped their feet in time to the lilting tunes: a regrettably vulgar 'comic' raised the spirits and lowered the tone of the gathering, making Mr. Jackson laugh out suddenly, to his own great embarrassment.

In the interval Mrs. Jackson craned her neck to see every one round about her.

'Who are those people behind?' she whispered. 'They're surely strangers.'

Mrs. Douglas looked cautiously round. 'You mean those two girls with their father and mother. They live in that house outside Langhope, "Langhope Towers," they call the house. Brunton is the name. Barbara has taken them up and wants us all to call, but I haven't yet....'

Mrs. Jackson took another glance at the family in question, and wondered what had brought them to this part of the world.

Indeed it was difficult to understand why the Bruntons had elected to make their home in a country place with which they had no ties, for they were suburban to their finger-tips. The girls adored tennis, and dancing, and bridge-parties, going into town for shopping and theatres, and coming back in happy parties.

Accustomed to a chatty, sociable life, they found Langhope deadly dull. They had expected great things of existence at Langhope Towers, and to find themselves restricted to the society of the minister, the doctor, the lawyer, the banker, and the respective wives of those genteel men, was a heavy blow. That the people round should not call had never occurred to them, but had they known it, the people round were quite unaware of the existence of the Brunton family. Langhope called *en masse* and at once, but that was all that happened.

Mr. Brunton walked about in the most correct of rough tweeds, with a dog. Ailsa and Christine walked about with two dogs, or motored themselves into Edinburgh to shop, or played golf on the nearest course, and confessed to each other that though *Langhope Towers, Langhope*, might look smarter on note-paper than *The Neuk, Coniston Road*, it was enormously duller. Mrs. Brunton was not so much to be pitied as her husband and daughters, for she had her house to fall back upon. She was a comely woman with a bright colour and twinkling eyes, who liked community singing and discussing the Royal Family.

Then, at a local Sale of Work, Barbara met the two girls and heard from the minister's wife that they were interested in Guides, and very willing to be useful. Thinking such people deserved to be encouraged, she called one day at Langhope Towers. She liked the family, who showed a most proper appreciation of her condescension, and made up her mind that they should be recognised by the neighbourhood, and as a beginning invited them all to lunch at Rutherfurd. It was not a particularly pleasant outing for the Bruntons. Barbara had sometimes an absent-minded way with her guests, an air of being rather surprised to see them, which was chilling at the start. Andy Jackson had not a great deal of small talk. Also, Rutherfurd itself had a sobering effect on Mr. Brunton who did not feel at home among all the dead and gone Rutherfurds in their frames, and was only reminded of one anecdote, and that a dull one. Mrs. Brunton said it reminded her a little of Queen Mary's apartments at Holyrood, which had always given her the creeps, and to which she attributed most of the ill-luck that pursued that tragic lady.

Barbara had not been very successful in getting her friends to follow her lead. Alison Lockhart refused at once, saying that it took her years to begin to like new people, and she saw no reason for trying to like the Bruntons.

Jean Douglas demanded to know why she should call.

'Well,' said Barbara, 'it would be kind.'

'I don't see it--. I might call, but if nothing happened after they'd have the right to feel aggrieved, and I can't be fussing them and having them here. Tom would hate it. All I'd do by calling would be to get myself disliked.'

'They are nice people,' Barbara persisted, her face assuming the sullen look it was apt to wear when she was not getting her own way, 'and willing to take an interest in things.'

'I don't want them to take an interest in me,' Mrs. Douglas said, and Barbara, exasperated, thought that her friend behaved sometimes more like a naughty schoolboy than a responsible middle-aged woman.

As they were leaving the hall after the concert, Barbara introduced her mother-in-law to her new friends.

'Pleased to meet you,' said Mrs. Jackson cordially. 'Wasn't it a nice concert? These wee Brownies selling programmes!... You're new to the place, I hear? I feel for you, remembering what it was like when I came first.'

Mrs. Brunton and Mrs. Jackson looked at each other and knew themselves sisters.

'Come to tea to-morrow,' said Barbara, remembering that Jean Douglas and Alison Lockhart were coming.

There was a touch of royal command in the invitation, but the Bruntons did not seem to mind that, and at once accepted.

They found Rutherfurd a very different place the second time they visited it. Barbara, to be sure, having asked them, evidently thought that nothing more was expected of her, but Lady Jane seemed full of gentle interest in their opinions, Nicole went out of her way to be pleasant, and Mrs. Jackson brooded over them like a providence.

It was a very happy afternoon for that lady. Here was she ensconced in her son's house, grandmother of the beautiful boy in the nursery, surrounded by dear friends who applauded her witticisms, showing kindness to a deserving family. In Mrs. Brunton she saw herself had she come to the neighbourhood unheralded and unfriended, and it not only gave her pleasure to play the patroness, but she thoroughly enjoyed having found a listener.

She told her new friend all about her old home in Pollokshields, about her first coming to Rutherfurd, about the kindness of Lady Jane and her daughter.

'Mrs. Brunton,' she said earnestly, 'there's nothing so pathetic as to see the decay of the real aristocracy.'

Mrs. Brunton glanced involuntarily at Lady Jane sitting near the fire, with her embroidery frame, smiling at something her companion was saying and looking in the soft light almost as girlish as her daughter; then her eyes strayed to Nicole perched on the arm of a chair bandying words with Jean Douglas, gay and alert, and fair like a morning in May.

'Well,' said Mrs. Jackson, aware of some incongruity, 'decay is mebbe hardly the word in this case, but you know what I mean. And it's wonderful, mind you, to see how happy Lady Jane and Nicole make themselves in Kirkmeikle. A house down on the sea-edge--ucha.'

From the old aristocracy it was but a step to the Royal Family, a subject in which both ladies were thoroughly at one.

'They're an example to the whole country, Mrs. Brunton, that's what I always say.'

Mrs. Brunton purred agreement. 'Everybody says the King's so affable; and isn't the Queen *regal*?'

'And yet so motherly! I like to see pictures of her with the little Duchess. That's a sweet creature, Mrs. Brunton.'

'*Isn't* she? And the baby! D'you know I think she's a great look of the Queen.'

'She has, I see it myself, but she has her mother's taking smile--You'll see *our* baby in a little. He's a great wee fellow.'

'You must be proud of him, Mrs. Jackson.'

'Proud! I'm sometimes frightened to think how much he means to us all: a baby's a frail thing to pin all one's hopes to, but indeed we're all poor creatures when trouble comes--Well, we can only pray that he will be spared....'

Mrs. Brunton agreed and let her glance wander round the room, at the walls clothed with little square Tudor panels now dark as ebony with age, at the plaster ceiling with its deep medallions and heavy enrichment of flowers and foliage, at the Adam mantelpiece whose marble nymphs and cornucopias had, like the ceiling, a dull ivory sheen; at the faded Mortlake brocades of the old chairs and settees; at the pictures of Rutherfurds--one by Jameson, in black armour and a gorgeous scarlet sash, another by Allan Ramsay, in a purple coat, a sprigged waistcoat and a steenkirk cravat. There was a Raeburn too, of a Lord of Session. All the pictures but one were of men. That one was framed in the panelling above the fireplace, a picture of a woman no longer in her first youth, with a mouth narrowed a little by pain and disappointment, but with great brown eyes full of the hunger of life. It was a replica of the Mierevelt of the 'Queen of Hearts,' Elizabeth of Bohemia. Looking down with her wistful, small face above the ivory of the mantelpiece, she seemed to make the marble nymphs fussy and ill at ease, for her beauty was rare and sweet and far from common loveliness.

'It's a beautiful place,' said Mrs. Brunton, 'but I'm not educated up to it. I like lots of things in a room--you know, photos and ornaments and pretty bits of china.... I doubt I'd never feel at home in a room like this.'

Mrs. Jackson nodded. 'You'd like our new house, Mrs. Brunton. It's got everything of the latest; there's not an old thing in it. You see, after living here for a while I just felt I'd had about enough of antiques. Hot and cold in my bedrooms. Every labour-saving appliance. Everything's so fresh and new, it's a pleasure to keep it clean, and the maids seem to feel that. I've got four real decent girls just now, and they just arrange the work among themselves and go out when they like. I'm past bothering about that sort of thing. My! when I think how I used to worry over servants!... You're well off to have daughters, Mrs. Brunton; what nice-looking girls they are, so fresh and healthy, and such a fine colour.'

Mrs. Brunton smiled deprecatingly, and presently asked: 'Who is the young lady in green?'

Mrs. Jackson glanced at Althea who was sitting a little apart in a high-backed chair, her hands folded demurely in her lap, watching and listening.

'That,' she said, leaning towards her companion, 'is Althea Gort: a sort of connection of Lady Jane's. *Her parents were divorced!* Ucha. Poor thing, I dare say she feels it, but she's not a nice type of girl. You never know whether she'll speak to you or not. And painted--isn't it a disgrace in a girl of eighteen?'

'A pity,' Mrs. Brunton admitted. 'But she's very distinguished-looking too. And that's Mrs. Douglas of Kingshouse, isn't it? I've seen her at meetings: she seems very nice.'

'Oh, she's a jewel. And that's Miss Lockhart next her. She's given over to horses. A woman of her age! You'd think she'd take to something more restful. Of course she travels a lot.... The gentleman talking to Lady Jane is Sir John Dalrymple. My daughter-in-law would like to make a match between him and Miss Rutherfurd. He's willing, any one can see that, but I've my doubts about Nicole--Never match-make, Mrs. Brunton, that's my advice to you; you burn your fingers every time. I know, for I've tried it.'

When the guests had gone Barbara invited Althea to go with her to the nursery to see young Andrew having his bath.

She had tried several times to make friends with the girl, but Althea had remained aggravatingly unresponsive. Barbara wanted to find out why she was staying at the Harbour House, what she thought of the life there, and on what terms she and Nicole lived together: this was her last chance, and she took it.

They went together to the nursery, an airy room gay with white paint and brightly coloured pictures and rugs.

Althea sat on a white wooden chair and watched Barbara hang rapturously over the baby, who was puffing and panting in the water like a young grampus.

'No, don't suck nasty sponge, darling. Mummy'll give 'oo nice fishy to hold. Oh, Althea, *isn't* he a darling?'

'Yes, he is.'

'Doesn't even trouble to smile,' thought Barbara angrily; 'these modern girls!' Aloud she said, 'Are you at all fond of children, or does the modern girl scorn such emotions?'

'I don't know about the modern girl,' said Althea. 'I like children quite well when they aren't being sick, or howling.'

Barbara and the nurse, both feeling outraged by such half-hearted sentiments, continued to lavish endearments on the unconscious Andrew, while Althea sat and watched them.

When the baby had been taken to the night-nursery and tucked into his cot Barbara came back and stood fingering the objects on the mantelpiece. Presently she said:

'It must be a great change to you to come from London to Kirkmeikle?'

'Yes,' said Althea.

'Such a dull little place, isn't it? Mrs. Heggie and the others.... It is just made

83

endurable by the Erskines and the Fentons--Of course the Harbour House is rather nice in a way, quaint and unusual, but after *Rutherfurd*--And yet Nicole pretends to like it?'

'Was Nicole fond of Rutherfurd?'

'Fond! My dear, she adored it; she was perfectly crazy over it. That's why I think it's rather an affectation to protest such fondness for the Harbour House. But she does take things so lightly, Nicole.'

'Does she?'

'Well, you see for yourself what high spirits she has, and when you think that she lost two brothers in the War, then her father, then Rutherfurd! And you know about Simon Beckett? No? Well, as a matter of fact no one was supposed to know; neither Nicole nor Aunt Jane ever mentioned the subject to me, which I couldn't help thinking strange considering I was there and saw the whole thing.'

Barbara paused and looked at Althea who said, 'Really?'

'Yes. When we left Rutherfurd and went to Kirkmeikle Simon Beckett had rooms there and was writing a book about Everest. He and Nicole made great friends over Alastair, who lived with his aunt, a tiresome woman who married later some man in Edinburgh. He was very good-looking--Simon, I mean, and very charming. I wasn't at all surprised that Nicole fell in love with him, but just before my own marriage he went off again on an expedition to Mount Everest and was killed....'

'I didn't know,' said Althea.

'No, how could you? Why, *I* was never told anything--but I'm certain they were engaged before he left.... And that explains why they have practically adopted Alastair. Simon was fond of him.'

'I didn't know,' Althea said again.

'Of course it was very sad,' Barbara continued, 'but I do hope Nicole's going to be sensible and take John Dalrymple. It would be such an ideal arrangement.'

'But if she still cares for----'

'Oh, that's nonsense; she can't. I mean to say faithfulness is all very well, but what's the use after all? And even if she didn't care greatly, in marriage there are so many compensations.'

'Are there?' said Althea.

Barbara glanced sharply at her. What an annoying girl this was with her eternal interrogations.

'Shall we go downstairs?' she said then. 'I expect you are longing to get back to London?'

84

'Ought I to be?'

'Well--it would be natural. You don't look much like Kirkmeikle. But perhaps you've been infected by Nicole's passion for the place?'

'Perhaps,' said Althea.

Chapter XV

'If music be the food of love, play on.'

TWELFTH NIGHT.

A few days later the Harbour House got back its inmates, and they were all glad to be home.

Alastair, lying on the hearth-rug hugging Spider, said:

'Rutherfurd's a lovely place: there's such a lot of room all about and so many beasts, and the burn, but--I'd rather have this.'

And Althea stretched in an arm-chair, poking with the toes of her slipper at the wriggling mass of boy and dog, said, 'I quite agree.'

Lady Jane looked up from the letter she was reading.

'My dear,' she said, 'I'm glad to hear you say that, for I hope it means that you haven't hated it all too badly. This letter is from Aunt Blanchie suggesting you should join her in Egypt. It seems her friend Lady Loveday is going out about the 20th and would take you.'

'Oh, Althea, what a lovely chance!' Nicole cried. 'Egypt in January! When we are listening to the wind skirling through the wynds.'

There was silence for a minute, then Althea said: 'I suppose I must go? I mean to say, you must have had more than enough of me?'

'Don't you *want* to go?' said Nicole, coming over and looking in astonishment at the girl. 'Why, Althea, I've felt so sorry for you putting in these months here, walking about on cobbled streets, sniffing bad smells, talking to people who were of no interest to you, deprived of music and lights and crowds....'

'Why should I want these things more than, say, you?'

Nicole sat down on the fender-stool.

'Well,' she said, 'for one thing you are nearly ten years younger and you've had a different upbringing. My home has always been in the country, I've always walked in quiet ways, but you are town-bred. Being a Scot, cold winds and grey skies are in my blood: you belong to the warm south. What is my food is your poison more or less.'

'I see,' said Althea. 'I dare say it's true. All the same, in Egypt I'll envy you the wind in the wynds. Yes, I'll even envy you the conversation of Mrs. Heggie. It's a morbid taste, I know, but there it is.'

Nicole jumped up. 'Mums,' she cried, 'do you hear that? Actually Althea *likes* Kirkmeikle!'

'In that case,' Lady Jane said placidly, 'she mustn't leave us. Althea dear, I was just realising how much we would miss you. You mustn't go if you'd care to stay. We welcomed the chance for your sake, not for our own. Isn't that true, Nikky?'

'Utterly true, Mums.... I feel this to be a proud moment both for us and for Kirkmeikle. No, I'm not scoffing. There's nothing so pleasing as to have people agree with one's likes and dislikes. Althea, we now bestow on you the Freedom of Kirkmeikle--Look at Spider registering dejection! I'm afraid he can't be entirely glad about our return. The Bat's embraces must be disturbing to his inside.'

'He likes them,' said Alastair. 'Don't you, 'Pider?' He gazed fondly at the small white object with the black patch over its eye and, 'I believe,' he said, 'that Spider's mother is a widow.'

'He has a bereft look,' Nicole agreed, 'but he has his merry moments--Isn't it nearly tea-time? I seem to be always hungry since coming back.'

'So'm I,' said Alastair, 'and so's Spider, only he never was away. Dogs are always hungry if they're not sick. I'll tell you the time on my new watch--it's twenty past four.'

'Isn't Mrs. Jameson coming?' Althea asked.

'It wasn't quite certain, so we needn't wait after the half-hour--Here is Effie and the tea, and I smell new scones.'

A minute or two later Mrs. Jameson came in, bright-eyed from the cold, and explaining that she was late because she had been shopping in Langtoun.

'It has been so dreary without you--you simply can't think what a difference it means to have the Harbour House shut up. Kirkmeikle without you people is like a room without a fireplace.'

'What a very nice way to put it,' Lady Jane said. 'I'm glad you missed us a little.... You were alone for Christmas, I think?'

Esmé Jameson undid her coat as she said: 'Yes, I was, although I had great difficulty in persuading those kind Erskines that I really wanted to be by myself. I dined at Queensbarns the next evening and found a large and very gay party, every one for miles round. The Erskines do help to keep the world going round--But do tell me, had you a good time?'

'We had, indeed.... Oh, here is Mr. Walkinshaw!'

'I say,' said that young man, 'are you only just back? Turn me out if you can't be bothered with me.'

'We came back last night,' Lady Jane told him, 'and we're delighted to see you. Have you come from golf?'

'Yes. I was lunching with the Fentons and we had a round, then I thought I'd run down and see if you were back.'

'Take that chair,' Nicole directed him. 'We're all perishing for our tea.'

Charles Walkinshaw managed to manipulate his long legs under a small table, and remarked cheerfully between bites of hot scone: 'Somehow I always think of this room at tea-time.'

'Yes,' said Esmé, 'it seems specially meant for the nicest hour in the day.'

'Well,' said Nicole, 'it is the room where it is "always afternoon"; we have tea here unless there are too many for these small tables. And I love our evenings, too, in this room, when it is so quiet you hear nothing but the water, or a far-away hoot from a ship at sea, or the cry of a sea-bird....'

'I think,' said Althea, 'that most of us feel more good-natured at tea than at any other time.'

'Yes,' Nicole agreed, and turning to her mother, said: 'Mums, do you remember the ploughman at Langhope Mains, who was left a widower with young children and thought he'd better marry the woman who was keeping house for him? Mr. Blackstocks, the farmer, told me he met him looking very downcast at having been rejected....

'"When did you ask her?" he demanded. "At breakfast-time? Man, what answer did you expect at that time of day? Try her again at tea-time and see what she says." And sure enough she said "Yes."'

'What a wise man that farmer was,' Esmé Jameson said. 'A breakfast-time proposal would be too bleak.'

'Not to me,' Nicole said boastfully, 'I'm at my best in the early morning.'

'You are,' said Althea bitterly.

Nicole laughed. 'I know, it's a horrible trait.... How is your mother, Mr. Walkinshaw? Did she have a nice Christmas?'

'I think she had. A young cousin spent it with us, just home from school in Paris, and so above herself with delight at being done with it that you could hardly keep her on the ground. Her people are in India, and she's not going out to them till next October, so we'll probably have her a lot with us. It makes an enormous difference having her, for everything amuses her, and her amusement amuses Mother. She's found heaps of little things that my mother can do, making flowers and things, and she tells her endless stories about the girls and governesses and what she did in Paris. It's jolly nice, I can tell you, for my father and me to hear my mother laughing and amused. I tell Belinda that we'll simply tie her up and keep her at Kinogle.'

'Belinda!' said Lady Jane, 'what a delightful old name.'

'It makes one think of Pope,' Nicole said. 'Did he not write about Belinda pressing her downy pillows...? Is she eighteenth-century looking?'

Charles took a bun and a lot of jam on his plate and confessed that he did not know what eighteenth-century looks were. 'She's a pretty infant,' he said. 'A little thing with a mouth that turns up at the corners. Now that I think of it she'd look rather well in powder and patches. We must remember that if there are any fancy-dress things. She's crazy to dance, of course.... I say, it's jolly to have you back again!' He looked at Althea for the first time since he had greeted her on entering the room. 'Had you a very gay Christmas?'

'Oh--quite. It was the depths of the country, you know. But we did go to a village concert.'

'That,' said Nicole, 'is a most misleading statement, Mr. Walkinshaw. There were two very enjoyable dances as well as various other small festivities. Althea was amused that we should take a village concert so seriously. But I'm sure you will agree that there are few more solemn things in life.'

'Few indeed! Talking about concerts reminds me there's something I want to consult you about. I wonder if you and Miss Althea would help me with a scheme I've got in my head? You know Cowdenden?'

'The grimy little town you pass through going to Langtoun?'

'Yes. As you say it is a grimy place, but there are a particularly fine lot of young people in it--miners mostly, and they have a struggling sort of musical society. They practise away at Gilbert and Sullivan, but they've never money to produce. Times have been so bad for years, and of course they're worse than ever now, and I dare say most people will cry out at the thought of spending money in producing--even in the humblest way--at a time when every penny is needed for bare necessities. But it would be such a cheer-up for those decent fellows, and something to interest them. It must be most demoralising to have to loaf all day. People tell me, "Oh, they like to idle." By Jove----'

Althea looked at the young man and asked:

'How do you know so much about them?'

Charles explained that as prospective Unionist candidate it was his job to get to know the young people in the district. 'Besides,' he added, 'I like these fellows apart

88

altogether from their votes. I wonder if you would come some night to one of their practices and see for yourself what good chaps they are!'

'But what use would we be?' Althea asked.

'Well, in the first place it's heartening to have some one take an interest--And then, I thought, if we could get some people to stand in and help with money they might be able to give a show. If we did it in a very modest way it wouldn't cost a great deal, and anything we made could go to local funds. Is that a quixotic scheme, d'you think?'

Nicole at once threw herself into the project.

'What we want is to get as many as possible interested so that we can be sure of an audience.'

'It would need at least three performances to make it pay,' Charles told her. 'The scenery and dresses are fairly expensive to hire. I find they knew all about it from other towns that have tried it. I forget how many other towns in Scotland produce Gilbert and Sullivan every year.'

'Then,' said Nicole, 'your musical society is quite capable of running the whole thing? All they want is backing? That should be quite easy. Cowdenden is within reach of the whole neighbourhood. Let's begin where we are! Mother, you'll be an honorary member, won't you? You and Mrs. Jameson?'

Both ladies turned--they had been deep in talk--to ask what was required of them.

'Nothing much,' Nicole assured them, 'simply a little time and a small sum of money. Mr. Walkinshaw will explain----'

'Oh, please, you do it,' pleaded the young man. 'I'm no good----'

'That's nonsense, but we needn't argue.... You know, Mums, that ugly little town we pass through motoring to Langtoun. You said once you wondered what the people did with themselves when they weren't working. Well, as you know, there isn't, unfortunately, much work just now to do, and to cheer themselves the young people run a musical society and study Gilbert and Sullivan. Mr. Walkinshaw--oh, may I say Charles? the other is such a mouthful--Charles says they are wonderfully good and so keen, and he wonders if we couldn't all help them to produce an opera--It's not a thing they could attempt without backing. I suggest that we get a good long list of honorary members who will subscribe and promise to go? Will you be one, Esmé? You and Mother and me--and Althea, if we can persuade her not to go to Egypt.'

'Egypt!' ejaculated Charles. 'You're not going *there*, are you?'

Every one laughed at his tone.

'Does it seem so absurd to you,' Esmé Jameson asked, 'that any one should leave the bleak Fife coast for golden sunshine?'

'Oh, it's not that; Egypt's all right, of course, but--I thought Miss Althea was settled here for the winter.'

Nicole came to the rescue of the abashed young man.

'And so she is, we hope. She has gone so far as to say she would miss Kirkmeikle.... Well, that's four members we've got and there must be heaps in this district if I could think of them. People are generally quite pleased to support a thing like that.... Will no one have any more tea?'

'I can't have any more,' said Alastair, 'for I haven't had any yet.'

'Neglected child!' said Nicole, pouring into a cup milk and water with a dash of tea, 'but if you will lie under the table with Spider....'

'And they've eaten lots, anyway,' Althea remarked.

At that moment Effie announced 'Mrs. Heggie.'

She stood in the doorway like a ship in full sail about to enter the harbour, murmuring:

'It's too bad, really, coming like this when you're only just home.... How d'you do, Lady Jane? How d'you do, Mrs. Jameson?'

'I can't get up, Mrs. Heggie,' Nicole cried. 'You know Mr. Walkinshaw?'

'No,' Mrs. Heggie said, as Charles placed a chair for her, 'I don't know him, but I've often heard of him.'

'Why, of course, he's your Unionist candidate! This is one of your supporters, Charles--you will vote for him, won't you, Mrs. Heggie?'

'Oh, certainly. Not that I'm much of a politician.... I'm terribly easily convinced. It's always the side I've heard latest that I believe in, and of course that's not the idea at all. And I really am a Conservative, you know?'

'So your vote is safe, whatever your opinions may be?' said Althea.

'Whatever your politics are we want you to become a member of a musical society in Cowdenden.'

Mrs. Heggie's eyes grew rounder. 'Cowdenden! I didn't know they went in for music there. It's a dreary looking place. I once had a cook from Cowdenden, a good cook she was too, but very ill-tempered. She wouldn't let the other maids bring a friend into a meal, and to keep them I had to part with her. I was sorry to do it, for she was clean and economical, and things went like clock-work.'

'That was very trying,' Lady Jane said. 'And I expect you had to replace her by a good-natured dirty one? I hope you had a very happy Christmas, Mrs. Heggie? We're in time to wish you all good things for the New Year.'

'And the same to you,' Mrs. Heggie said earnestly. 'I've been picturing you all at

Rutherfurd. It must have been lovely. I never think it's a real Christmas unless there's a baby.... But a little trying for you, dear Lady Jane.... Life gets sad as we go on.... Yes, we had a nice time. Quiet, of course. I tried to gather all the unattached people in the place to our Christmas dinner. Dr. Kilgour and his sister and all the Lamberts-- We had it in the middle of the day for the children.... And I've had an old cousin staying, Joan doesn't much care for having her, but she's old and alone and lives in rooms all the year round, so it's a change for her to come here....'

'If she's still with you, do bring her to luncheon or tea!'

'Oh no, Lady Jane, thank you. That's not at all necessary. I mean to say she wouldn't expect such an attention. She's a plain old body and a run into Langtoun in the car is her idea of a treat. But I'll tell her you asked her and she *will* be pleased--What is it, Miss Nicole?'

'Will you, kind lady, pay ten shillings a year to be an honorary member of Cowdenden Musical Society?'

Mrs. Heggie immediately began to fumble in her bag. 'Oh dear me, yes. More if you like. I'm heart sorry for the miners, though, of course, they did----'

'No,' Nicole interrupted her. 'Don't say it was their own fault, *please*. I'm so tired of hearing that, and it doesn't get anywhere near the root of the matter....'

Chapter XVI

'Bid the players make haste.'

HAMLET.

After the orgy of present buying and receiving that prevails in December, after the family gatherings and the determined lightheartedness of the so-called festive season, a curious flatness is apt to pervade the first month of the year.

Then it is that those who had meant to see the winter through in their own island begin to waver in their determination, and tentatively enquire about hotel accommodation on the Riviera, or dally with the thought of a cruise to find the sun.

Kirkmeikle and its neighbourhood was not exempt from this unrest. The Erskines went off to Cannes, the Bucklers left Lucknow for Switzerland, and Joan Heggie tried to get her mother to consider the desirability of spending a few months in Madeira. But that lady held on stubbornly to Knebworth, giving as her chief reason for refusing to leave, that she could not bear to be buried at sea.

In vain her daughter pointed out that there was no reason why she should be buried at sea, that the voyage was a short one, the ship equipped with every comfort including a reliable doctor, but Mrs. Heggie was adamant. She was too large, she said, too heavy to be really happy on a ship; the very thought of a bunk made her sick, and there was always the smell of oil and cockroaches.

'But think of the sunshine,' Joan pleaded.

'Sunshine's not everything,' said Mrs. Heggie. 'If we haven't much sun in Kirkmeikle we've other things--good beds and nourishing food and warm fires. The misery of those foreign hotels! I know them!'

'But that's just what you don't do. You've hardly been anywhere, and it would do you all the good in the world to see new places and meet new people and widen your outlook on life.'

Mrs. Heggie sniffed. 'My outlook on life is as wide as I want it to be. At my age one has made up one's mind about most things, and it would be very unsettling to have those views changed. I'll stay quietly at home, thankful that I've a comfortable house to stay in, and kind neighbours. But you go, Joan. It's a chance when your friends the Colsons are going. I suppose you'd be quite safe with them? I'll be glad to think of you happy in the sun. The trip will be my birthday present to you, and I'll get your room papered and painted while you're away and have it nice for you to come back to.'

'Well--' Joan shook her head in astonishment. 'You have the oddest ideas of enjoyment, Mother. I verily believe you think it more amusing to mess about at home with painters and charwomen than go out into the world and *live*.'

'Yes,' her mother said placidly. 'I do. Travel *sounds* very well. What could be more delightful than these pamphlets about cruises: oranges and roses and blue lakes? But it's all very different once you start. Oh, I know. I once went a cruise with your father. The bother about luggage--what to take and what not to take, and whatever you decide you're always wrong: the fussing, the arranging, and when you do get on to the steamer, the queer squeamish feeling that never really leaves you till you get off again. The way the water sways in your bath.... And the cold-storage food that always tastes the same; they may call it anything they like on the menu, but fish, flesh, or fowl, it's all alike.... And when you land it's pretty dreary work looking at scenery and churches and picture-galleries!'

'All I want,' said Joan, 'is simply to *steep myself in sunlight*.'

'Well,' Mrs. Heggie said, picking up a dropped stitch in the scarf she was knitting, 'take care and not bring on a trouble in your skin! I knew a girl--I don't know whether she's alive now or not, I've lost trace of her--Agnes Parsons was her name. Have you heard me speak of her? She married a banker, and had no children. A restless couple they were, always travelling about. *They* went off one winter to look for sunshine, and she got bitten by a mosquito--poisoned, I suppose. Her face went all black and blue and both eyes were closed, and she came home from the trip a wreck. That put me off hot climates.... But I dare say Madeira'll be all right--I'd like you to get some nice new clothes before you go; people are very smart in these big hotels. And couldn't you do something about your hair? It's inclined to be endy. I notice some people can make their hair fit into the shape of their head very neatly. D'you not think a permanent wave might help yours?'

Joan shook her rather shaggy shingle. 'I don't like the artificial look of a permanent wave.... I'll need a new dinner-dress, and some other things--thin things. One so seldom wears real summer clothes in Kirkmeikle.'

She paused, and then with an effort, for it was never easy for Joan to be gracious, she said:

'It's frightfully good of you, Mother, to stand me the trip. I'm sorry you won't come too, but perhaps you wouldn't care much for the Colsons as travelling companions. They're not your sort.'

'They are not. That time they lunched with us at the hotel in London I could hardly find a word to say to them. Silly, I thought they were, calling each other pet names.... And their real names are ridiculous enough, Hulbert and Delilah! I expect Mrs. Colson's responsible for the names. Have you any idea what Mr. Colson did when he was alive?'

'I haven't,' said Joan, 'but I think it was some sort of business.'

Her mother nodded.

'Lucky for them that he could leave them so comfortable, for I don't believe the young man'll ever support himself by his pictures. *Hulbert*----'

She repeated the name, laughing sardonically, and added: 'Delilah, too. Why not Jezebel? But they're your friends, and I don't want to say anything against them. I'm sure I hope you'll enjoy their company.'

Those who were left in Kirkmeikle drew closer together.

Esmé Jameson remained at Windywalls, too enamoured of her new home to think of leaving it. The Walkinshaws, weary of wandering, were only too happy to stay at home. Althea Gort did not go to Egypt, in spite of many persuasive letters and cables from her aunt. It was obvious that, glad as Lady Elliston had been to get rid of the girl, she was now just as eager for her companionship.

Althea said, 'If you'll have me I'd like to stay, Aunt Jane.'

'I want you to stay, my dear, but I'm just afraid Blanchie will think me selfish keeping you.'

Althea sat down by Lady Jane and began to play with the many coloured silks in her lap.

'Don't worry about Blanchie,' she said calmly, 'she's too thoroughly selfish to give a thought to any one but herself. All the Careys are like that.'

Lady Jane was silent, and the girl went on: 'D'you suppose when she planted me on you she cared whether it was for your happiness or mine? Not she. I had got myself talked about, she wanted to get rid of me--My mother was selfish too. As a family I despise the Careys.'

'Althea dear...'

'Oh, I know it's shocking taste to speak like that. You and Nicole never err in taste--. I beg your pardon, Lady Jane, I'm impertinent.'

She rose, and going over to the fireplace, standing with one arm along the mantelshelf, she surveyed her companion. Then, 'Be patient with me,' she said. 'I have improved a little since I came to the Harbour House, don't you think? Though, of course, I'll never be like Nicole.'

Lady Jane did not ask if she regarded this as a fact to be deplored. She smiled at the tall girl standing in the glow of the firelight and said:

'Nobody wants you to be like Nicole, we like you as Althea.... I believe the rain has stopped.... Let's go out and get a blow of salt air before tea. One feels so un-aired sitting all day in the house.'

'Yes, let's.' Althea dropped on her knees beside the small black-and-white terrier on the rug. 'And you will come too, my beautiful Spider, best and loveliest of hounds, wisest and most affectionate of canine friends.'

'Absurd child!' Lady Jane said as she laid aside her work. 'You're affronting Spider; remember he's a Scots dog.'

* * * * *

Charles Walkinshaw had not allowed his plan about the Cowdenden Musical Society to languish; with the help of Nicole he had managed to get quite an imposing list of honorary members, and he had also got promises of substantial help from his father and one or two others. One evening he came to dine at the Harbour House, and took Nicole and Althea to see a rehearsal afterwards. He looked anxious and absorbed all through dinner. When Nicole said, 'Isn't it exciting to be dining before the play?' he did not smile.

'I hope you won't think it too bad,' he said rather wistfully. 'Perhaps I've bucked too much about them.... They may seem to you very rough, and, of course, they need endless rehearsals....'

'It's *Iolanthe*, isn't it?' Althea said. 'Almost my first favourite.'

'It *is* jolly. And really, you know--But you'll judge for yourselves. I'll only put you against them if I over-praise.'

'When shall I expect you back?' Lady Jane asked.

'Not much after ten,' Charles said. 'It's a beastly night, so I brought the Daimler, chauffeur and all.... It's rather an awful hall they've got to practise in, but it's expensive hiring places, and this does all right. Well--shall we go?'

When they reached their destination, a back street in Cowdenden, Charles hurried them out of the car. 'I'll go first with the flashlight,' he said, 'for the stairs are broken in places, and it's a regular trap for the unwary--Hullo, you were nearly down that time. We'll be lucky if none of the performers break heads or legs before the show comes off.'

'I feel like a conspirator,' Althea said, as she groped her way up the steep stairs, and she laughed. Nicole, hearing her, thought, 'That's the first time I've heard Althea giggle like an ordinary girl.'

'Here we are,' said Charles, throwing open a door and letting out light and the sound of music.

* * * * *

A couple of hours later the girls were back in the drawing-room at the Harbour House, drinking tea by the fire.

'But where is Charles?' Lady Jane asked.

'Gone home,' Nicole told her. 'We asked him to come in but we didn't urge him, for it was time he was home and we felt we had had enough of him for the time being! Men are such innocent things: he was so keen that we should be impressed by his protégés.'

'And were you?'

'I was. Weren't you, Althea?'

Althea nodded in her grave way. 'They struck me as being wonderfully good, especially the men. I don't know why it should be, but men as a rule act better than women. But they all acted as if they were enjoying it.'

'Oh, they did. Mums, you'd really have liked it to-night. We went up a very broken and exceedingly dirty stair into a small hall with a piano and a few chairs and forms. Not very inspiring, but the only place they can afford. The girls looked so nice in their jumper suits; and such neat heads! An amazingly high average of looks. I've seldom seen so many pretty ankles and legs gathered together. Weren't you struck by that, Althea?... When not required, the young men are apt to stand outside on the landing, and talk and smoke, but the girls sit demurely sewing or knitting, and listen. It was frightfully nice to see Iolanthe lay down her work, pull down her frock, and become a fairy.'

'But,' said Lady Jane, 'I can't quite see--Does Gilbert and Sullivan not sound rather odd in a Fife accent? How do they manage the libretto?'

Nicole laughed a little. 'Well, that is rather a difficulty, I confess. Charles very delicately hints now and then that certain words are not being pronounced in the usual way, and they take it delightfully. As one man remarked to me with great cheerfulness, "Mine's Fife English."'

'But--' Lady Jane still looked dubious. 'Strephon, for instance? Have they any one who can play the part properly?'

'Yes!' said Althea. 'By great good luck there is a slim fair boy who can both sing and act, and what is more, he looks the part.'

'He does indeed,' Nicole agreed. 'A light-foot lad! He and the girl Phyllis do very well together. Even now in their ordinary clothes they looked nice, and when they get on the white satin and blue and coral ribbons of their parts, they will look like Dresden china figures. And Althea has promised to help them a bit with their dancing.'

Lady Jane looked kindly at the girl as she said: 'There's no one better fitted, my dear.'

'Oh, I don't expect to be of much use, but they are more likely to take hints from an outsider than from one of themselves. It's a pity they couldn't see the D'Oyly Carte Company. Aren't they to be in Edinburgh before March?'

'That's an idea,' said Nicole. 'We might find out. It would be such a good thing if the principals could see it.'

'It would certainly make it easier for them,' said Lady Jane, 'but wouldn't they be apt to copy what they saw? I should think their own interpretation would be more interesting.'

'Ye-es,' Nicole said doubtfully. 'But you see, they're so new at the job. It would give them confidence to get a lead.... The stage-manager has seen *Iolanthe* done, and tries to convey to them what struck him about the parts.... It must be terribly difficult to train a chorus; to get a crowd of untrained people not only to sing in time and in tune, but to stand and move properly--Althea, I can see that the poor man looks to you to help him to save the situation.... Oh dear, I had forgotten what delicious fooling *Iolanthe* is! The plea of blue blood, *Spurn not the nobly born*. And the chorus of peers!'

'What were they like, the peers?' Lady Jane asked, and Althea answered her, 'A good deal better-looking than any peers I ever saw.'

'I dare say,' said Lady Jane. 'Well, it must be good for those young people to study such witty words and music!'

'Good!' said Nicole, 'I should think so. I hadn't realised it, but Gilbert and Sullivan are the cure for Communism. To hear those men singing with such gusto:

'Bow, bow, ye lower middle classes,
Bow, bow, ye tradesman, bow, ye masses!

One who sang most lustily, Charles told me, is a leading Socialist, red as blood, a leveller. But I expect after this when he thunders at meetings he won't be able to be so bitter, and perhaps will laugh a little at himself.'

Nicole got up in her vehemence, and stood before the fire. 'Good for them, yes, and jolly good for Charles Walkinshaw. He and those men are getting to know each other, learning to understand each other. I never liked Charles so well as I did to-night, seeing him so eager among those people, so keen that they should do well, so anxious to help them to do themselves justice.'

'I believe Nicole's a Socialist,' Althea said, ruffling Spider's woolly white coat.

'Only so far as every decent person is a Socialist,' Nicole said. 'I'm a Tory Democrat, if there is such a thing.'

Althea smothered a small yawn. 'I wonder if I shall have a vote next election!-- meantime, what about bed?'

Chapter XVII

'Hast any philosophy in thee, shepherd?'

'No more but that I know... that he that wants money, means or content is without three good friends....'

AS YOU LIKE IT.

Perhaps it was because the dining-room in the Harbour House was such a pleasant morning-room that the Rutherfurds had got into the habit of lingering there after breakfast, discussing the news the letters brought.

'Aunt Jane,' said Althea, 'you do get a budget every morning. How is it, I wonder?'

Lady Jane only smiled, but Nicole said: 'My dear, can you wonder? Mother has a host of friends, and when any of them are glad they write to her, if they are sad they write to her, if they want anything, from servants to sympathy, they write to her. And Mother is one of the few people left alive who writes real letters, long newsy sheets. I assure you the recipients bequeath these letters as heirlooms to their descendants.'

'Then you must *like* to write letters,' Althea said in awed tones.

'Nicole is talking nonsense,' Lady Jane said. 'I only write necessary letters, and even those sometimes very unwillingly.... To-day I have a very uninteresting post--chiefly bills. Have you fared better, Nicole?'

'Mine,' said Nicole, 'seem chiefly invitations. Jean Douglas wants Althea and me to go to her for the Hunt Ball--we must talk about that anon. A note from Kinogle asking us to luncheon on Friday--that's the day we're going to Edinburgh, *and* an invitation from Mrs. Jackson to stay with her for a week at The Borders. She says she will not take a refusal this time.'

'Well,' said her mother, 'why don't you go, Nikky?'

Althea stopped feeding Spider with toast to listen.

'I don't know,' Nicole said slowly. 'I've a sort of reluctance. I like Mrs. Jackson, but...'

'Why d'you like her?' Althea asked. 'A vulgar old woman! You might as well go and stay with your cook.'

'Well, for that matter, I can imagine many worse people to stay with than Mrs. Martin.... But Mrs. Jackson isn't vulgar, she's a comic; you must learn, Althea, to differentiate between the two.'

'She's got money,' said Althea, 'that's all the difference really between her and all the thousands of women who live in the rows of little suburban houses, and do their marketing in bags.'

Nicole laughed. 'Oh, but I assure you, Mrs. Jackson wouldn't mind in the very least a marketing bag or a little house or anything like that. Why should she? But vulgarity doesn't necessarily accompany these things. The vulgarest woman I know is a lovely creature with a pedigree extending back to the beginning of time. You'd shudder at the things she says and does. You'd never shudder at Mrs. Jackson, but you'd laugh-- often. She helps every one, she hurts no one, and the more she makes you laugh the better pleased she is.'

'Then,' said Althea, 'if she's so amusing, why aren't you more pleased at the thought of visiting her?'

'Here we are back at the beginning! I don't know, unless it is that I'm still sore about Rutherfurd--and that would be too silly.'

'Andy Jackson struck me as rather nice,' Althea said, 'but all the same he has no business to be in Rutherfurd, he's not the least like the place. But of course it's what you see all over now; new people in the old places.'

Nicole nodded. 'Dear me, yes. We've had our shot, it's somebody else's turn now.'

Althea looked thoughtfully at her as if trying to make up her mind if Nicole spoke sincerely, while Lady Jane said, and she sighed as she said it: 'Oh yes, we have had our shot, Nikky. All I ask is that the new people will try to establish relations with the people who serve them. That's apt to be where the difference comes in. There is no link between them of shared experience. The new people are mostly people who have made their own money, and they look at everything from a business point of view, which means that they want their money's worth and have no use for sentiment.'

'Their money's worth!' said Nicole. 'That's the snag with all the new rich. Why, look at the Erskines! They're overwhelmingly hospitable, they'd feed you with their best, they'd even give you their finest brand of champagne and enjoy seeing you drink it, but ask them for a pound for some good but obscure cause, and see how they squirm. And yet they'll give to almost any extent in a public way, feed a multitude at a Unionist Demonstration, head a subscription list and never grudge it. Mr. Erskine talked to me all through dinner one night about how he had managed to beat down a local tradesman and make a few shillings. He expected me to applaud, but what I really wanted to say was, "My poor fellow, what d'you suppose is going to happen to that huckstering little soul of yours when you are done with buying and selling?"'

Althea laughed aloud. 'Poor Mr. Erskine!' she said. 'He wouldn't be in Queensbarns now if he hadn't beaten down lots of people. But, Nicole, when you plume yourself on your open-handedness--oh yes, you do!--just consider how much of it is generosity and how much mere carelessness.'

There was a silence while the two girls looked at each other. Nicole's face flushed. She turned to her mother and nodding towards Althea said: 'She's a wise child, isn't she, Mums?... Well, Mrs. Jackson has led us into quite a discussion, but you haven't given me any advice about her most kind invitation.'

'Don't go,' Althea advised, 'unless you think you'd be amused. To go to give pleasure to Mrs. Jackson would be a horribly priggish thing to do.'

'So it would,' said Nicole, and laughed.

'Here,' said Lady Jane, 'is another invitation, to dine at Windywalls on Thursday to meet Mrs. Heggie.'

Althea made a face, and Nicole said: 'What fun! Now Mrs. Heggie will get an opportunity to put on her new evening dress. She confided to me that she thought she'd have to go to a Hydro to get a chance to wear it. She got it in Edinburgh, and it's evidently very smart.'

'Will that be the evening's entertainment?' Althea asked; 'admiring Mrs. Heggie's new dress?'

Lady Jane looked up from her letters. 'Did I hear you say you were going to Langtoun this morning?'

'Yes, Mums. Althea's helping me to make an evening dress and we're going to try to match something. Can we do anything for you? These silks.... If we can't match them, will the nearest thing do? or would you rather send to London? Oh, very well... we won't be back till after one, for we've some calls by the way--What about Spider? Shall we take him?'

'Of course we'll take him,' Althea said. 'He adores a jaunt in the car, especially to Langtoun, where he knows all the dogs who take the air with their mistresses of a morning in the High Street. See, he understands what we're saying: he's registering satisfaction.'

99

'He's doing what Effie calls *spurling* on the carpet. She complains that he ruins all the carpets.... Mother, I'll get the things for Alastair's box, shall I?'

'Oh, please, and just ask if Mrs. Martin needs anything....'

When the girls had left the room Lady Jane took up a letter and re-read it carefully. It was from Jean Douglas, and ran:

'I've written to Nicole to ask her and Miss Gort to stay here for the Hunt Ball, which was put off, you remember, from December to the beginning of February. I know quite well Nicole won't want to come. I can understand how hard it is for her to come back to this neighbourhood, I can see how she shrinks from meeting the old friends, all the same I think you will agree with me that it is time she got over that, and it is easier for her to be at Kingshouse than at Rutherfurd. I've been to see Barbara. I told her I so much wanted to have a party for the Ball, that I particularly wanted it to be as much as possible like old times, and would she mind if I asked Nicole to be my guest. She looked offended at first, and said people would think it so odd and might imagine there had been a quarrel, and so on, but I said a great many smooth things-- some of them true--and before I left she had got quite used to the idea.

> 'It may surprise you, this sudden burst into entertaining on my part. I confess it never entered into my head to have a house-party until John Dalrymple *asked me to have him and Nicole*. So now you know! And, dearest Lady Jane, won't you use your influence to get Nikky to Kingshouse?...'

Lady Jane sat with the letter in her hand and looked out of the window. Spider was having some exercise before departing from Langtoun. On the long stretch of firm sand he was careering wildly round in circles, while Althea stood like a circus-master in the middle of the ring, encouraging him. Nicole, on the low wall, her hands on her sides, laughed at them both. How carefree they looked, the two girls, laughing in the winter sunshine.

Lady Jane's thoughts slid back to the past, that past which was almost more real to her than the present. John Dalrymple, Ronnie, Archie--they had all grown up together. It had been her husband's dearest wish, and her own, that Nicole would go to Newby as a bride, and it had been an end of many hopes when she had sent John away--. Now John had come back, still, it seemed, faithful to his first love. How ideal it would be! Newby was almost as full of associations as Rutherfurd; John had been like her own.... Jean Douglas, kind woman, thought all she had to do was to give John a chance; but she didn't know what Nicole's mother knew, that there was something in the way. The face of Simon Beckett rose before her. No dog in the manger this, those eyes could never be resentful; but wasn't it just that utter unresentfulness that gave the old love its strength? Well, time would tell....

* * * * *

On Thursday evening the three ladies at the Harbour House all appeared in their best clothing, ready to dine at Windywalls. Each seemed rather surprised at the appearance of the others.

'I call this simply silly,' Althea said, 'dressing up for old Mrs. Heggie. Why, Aunt Jane, you've actually got on your emeralds! And Nicole's wearing a dress she should have kept for an occasion.'

'I notice,' said Nicole, 'that you're not conspicuously shabby yourself, my dear.'

'Oh, this old thing! I thought I might as well wear it out, though it is too smart.'

When they got to Windywalls they found that they were the only guests, except for an Irishwoman staying in the house, and Mrs. Heggie. But their hostess wore her smartest frock, and the dinner was so carefully thought out, so perfect in every detail, that they knew special pains had been taken with it.

Mrs. Heggie sat in the place of honour, and, Joan not being there to look at her disapprovingly, talked to her heart's content. The Irishwoman, a Miss Barbour from Donegal, middle-aged and jovial, entirely undamped by the very troublous years she had lived through, was obviously delighted with her and encouraged her to further efforts. It was as well that Joan, enjoying sunshine and the cultivated society of Hulbert Colson in Madeira, was unaware of some of her mother's speeches that night.

'Oh yes,' she said in reply to some one. 'I'm getting on quite well without Joan, though of course I miss her. It's a good chance to get her room thoroughly cleaned. We daren't touch it when she's there! It's as much as my life's worth to displace a book! But I just told the servants to carry everything as it was, into a spare room, and got in the painters. It's all plain cream. I'd have liked to put on one of these lovely new papers with hanging flowers in the corners, if I hadn't known Joan would hate it--. But anyway, it's clean from the foundations.... Oh yes, I think she's enjoying herself. She bathes and lies about all morning. I'm glad I didn't go, for she tells me she never gets anything for her tea but a stale biscuit. Fancy! Cake seems unknown.'

'Your daughter's with friends?' Mrs. Jameson said.

'Oh yes, from Chelsea. I've only met them once. Their name is Colson. There's a mother, a widow, about my own age, and a son and daughter--Hulbert and Delilah. Did you ever hear such names?... They're all either literary or artistic or both--even the mother. Isn't it awful when quite elderly people are like that?'

'Awful!' agreed Nicole. 'And do you suppose they sit all the time in the sunshine, talking about Art? It's a solemn thought.'

'Sometimes,' said Mrs. Heggie, 'they go expeditions: picnics, I expect.'

'I wonder,' said Mrs. Jameson, 'if they ever toboggan down from the top of the town. Long ago, before the War, when I was a young girl, I went with a party of friends, on a cruise round by Tenerife and Madeira and a lot of other places: Lisbon and the Azores. One of the things I look back on with pleasure was sliding down the

101

cobblestones at Madeira.'

'It sounds dangerous,' Mrs. Heggie said.

'Is that an interesting cruise?' Lady Jane asked. 'We've sometimes thought of taking it.'

Esmé Jameson helped herself to the dish that was being handed round, and said: 'It ought to be very interesting, but my chief impression seems to be that it was very stormy at sea and very hot on land; and I don't think our party--of which I was a very young and unimportant member--behaved very well. We rather held ourselves aloof from the life on board, and sat about and invented descriptive names for the other passengers. A group of sketchily clad young women who had a trick of standing against the sky-line were *Nymphs surprised while bathing*, and a small fat man who suffered from the motion of the boat was *The Seasick Piglet*. It was very rude and not at all witty.... There were a great many wealthy Lancashire people on board.... I'm afraid we were deservedly unpopular.'

'I expect,' said Nicole, 'you'd simply have loved it if you'd let yourself go and been friends with all and sundry. I've always longed to go on one of those cruises, or better still a Munn's Tour.'

'Awful!' said Althea.

'Lovely!' said Nicole, 'I've watched them at Calais and Boulogne, all with their labels neatly stuck on their cases, getting into the train for Rome, and been filled with envy. Probably most of them had saved for it for years, and how much pleasanter to go with people who are determined to get every ounce of enjoyment out of everything than with a party of blasé creatures who are only killing time.'

Althea shook her head. 'You might think it fun for one day, but it would soon become insupportable. Just think how the people would get on your nerves!'

'Why should they? I'd be more likely to get on theirs.'

Miss Barbour turned to Mrs. Heggie, with a wave of her hand at the two girls.

'These young things talk away, but it's the older ones that should go and see the world. Now you and I, Mrs. Heggie dear, would make grand travelling companions. What do you say to starting off somewhere? You're free and I'm free. We've got to the time when we need to see life from a new angle. I've never been to America. Will you accompany me there?'

'Not to America,' said Mrs. Heggie firmly, 'nor anywhere in a ship. As I told Joan when she spoke about Madeira, I will not be buried at sea.'

'Well now, doesn't that curb us a good deal, for the British Isles are not very tempting in the winter.'

Mrs. Heggie looked doubtfully at her new friend. She liked her broad, good-natured smile, and the hint of a brogue that gave such a rollicking touch to everything she

102

said, but she could not but feel that the lady was a trifle precipitate. 'I once met a lady in a train,' she said, 'travelling from London to Edinburgh, and she asked me to come and stay with her and hunt--she was Irish too.'

'It accounts for almost anything,' Miss Barbour said with a chuckle. 'Then you don't regard me favourably as a travelling companion.'

'It's not that,' Mrs. Heggie said earnestly, 'I'm sure you'd be ideal, for you'd always make the best of things, but the fact is I prefer to stay at home. I doubt my travelling days are done.... But I'd be more than pleased if you'd come to a meal with me while you're at Windywalls. Perhaps lunch would suit you best. I'll arrange with Mrs. Jameson.'

In the drawing-room after dinner they talked and played at games, and every one was surprised when it was time to go.

Before they left, Esmé Jameson said to Nicole: 'I felt it rather unkind to ask you and Miss Gort to such a dull party. I really hoped to have two cousins staying with me, rather interesting men, but when they failed me I thought I'd have no men at all and make it Mrs. Heggie's party.'

Nicole laughed as she said, 'I'll confess to you I loathe going out to dinner, time seems to me simply to *crawl* in other people's houses between eight and ten. I keep trying to see the clock, and wondering if it has stopped. But to-night I've never wanted to know the time. It's been fine, hasn't it, Althea?'

The girl smiled at her hostess. 'It rather looks,' she said, 'as if the boredom came with the men.'

Chapter XVIII

'Give me audience, good madam.'

AS YOU LIKE IT.

It would have been easier for Lady Walkinshaw simply to have given up, to have become a complete invalid, keeping to her own room, her interests bounded by the four walls of it, her daily companions doctors and nurses. But she saw life as a battle to be fought, and every morning she buckled on her armour.

No one knew what it cost her to keep that serene face, that gay smile, to get into the pretty clothes that her men-folk liked, to endure having her hair done in the way that best became her, to be wheeled in her chair to her place at table. It kept her up, they said, to attempt things, but to her every hour was an engagement. The talk with the

103

gardener, the half-hour with the cook, the luncheon-party, the afternoon call--if she got through smiling it was a victory, if she let pain and discouragement become apparent she had been worsted.

She was helped in her battle by the fact that her husband and son did not realise how hard it was for her. They were 'glad she felt well enough' to make the effort to be with them in their daily life. And Belinda, her young niece, frisked round like some happy young animal, charming to behold, amusing to listen to, and with no thought of any one but herself. But though Lady Walkinshaw felt that anything was better than being fussed over, she found it a relief sometimes to relax before the understanding in certain eyes.

There were visitors who bustled in evidently impatient to be off again; who said 'Is the pain *very* bad? No, don't move, *please*,' who sat just where it was torture for her to look at them, and then, in a few minutes jumped up saying, 'Now I must rush.' This they called 'cheering up poor Lady Walkinshaw.' But there were other visitors more acceptable, who came as to a pleasure, who talked to her as if she were an ordinary being like themselves and interested in rational things, who told her when they found a book that pleased them, a new recipe, an interesting acquaintance.

When Nicole Rutherfurd rang up to ask if she could see her on a certain afternoon, Lady Walkinshaw said 'Yes' at once. Her husband was in Edinburgh, Charles in London, Belinda was spending the day with some friends; it would be pleasant to have the girl to herself. She had seen a good deal of her, and had heard more from Charles, who spent, she knew, much time at the Harbour House. Nicole and he seemed good friends and he was always willing to speak of her: it was the other girl, Althea Gort, of whom he said little.

His mother, of necessity a great deal alone, utterly impotent to help or hinder, brooded much on this girl, and listened eagerly to all she heard of her.

Belinda's opinion had been frankly given after her first visit to the Harbour House.

'Lady Jane is a darling,' she said, 'but not quite of this world: the daughter Nicole's *too* fascinating, but the other girl's a dark horse.'

'Didn't you like her?' her aunt asked.

'Not at first, I didn't. I thought she was a cold, snubbing creature. But there are nice bits in her. I don't think she's a cat, and her smile's the prettiest thing I ever saw. I can't think why she doesn't smile all the time when it makes her so attractive. I don't mean that she isn't always definitely pretty, she is--but it's a cold prettiness until it is lit up. You should see old Charles's face when she smiles at him!! But for goodness' sake don't say I said so.'

Lady Walkinshaw had not thought Althea cold the few times she had spoken to her. She had seemed to her surprisingly gentle and understanding for a young girl, and she had rather wistfully wondered how she could become better acquainted with her.

Nicole arrived in her little car known as The Worm, because so far it had never turned. She was, she explained, making a round of farewell visits because she was going away for a fortnight.

'But what will you do without Kirkmeikle?' her hostess asked.

'What, indeed? I become more *thirled* to it every day--isn't that a good word? John Grumblie at Windywalls taught it me--and the thought of leaving it for a fortnight almost breaks my heart.' Lady Walkinshaw smiled with pleasure at the prettiness of the girl, her face flushed by the cold wind, her eyes grey as glass under her little scarlet hat.

'Then why go?' she said.

'Well, because one can't always be refusing invitations when people mean to be kind.... First of all, Althea and I are going to stay with old friends of ours on Tweedside, for a ball. No, I don't think it will be very nice. I'm a bit old for balls, but I'm hoping Althea will enjoy it. It's pretty quiet for her here.'

'But it isn't her first ball?'

'Oh--*no*. Althea's had a London season and she's travelled about a tremendous lot and seen life. She's barely nineteen, but she's old for her years. Why, Belinda's only about a year younger and she's a mere child. It's the difference in the way they've been brought up.'

'Yes,' said Lady Walkinshaw, and added after a pause: 'Althea is your cousin, isn't she?'

'No, no relation really.'

The woman and the girl looked at each other. Nicole quite realised that her companion wished to know all there was to know about Althea, to satisfy herself that she was the sort of girl a mother would like to see her son marry, and in ordinary circumstances she would have enjoyed the situation. With a suspicious, worldly-minded woman a fencing-match might have been quite amusing, but in this case--she looked round the gay room with its flowers, its fresh chintzes, its twittering love-birds, and her eyes stayed on the woman in the wheeled chair, who smiled so indomitably through her pain, whose pretty clothes were about as comfortable as the hair shirt of a saint. No, she couldn't fence with one so defenceless.

She leant forward, laying one hand on the arm of the wheeled chair.

'Lady Walkinshaw,' she said, 'I expect you know that Charles comes a lot to the Harbour House and that he seems to be keen on Althea? Remember, I haven't a notion if she cares for him, but--you must wonder a lot, and perhaps if I tell you all I know it may make you understand the whole position better.'

Her companion did not speak, and after frowning at the fire for a moment, Nicole went on.

'Till last October I had hardly heard of Althea's existence. I knew vaguely there was such a girl, but my mother has such a host of relations and connections by marriage that it's difficult to keep track of them all. Then last October, my mother had a letter from her sister-in-law, Lady Elliston--Blanchie we call her--asking if we'd have Althea on a visit. Althea is her niece, her dead sister's child. She had brought her out and was taking charge of her, and any one less capable of taking charge of anything you could hardly imagine! She's quite a decent woman, but that's all, and her sister wasn't even that. She divorced Althea's father, Freddy Gort, or he divorced her, I really forget, but anyway, it doesn't matter, for they were both as bad as could be. So that's poor Althea's short history. Tossed between worthless parents like a shuttlecock. Can you wonder that she seems cold and suspicious? Why, she doesn't know disinterested kindness when she meets it; she's never had a home or family affection or anything.'

Still Lady Walkinshaw said nothing, and Nicole hurried on.

'I don't pretend that I wanted her to come. I pictured an unpleasant type of the girl of to-day--and when I saw her she was worse than anything I had imagined! She was obviously furious at having been sent, and wanted to make the very worst of herself. Her manners! Her little painted face!... You see, the poor babe had been dragged away from some man she fancied herself in love with, a low fellow who didn't trouble to follow her into captivity, who didn't even trouble to write to her after the first week or so. No wonder we found her difficult--But now we know her we'd hate to lose her. There's something rather delightful about her, and--oddly enough--something straight and scrupulous. She must be a throw-back to some decent ancestor.... Forgive me telling you all this, because you may never need to know Althea better; as I say, I haven't an idea whether she cares for your son or whether he cares seriously for her, but I thought you might be wondering--Oh, have I been officious?'

'No--Believe me, I am very grateful. It isn't easy to be a prisoner when things are happening. I dare say I'm not more fussy about Charles than any mother with an only son but'--Lady Walkinshaw laughed a little--'the hen on the bank with the young ducks has my profound sympathy.... I sit here and think and wonder--having so little else to do!--and most of my thoughts are about my boy. It matters so much to a young man the sort of wife he gets, so much that sometimes one trembles.... I think he will be lucky if he gets Althea. And I shall count myself lucky. She would be a much more interesting daughter-in-law, and for that matter a much more interesting wife, than a petted, indulged young creature who knew nothing about life and the hard things. Funnily enough, the thing that struck me about Althea the only time we really had a talk together was the understanding look in her eyes, as if she knew what suffering meant--Well now, while we're having tea, tell me something more of your doings. You are both going to a ball?'

'Yes, and we've both got new frocks: rather divine! We stay a week at Kingshouse--a place on Tweedside near our old home--and then Althea comes back to be with

Mother, and I go on to Glasgow to visit a friend of mine, a Mrs. Jackson.... Oh, and we haven't talked about the Cowdenden Musical Society. I do hope it's going to be a success. How I wish you could be at the rehearsals. Charles's efforts to correct wrong pronunciation! There is one girl who will say "audocity"--a lovely word. But he is delightful with them, a man and a brother; they'll take anything from him, he has such a nice human way of going into fits of laughing over mistakes and awkward moments. Althea is really very useful with the dancing, she dances so beautifully herself.... Isn't it a blessing Mr. Baldwin is going to give the girls votes before the election? The Cowdenden chorus of *Iolanthe* will vote solid for Charles.'

A few minutes later, when she was leaving, Nicole said:

'I greatly fear I've talked too much and tired you. Please try and not be the worse of me or Sir James won't let me come back.'

'My dear, I am greatly the better of you. You've given me lots to think about, and that's what I want. Dr. Roberts keeps saying "Interest yourself," but it's not so easy. He's profoundly uninteresting himself, poor man.'

'I wish you had Dr. Kilgour,' Nicole said earnestly. 'He finds life so thrilling he'd interest you himself, and he'd interest you in all sorts of people and things.... Oh, have you read this? *Letters of Dorothy Osbourne?* It's one of Mother's favourite books, and she sent it to you on chance. No, you're to keep it, she got that copy especially for you....'

* * * * *

When Nicole reached Kirkmeikle she looked up at the clock-tower and saw that, as it was only half-past five, she would have time to look in at the Lamberts. Leaving The Worm in a side road she went through the green door in the wall, through the dark wintry garden to the square grey house. The blinds were not drawn in the study and she could look in on the fireside scene--the minister in an arm-chair with a book, Mrs. Lambert mending at a table with a lamp, the two little girls intent on some game.

'You looked so peaceful,' she said, when the maid had admitted her, 'that it seemed a shame to disturb you.'

Mrs. Lambert pushed aside her work and rose to welcome the visitor, saying:

'We can put up with a lot of this sort of disturbing.... Move your bricks a little, Aillie. Sit into this chair, Miss Nicole.... I'm so glad you've come in now, for it's the hour of the day we enjoy most. John's congratulating himself on not having to go out to-night. He's deep in the last book you lent him.'

The little minister came forward, after carefully marking his place in the book he had been reading.

'I'm afraid,' he said in his hesitating way, 'I'm afraid you've done me a bad turn, Miss Rutherfurd. I c-can't lay it down. The *very priests of God are reading comedies, singing the love-songs of the bucolics.'*

For a moment Nicole looked blank, then her face lit up.

'Oh, *The Wandering Scholars*! Isn't it a delicious book? I suppose one would need to be learned really to appreciate it, but I adore the richness of it, the plums one can pick out--poems and lovely sentences that are like balm to remember.' She turned to the minister's wife. 'I know how precious your time is and it's a formidable work to tackle, but I believe you'd love it as much as I did.'

Mrs. Lambert nodded. 'Oh, John's been reading bits to me. I sit here knitting or sewing with my mouth open like a young bird's for the morsels he gives me. I enjoy them like that much better than reading them for myself.'

'Of course you do; it's the perfect way of acquiring knowledge.' Nicole dropped on the floor and began to help the little girls to build their tower.

'What is it?' she asked, 'the Leaning Tower of Pisa?'

'No,' said Aillie, 'it's the Tower of Babel.'

'I see. Well, Betsy, we'll have to make it strong, for I expect all the people had a free fight when they found they couldn't understand each other.'

'That's not in the Bible,' said the small Betsy stolidly.

Nicole smiled up at the children's parents. 'Isn't she staunch?' she said. 'Mrs. Lambert, I'm so sorry I shan't be at the "Mothers" on Wednesday; I'm going away for a fortnight. I keep saying, "I'm going away for a fortnight," in the hope that you'll mourn with me. I do hate going away.'

'The Mothers will miss you,' Mrs. Lambert said, 'as indeed we all shall,' while her husband remarked, 'I hear you've been walking in d-devious paths, Miss Nicole. Jimmy Greig tells me you went to the Gospel Hall meeting the other night.'

Nicole dusted her hands as she said: 'Oh I did, I did. Jimmy had so often asked me to go that I was quite ashamed, so last Sunday I managed to persuade Althea to accompany me in order to keep me in countenance. It's a nice meeting. I liked the harmonium and Sankey's hymns, but it was the familiarity of it all that unmanned me. The prayers, you know. The intimate friendly way that just anybody got up and prayed to their Maker. Like this--"*O Lord, as Thou knowest, dear Sister Simpson is not just so well to-day. Lord, make Thou her bed beneath her...*" We weren't prepared for the *easiness* of it all.... And there was a man from Leith who sang solos. Providence had not intended him for a singer, but that in no way deterred him. He got up and bellowed a hymn beginning:

'I'm one of the sorrows of Satan...'

'N-no,' Mr. Lambert objected. 'Now you're making fun of it.'

'Oh, but I assure you that was what he sang. Ask Jimmy Greig. Jimmy was much impressed both by the hymn and the singer--D'you think a meeting like that does good?'

Mr. Lambert rubbed his forehead perplexedly as he said:

'I wouldn't like to say it didn't. Anyway, it gives great pleasure to the little band who run it. They seem to crave something--something warmer than our church service, and this meeting supplies the want. I sometimes go to it myself when they are in need of a speaker, but I always feel that my utterances must sound stilted and cold after what they are accustomed to.'

'I wish,' said Nicole, 'you had seen Althea Gort's face,' and was promptly overcome with laughter at the recollection. They all laughed with her, so infectious is uncontrolled mirth, until Nicole, wiping her eyes, said she must go.

'How is Spider?' Aillie asked.

'Ah, that reminds me, would you and Betsy take him for a run on the sands when you've time? That would be kind. Well--I suppose a fortnight will pass!'

Chapter XIX

'It is a truth universally acknowledged, that a single man in possession of a good fortune must be in want of a wife.'

JANE AUSTEN.

Jean Douglas came in from her morning walk, fresh and rosy with the frosty air, and feeling somewhat relieved in the mind that the ball was over, that the house-party had departed, that peace had descended once again on Kingshouse. She was met in the hall by the butler, who told her that Miss Lockhart was waiting for her in the boudoir, so there she repaired, followed closely by her two faithful followers, Gay and Merry.

'*Well!*' was Alison Lockhart's greeting, 'you are an early bird! I came here before eleven thinking I'd be sure to find you in, and I've been waiting for an hour. Where on earth have you been?'

Jean Douglas unwound her woollen scarf as she replied: 'On the top of Laverlaw. I haven't had a decent walk for a week, and I did want to feel the hill air on my face.... Why didn't you come to meet me?'

'Not I, forsooth! I've read *The Scotsman* from beginning to end, eaten some black-striped balls out of that beautiful glass jar--was it a Christmas present?--and was in the middle of *The Queen*.... Hullo, Merry, old man. Good Gay, good dog!'

'Put them off the clean chintzes, Alison.'

'Oh, they won't do any harm. How d'you keep them so white and woolly? They're disgustingly clean and tidy to have come in from a walk. I believe they have their paws sponged by Donald the footman before they enter the front door.'

Mrs. Douglas sat down on the large chintz-covered sofa beside her friend, remarking, 'Your jibes, my friend, leave me untouched. If it's not a rude question, might I ask what brought you here so early? Was it merely a desire for company, or had you an ulterior motive? Anyway, you'll stay to luncheon and see Tom?'

'Thank you, yes. I hoped you'd ask me. The truth is, I suddenly found myself very tired of the cooking in my own house. There is no element of surprise in the meals, and there ought to be, for I leave it entirely to the cook. But she has a stodgy mind, decent woman, which is reflected in her dishes. The lightness of your Mrs. Fraser's touch will be a welcome change.'

'I hope you aren't accusing Mrs. Fraser of frivolity because her soufflés and omelettes are so light. But I know what you mean. One sometimes tires of meals in one's own house, and any change seems for the better. It's the company, my dear, that really makes the difference. Eating alone is an unnatural thing.'

'Considering that for the last week I've had eight at each meal--The last lot left this morning. I don't pretend to grieve. I'm quite willing to be hospitable, but people staying in the house are a dreadful bore. It isn't so bad if they're keen on bridge, and will sit planted for hours, but when they want to be routing about all the time--And young girls are really the limit--However, it's over, and nothing more can be expected from me for a long time. Anyway, I'm going off in another fortnight.'

'Again!'

'Yes, I've got wandering in my blood. All the time I'm away I think how beautiful my home is and what a fool I am to be missing the loveliness of each succeeding season on Tweedside, and when I am at home I think of the swiftness of the passing years and how wide the world is, how much there is to see while it is still day. I remember that, if I live there will be long years when I shall be compelled to stay in my own quiet glen, and that then I shall be glad to think on all I've seen and done.... This time I've planned quite a far trek--but I'll tell you about that afterwards, and you'll have the goodness to listen, but what I want to know now is, *what happened last week?*'

Jean Douglas rose and dislodged Gay and Merry from two arm-chairs, then leaning one arm along the narrow shelf of the Adam mantelpiece, she looked down at her friend with a half-rueful, half-quizzical smile, and said: 'What happened? Nothing: nothing at all.'

Alison Lockhart snorted. 'What? After all your trouble and planning? Whose fault was it?'

Jean Douglas shrugged her shoulders. 'My dear, I know nothing.'

'But--surely you've *something* to tell me?'

'Lots, but nothing of importance. Last Thursday Nicole and Althea Gort arrived, and John Dalrymple came over from Newby. As you know, I asked two other couples, and a young man for Althea, thinking that that would throw Nicole and John very much together: as old friends that would only have been natural. And it all seemed to work out very well. Althea and her young man got on famously--she has a way with her, that girl, as was to be expected. The two couples had much in common, and Nicole and John walked and talked and played together on what seemed the easiest and friendliest terms. Much too easy and friendly for my liking. She treated him like a brother. "John, d'you remember this?", jokes from nursery days; pranks recalled--It was very pretty, and rather terribly pathetic when one remembered the changes the years had brought....'

Mrs. Douglas's voice sank, and there was silence for a minute, broken by Alison Lockhart, who said:

'I've been seeing a good deal of John Dalrymple these last months, and every time I've seen him I've liked him more. He's not easy to know; that impassive way annoys one often, but he isn't really dull, he has rather a delicious dry humour, and he's got a good honest heart. He would be very wrathful if he knew I know, but I heard from my old nurse in Lowden village that he keeps all the old people in the place in great comfort: actually writes to them when he is away and visits them regularly when at home. "Maister John" is a god to the old Newby servants--I must say I was rather surprised, for he certainly has the appearance of being aloof and indifferent, don't you think?'

'I've known him since he was in petticoats,' said Mrs. Douglas, as if that explained everything. 'He's thirty-four now, and it's high time he was settling down and giving Newby Place a mistress. Well, I've done my best. When John said good-bye to me yesterday--I need hardly tell you I asked no questions--he said "Mistress Jean" (that's what Nicole always calls me and he has adopted it too), "Mistress Jean, you've been amazingly kind. I can never thank you enough for this week. Whatever happens, I've had that."'

'Mm--Doesn't sound too hopeful? What of Nicole?'

'Oh, Nikky went off as blithe as a bird to stay with Mrs. Jackson in Glasgow! It will really be desperately annoying if she turns down John. Nothing more suitable could be imagined. It's almost absurdly suitable. It would bring Jane Rutherfurd back to the neighbourhood, where she's badly needed. I tell her--and it's the truth--that we've deteriorated without her. It would make Newby Place a centre of hospitality, for Nicole has all her mother's social gifts, and it would keep Barbara Jackson in her place, for that young woman is getting quite above herself.'

Alison Lockhart gave an impatient sigh. 'It will never come off,' she said, 'you will see, something will happen to prevent it.... Odd, isn't it, how Barbara Jackson rubs people the wrong way. There's something so condescending about her affability, and have you noticed she asks kind questions but never listens to the answers?--her eyes are looking over your shoulder in case she misses higher game. That is not a trait that makes for social success.'

'She doesn't look to me a happy woman, in spite of all the possessions she delights to flaunt. I just hope she makes that decent fellow Andy happy. Anyway, he has the boy. It's rather pretty to see how his face lights up when you ask about his small son.'

Alison Lockhart yawned. 'Sorry. I seem to want my lunch.' She looked at the clock. 'Still half an hour away! How did you think the ball went?'

'Have another striped ball? No, well, perhaps it would spoil your luncheon--Oh, I thought everything went very well. The decorations were quite pretty; the supper was good, and it wasn't too crowded. Of course it would have been infinitely cosier in a private house, but the numbers were too great. I quite enjoyed it, and Tom found a lot of cronies and didn't keep fussing to get home. The dresses were pretty, didn't you think?'

Miss Lockhart stretched her skirt to conceal the fact that Merry had crawled on to the sofa beside her, and said, 'Some of them. Tilly Kilpatrick was a sight. One would think that with those stout legs of hers she would take advantage of the long evening skirts, but no! Everything possible revealed--poor soul!'

Jean laughed. 'She was quite happy. It seems to me it's the forty-ish and even the fifty-ish that are keenest about dancing. The very young tell you they rather prefer a quiet evening at home! I thought Barbara Jackson looked very well: the line of her velvet dress gave her dignity: she really is a very handsome woman in an uninteresting way.'

'Oh yes,' Alison Lockhart agreed indifferently. 'I never see her but she torments me to go and call on those protégés of hers--I forget the name, Brunton, is it? I told her nothing would induce me when she began again about them the other night. She's a most tenacious creature when she gets an idea in her head. Have you been persuaded?'

'I have. I know it was weak of me, but it was less trouble than to keep on refusing. They're perfectly nice people, but I found conversation difficult. I can quite see why Barbara has taken them up. They give her the adulation that she feels is her due, an adulation that's disappointingly absent in the rest of her neighbours. "Gracious" was the word Mrs. Brunton used about her. Barbara would appreciate that; there's a queenly touch about it!'

'Talking about the queenly touch,' said Alison, 'I thought Nicole looked like a ballad queen the other night. That long parchment-coloured frock opening over gold lace, and the crystals binding her hair and coming down on her forehead--fire and dew. She always had moments of great beauty--But the other girl, Althea, is a *pukka* beauty.'

'Oh yes, hers is the beauty of feature and line and colouring: it has nothing to do with temperament. I was really rather proud of my party the other night. I thought they compared favourably with any other....'

A barking of dogs was heard outside.

'Here's Tom. Quiet, Gay. No, you're not going out, and Tweed and Yarrow are not coming in, so there's no necessity to make a fuss. Alison, come with me while I wash my hands and tidy a bit.'

Miss Lockhart got up and surveyed herself in the mirror. 'Indeed,' she said, 'a little tidying wouldn't come amiss to me either. I can't help thinking your mirrors at Kingshouse are very unflattering. When I glance at myself I'm always surprised to find how plain I'm looking, and at home I'm quite passable. It's wise to have a flattering glass, for it sends you out to meet a cold and critical world warmed and cheered, whereas----'

'Yes, I quite agree,' said Jean Douglas, moving to the door, 'but Tom likes his meals to the minute, and the gong has gone.'

'Life without a man has its compensations,' Alison remarked, as she leisurely mounted the stairs, while Tom trumpeted in the dining-room.

Chapter XX

'I hope I never ridicule what is wise and good. Follies and nonsense, whims and inconsistencies do divert me, and I laugh at them whenever I can....'

JANE AUSTEN.

Mrs. Jackson sat behind the breakfast-tray in the dining-room of The Borders and remarked: 'Well, Nicole'll be here to-day. Isn't that nice?'

Her husband looked up for a moment from the pages of the *Glasgow Herald*, but did not commit himself to any opinion.

'Thursday this is, till next Thursday. One week. It's little enough for all I'd like to show her. Let me see, she comes to-day about four, so after tea we'll look through the house--No, we'll keep the house till next morning when she's fresh and when she can see it in the morning light. Tea and a rest and dinner and a good talk--that'll be the first night. I thought mebbe a theatre on Monday or Wednesday--What's on next week, Father?'

'Eh?' said Mr. Jackson, again deep in his paper.

'It's the theatre I'm speaking about, but never mind just now. I'm going into town this morning anyway, and I'll arrange about seats. I think a box would be best--more exclusive.... To-morrow night we're having those people to dinner that we've been owing so long. You know--the Ralstons. It's a chance to have them when Nicole's here to talk to them, for Mrs. Ralston's not our style, though always quite pleasant. Saturday I thought we'd go a good long motor-drive and have a quiet evening seeing it's your night in, Father. Sunday: I'm sure I don't know what we could do on Sunday. I like my Sunday quiet, but then, of course, I'm old-fashioned. I believe she'd be quite happy to read. You might order a lot of new books, for she goes through them like anything. Monday we're having an evening party, paying off a lot of people for things like tea-parties and whist drives, you know. Should we try bridge, I wonder, or just talk and have a little music? I dare say I'd better engage a pianist and a singer or two anyway. What d'you think?'

Mr. Jackson did not look up, and his wife continued her monologue.

'And then, of course, I must take her all about, for she's never been to Glasgow before. I do hope it's decent weather and I can take her down to Gourock, and out to Stirling, and then there's the Rouken Glen and the Art Galleries and the Municipal Buildings and all the sights. Uch, a week'll never do it!'

'What's that you're saying, Bella?'

Mr. Jackson had laid down his paper, which he invariably opened and glanced through when he had finished his first cup of tea. 'You seem quite excited.'

'Well, I am, and no wonder. Nicole Rutherfurd's coming here to-day, and I've an awful lot of things to show her. She's never stayed in Glasgow in her life--fancy that! So it's all new to her. It'll be a fine change after Kirkmeikle, and I want to give her a real good time.'

Mrs. Jackson came round the table with her husband's second cup, put the toast within his reach, the butter and the marmalade, and looked complacently round the room. 'My! what will she think of this house after that queer old place by the sea? *By* the sea! It's very nearly *in* the sea!'

Mr. Jackson laid a spoonful of marmalade on a piece of toast, and while munching it, said: 'She'll not likely think much of it. These kind of people are all for what's old and shabby, and this house is neither the one nor the other.'

He, too, looked complacently round the room which, truth to tell, was remarkably like a show dining-room in a furniture warehouse.

'It's handsome,' said his wife, 'and so convenient. Everything made to our own design. So easy to keep too: that wood needs no polishing to speak of, and what with vacuum cleaners and one thing and another, the maids need hardly dirty their hands. Telephones, wireless, electricity--I'm just afraid we go up in a blaze one of these days.'

'No fear,' said her husband. 'Well, be sure and give Miss Nicole a good time. It'll be quite a treat for her to see Glasgow; it's a place where there's always lots going on--Good-bye then. I'll not be in till near seven to-night; I've all manner of committees.'

He said it in a satisfied voice, not at all as if he were sorry for himself, and his wife helped him with his coat and patted him on the back, saying, 'I'm sure I don't know what they'd do without you. The amount you get through! And all free, gratis, and for nothing too. Public-spirited, that's what you are. Well, good-bye then. Be sure and have a good lunch in case you haven't time for tea.'

* * * * *

When Nicole jumped out of the train that afternoon and saw Mrs. Jackson's welcoming face, she said:

'No wonder the sun doesn't trouble to shine much in Glasgow; you don't need it when you have such beaming faces!'

'Tuts!' said Mrs. Jackson, pleased but rather affronted. 'We get plenty sunshine in Glasgow. It's been shining like anything to-day and it only the beginning of February.... Well, well, and how are you? I needn't ask, you're blooming. The sea air seems to agree with you.' Without waiting for an answer she went on: 'And your dear mother? As placid as ever of course. A wonderful faculty she has of accepting things as they come! Nothing ruffles her. I'm sure I envy her: there's no patrician calm about me.... Where's our porter gone? Is that him? Isn't it queer how difficult it is to know one porter from another? Like shop young ladies.'

'And waiters,' said Nicole.

'Yes, waiters. Ay, that's our man. No, we don't want a taxi: our car's waiting--yes, the end one....' Mrs. Jackson turned to her companion and said: 'I'm so glad we've got our new car in time for your visit. Yes, it's a beauty, the very latest model, but a wee thing low in the roof for me. You're meant to crush away down, but I haven't the figure for that. I do better bolt-upright, and the old-fashioned kind suited me.'

'It's delightfully comfortable,' Nicole said, sinking into her corner, 'the last word in luxury--Is it far to The Borders?'

'Uch, no. I'll tell you all the places as we pass. We're crossing Jamaica Bridge. Yes, that's the Clyde.'

'Oh, but how lovely!' Nicole cried.

'Oh, the Broomielaw's a dirty place, but it's very bonnie down a bit. I'm going to take you down to Gourock and you'll see across the Firth.... This long street's Eglinton Street. We turn up at the Toll for Pollokshields. It's a big suburb, roads and roads of villas. It's mebbe not so smart as out West, but I like it better; the air's fine, and where we are is very nearly the country.'

'There must be a great deal of money in Glasgow,' Nicole said, looking at the never-ending line of large comfortable-looking houses each in its own garden.

'Uch, yes--though, mind you, we've been hard hit these last years. You wouldn't think it going through the shops and seeing crowds of well-dressed people, and all the lovely cars and fine houses out West, but works are standing idle that used to be busy, and there's no doubt there's a good deal of privation. I'm not one of those who say the men don't want to work. People speak as if the dole was a fortune! It must be desperate for decent couples who've held their heads up, to see their wee bits of things disappearing, and the children needing things they can't give them. I often lie awake at nights and think about them--. You see, though Mr. Jackson has been so successful and we live in style and all that, we're plain people, indeed it's not so long since we were working people. My own father rose from being a workman to a master, so did Mr. Jackson's. It's just the way of the world, some rise and some go down. I wasn't envious when I was down, and I hope I'm not proud when I'm up--. Well, well, how I do run on. And I was thinking you'd come from Kirkmeikle, forgetting you've been at Kingshouse--what took you there when there's always a room for you at Rutherfurd?'

'Oh well--Mrs. Douglas is such an old friend, and she made a particular point of us going for the Hunt Ball. It was put off, you remember, from Christmas week? But we lunched one day at Rutherfurd and got all sorts of messages for you, and a kiss from the small Andrew.'

'Bless him! Did you know a difference on him? Has he grown any?'

'In five weeks! But they did tell me how much he had put on--so many pounds, or would it be ounces? Anyway he's a picture of a baby, and was most urbane to me when I held him for a bit. He's a real Jackson.'

'You see it too? You tell Father that, he will be pleased.... We're getting near our place now.'

'Why, you're quite in the country.'

'Yes, and yet so near town that it's nothing to run in for a play or a concert.' Mrs. Jackson was sitting looking out, and she now cried: 'There!' and Nicole found that they were in a short, perfectly-kept drive, approaching a large, many-turreted red house, and she pulled herself together for her task of admiring, to the satisfaction of her hostess.

As they entered the front door, 'See,' Mrs. Jackson said, '*marble*!'

'So it is! How cool it looks and clean!'

'And don't the red rugs look cosy on it? These were all made to order, and the stair-carpet too. The man said to me, "Believe me," he said, "in forty years there won't be a bit of difference on them." "Mebbe not," I said, "but there'll be a difference on me." He *laughed*.... I'm awful fond of red carpets, they're so cheery.... I keep magazines on the table there, like Rutherfurd, but Father and I never sit in the hall. I don't see much sense in it, and it's apt to untidy things and give people a bad impression of the house.... You see, it's all as compact as you like; the dining-room here, the pantry, and

116

then through to the kitchen; on this side the drawing-room and Mr. Jackson's own room, and the billiard-room. But you'll see it all later, there's plenty of time, and you want your tea just now. Come away and get your hat off.... You see they're very easy stairs? I insisted on that. And this conservatory gives the landing a nice finish, don't you think? The flowers give the same red-and-white note as the red rugs and the marble, though hyacinths are not as successful in that way as geraniums.... If you're a bit stout and short of breath the flowers give you an excuse to stop and rest on your way upstairs! We've just the four bedrooms (of course with dressing-rooms), just enough to take in Barbara and Andy and the boy, but we've *three* bathrooms, not to mention the one for the maids. Beauties--marble floors and tiled-you'll see. Father just said, "We'll have a small house but it'll be perfect!" And it is. Hot and cold in every bedroom: fitted-in wardrobes, and cupboards galore, and the very latest in spring mattresses. The maids' rooms are just as nice, and the kitchen's a fair treat! A sitting-room, too, for the maids to entertain their friends, and a wireless; the plumbing perfect and the pipes all copper. But here I go on talking and you wearying for your tea--. This is your room: I thought of you when I chose the things for it, and hoped you'd often sleep in it.'

She stopped, expectant of raptures, and Nicole did not disappoint her.

There was much to praise. Never had Nicole walked on softer, more opulent carpets, or seen a more inviting bed, with its rosy eiderdown and curtains. Mrs. Jackson turned back the sheet and showed pale-pink blankets bound with broad satin ribbon. 'Aren't they a conceit?' she said. 'I saw them in a shop in Bond Street, and I just said to myself, "The very thing for the pink room," and there they are! Of course I don't know how they'll wash.'

'Wouldn't it be safer to send them to the cleaners? They are so beautifully soft and light. And the embroidered curtains! Did you get them in Bond Street too?'

'Yes, all the wee tasty touches, but everything else in Glasgow; the furniture and carpets.' She looked round and added, 'and very nice they are!'

Nicole often said that she hated to stay with people for she was always either cold, or bored, or both, but with Mrs. Jackson she was neither the one nor the other. She delighted in that lady's comments on life, and enjoyed going with her to see fresh places and hearing her tales of people. Mr. Jackson she found quite unexpectedly interesting when he suddenly broke into talk about his own city, for which he had obviously a deep, if almost an ashamed, affection. She enjoyed, too, meeting the Jacksons' friends.

On the Friday morning Mrs. Jackson said: 'We're having a couple to dinner to-night, a Mr. and Mrs. Ralston. I've been waiting for your visit to ask them, for they're not my style at all. Clever, you know. Mr. Ralston's very learned, I'm told, though he's in business: I'm not sure that it's not tobacco; but so old-established that it hardly counts as business--you know what I mean. And his wife is very tall and--oh, I don't know, you'll see for yourself. I'll away to see cook just now, for I'd like everything to be very perfect. We dined there one night, and there was something very tip-top about it. I'll ask your advice later about what to wear. I'm depending on you to get me through this evening, mind that!'

When evening came they waited in the drawing-room for the expected guests. Nicole had wiled her friend away from a much ornamented green satin, and had coaxed her into a black velvet gown, greatly against that lady's own wishes.

'The green's quite new,' she wailed. 'I was keeping it for an occasion; and I'm so dingy in black.'

'Dingy!' said Nicole, 'with your pearls, and your lovely white shoulders and arms! Keep the green for some big reception: this velvet is perfect for a small dinner.'

'Oh well--' Mrs. Jackson was not convinced, but she gave in. 'But you'll make yourself smart, won't you? You see the Ralstons are never likely to see you again, and I'd like you to look your best to-night.'

So Nicole put on the parchment-coloured silk with the gold lace, and bound the crystals round her forehead to please her hostess. She knew she would have to work hard this evening, for she had some experience of the way Mr. Jackson relapsed into almost complete silence when strangers sat at his board; his wife, on the contrary, when unsure of herself and awed by her company, was apt to babble.

She began at once, when the door opened to admit the expected guests. 'How d'you do, Mrs. Ralston? How d'you do, Mr. Ralston? Chilly, isn't it? This is Miss Nicole Rutherfurd who's staying here. I don't know if you ever heard that we bought a place on the Borders? Well, it was Miss Rutherfurd's home we bought. Our son lives there now, you know. Uch, married, yes, to a cousin of Nicole's there, and they've got a fine wee boy. But Miss Rutherfurd lives in Fife....'

The stream of talk went on while Nicole shook hands with a very tall, youngish woman and her husband who was much shorter and had a smooth, egg-like face; it eddied round them, washed over them, and it was with a sensation of relief that, at last, Nicole found herself seated at the round table in the dining-room between her host and Mr. Ralston, neither of whom seemed inclined to utter a word.

Mrs. Jackson was flapping out her napkin, and asking Mrs. Ralston a stream of questions, to make her forget, no doubt, that her host seemed to have forgotten his duty, and also, Nicole knew, because she would rather make conversation with the wife than try to tackle the husband who was her rightful partner.

Nicole looked at him. He seemed to be enjoying his grape-fruit, so she began a gentle sort of monologue which called for nothing much in the way of response, about the interest of first beholding a great industrial centre like Glasgow, her hopes of seeing something of the beauty of the Clyde; and went on to compare the East and West Country. It was all delivered in a voice soft as 'doves taboring upon their breasts,' and Patrick Ralston, beginning to feel soothed and comforted--he had hated the idea of driving miles to dine with a couple like the Jacksons--got interested, and presently he

118

was doing all the talking and Nicole had only to murmur a comment now and again and look appreciative, and had time to observe the other members of the party.

'Five's an awkward number,' Mrs. Jackson was saying. 'I should have had another man, but to tell you the truth, I couldn't think of one that would fit in. Not that we don't know lots of young men, nice hearty fellows they are too, but you see with Miss Rutherfurd--Well, I didn't know how they'd *mix*, if you know what I mean.'

The eyes of Mrs. Ralston met Nicole's across the table, and the light of laughter shone in them for a second.

'I think we're very comfortable as we are,' Mrs. Ralston said. 'May I tell you how I love your house? I had no idea we were to see anything so original and charming.'

Mrs. Jackson beamed. 'Well, you see, it's quite *new*. Mr. Jackson really designed it himself, and he knew just what he wanted.'

'Hot and cold in every bedroom,' said Mr. Jackson, helping himself in a resigned way to vegetables.

'A wireless in the maids' sitting-room,' added his wife.

'Copper pipes everywhere,' said Mr. Jackson.

'Splendid,' said Mrs. Ralston. 'You'll make us sadly dissatisfied with our own house, with its basement and other evils.'

'Oh, Mrs. Ralston, I thought your house was awfully uncommon that night Mr. Jackson and I dined with you. I'm sure you needn't envy any one.'

'Needn't I? Well, I do. Do you know whom I envy? Every one who has got a small place in the country. Quite a small place in the real country. I've been looking for one for years, but when I like a neighbourhood and its people, there's nothing available, and if I find a suitable place somebody I simply can't bear is sure to have settled near. It's very trying.'

'So it is,' Mrs. Jackson agreed. 'We bought a place in the country, I was telling you'-- she glanced at Nicole--'Rutherfurd. But we got very tired of it. When our son married we were real glad to get back to Glasgow. I don't think you belong to Glasgow, Mrs. Ralston. English, aren't you?'

'Oh dear, no. I'm a Scot, born and bred.'

'Fancy! It was just the accent I was going by. Miss Rutherfurd's half English, but she can talk the broadest Scotch, can't you, Nicole?'

At this moment, Mr. Jackson was heard to remark without apparent relevance, 'Life's never the same after you get a plate.'

He looked searchingly at Mr. Ralston as he spoke, and that gentleman said stiffly as if it were no affair of his, 'Indeed!'

'And I always know false teeth when I see them,' Mr. Jackson went on. 'You can't cheat me with them,' he added, with a little wistful smile.

'Well, I'm sure, Father, that's a poor boast,' said his wife, hotly ashamed of such a topic of conversation being introduced at her table.... 'Will we make a move, Mrs. Ralston, and leave the gentlemen to their cigars?'

It is to be presumed that Mr. Jackson talked more when left alone with his guest, for it was quite a long time before they joined the ladies in the drawing-room.

Nicole did not feel the time drag, for she was enjoying her talk with Mrs. Ralston. She liked everything about her, the long, slim figure in its clever grey draperies, the interesting face that ought to have been plain but somehow wasn't, the pretty hands, the voice which made her think of champagne, so light it was and golden. She was hearing from her of Glasgow life.

'Of course,' her new friend told her, 'it's very possible to get badly bored with Glasgow. A course of gentility is the best cure for that; a few weeks with the ultra-refined, the persistently highbrow, and you come back gladly to the frank naturalness of your own city. I don't really belong to it, so I can speak without prejudice. My husband's people have been here for centuries, and I used to like to hear my mother-in-law tell of the Glasgow she dimly remembered. Her family and her husband's belonged to Glasgow, their fortunes were bound up with the city's, their grandfathers had sent laden ships from the Broomielaw. Yes, the old Glasgow sounded so delightful.... Mrs. Jackson has gone to sleep. Don't let's disturb her.'

Nicole looked undecided. 'I think I'd better wake her,' she said. 'She wouldn't like to think she had slept....' She raised her voice. 'Your dress is Paris, isn't it?' She drew her chair nearer her sleeping hostess. 'We're talking clothes, Mrs. Jackson. I'm telling Mrs. Ralston that I'm sure her dress is from Paris.'

Mrs. Jackson sat up with a little start. 'Oh yes,' she said, 'Paris, of course.'

'And,' said Mrs. Ralston, 'I am telling her "No such thing." This dress was made in Glasgow. Yes, indeed it was. Didn't you know that Glasgow had frightfully good shops, Miss Rutherfurd?'

'Well, I had always heard so, but that frock's so clever.'

Mrs. Jackson was now thoroughly awakened. 'I don't think much of Paris gowns myself. It was a queer thing, once we were motoring through England and we stopped for the night at a town--I don't even remember the name of it, but I saw a neat little shop with a French name and I went in. I found the woman made dresses, and I just took a notion to get one. She said one fitting would be enough, and when she was fitting me I asked what she was doing in a little English town, and her French, and she told me she had married a gentleman in the Post Office.... She said she would post the dress to Glasgow in a fortnight, and it came to the day!'

'And wasn't it a success?' Mrs. Ralston asked.

'Uch, it fitted all right, but it was all lined with red silk! I don't care for French taste....'

Before they left Mrs. Ralston asked Nicole if there was no chance of their meeting again before she left, but Nicole shook her head regretfully.

'I rather think Mrs. Jackson has filled up every moment. But I'll always remember this evening with pleasure, and some day you might find yourself near Kirkmeikle.' She added, 'I'll like to think that Mrs. Jackson has got you to support her sometimes when she attends functions. Give her a kind look when you can. She's shy and people scare her, though perhaps you'd hardly think it. She and I are friends, and she tells me things.'

* * * * *

Mrs. Jackson told her friend many things in that week, but the most important was kept for the last night.

They were together in Nicole's bedroom, and Mrs. Jackson was deploring the girl's departure.

'I'm glad,' she said, 'you've had a happy time, and the sooner you come back the better pleased we'll be. And, mind you, I'm speaking for Father too--Yes, I must say I'm enjoying this part of my life. There was a time before we went to Rutherfurd when I almost felt that I had lost Father. He seemed so taken up with business that he had neither time nor patience for me, but now, whether it's Andy being away or what, I don't know, but anyway, he makes quite a companion of me.'

There were grateful tears in her eyes as she sat on a high chair, one hand on either knee, and Nicole bent down and kissed the kind, comical face.

'I'm glad,' she said.

'Thank you, my dear. And there's another thing that's making me very happy, though I'm almost afraid to speak about it. It seems far too good to be true, and I'm not letting myself count on it, or even mentioning it to a soul, for it would be an awful begunk if it didn't happen, but I know you'd never breathe it to anybody....'

She paused, and then in tones of almost solemn joy she said: 'Listen, *Father's likely to be made a knight.*'

Chapter XXI

...*'Sounds and sweet airs that give delight and hurt not....'*

THE TEMPEST.

The Musical Society of Cowdenden took more time than Nicole and Althea had bargained for. All that Charles had asked was that they should show an interest by now and again attending a rehearsal, but one night every week found the girls in the dirty little hall in the back street. Generally they went alone in The Worm, for Charles found his time more and more engaged with political work, but it was surprising how often he managed to arrive before the end of the practice. All three took an intense interest in the coming production.

Althea had turned out a most competent dance instructress. It seemed to Nicole little short of miraculous the order she had produced out of chaos. Her rather tired smile and languid manner concealed much energy, and her patience was boundless. 'It's rather fun,' was all she said, when Nicole suggested that the rehearsals were absorbing much of her time, 'and it isn't as if I were one of the world's workers. If these girls can do it after blacking grates all day, surely I can.'

And Nicole told her mother, 'You'd be surprised, Mums, how the girls obey her slightest wish. She never makes a fuss of them, when they've tried their hardest and look to her for commendation she merely gives that weary little smile.... I think they like her, indeed I'm sure they do, but she's a puzzle to them as she is to me. Most young girls are rather like champagne, frothing over, bubbling about their own successes, with bursts of ardour about this and that; bursts of giggles and silliness-- but Althea's still, like a deep pool.'

'I'm glad,' said Lady Jane, 'that the child is interested in this. Anything is good that takes her out of herself.'

'Yes, and working with Charles is good for her; he's so frank and cheerful and on the surface (I don't mean that he hasn't depths as well), and I'll tell you another thing that's good for her--Belinda being at Kinogle. Charles is quite frankly amused and delighted by Belinda and her ways. I don't wonder, she's as charming in the house as a Persian kitten.'

'But you think it is Althea he really cares about?'

Nicole nodded. 'I'm sure of it. But I hope he won't ask her for a long time, until she's had time to forget the other man. What a cruel thing it is to take away a girl's self-esteem.'

'But won't Charles's adoration restore it?'

'It ought, but perhaps she won't allow herself to believe in it.' Nicole gave an amused grin. 'Aren't I talking just like a maiden aunt? But, really if you think of it, it's a perfect arrangement. They're so suited to each other. Charles's exuberance would be curbed by Althea's calm, and she would be warmed by his enthusiasm. And Lady Walkinshaw's helplessness would bring out all that's gentle and kind in Althea. It's the feeling that she has no real home, no real niche, that hurts the child--But there's absolutely not one single thing we can do to help things on. We must fold our hands and wait, my dear.'

'I'm no believer in match-making,' Lady Jane said. 'There is something rather revolting to me in planning and plotting about such things.' She looked at her daughter rather wistfully as she added, 'Perhaps I've failed in my duty....'

Nicole took her mother's hand and kissed it.

'You don't know how grateful I've been for your adorable reticence. It's almost the nicest thing about you. When I see some mothers--But let's struggle out of this morass of sentiment.... You will come and see *Iolanthe*, won't you? I'd like you to come behind the scenes and be introduced to some of the performers.'

'I'd like that too. I seem to know them quite well.'

'The clothes are to arrive to-day: they're to try them on to-night, so the excitement is intense. Most of them have never dressed up before.... I think there should be good houses all three nights. It's a pity so many people are away, but every one who is at home has promised to be there, and Mrs. Heggie tells me that there's quite a large contingent coming from Langtoun and, as she puts it, "They're all five-shilling people!" We had to make the rest of the seats very cheap, for money, alas! is scanty in Cowdenden.'

Lady Jane sighed, for, like Mrs. Jackson, she too lay awake at night and thought of the hardships of her fellow-men.

'Can it possibly pay itself?' she asked.

'Oh, we'll see that it does. Of course the hiring of costumes and scenery is very expensive, but Sir James is going to help with that. We hope to have something over after the performance to lay aside as a nest-egg, they're so keen, I'm sure they'll want to go on.'

'Of course I must see it,' Lady Jane said. 'The last time I saw *Iolanthe* was at the Savoy, I think, in 1908. We were on our way to Switzerland, and we took the boys. You were only a little thing and were left at the hotel with Nannie. I think perhaps it was rather beyond Ronnie and Archie too, but your father was in ecstasies over it. Dear me, that's a long time ago!'

It was a hectic evening that of the dress rehearsal, what with clothes that went astray and clothes that were misfits, scenery that arrived damaged, and properties that failed to arrive at all. It was not surprising that tempers gave way under the strain. The janitor of the town hall, which had been hired for the occasion, quarrelled with the stage-manager of *Iolanthe*. He complained to Nicole: 'That chap's chippin' at me. As if I didna ken hoo to pu' up a curtain an' pu' it down again withoot his interference! I dinna haud onyway wi' thae theatricals. Pentin' their faces an' lettin' on they're lords an' what not! Fairies tae! This'll dae an awfu' harm in Cowdenden. They're licht enough as it is, what wi' pictur-hooses an' dancin', an' whist-playin' at the Bible Class Social, but this'll fair pit them ower the edge. Ay, it's a peety when ye think on't.

Here's the ministers in the place tryin' their best up to their lichts tae keep the folk in the Narrow Way, an' they get the legs ca'ed frae under them by an opery.'

'It's perfectly harmless,' Nicole protested, but the janitor shook his head.

'All is vanity, as Solomon said, an' he kent what he was speakin' aboot.'

Feeling rather dejected, Nicole looked round at the scene. It certainly did look rather odd. Peers were wandering about hugging coronets (one complained to another as they passed her, 'Aw here, I've lost ma breeks'); fairies got into the way, principals trotted about chattering vaguely.

'Nikky,' said Althea, coming up with a bundle of things in her arms, 'it's absolute chaos. They seem to have forgotten all they've learned: they don't recognise their positions on the stage.... For goodness' sake come and take hold with me.'

Out of a crowd of performers oddly unfamiliar in their make-up, peers and fairies, all confused by new surroundings, dazzled by the unaccustomed footlights, awkward in their new costumes, order had to be brought.

Between despair and helpless laughter the two girls and Charles and the stage-manager wrestled, and the performance was got through somehow.

When the curtain had fallen on the last scene they all looked at each other rather disconsolately.

'Well,' said Charles, 'that's that. You saw where you failed to-night, and I've no doubt you'll watch all these points to-morrow. Remember, please, people are paying to see a good performance, not a dud, so it's your very best we want.'

'Phyllis' (who had stuck twice) complained to Nicole, with large tears standing in her eyes, that her dress was so tight that she could hardly breathe, much less sing.

Nicole comforted her, told her how sweet she looked, and that an inch in the waist would make all the difference. They all seemed to need a heartening word, and Charles said, with his encouraging grin, 'A bad dress rehearsal always means a successful performance. You'll see, to-morrow night it'll go with a bang, only--don't rush it, say your words correctly and distinctly, and whatever you do, keep a grip of yourselves.'

But even Charles was rather dejected, and accepted gratefully Nicole's invitation to come in and have some coffee.

'Pretty awful,' he said in reply to Lady Jane's question about the performers. '*Pretty* awful! If they don't find themselves before to-morrow night the show'll be a fiasco. They seemed so well up in it at the rehearsals, but to-night they'd forgotten everything they'd been taught, fumbled about in the most uncertain way, sang flat, missed their cues, went back to their original pronunciation which we thought we'd cured them of--It *was* awful, wasn't it, Miss Althea?'

That young woman seated on her favourite fender-stool, munching a sandwich, shook her head.

'You'll see,' she said, 'they will go through with it to-morrow night without a hitch. To-night'll steady them and put them on their mettle.'

'I believe Althea's right,' said Nicole. 'If they had done well to-night they might have been filled with vain-glory and got careless; now they know they must put every ounce of themselves into it--But a lot will depend on the audience. We must see that the points are taken up. A few in the front rows applauding vigorously and laughing intelligently at the right places can do a lot. Of course really to enjoy Gilbert and Sullivan you want to know every note of the music and every word of the libretto.... Did you hear the janitor, Althea? He was very stern with me, and said the harm we had done, morally, to Cowdenden by producing *Iolanthe* was incalculable!'

'Oh, surely not!' said Lady Jane, 'anything less harmful--"Sweet airs that give delight and hurt not...."'

'On the contrary,' Nicole went on, 'he said that they had been "light enough" before, but this would simply push them over the edge--That's you, you see, Charles! With the best intentions in the world you've corrupted a whole town.'

'And to no purpose,' said Charles, 'if the show's a dud.'

'Quite a Gilbertian situation,' said Althea, handing her empty coffee-cup to the young man.

Althea proved a true prophet. From the moment that the curtain went up on an obviously palpitating chorus of somewhat substantial fairies to the grand finale of Peers and Peris, the performers went with vigour and accuracy. The principals, one and all, played well, and the audience was quick to take up the points, and generous in applause.

Quite a number of 'the five-shilling people' met later for some slight refreshment in the Harbour House.

'It was fine,' said Mrs. Heggie. 'Tea, please, I wouldn't sleep a wink if I took coffee--I enjoyed every minute of it. D'you mean to tell me that those were all Cowdenden people, all those peers and pretty girls? I wouldn't have known them from real actors. And such fine English accents.'

'Well,' said Charles, 'I wouldn't say too much about the accents.' He turned to Althea, 'Did you hear "audocity"?'

Althea smiled. 'It's always the way. In the strain of performing in public they're apt to go back to their original pronunciation. The girl would probably have stuck if she'd tried to get it right.'

'Anyway, it was lovely,' said Mrs. Heggie.

Nicole appealed to Mr. Lambert. 'You don't think, do you, that a performance like that could do any one harm--morally, I mean?'

125

Mr. Lambert blinked. If addressed suddenly he always looked dazed, like an owl in daylight.

'I d-don't see how it could,' he stuttered, 'it's such delightful fun, and there's more than a little wheat among the chaff. No, I think it is calculated to do the p-performers good rather than harm.'

Althea turned to Charles, who was beside her, and said: 'I'm glad they have the other two nights. I hate to think of them folding away their pretty clothes and going back to their workaday things. They do love doing it.'

Charles nodded. 'And you helped them enormously. I do think it's worth while, don't you? It'll be all over in another couple of nights, but they'll have the memory of it. They've been kings and queens of a golden land for an hour or two! They've got the music in their minds, and the charming words; they've had all the fun of working together--and team-work's good for us all; and they're already looking forward to another show next year.'

'Yes,' Althea agreed, 'it's been well worth while. I think we all enjoyed working together....'

Chapter XXII

> *'And what wad ye do there,*
> *At the bush aboon Traquair?*
> *A long dreich road, ye had better let it be.*
> .   .   .   .   .
> *They were blest beyond compare*
> *When they held their trysting there*
> *Amang thae greenest hills shone on by the sun:*
> *And then they wan a rest,*
> *The lownest and the best,*
> *I' Traquair kirkyard when a' was dune.'*

JOHN CAMPBELL SHAIRP.

One Sunday evening Mr. Lambert made a sudden descent upon the Harbour House.

It was about eight-thirty, and they were finishing dinner, when Effie announced that the minister was in the drawing-room.

Nicole, leaving her coffee, hurried upstairs and found the little man perched on the edge of a chair, nervously smoothing his felt hat which he had laid on his knee.

He let it drop as he rose to shake hands and apologised for coming at such an odd hour.

'B-but I c-couldn't put it off,' he explained. 'I p-promised Mrs. Curle.'

'Mrs. Curle,' repeated Nicole. 'Of course--how stupid of me! Mrs. Curle in the Watery Wynd. We know her best as Betsy.... She isn't ill, is she? I saw her a few days ago.'

'She took suddenly ill last night--a heart attack, and she is fretting herself into a fever about something she wants to say to your mother. I suggested that I might do as well, but she treated the suggestion with the scorn it no doubt deserved.'

Nicole smiled, well able to reconstruct the scene, and said: 'I hope the poor dear isn't seriously ill?'

'Well--she made Dr. Kilgour tell her just how ill he thought her. It seems another attack like this would probably be the end.... Illness has done nothing to subdue the vigour of her tongue, and I simply dare not return without saying I have seen Lady Jane and got a p-promise from her.'

'Here is Mother--Mums, poor old Betsy is ill and wants to see you very particularly.'

'They can't quiet her,' Mr. Lambert said. 'She has already told Dr. Kilgour that he is an idiot, and she thought even less highly of me, and when I tried to p-pacify her'--he helped out the word with little pats on his knee--'she says that there is something that she can only say to you, Lady Jane, and she can't rest till she says it. M-may I tell her that you will see her to-morrow?'

'Why, no, Mr. Lambert, I'll go to-night. It may help Betsy to sleep. It's only a step. Get me a cloak, Nicole, please.'

'Yes. I'm coming with you, Mother. I'll wait outside the door and Betsy won't know I'm there.'

Mr. Lambert trotted before his companions over the cobblestones and up the steps of the outside stair. 'Be careful here!' he advised, 'there's a broken place, and the rail is shaky too. The p-place is a trap on a dark night....'

Betsy's single room was lit by a small oil lamp placed on a table near the bed, beside a drinking-cup containing some nourishment. A kettle sang on the hob and a woman was moving about, but as the minister entered she threw her shawl round her head and, saying 'Aweel, then, Betsy, I'll awa' the noo, but I'll be back or it's lang,' made her way out.

The old woman lay high on the bed, propped up with pillows. She seemed unaware of what was going on, but when the minister went up to her she opened her eyes and said: 'Is her leddyship here?'

Lady Jane came forward. 'Yes, Betsy, I'm here.'

'That's a' richt,' Betsy gave a satisfied sigh and said to the minister, 'Will ye gang awa' noo, sir?'

Mr. Lambert obediently withdrew, and Nicole went with him to the stair-head.

'I've been dismissed,' he said, 'but I'll return shortly and take you and your mother home.'

'Indeed you won't. Surely two able-bodied women can be trusted to find their own way home! You must be tired after your long day, and I know how your wife looks forward to Sunday evening--so return at your peril! No, really, Mother would be truly sorry if you waited. Good-night, and thank you.'

Nicole went softly back to the kitchen and stood at the door in the shadows. She did not want to listen, but on the other hand she did not think Betsy would mind if she did overhear.

Her mother was sitting holding Betsy's hand, and the old woman was speaking earnestly, breathlessly:

'In ma Bible,' she was saying, 'it's oor family Bible, an' ma faither made a leather cover for it an' keepit a' sorts o' papers in the flap, birth-certificates and marriage-lines--It's a fine place tae hide onything, for folk dinna fash the Bible muckle thae days.' She gave a grim chuckle and for a moment choked for breath.... 'There's twae five-pound notes. I've been scrapin' for years an' Dr. Kilgour changed ma bawbees into notes for me. Mebbe he guessed what it's for--I dinna ken. *Is't eneuch, think ye?* I ken it taks a lot to cairry a corp.'

'Yes, yes,' Lady Jane said hurriedly, 'I'm sure it's enough. I hate to think that you denied yourself to save....'

'It was a *pleesure*....' There was triumph in the weak voice. 'Ma gude-dochter thinks that when ma time comes they'll cairt me tae their cauld kirkyaird, and hap me awa' an' hae dune wi' me. She little kens I'm gaun tae traivel back tae ma ain countryside.' She raised her voice anxiously: 'They'll no mak' nae objections, surely, tae me lyin' aside ma folk? It's no like a toun graveyaird whaur ilka inch counts. There used to be walth o' room at Langhope Shiels, an' it canna hae changed that muckle.'

'I'm sure there will be room.'

There was a silence for a minute, then Betsy spoke again.

'The Book says, ye maun leave faither and mither and cleave tae yer husband. I'm leavin' mine lyin' here.... Ay, but folk are made different an' ma ain countryside and ma ain folk were aye mair tae me than ma man.... "There's little sap amang the shavin's," ma mither said when I mairret him--him bein' a joiner to trade--an' Tam was aye a dry stick, though it ill becomes me to speak ill o' the deid '--her voice sank to a whisper--'*me that's sae near them!*'

Nicole felt a coldness come over her as she watched the scene--the yellow face on the pillow, with the dark sunken eyes, her mother's face white in the shadow, the light from the lamp falling on her delicate hand with its gleaming rings: the fire whispering to itself: outside the beat of the sea and the crash and blatter of the March wind.

'Try and sleep now, Betsy,' Lady Jane was saying.

'Ay, I'll sleep now.... Ye'll see t'it that they tak me straight back to Langhope Shiels, and Mr. Lambert'll mebbe say a prayer ower me afore I stert.... As near ma mither as ye can get me.... I kent ye wad understand. I couldna lie in Kirkmeikle, me that belongs to Tweedside. The sea wadna let me sleep.'

'Sleep now.' Lady Jane was stroking her shoulder and hushing her like a child.

Betsy gave a small, tired smile. 'That minds me o' ma mither when we were bairns an' no-weel. "Sleep, ma dearie, an' ye'll be better gin mornin'."... She was a brave body, ma mither, an' feucht awa' a' her days wi' a big family an' little means, but at the end--she was eighty, mind ye--she was vexed tae gang. She said she had likit her life rale weel.... But she was aye amang her ain folk; her hert was at rest; it's frettin' wears a body oot.'

There was a step on the outside stair, and Nicole found herself put gently to one side, as Dr. Kilgour in his Highland cloak stalked into the kitchen.

As he stood warming his hands, he gazed under his bushy eyebrows at his patient lying there with a look of triumph on her face.

Nicole noticed how gently he took Betsy's hand. It interested her, for she had wondered how the brusque doctor comported himself in a sick-room.

'Well, Betsy,' he said, 'you're a wonderful woman. We all obey you, even when you make us leave our own firesides on a Sunday night.'

Betsy replied with a satisfied sigh. 'Her leddyship's gaun tae pit a'thing richt. I've got the better o' the sea noo.'

The doctor shook his head at that. 'Tuts, woman, you haven't the sense to appreciate your mercies. I could lie content nowhere out of the sound of the sea. What's about Tweedside that it draws folk back not only in life but in death?... But you're better to-night.'

'Ay, I'll mebbe no dee yet, so Tam's wife needna plan whaur she'll pit ma bits o' things in her hoose.... Ma gude-dochter's a gude gear-gatherer. She was a Speedie, ye ken, an' they're a' hard.... But she's welcome tae onything o' mine. I'll hae got a' I want afore she taks what I've dune wi'.'

The woman in charge came back, and Nicole took the opportunity to make her presence known.

'I'm sorry you're ill, Betsy,' she said, 'but you mustn't talk about leavin' us.... If you lie still and take Dr. Kilgour's horrid bottles and Agnes Martin's good soup you'll soon be all right.'

'Mebbe.' Betsy's tone was enigmatical. 'Tak her leddyship hame. It was rale forritsome o' me to send for her. I dinna ken hoo I hed the impidence.'

Lady Jane laid her hand on the wrinkled hand that lay on the coverlet. 'Good-night, Betsy. Thank you for sending for me. I'll be round first thing in the morning. Come, Nicole.'

* * * * *

Betsy rallied, and for three days was her old sharp-tongued self, but on the evening of the third day she turned her face to the wall and died.

Dr. Kilgour came to the Harbour House at breakfast-time. The March sun was flooding the little dining-room, with its white-panelled walls and Hepplewhite chairs and striped curtains. A blue bowl of daffodils stood on the round table, which was covered by a checked blue-and-white breakfast cloth: there was a cheerful morning smell of coffee and sizzling bacon.

The door opened and Lady Jane came in. She walked quickly up to the doctor and 'Is it Betsy?' she asked.

Dr. Kilgour nodded. 'She got away at the turning of the tide. Very peacefully. I've seen many a one resigned to go, but I don't think I ever saw any one so welcome death. She shut her eyes as I've seen a bairn do on Christmas Eve--determined to sleep to bring the morning nearer. And mind you--' Dr. Kilgour pulled his eyebrows together and glared at his companion as if daring her to find anything sweet or touching in what he said--'Mind you, I don't believe that she cared about Heaven or anything like that. Her one idea was to get back to Tweedside to lay her dust beside her kin.'

Lady Jane smiled while tears stood in her eyes.

'Dear Betsy! We needn't worry about her motives, the God who made her understands.... She was a good woman and a loyal friend and I'll miss her greatly--. Nicole,' as her daughter came into the room, 'Betsy has got away.'

The girl stopped short. 'I'm glad,' she said after a moment, 'at least I'm more glad than sorry. She did so hate Kirkmeikle and her daughter-in-law and the inquisitive neighbours, and now she's done with them all and nothing can vex her any more.... Dr. Kilgour, you must have some breakfast. Do you take coffee? We'll get tea in a minute.'

'Bless you, girl, I had my breakfast an hour ago. I must be off. I knew you'd want to hear about Betsy.'

'Before you go,' Lady Jane said, 'we must arrange things.... You know I promised Betsy she would go home? I'll wire to Andy to make all arrangements at Langhope Shiels--I know he won't mind the trouble--but I don't know how to manage at this end. I suppose there is an undertaker?'

'That'll be all right,' Dr. Kilgour assured her. 'I'll see about everything and let you know trains and so forth.'

'I must go with Betsy,' Lady Jane said, 'and see her laid beside her mother.'

'Oh, Mums!' Nicole protested, 'it's such a long journey.... Still, if you want to go, I'll go with you.... I don't expect the son will think of going, his wife won't let him. He's a weak soul. "Young Tam," his mother always called him, though he must be about fifty.'

Langhope Shiels churchyard was beautiful beyond words that March day when Betsy came home. Snow-drops still lay in drifts among the graves, while celandines were vividly yellow and green in the withered grass. The whins and heather were burning--these sacrificial fires of spring! Wisps of white smoke drifted across the blue hills, and Tweed ran silver in the sunshine.

Nicole, standing beside her mother, took in the whole scene, the almost unbearable beauty of the spring day in these uplands, the coffin covered by a great cross of daffodils, the little group of mourners, the minister reading the Bible, the grey headstones that seemed to be leaning forward to listen.... She read the names on the stone nearest her:

'JOHN SANDILANDS, TENANT FARMER OF LANGHOPE MAINS ...HIS WIFE, ELLEN... THEIR DAUGHTER, JESSIE...'

That must have been long ago, she thought, for the farmer she had known in Langhope Mains was a decent man called Blackstocks, who had lost his two sons in the War.... There was a grave marked only by a jelly-pot with some snowdrops.... She looked up and found John Dalrymple's eyes fixed on her. Andy must have told him, and he had come out of respect. How like him! Looking so morose, too, in his funeral blacks! And Andy too, so serious! What a decent, kind soul he was, incapable of grudging the time spent in attending the burial of an unknown old woman. Betsy would have been proud, *was* proud, Nicole felt, for she could not rid herself of the idea that her old friend was watching the proceedings....

In sure and certain hope of a blessed Resurrection....

They stood, the little group, with bowed heads, listening. What were they thinking of, Nicole wondered? Were they hearing at their backs Time's winged chariots hurrying near, and thinking great swelling thoughts of eternity? Or were they merely grateful that they were still in this warm kind world and would soon be at home drinking tea and discussing the price of beasts at the market?

It was soon over, and as they turned to go she heard an old man say to his companion: 'Ay, she's been dacently pit awa'. Her leddyship an' twae lairds, nae less!... I hevna seen Betsy thae forty years. Efter she'd been mairret to Curle for a while she gaed awa' aboot Fife.... She was a wiselike wumman when I mind her. Weel, she's awa', an' it's the road we maun a' gang. What did ye tell me they wanted for the coo, Elick?'

They hobbled away discussing temporal things, and Nicole turned to find John Dalrymple at her side.

'Hullo, John, it's nice to see you--. Did Andy tell you about Betsy?'

'Yes. I saw Jackson yesterday, and he happened to mention that you and your mother were coming. And then I heard that your old friend had two nephews at Newby Place; they're here to-day.... She must have been a loyal old woman to be so keen to come back and lie by Tweed--Oh, here is Lady Jane.'

'Why, John, this is very pleasant. No, we're not staying, alas! Barbara is giving us tea, and Andy is motoring us to Galashiels and we'll soon be home. I wish we had time to go to Newby--But when are you going to pay us a visit?'

'When you ask me.'

'There's nothing for John to do at Kirkmeikle,' Nicole broke in, 'he'd be bored to death.'

'I don't believe he would,' said her mother, 'he could always play golf. But anyway, John, you must come to us in September wherever we are on holiday. You will? That's a promise. Yes, Andy, I know we have very little time.'

'Good-bye, Nicole,' said John, 'till September.'

'Good-bye, John,' said Nicole.

Chapter XXIII

'We, in our dreams, behold the Hebrides.'...

Easter brought The Bat back to Kirkmeikle, and Spider, who had begun to lose his figure, padded many miles on his woolly white legs behind his master. There never was a busier boy than Alastair; he went all day from one ploy to another, absorbed in his own inventions.

'That child,' said Nicole, 'grows more Puck-like every day. Did you ever see anything so quaint as those tilted eyes and that mouth? And impudent!'

'Oh no, Nikky,' Lady Jane protested, 'Alastair is never pert. I detest pert children.'

'Well, I don't know what you call pert, but when he brought in those primroses that "Roabert" sent to you this morning, and you said, "Darling, how lovely!" and kissed him, didn't I hear him remark resignedly, "If you must kiss some one, couldn't you kiss Roabert?"'

'Oh well!' Lady Jane laughed. 'I should have remembered that boys detest being kissed.... But I do wish there were more children here for him to play with. There's a shocking dearth of boys, in fact the only children about are the small Lamberts. They are dear little girls, but so gentle they let Alastair lord it over them. When they came to tea yesterday they had to crouch on the floor most of the time while he strutted about like a cock in a farmyard. He was Sir Patrick Spens, he explained to me, and they had to do that because of "*O lang, lang may the ladies sit!*"'

'I expect,' said Althea, 'that he thought it was a good way of keeping them quiet, while he played in his own way. And you needn't pity the Lamberts, Aunt Jane. Their mother tells me they adore Alastair's games. They would rather be neglected by him than fussed over by anybody else.'

'Anyway,' said Nicole, 'he'll have Barnabas for the summer holidays and that'll mean six weeks' bliss for both.'

'Yes,' Lady Jane said, 'I can't but think it fortunate that Barnabas's parents are going on that long trip. I love having the boy.... Dear me, how untidy my silks are; I must put them right before I go any further--The question is, where are we going to spend the summer? We went south last year. Shall we go north this year? What do you say, Althea?'

Althea turned--she was watching a Norwegian ship that had come into the Harbour--'I?' she said. 'Shall I be here?'

She looked straight at Nicole as if trying to read what was in her mind, and Nicole replied with obvious sincerity:

'Well, I hope so. Having wintered us, you must summer us. And Blanchie is always heavily booked for the summer months, so we needn't worry about neglecting her. What a blessing that these new friends she met in Cairo have kept her so contented all these months! Otherwise she might have suggested coming here!'

'Nikky!' said her mother reprovingly, 'we would be glad to have had Blanchie here.'

Nicole looked sceptical. 'Mmm... only moderately glad, I think. Personally, I can't imagine anything more terrible than a visit from that dear lady. She is delightful in her own setting, I grant you, but perched on the rocks of Kirkmeikle she'd be a complete failure. Can't you hear her plaintive "But, Jane darling, so *triste*, is it not? No brightness, no variety; always the sea." Can't you see her picking her way over the cobbles in the Watery Wynd--? And, a thousand times more difficult than her mistress, the superior Hopkins! Imagine her pained surprise when she was introduced to what we are pleased to call shops in Kirkmeikle, when she found no servants' hall in the Harbour House, no bridge of an evening (Mrs. Martin has a horror of playing cards and sees no reason why people should not amuse themselves in their leisure knitting a stocking!), no picture-house nearer than Langtoun, no theatre nearer than Edinburgh! I think if Blanchie ever did come here it would be a short visit: Hopkins would see to that. She would find that the sea air did not suit her lady's health and they'd depart thankfully together.'

Lady Jane looked admiringly at her tidy silks as she said:

'Hopkins has her faults, but she's a faithful creature and Blanchie would be lost without her.'

Althea suddenly spoke vehemently. 'Hopkins is lazy and greedy and desperately jealous. If I took the trouble to think of her I'd hate her. She's been a beast to me always, and Blanchie listened to her tale-bearing....' She stopped as if ashamed of having shown so much feeling, shrugged her shoulders, and finished: 'So you see I don't care much to go "home." Anywhere else, north or south, would please me.'

'Well,' said Nicole in a very matter-of-fact tone, 'you haven't seen the north--that's a very good reason for us choosing it this summer. It would be fun to go somewhere that is new to us all.'

That afternoon, when Esmé Jameson came in as she often did, for tea after a round of golf, she was asked for her advice.

'You see,' Nicole explained, 'we generally either stay with cousins in England or join with them in taking a place in Ross-shire, but this year they've gone a long voyage, so we are on our own. We don't want a big place, nor too far out of the way, but we'd like some fishing, and if possible, some rough shooting for the boy cousin who will be with us. But I'm afraid such a place is almost impossible to get.'

Esmé Jameson nibbled a scone, and thought. Presently she said, 'What about the Island of Mull? It's a longish journey and that puts people off, but it's quite easy to reach, and there are some delightful small places to be had there. In fact,' she waved her scone excitedly, 'I rather think I know of one.'

'Cheers!' cried Nicole, while Spider barked in sympathy.

'Yes, friends of mine had it last year and took it again for August and September, but the last I heard they were doubtful of being able to go. Of course they may have sublet it. Shall I write and ask?'

'Let's wire,' said Nicole, 'we can't afford to lose a minute. Dictate to me, please, and Effie will fly with it.'

'And now,' said Esmé, when the business was done and Effie accompanied by Alastair and Spider had flown, 'may I finish my tea in peace?'

'Poor dear, you may,' Nicole said graciously. 'I'm sorry, but the matter was urgent. I like the thought of the Island of Mull.'

'Mull,' said Lady Jane vaguely, 'I'm afraid I don't quite know where it is.'

'Just across from Oban,' Esmé told her. 'Nothing of a sail. I've never been there, but I'm told the island is lovely--lochs and mountains and heavenly colouring.'

'And rain,' said Nicole. 'They all go together, don't they?... Don't you think, Mums, it sounds the sort of place we want? And it would be new to us all, which is such fun--Where are you going this summer, Esmé?'

'Well--I don't know. I'm so stolidly satisfied at Windywalls that I can't be bothered making any plans. My rock-garden grows apace. John Grumblie actually begins to take an interest in it, in fact it's rather embarrassing, for we daren't disregard his advice! I find that both he and David are so much more keen on stones than plants that it's more rock than garden. My spring garden, too, is beginning to show what some day it may be.'

'The snowdrops under the beech-trees were lovely,' Lady Jane said.

'Yes, and now the daffodils are beginning, and soon the wild hyacinths will be out. Mrs. Erskine was very kind sending me.... I *knew* I had something to tell you. Vera Erskine is engaged. Yes. Her mother wrote to me about something and mentioned it by the way.... I expect she will be writing all details to you. She seemed pleased--a Mr. Marshall, I think that was the name--a very pleasant young fellow, she said.'

'Now this is thrilling,' said Nicole. 'It will be such fun for the Erskines. Can't you see Mrs. Erskine flinging herself into the preparations? The question is, will the wedding be here or in London? They could make more of a splash in London with bishops and decorations, but there would be more real interest here.... Vera's a nice girl: I hope she's very happy.'

At that moment the afternoon post was brought in.

'A letter from Mrs. Erskine,' said Lady Jane.

'And I've one from Vera,' Althea cried, 'so now we'll know.'

While the letters were being read another visitor arrived--Mrs. Heggie.

As usual she was apologetic about coming, murmuring, 'Now don't let me disturb you--No, I've had tea, thanks. I just came in for a few minutes, it was such a lovely evening for a walk, and I hadn't seen any of you for some time.'

Nicole put her into a high chair and assured her that she had come at a most fortunate moment.

'We've just heard that Vera Erskine is engaged, and letters have come giving details. Isn't that exciting?'

Mrs. Heggie's face glowed, news was the breath of life to her. 'Miss Vera Erskine! That's the older one, isn't it? A handsome girl: I've met her here. Well, well....'

Althea laid down her letter.

'Happy?' asked Nicole.

Althea nodded. 'Quite definitely: the wedding is to be in London in June and she asks me to be a bridesmaid. There are to be eight, and two train-bearers. She says she always meant to marry so as not to miss anything in life, but it adds greatly to the fun of it that she cares so much for Basil. She says he is rather plain, and an only son; twenty-eight, and a little bald, keen on games and dancing and likes the country-- Now that I think of it I've heard Vera speak often of "Basil." She's known him some time.'

'It all sounds very suitable,' Lady Jane said, laying down her letter and taking up her work. 'Mrs. Erskine says the young man is all they could desire in a son-in-law.'

Lady Jane smiled at Mrs. Heggie, but she could not help wishing she had chosen some other time for her visit. It was nearly six o'clock, and at that hour Lady Jane liked to put away her work and go to her own room and sit for a little by the window, very quietly with her hands folded in her lap. This was the time she and Walter had always spent together in her little sitting-room at Rutherfurd, talking over things, planning for the children, laughing over their wild ways and their odd sayings, and this hour she still kept for thinking....

'I wonder,' said Esmé Jameson, 'if he has a job or if he's a gentleman of leisure?'

'Basil sounds leisurely, somehow,' Nicole said, and Althea remarked, 'Blanchie had a Sealyham called Basil, a most engaging creature.'

'It would be better, though, if he had some business or profession,' Mrs. Heggie said earnestly. 'It somehow seems to me so unnatural that a man shouldn't go away every morning and work. I can't bear to see a man come to breakfast in his slippers, a young man, I mean. Of course retired men have earned their slippers so to speak. And it's much nicer for the wife too, she can get on with her housekeeping, and do her shopping in peace. But of course, my ideas are old-fashioned, as Joan is always telling me.'

'They're very sound ideas, I think,' Nicole said. 'An idle man must be a horrid bore. Let's hope that if Basil is a gentleman of leisure, at least he'll be keen on golf and anything that keeps him outside. Vera will make a charming bride.... Will you be her bridesmaid, Althea?'

'Not I,' said that young woman.... 'No, Aunt Jane, I promise you I won't be ungracious. I think it's very sweet of her to ask me, and I'll invent some excuse that will be sure to carry conviction, but I won't go to a crowded London wedding.'

Mrs. Heggie shook her head. 'Well, well, girls have changed since my day. I would have thought it would be the greatest treat. I always wondered if Mr. Charles Walkinshaw wouldn't make a match with one of the Erskine girls: neighbours and very friendly, as they are--but some one was telling me he's likely to marry that pretty little cousin who stays so much at Kinogle. Is that true, d'you think?'

There was silence for a moment, then Nicole said:

'Don't you think it's the sort of rumour that would be almost bound to be circulated? Not that I know anything about it. Charles has been away for the last few weeks, so we're rather out of acquaintance--That reminds me I've got a book Lady Walkinshaw wants. Don't let me forget to take it to her to-morrow.'

* * * * *

Althea laughed more and talked more that evening than was usual with her. When she slipped off to bed rather early, Lady Jane looked after her, saying:

'The child really seems to be happy here, Nikky.'

'Yes,' Nicole agreed. 'She's beginning to be happy--though I hardly think this has been one of her cheeriest evenings.'

Chapter XXIV

'How could such sweet and wholesome hours
Be reckoned, but with herbs and flowers?'

ANDREW MARVELL.

One May day the family from the Harbour House went out to lunch at Windywalls and see the garden. That part of the world is late in waking from its winter sleep, spring comes slowly up that way, but by the end of May it is decked like a bride, and Esmé Jameson was enchanted with her new possession. Proud, too, of the changes she had wrought. The hollow through which the burn ran at the foot of the wide sloping lawn was blue with forget-me-nots; a mist of wild hyacinths shone through the snowy blossoms of the wild cherry as she had planned, and beds had been made and filled with polyanthus, pale yellow and oranged terra-cotta. Laburnum, and lilac, and copper beeches shone glorious against a background of firs.

Old John Grierson was now more or less reconciled to the new order of things. He had put in a bad winter with rheumatism and other ills, and had found his new mistress both kind and thoughtful. She was not, and never could be, like his old mistress, still--she had points, as he told Dr. Kilgour.

'Mistress Jameson hes a'thing to learn aboot a gairden, an' that keeps her humble.... I'm no as souple as I once was, but she says I'm worth mair than ma wages for advice, an' I'm sure that's true. I'll say this for her, she's no aye worryin', she kens a gairden's an endless job, needin' baith time an' understandin', siller, tae--she never grudges that. Oh ay, we micht hae got waur--ane o' thae hen-heided females, screechin' like a pea-hen, never puttin' in but aye wantin' oot.... I whiles think I'd like to tell the Mistress that things is gettin' on no that bad; she was sweir to leave me an' the gairden.'

The visitors had heard so much of the old gardener, both from Esmé and Dr. Kilgour, that they were delighted to meet him in the flesh.

He shook hands with some condescension, and when Lady Jane, after congratulating him on the beauty of the place, remarked that they had no garden to speak of at the Harbour House, he said kindly:

'Well, ye're spared muckle anxiety.' He stopped to mop his brow with a red handkerchief, and continued: 'Mony a nicht I loss ma sleep ower frost an' rabbits, no to mention slugs.... Oh ay, it's no a bad gairden: I've devoted fifty-eight years o' ma life to't, for I cam here a laddie o' sixteen. Changes? Haud yer tongue! Naething but changes, an' *aye for the worse*.... Ay, it's the truth. Juist tak thae lawns, we used to scythe them and keep them like velvet. Then they startit lawn-mowers an' a pony--no hauf as guid as the scythe. Noo, if ye please, it's a motor machine tuff-tuffin' aboot the place, makin' the horridest stink. Oh ay, an' rock-gairdens an' every known thing.... Weel, I'll sune be done wi' it, an' I never heard there were ony gairdens whaur I'm gaun, although we ken the Almichty likes them fine, for ane o' the first things He did was to make a gairden an' walk in't in the cool o' the day. The mistake He made was pitten Adam and Eve in't. Adam himsel mebbe wadna hae dune muckle ill, but...' The old man looked round at the four women and, judging that discretion was the better part of valour, merely shook his head, remarking:

'It's ower late in the day to fash aboot the Gairden of Eden.'

'Well,' said Lady Jane soothingly, 'anyway there's no serpent in this Paradise.'

'Is there no?' said John Grumblie darkly, and hobbled away.

'Now, what did he mean by that?' asked his mistress. 'Is it me or David, or perhaps poor Tam? When we cross him he always harks back to the old days, poor dear!... Now here is my much-talked-about rock-garden. No, it's not bad, is it, for a beginning? and of course the burn is a tremendous help. There's simply no end to what you can do with a burn. I can see that it'll keep me happily employed for years.' She looked at her wrist: 'Why, it's after the half-hour. I shouldn't have waylaid you and brought you to the garden first. You must be fainting for your luncheon.'

They walked up the sloping lawn to the house, still talking about gardens.

Lady Jane said: 'I enjoy hearing people talk of gardens, and I enjoy reading about them. You know *Autumn Crocuses*?'

Esmé nodded. 'It's one of my bedroom books. Only very special books find a place there.'

'D'you remember the story about the pansies?' Althea asked. 'The garden the sick lady came back to always makes me think of Mrs. Heggie's, with all the rambler-roses and the pergolas... such a hot little garden!'

They were seated round the table in the cool dining-room with a great yellow bowl of polyanthus to look at, enjoying cunningly prepared grape-fruit, and still they talked of flowers.

'Just now,' said Esmé, 'my bed book is *Elizabeth's German Garden*. I haven't read it for years, and I'm adoring it. I love her "happy struggles and failures," and the gardener who gave notice regularly on the first of every month! When I finish it I'll begin the *Solitary Summer*, then *Elizabeth in Rügen*, then *Fräulein Schmidt*.'

'And stop there?' said Nicole. 'I think you're right: these books finish a period.... I do like living with a writer till I become soaked in the atmosphere she--or he--creates. How much do you read at night? Only a chapter or two? Then these books will keep you happy all the summer nights; and talking of summer plans, we've arranged to take Ardmore for August and September. Mother liked the sound of it--didn't you, Mums?'

Lady Jane finished helping herself to salmon, and said: 'It sounded most desirable, and your friend Mrs. Wolsley has been so kind giving us all manner of details, just the little things that are so important.'

'I'm glad,' said Esmé, 'The Wolsleys adore Mull; they've gone every year for about five years: first to a place on the coast, and then to this house, Ardmore, which seems to be on a fresh-water loch. It's a good many miles from the place you land, but it's quite a good road, and once or twice a week vans actually call, I'm told, from Tobermory. And I dare say you could get things sent over from Oban; there will be a Store too, I expect, in each village.'

'The house sounds all right for size,' Lady Jane said. 'Seven bedrooms and good servants' accommodation: two living-rooms and a billiard-room. Plainly furnished, Mrs. Wolsley says, but quite comfortable, and what more do we want? The plainer the better. I can imagine nothing more miserable than looking after other people's treasures. The billiard-room will be a great help on bad days. Mrs. Wolsley says there is a boat on the loch, and a gillie, a very good man, who can be trusted with the care of boys. That is a real comfort. I should never know a moment's peace if they were out alone.'

'Barnabas can swim, and The Bat is learning,' Nicole reminded her, but Lady Jane insisted, 'If the loch is any size they would never reach the shore. No, the gillie is the best thing I've heard about the place.'

'It seems so cheap,' Nicole said, 'for a decent house and good fishing.'

'That,' said Esmé, 'is why the Wolsleys go there. They say that the great point about Mull is that it's not fashionable. There are no great grouse moors to bring the very wealthy, and it's too far out of the way for business men to travel back and forward to, so it's unspoiled. They find it a splendid place for their three boys, no end of things to do, and a glorious free life.'

'I can imagine how Alastair will love it,' Lady Jane said, smiling at the thought. 'He has fished a little at Rutherfurd, but with Barnabas and a gillie and a boat he will feel himself a man among men.'

'And we'll take the little car, Mums, and drive you about to see all the new place, and

Althea and I'll walk and climb hills and explore--what fun!'

'Did Betty Wolsley tell you that she only took from London the cook and chauffeur and her own maid? She said she found it quite easy to get local girls who made excellent parlour and house maids?'

'I know,' said Nicole. 'Mull sounds like the Islands of the Blessed, with trained domestic servants on tap! And Mrs. Wolsley kindly offers to send names and addresses.'

'We are really immensely obliged to your friend,' Lady Jane said. 'I have written, of course, but will you please tell her how truly grateful we are for all the trouble she has taken. And you too, my dear.' She touched Esmé's hand and smiled at her. 'You have been so helpful.'

'Not a bit, but don't any of you get drowned in the loch, or I'd feel horribly responsible--By the way, are you going to the Erskine's wedding?'

'Only Nicole,' said Lady Jane. 'Althea didn't want to be a bridesmaid, and it would take more than a wedding to tempt me to London. Are you going?'

'No, oh no, but I've got rather a nice present for Vera, at least I hope she'll like it.'

'May we know what it is?' Althea asked.

'I went on the plan of doing to others as you would have them do to you and got her one of those models of sailing ships. An old one, a real beauty. I'd like to keep it for myself: there's a place in the hall where it would look just right.'

'Keep it then,' Nicole advised, 'and send her something out of a silversmith's. Unless Basil has a taste for such things it'll be rather thrown away, I fear--wouldn't you say so, Althea?'

Althea considered. 'Yes, I think Vera has inherited her mother's taste in furnishing. What about some personal thing?'

'Such as?'

'Well, Aunt Jane and Nicole are giving a chain of lovely amber, and I've got her a jade pendant.... I had to spend more than I wanted to, for my conscience wasn't quite easy about refusing to be a bridesmaid. That's how one's sin finds one out!'

Esmé Jameson laughed. 'How true! But I think I'll keep my lovely ship and send a hat-brooch or something. I hear from Mrs. Heggie--though what her source of information is I don't know--that there are to be hundreds and hundreds of guests, so there will also be a wilderness of presents. There is really something rather distasteful about these large weddings.'

'Oh, I don't know,' Nicole said. 'The crowd after all is only a background. To the bride it's the few intimates round her that matter--The Erskines with their lavish hospitality must have an enormous circle of acquaintances who will all expect an invitation. It's

140

a funny thing the social game!'

'I wonder,' said Lady Jane, 'if we may see through the house to-day? I've always wanted to explore Windywalls inside and out, but there never has been time before.'

Her hostess rose with alacrity. 'How kind of you to ask!' she said. 'Nothing gives me so much pleasure as personally conducting a party through my domain. Let's begin at the top and work down, and I won't spare you so much as a cupboard.'

Chapter XXV

'...The time will bring on summer,
When briars shall have leaves as well as thorns,
And be as sweet as sharp.'

ALL'S WELL THAT ENDS WELL.

'It's a very odd thing,' said Mrs. Heggie, 'how quickly the summer flies. Before you realise it's here we've got to the shortest day, and after that, no matter how good the weather is, you've an uneasy feeling that we're posting back into winter.'

She was sitting on a solid chair--her weight did not permit her to use a canvas one--in the middle of the lawn at Knebworth, looking over the top of her delphiniums to a sea that was almost as blue.

'This is only the second party I've had this summer,' Mrs. Heggie went on, 'and I bought all those new garden things to be ready.'

Joan looked round at the orange glasses and jugs, at the bright cushions and rugs, and her mother added:

'I forgot about the rambler-roses when I got them. I'd have been better with rose colour.'

'Green is always the safest choice,' said Joan.

Mrs. Heggie and her daughter were waiting for the guests to arrive to a tea-party, and Joan was making no effort to conceal her boredom at the prospect.

'Who are coming?' she asked, lolling back in her chair and displaying unexpectedly stout legs.

Her mother mentioned the names of a few Langtoun ladies, and added Mrs. Lambert from Kirkmeikle.

'I had the others,' she said, 'the Rutherfurds and Mrs. Jameson and the Dundases from

St. Andrews, that lovely day a fortnight ago. That was a very successful party.'

'This isn't one of your higher efforts,' Joan suggested.

'I don't know what you mean, Joan. They are all people I'm fond of and glad to see. Indeed I'm looking forward to this party very much, for there will be no strain about it. I mean, we're all the same sort of people who have been brought up in the same way and look at things from the same standpoint. Sometimes with Lady Jane and the others I feel a little confused. Out of my bearings--is that the expression? But--Oh, here comes Mrs. Lambert. Come away, my dear. First comers get the choice of the best seats. Is Mr. Lambert well? And the children? That's good.'

Mrs. Lambert looked round and remarked on the gaiety of the scene.

'Yes,' said Mrs. Heggie, 'it's pretty enough, but I was just saying to Joan that the summer's hardly here before it's away.'

'I know.' Mrs. Lambert gave a small sigh. Summer in Kirkmeikle is only a glimpse and winter is so long and real.'

'I escaped it last year,' said Joan, 'and I mean to do the same again. What it means to bask in sunshine and know that all you poor creatures are starving under a pall of fog and cold!'

'Perhaps you may be able to persuade your mother to go with you next winter,' Mrs. Lambert said.

'She will never do that,' said Mrs. Heggie, rising to greet three other ladies who were making their way across the lawn. 'Mrs. Lambert, you've met my friend, Mrs. Stark from Langtoun, and her sister, Miss Grant, and Mrs. Burnett who is staying with Mrs. Stark?... Yes, well we've been discussing wintering abroad, and I was just saying nothing would induce me to leave my home. I don't really mind the winter. It's dull sometimes and I could do with more people dropping in for a meal or a chat, but anything's endurable when you're in your own home. It's the utter weariness of living in hotels and having nothing to do. Of course you can talk to the other people, but that's dull work. If you play bridge I dare say it's bearable, or if you write books or paint you'd be driven to work out of sheer ennui.'

'I suppose,' said Mrs. Lambert in her small, gentle voice, 'that it must be tiresome to have nothing to do, but it would be very pleasant to try it for a change.'

Mrs. Heggie looked with understanding sympathy at the fragile little woman, as she said: 'I wonder when you had a rest, my dear! So long ago that you can't remember it?'

Mrs. Lambert flushed as if she feared she had been found complaining. 'Oh,' she said, 'summer's a very easy time for us. No meetings and a month's holiday. We're going to Speyside for August.'

'But it's no holiday if you take your burdens with you.'

'Burdens?'

Mrs. Heggie laughed good-humouredly.

'Oh, I know what you're thinking. But what you need is to get away by yourself and never to have to give a thought to a house or a meal or a child. Speyside is lovely, and a fine change from Kirkmeikle, but if Mr. Lambert's taking the services you'll be in the manse and it'll be a strain all the time, keeping the children from kicking the paint and destroying the furniture, then getting it all cleaned up at the end; and your own house to be freshened up when you get home--what kind of holiday is that?'

While Mrs. Heggie had been talking, maids had brought out tea and put a table conveniently near each guest, and carried round eatables while their mistress filled the cups.

Mrs. Lambert was dumb before such a flood of facts, but Mrs. Heggie was not to have it all her own way. Mrs. Burnett, who had come with Mrs. Stark, leant forward with her cup in her hand and said briskly:

'A very good holiday indeed. Forgive me butting in, but I'm a minister's wife myself, and I know all about it. We couldn't have had a holiday at all when the children were young if my husband hadn't preached for a house--and grand holidays we had. Manses aren't as a rule so handsomely furnished that you have cause to be nervous,' she grinned cheerfully at Mrs. Lambert as she spoke, 'but once--once my spirit was nearly broken. It was a seaside manse owned by rather a pernickety couple with one child, a boy. They had private means, so the house was very well appointed, china and glass that it would have been difficult to replace, and that kept me nervous. I had six children, four of them boys, and all of them full to the brim of original sin.' She stopped to eat a scone and drink off her first cup of tea, and while her cup was being replenished she went on:

'It's always been my boast that we left a house as clean as we got it, indeed, sometimes we left them a good deal cleaner than we got them, but we came lamentably short with the M'Andrews' manse. This only boy of theirs had beautiful and expensive toys, such as our boys had never seen or imagined, great things that couldn't be locked away. We made rules about touching them, but one day, in some cupboard, they discovered something that no rules had been made about--an aeroplane or parachute, or something of that kind. Away they rushed with it, climbed a high wall, and let themselves go. In a second the thing was wrecked, and one boy had a broken arm and another concussion.'

'Dear, dear,' said Mrs. Heggie with great enjoyment, 'did they get all right?'

'Oh yes, in a few days they were ready for more mischief--It was very wet weather, and they were constantly in and out of the house, which accounted for some of the damage, but most of it was sheer ill-luck. There was a Chippendale sideboard----'

'Yes?' Every one listened breathless.

143

'Those things are too delicate for a family,' the strange lady said resentfully, 'such spindley legs.'

Mrs. Lambert's eyes grew large with horror. 'You didn't----'

'Yes, smashed a leg. I think myself it was worm-eaten, but there's no doubt Johnnie was a clumsy fellow. Then Jessie knocked Robert's head through the stained-glass panel in the front door. How she did it I don't know, for the thing was all leaded in squares, and I can't tell you what we didn't pay to have it replaced. But we did keep the glass and china whole until the night before we left. Some people were coming to supper, the table was all laid, when the littlest boy threw a ball....'

Groans burst from the audience while Mrs. Burnett proceeded to make a very good tea, which she doubtless felt she had earned. Mrs. Stark looked encouragingly across at Mrs. Lambert, remarking: 'Mrs. Burnett's was a particularly riotous family, and you have only two gentle little girls.' She turned to her friend and 'Did you ever get the same manse twice?' she asked.

Mrs. Burnett seemed amused at the question. 'Of course we did; we were great favourites, I assure you. Sam can preach, you know.'

Every one, it seemed, had a story to tell about letting houses, and in the riot of talk that followed no one noticed a tall girl in white come across the lawn, till Mrs. Heggie, looking up, cried in a happy fluster, 'Why, it's Miss Nicole!'

'I told the maid I'd find my way out to you,' Nicole said, 'but I didn't know you had a party. I hope I'm not interrupting horribly?'

'Not at all. I don't think you've met my friends.' She named the three friends, adding, 'Mrs. Burnett has been telling us her experiences of houses she has been in in the summer--very entertaining.'

'I wish I'd heard them,' Nicole said, turning to smile at the big bright-eyed woman who looked fit to cope with any situation. 'We've no experience at all of living in "letting" houses, but we've taken one this summer.'

'I heard that,' said Mrs. Heggie. 'In Mull, isn't it? I know nothing about that part of the world, but I've heard it's very wet.'

'You've probably heard aright,' said Nicole, who did not seem cast down by the prospect, 'but nobody minds rain in the West Highlands.'

'Not a bit,' said Mrs. Burnett, 'we were in Tobermory one August, it rained the whole time, but that didn't matter for the children were never out of the water anyway.'

'We're about fifteen miles from Tobermory,' Nicole said.

'Is it a nice house?' Mrs. Heggie asked.

'We hope so, but we've never seen it, it's a pig in a poke. But whatever the house is like we'll have lovely surroundings, lochs and mountains.'

Mrs. Heggie shook her head. 'I hope the kitchen range will be all right,' she said. 'That's more important than a view when all's said and done.'

Nicole laughed and said, 'I wonder,' while Joan remarked that so far as she was concerned kitchen ranges need not exist, so little did she care what she ate.

'Well, Joan,' her mother reminded her, 'there's no one makes a bigger fuss when the bath water isn't boiling hot,' but Joan looked out to sea and pretended not to hear.

'Once in Arran,' said Mrs. Burnett, 'I had to cook on an open fire without a vestige of a boiler: every drop of water had to be boiled in a pot. But we managed beautifully. When you're young you can put up with discomfort, but I confess that now I'm beginning to feel I'd like to take things easy.'

'What about servants?' Mrs. Heggie asked Nicole; 'are you taking your own?'

'Mrs. Martin is going--quite wants to go: and Harris, too, is eager to see a new part of the world, but Effie and Jessie will have their holidays, and we are to get local girls to do the housework.'

'I see.' Mrs. Heggie turned to look after her other guests, and Nicole found herself alone with Joan.

They talked together of Madeira and of Joan's friends the Colsons. From the Colsons it was only a step to poetry, and Nicole was amazed at the way her companion's face lightened and beautified when something interested her. Kirkmeikle regarded Joan as both dull and difficult, but Nicole realised in those few minutes, as she had never done before, that in Kirkmeikle Joan felt herself in prison: she realised what a different creature she must be amid other surroundings, in more congenial company, and she felt sorry for both Joan and her mother.

Nicole got up to go in a few minutes, saying: 'I really came to tell your mother about Vera Erskine's wedding--I wonder, could you both lunch with us to-morrow? We so seldom see you. I know, of course, you have your work, but if you could spare an hour or two it would be a real pleasure to us.... No, don't trouble your mother just now when she's so engaged. If we hear no word we'll expect you both at one-thirty.'

Outside the garden-gate Nicole met Charles Walkinshaw who stopped the car and suggested he would drive her home.

'I haven't seen you for ages,' he complained, 'you always seem to be out. I've called thrice with no luck.'

'We met last at the wedding,' she reminded him.

'So we did. That was a great show. Why did Miss Althea not go?'

'I forget what reason she gave.--How is your mother?'

'Pretty much as usual. She likes to be out in the garden in this weather. All yesterday afternoon she sat among the roses. She declares being out is worth the effort--but it is an effort.'

Nicole nodded. 'She is a very gallant woman, your mother. I wish Joan Heggie knew her. I somehow feel that your mother would be able to do something for Joan.'

'Joan Heggie? Is that Mrs. Heggie's forbidding daughter? She writes poetry, doesn't she?'

'Yes, good poetry--Why, here we are already. Come in, won't you?'

Charles was obeying with alacrity when Nicole said: 'Mother and Althea have gone to St. Andrews. I'm afraid they won't be home much before dinner.'

'Oh--D'you know I think I'd better be getting home? It's later than I thought it was.'

Nicole stood on the doorstep and smiled at the young man, cheerfully malicious.

'Shan't we see you, then,' she asked, 'before we go away?'

'Aren't you to be here for the summer?' Charles asked blankly.

'Didn't you know? We've taken a little place in Mull.'

'*Mull!*' The dismay in his voice softened Nicole's heart.

'Do you know that part? I tell you what--why not come and see us there? Come and spend a week with us.'

'I say, d'you really mean it? Wouldn't Lady Jane and Miss Althea mind? I mean, wouldn't I be a nuisance?'

'You'll be a great help, if you don't mind a household of women and children, and no sport to speak of. Well, that's settled. We'll write and let you know time and steamer and so forth. But come to luncheon one day next week and say good-bye.... What about Wednesday?'

Charles drove off with a satisfied look on his face, while Nicole, as she went into the house, said to herself, 'John Dalrymple expects to be asked. He and Charles will come together and entertain each other,' and she, too, wore a satisfied look.

Chapter XXVI

'I should have then this only fear,
Lest men, when they my gladness see,
Should hither throng to live like me.
            And so make a city here.'

ABRAHAM COWLEY.

It was arranged that Lady Jane, accompanied by her maid Harris, and Mrs. Martin, the cook, would go by train to Oban, while Nicole and Althea, with Barnabas and The Bat, would make the journey by road in The Worm.

'If you stay the night at the station hotel,' Nicole said to her mother, 'we'll all arrive in time to cross with you in the boat at one-thirty.'

Lady Jane suggested that it would be as well if she and her fellow-travellers went straight across the same day.

'It's a Wednesday,' she said, 'so the boat leaves at half-past five, which would just give us time.'

But her daughter would not listen to such a plan.

'I'd hate to think of you arriving alone in a strange house.... You'll be all the better of the night's rest, and Harris would like to see Oban; she collects picture-postcards and little china dishes.... All the luggage must go with you: we can only take things for the night. Althea and I'll take turns at driving, and I just hope we don't land The Worm in Loch Awe or any other deep water.'

'I can *almost* swim,' said Alastair.

'I could rescue myself,' said Barnabas, 'but--' measuring the two tall girls with his eye, 'that would be all----'

'Nothing else would be expected of you,' Althea assured him. 'As a matter of fact I'm rather an accomplished swimmer myself, and I could even manage Nicole.'

'Don't, please, talk as if I were a behemoth,' Nicole protested. 'I only weigh eight and a half stone, and I'd promise not to cling round your neck.'

'The way to rescue people,' said Barnabas, 'is first to fell them, then grip them by the hair.'

'Brutal child! Let's hope your victims aren't shingled.'

'Let us hope,' said Lady Jane's gentle voice, 'that such desperate remedies will not be required. But do, please, try to arrive in good time. I don't want to have too much time in Oban with Mrs. Martin and Harris.'

'But there are heaps of shops, Mums. Chalmers has delightful things. You might occupy yourself buying Althea and me jumpers if you have time to put off--. I don't suppose we'll need anything but the countriest of clothes at Ardmore? Tweeds and woollen stockings will be the only wear. Like Kirkmeikle, only more so. I wonder if there will be tennis and neighbours....'

'What shall we take for evening?' Althea asked.

'Oh, any little frocks.'

'I like you to look nice in the evening,' Lady Jane said.

'That we *always* do, tactless one!' her daughter replied. 'But half-soiled dance dresses would look horribly out of place in a bare shooting lodge. To be clean and neat is our ideal.'

'Like Spider,' said Barnabas, who adored that small dog. 'He'll come with us in The Worm, won't he, Nikky? He'd feel it dreadfully if he were sent in charge of women-- I'm sorry, Aunt Jane, but there's nothing of the lap-dog about Spider.'

* * * * *

All things worked together for good with our travellers and the party at the station hotel, for at eleven o'clock The Worm drew up at the door and there was time for every one to see the shops: the boys being particularly eager to lay in a stock of fishing-tackle and sweets.

The sun shone and the sea had hardly a ripple when, after lunching heavily at the hotel, they meandered down to the Mull boat, where their luggage had preceded them.

Althea drove The Worm on to the boat, anxiously watched by the boys; Mrs. Martin and Harris sat in the saloon clutching their hand luggage, while Lady Jane stood watching the gulls as they dipped and swooped about the boat. Presently the two girls joined her, and the boys ran up at intervals to tell of new marvels they had found.

'The luggage is all right,' they announced. 'It's down on the lower deck, and there's a cow tied up beside it.'

'A cow!'

'Yes, a nice brown cow. It's eating Althea's hat-box now.'

They rushed away but came back presently to ask if they might have money to take the tickets.

'We won't take first-class ones,' they said, 'steerage is much cheaper.'

'But Mrs. Martin and Harris are sitting now in the saloon.'

'Well--' reluctantly, 'that'll be two firsts, but the rest of us should go steerage, it's much *nicer.*'

At the first stopping-place they watched the ferry-boat come out and take off passengers and row away back towards the jetty, and the green knoll on which stood a white-washed inn and a church and a manse, all as simple as a child's drawing.

Their own landing-place had a pier of sorts, and intense excitement prevailed while The Worm was being induced to land. It proved so refractory and developed so unexpected a spirit, that Nicole said its name would be there and then changed to 'The Sheik.'

'The brown cow gets off here too,' said Alastair solemnly.

'It's a great day for the Isle of Mull,' Althea remarked.

At last they were all landed, and Nicole breathed a relieved sigh. 'That's that,' she said, 'and now to see if anything has turned up for the luggage. That lorry----'

She came back announcing that all was well. The lorry and the Ford car were both for their party.

'It's only about six miles. I'll take you, Mums, and Althea; the others will go in the Ford. We'll let them go first to show the way. Now, *is* that all our luggage?'

'It looks a lot,' said Lady Jane, but Harris was able to say with absolute certainty that the whole pile belonged to them. Presently Spider, who had been throwing himself about in transports of self-importance, was packed into the Ford, along with the boys and the two slightly bewildered women.

Nicole cried, '*"On, on," said the Duchess!*'

'We'll see Ardmore first,' shouted Barnabas as the car he was in bucketed away.

They drove through the village, where they saw a hotel, a post-office, a general store, a baker's shop, a hall and two churches, out to a smooth road running between very green fields, backed on one side by steep mountain sides, and little copses of rowan-trees and larches, over narrow hump-backed bridges, until they stopped at a gate which the boys had leapt out to open. The rough drive was about half a mile long, and after a second gate had been opened and shut, they drove across a wide expanse of turf and found themselves at the door of a low rambling white-washed house.

The Ford had hardly stopped when the boys flung themselves out, almost knocking over the elderly woman who stood on the doorstep, and who began to explain very rapidly that she was the caretaker, and would be glad to show them everything before she retired to her sister's house in Tobermory. She also said that the two young girls were waiting--Morag Campbell and Ellen M'Wharrie--and tea would be ready whenever they wanted it, for the kettle was boiling this minute.

Mrs. Martin was thrust forward to deal with the situation, and she and Harris followed the caretaker into the kitchen, while the others stood and looked round.

The house stood on a promontory running into the loch which was surrounded by high mountains rising steeply from the shore. A clump of pine-trees sheltered the house at one side: a tall fuchsia hedge hid the out-houses: the jetty was only a few yards from the front door.

'It's rather like a chapel,' Althea said, 'with that wide arched doorway. What is the Latin, Barnabas?'

That youth spelt it out--'Something about "*Small house--much peace,*"' he said, turning to follow Alastair who had made for the jetty.

'They will never be out of the water,' Lady Jane said prophetically.

'Never!' Nicole agreed. 'I hadn't realised that we are practically on the loch: we've water on three sides of us. But isn't it lovely! The way the mountains come down on either side, and the sweep of heather and bracken. Obviously no garden. I rather like that. A garden would be out of place on this wind-swept promontory. The only decoration is the fuchsia hedge!'

'Where are we to get vegetables?' her mother asked.

'Where, indeed! By post from Oban, I should think. But perhaps we may be able to buy them at the cottages we passed.... Let's explore the house. Come, boys, and choose your rooms. There's no hurry to get out the boat.'

They found a wide hall with the dining-room on the right-hand side, then two shallow steps leading to the drawing-room and the billiard-room. There was one large bedroom next the dining-room, and upstairs six other bedrooms and two bathrooms.

Two of the bedrooms were small, with chests of drawers filling them almost entirely, and these the boys claimed for their own.

'But why?' asked Nicole, 'they don't look anywhere; they're miserable rooms. Have the big one with the two beds.'

But the boys were firm, and it transpired that the two rooms were connected by what Barnabas called 'a burglar run' made by the roof of the billiard-room, and that was the attraction.

'The downstairs room is really the best,' Nicole said, 'and ought by rights to be yours, Mother, but I don't like the thought of you sleeping on the ground floor. A kelpie might come in from the loch, or a water-horse.... We'll keep it for visitors.'

'Won't a kelpie be as likely to attack a visitor?' Althea asked, while Lady Jane remarked that Nicole's hospitality did not go very far.

'Quite far enough,' Nicole retorted. 'Visitors must take the rough with the smooth, so to speak. There are three rooms looking on to the loch and one looking up Ardmore. Who wants which?'

'If no one else wants it,' Althea said, 'I'd like the Ardmore one. There are waterfalls rushing down the mountains that will make a most lulling sound at night. Besides, it's not so exposed to the elements. I like the things to remain on my dressing-table, which they won't do with winds blowing in from the loch.'

'Take it and welcome. Mother, you have the one with two beds: it seems bright and sunny.... We're none of us far from each other, which is a blessing. The bathrooms are the isolated points. They have evidently been built on, with the billiard-room.... Oh, Harris, how do you find things?'

'Quite comfortable, miss, thank you. Mrs. Martin's satisfied with the kitchen range, and there's a servants' hall, and nice bedrooms. There's a post-office two miles away, besides the village we landed at, and carts come once or twice a week from Tobermory, so we're not exactly cut off from civilisation as you might say. Is this your room, miss?'

'No, this is Miss Althea's, mine is across the passage.'

'And her ladyship's, miss?'

'Is that Harris?' Lady Jane called. 'Tell her to get tea before she thinks of beginning to unpack. Oh, Nicole, come here--look at this book-case full of all the books I like best; books of my girlhood that I always meant to read again but couldn't lay my hands on. I shall have a feast.'

'There's a book-case in each room and one on the staircase,' Nicole said. 'It's a wonderful rich house for books. *What's that?* Oh, it's the gong for tea. But what a tocsin!'

Later they discussed what could be done with the drawing-room.

'It needs flowers, for one thing,' Althea said.

'There are no flowers, and no flower-glasses so far as I can see,' said Nicole.

'Branches of rowan would help, stuck in these blue jugs, and wild flowers. Let's make a complete rearrangement of the furniture. It's a big room and a light one, with these two gigantic windows, surely we can make something out of it.... This big old sofa before the fire? A writing-table for Aunt Jane in this window looking out on the loch.'

'There are no end of tables,' Nicole said. 'I counted four writing-tables in the billiard-room, one in each window; and there are at least two in my room and two in Mother's, and we don't need more than one.'

'Well, then, we can each have a writing-table.... And the round table had better stand just behind the sofa, for we shall need the lamp on it in the evening. And small steady tables on each side of the fireplace with two other lamps.... That's a horribly shabby hearth-rug. I saw one in the downstairs bedroom that would be much better. Then shall we draw those arm-chairs up to the fire?--that makes an oasis.'

Althea moved about remaking the room, while Nicole watched her with interest.

'Let's go through the house,' she suggested, 'and bring everything pretty we can find into the drawing-room, for this is where we'll spend most of our time. I can't say I admire the walls much. Those salmon painted on them--As a record of sport obtained, they're all right, but they seem to me to fail as decorations.'

'Would the people who own it object, d'you suppose,' said Althea, 'if we continued the scheme of decoration? Painted mountains for a background and water? The salmon look so stark alone.'

151

'That boat is very well done,' Lady Jane said, studying the sketches done on the distempered wall. 'The figures are so alive. I wish we knew what they all meant.... I expect happy young people did them long ago.... Where are the boys, Nicole, my dear?'

'They've gone on the loch with Dugald M'Lean. Oh yes, he looks thoroughly reliable--Mother, I think we should write for some cheap flower-glasses, and Mrs. Martin's got quite a long list of things that are necessary in the kitchen, small things, you know, like apple-corers and so forth. Shall I write?'

'Yes, darling.' Lady Jane was standing in the window, looking over the loch now shining in the peace of a perfect August evening. She turned, and it seemed as if the peace were reflected in her face as she said:

'No matter how bad the weather may become, though it mists and rains and blows, we've seen it once look its perfect best.'

Chapter XXVII

'...Summer's lease hath all too short a date.'

SONNETS BY WILLIAM SHAKESPEARE.

There followed a halcyon time. True, there was nothing much to do, but time hung heavy on no one's hands. They fished in Loch Ard in the morning, came in ravenous for luncheon, went out in the afternoon to Loch-na-Keal to find the exquisite little shells, yellow and blue, that abounded there, or took The Worm round the island, choosing some delectable place to make tea in.

It sometimes rained, but rain in Mull matters little, it is a gentle beneficent rain. But if it got too bad there was the drawing-room fire and books, and billiards if people could be persuaded to play.

The boys enjoyed Dugald more than anything. He spoke to them as man to man, he told them the legends of the countryside, he taught them the Gaelic names of the birds and beasts, he made ships for them to sail on the loch, so that they had quite a navy in the backwater by the jetty.

Lady Jane wrote endless letters at her own writing-table in the drawing-room, but often she sat, not writing, but simply looking at the water with its fringe of bright green turf, and thinking.

The days went past so quickly that it was September before they realised it. They had had no visitors except some friends from the South who happened to be yachting near, or going on to stalk, and they were only a night or two at a time, but in the first week of September they expected John Dalrymple and Charles Walkinshaw. It was Nicole's plan that they should come together.

'Best to have them together,' she said, 'and they can support each other, and also entertain each other. They will fish, I hope, and we've been promised at least one day's stalking for them.... We might go to Iona one day. Oh, a week will soon pass.'

'We would have been much happier without them,' Althea said.

'Ungrateful creature!' Nicole retorted. 'Haven't they been asked simply and solely to amuse you? *I* don't like having men staying in the house, they're always on one's mind. Of course it's different if there's a man in the house to arrange ploys for them and take them out, but I shan't know another really comfortable happy moment until they go.'

Althea laughed and advised Nicole not to worry. 'Mrs. Martin'll feed them well,' she said. 'They can fish or walk or stalk all day: there's always hot water for baths, and a good fire in the billiard-room: what more could they want? They'll be quite happy. Men are easy things to entertain: women are a very different matter--. Where are the boys?'

'They've gone to the top of the loch with Dugald and Spider and their lunch. What a blessing they've both got so keen on fishing, it keeps them outside, happily amused for hours at a stretch, and they do really catch fish--Alastair was pulling in quite good trout the other night, and Barnabas got a salmon--it's a splendid life for them. Perhaps it's more Dugald than the fishing that fascinates them. He teaches them so much, and they love him for appreciating Spider. He calls him, they tell me, "The Captain, the wee game captain." It's funny to hear Barnabas trying to speak like Dugald. It's The Bat who is the real mimic. He can not only speak like people, in some curious way he can make himself--just for a second--*look* like them. He's an imp beside stolid Barnabas, but they are very good friends.'

'They are one,' said Althea, 'in a dislike for all forms of learning, but Barnabas likes Alastair to tell him stories while he's hollowing out a boat or laying railway lines. Have you seen the railway and siding he has made? It goes from the garage to the jetty. It is wonderful to be made out of nothing, frightfully neat: that boy must be some sort of engineer when he grows up. Alastair will play for hours, shunting up and down, or being a non-stop express, while Barnabas rings bells and pulls signals.'

'Oh,' said Nicole, 'that explains the interest in Gamage's catalogue, and sundry hints about the lack of funds to buy necessaries! I expect they want rails, and all sorts of gadgets--. Barnabas is a great playboy, but he doesn't like to be observed. And how he hates strangers! The Bat would go off quite happily to those parties and picnics that they are invited to if he got any encouragement from his friend.'

Lady Jane turned round from her letter-writing and said:

'Are you talking about Barnabas? That's a funny boy. He tells me he hates "civilisation," and his one thought is to get away from the haunts of men. A lecturer had come to the school, and describing some wonderful place in Canada, said that if some enterprising person built a good hotel there it might soon become a popular resort. Barnabas looked into my face and said so earnestly, "Aunt Jane, was that not a *foul* thing to say?" This, he thinks, is the best place he ever was in, for he can look round for miles and see nothing but heather and water. I mildly suggested that it would be better for the island if there were more houses and more people, but he refused to see it.'

Nicole laughed, but said: 'It is sad to see those empty cottages. I wonder why the people are going away. Can't they live on the land?'

'Perhaps,' Lady Jane said, 'there are too many deer forests--I don't know. Is anybody going to the post-office before luncheon? I need stamps, and hadn't you better wire to John, and Charles Walkinshaw, at Oban to get off at Craignure instead of coming on to Salen?'

Nicole looked up from collecting the books and magazines which the boys were apt to spread over the sofas and chairs and even the floor. 'I'll go to the post-office with pleasure, but d'you think we need wire? They may as well come on to Salen and we'll send M'Cunnisty's car to meet them. The Worm would certainly turn at such a load.... Are you coming, Althea? We've just time before luncheon if we take the short cut through the nut-wood.'

Althea looked up from the magazine she was reading to the wind-swept loch, and said: 'It's very blowy. Why not take The Worm?'

'My girl, you'll lose the use of your legs altogether if you don't walk more. It's lovely in the wind.... Are these all the letters, Mums? Two postal orders for twenty shillings each--Yes.' Nicole stuffed letters and money into the pocket of her tweed coat; and said 'Come on, Althea. This is almost the last walk we'll get in peace. After to-morrow those men will always be on our minds.'

'There's something so truly hospitable about Nikky,' Althea said, as she went to get a coat, and Nicole turned to her mother, saying: 'You know, Mother, I *am* getting inhospitable, it's quite true. At Rutherfurd visitors came and went most of the time; we entertained as a matter of course, but living our quiet life in one small house, I find myself apprehensive about entertaining. I remember that cold weather I was in India, on tour with Uncle Nigel, we met a man--he came to dine--who told me he had been almost sick with fright about coming among his own sort of people: he lived in some out-of-the-way place, meeting only a few men and rarely a white woman. I was sorry for him at the time, but I'm sorrier now, for I understand better what he felt. To-day I can see no light in life because two harmless men are coming to stay! How did we come to ask them, Mums? And probably the poor creatures are just as badly bored at the prospect as we are, and are wondering at this moment why they ever accepted--Anyway it's kind of the Glenulva people to take them stalking, and... Yes, I'm coming, Althea.'

* * * * *

In spite of Nicole's forebodings nobody looked either bored or apprehensive after dinner that evening, as they sat round the drawing-room fire. The room was much more habitable now. There were flowers, for Dugald M'Lean's mother had a cottage with a garden full of old-fashioned, sweet-smelling flowers, and every day he brought a nosegay of pansies and mignonette and sweetpea to Lady Jane; there were piles of new books and magazines; branches of rowan and bracken hid the worst parts of the walls: the chairs were worn but comfortable, and there was always a bright fire burning on the hearth.

They were talking lazily, Lady Jane had many questions about old friends for John Dalrymple to answer, while Althea fenced verbally with Charles, and Nicole laughed at them both.

'What would you like us to do to amuse you, John?' she asked presently.

'Do I look as if I needed amusing? What do you do when you are alone?'

'Why, nothing; just read, and talk or don't talk, and presently go to bed.'

'And very nice, too,' said John. 'Why attempt anything else?'

'Seeing it's your first night I feel we ought to make some sort of effort. Charles, what about an intellectual game? We have one, a very searching one, which some one sent us.... If you all play I'll read the correct answers out of the book.'

Charles groaned, and Althea protested. 'I'll not play that game again, it stripped me of every atom of self-confidence.'

'Give me a pack of cards,' said Charles, 'and I'll teach you a game called "*Thank you, Darling*." It is warranted to break the ice in the stiffest house-party.'

No one looked enthusiastic and Lady Jane said: 'I'm afraid we haven't card minds: I'm a fool at bridge.'

But Charles assured her that for this game no skill was required, merely good manners, and being given a pack of cards he began gravely to instruct them in the rules.

'First of all, the cards are given names. Spades are "Spadicums," diamonds "Finklesteins"--but I'll tell you as we go along. The King is always "Papa," the Queen "Mamma," and when you get a card from any one you must say "Thank you, darling." That's the point you see, "Thank you, darling." It puts every one on an intimate footing at once.'

'I don't think it does,' John protested. 'It must absolutely prostrate shy people.'

After some more instructions Charles dealt the cards.

'I shall never learn this,' John Dalrymple said with conviction. 'It's a game for a master mind.'

'I'm glad to hear you say it,' Lady Jane told him. 'I never heard anything more confusing.'

'Perhaps,' said Althea, 'the confusion is more in the explanation than in the game.'

'Cruel!' murmured Charles, pausing in his task of dealing the cards. 'I think there's a mistake here--How many cards have you, Dalrymple?'

That gentleman counted patiently, and said he had twelve.

'Does your mother play Patience, Charles?' Lady Jane asked.

Charles turned a puzzled frown on his hostess.

'Yes,' he said vaguely. 'Oh yes. I mean No, she doesn't. How many cards have you, Nicole?'

'Eleven.'

'Oh, you can't--count again.'

'How is Mrs. Heggie?' Nicole asked, bending down to pat Spider who, having made a cushion of her feet, lay fast asleep on the rug.

'How should I know? *How is Mrs. Heggie?* What a question to ask a man struggling to teach unskilled players a game.... There's a card lost out of this pack.'

'The boys had it,' Althea said carelessly, 'and they're capable of losing any number, or perhaps Spider ate it.'

'Does it matter anyhow?' Nicole asked. 'I thought this was only a friendly game--We don't pretend to play cards seriously, you know.'

'Thank you for telling me,' said Charles.

'Come and look at the loch in the moonlight,' Nicole said, consoling him. 'I like to stand in this window at night: we never pull down the blinds--How odd it seems, this little lighted room with little humans talking and laughing, in the midst of the blackness and the bigness of mountain and loch!'

Chapter XXVIII

'...annihilating all that's made
To a green thought in a green shade.'

ANDREW MARVELL.

These September mornings at Ardmore seemed to Nicole about the most perfect things she had ever known. When she woke on the morning after the expected guests had arrived the sun was shining in at her window, so that she had to lean out at once and savour the delight of it--the loch like a silver shield, the scarred peaks with wisps of white mist floating round them, the little woods of rowan with here and there a flaming branch, the lap of the water against the jetty, the smell of wood smoke and frying bacon, Spider trotting round the house, Barnabas and The Bat looking incredibly clean and well brushed, Dugald carrying a lobster and a bunch of garden flowers--What a jolly time the morning was! Bath-water running, knocking at doors, tinkle of tea-cups, every one astir for the new day.

'We're going to Iona to-day. We are, aren't we, Nikky? It's a good day, and Aunt Jane said, the first good day.'

The Bat was anxiously studying the faces of the company, for corroboration of his statement. 'We are, aren't we?' he repeated.

'It's a lovely day,' Nicole admitted, 'we'll see what Mother says.'

'How far is it?' John Dalrymple asked, coming back from the sideboard with a plateful of sea-trout in one hand and a cup of tea in the other.

'Brown bread?'--Nicole offered a piece--'or toast?... Let me see, it's about thirty-five miles to the Ferry, and then you cross in a motor-boat. Would you care to go? None of us have seen Iona. It might be rather fun--Good-morning, Mums. It seems you promised the boys to go to Iona the first good day.'--Nicole waved her hand to the glory outside--'So what about it?'

Lady Jane smiled a greeting to every one and sat down in her place.

'Yes, please, a little porridge--No, John, thank you. I don't take sugar: I may be English but I haven't that on my conscience. Nor cream.... It is a perfect day. Well, who cares to make the expedition?'

'The question is,' said Nicole, 'how many we can pack in. We can hire two cars, so we needn't take The Worm--it's beginning to show signs of encroaching age anyway-- How many is that? I suppose we may take it that Althea will go, and Charles? Where are the lazy creatures?'

'Spider *must* go,' said Barnabas.

Protests arose from Lady Jane and Nicole. 'You know he hates long journeys--he'll be a nuisance,' but Barnabas pleaded:

'He loves a jaunt. It breaks his heart to be left at home. I'll hold him in my arms all the way and he won't be sick.'

'Oh, all right,' said Nicole, 'it's your affair--. Now I must whirl down and engage the cars. Who'll come with me and open gates?'

'Me,' said The Bat.

'Why should you go?' John Dalrymple asked, getting up, napkin in hand. 'I'll take The Worm to the village.'

'Sit down, both of you,' Lady Jane commanded, 'and finish your breakfast. It's absurd of Nicole to rush off like this. What does half an hour matter?'

'It may simply mean that the cars are taken by some one else,' Nicole said, and the eager watching faces of Barnabas, The Bat, and Spider all registered dejection.

The door opened and Charles came in.

'Anything happened?' he asked after greeting his hostess.

'Hurry up with your breakfast,' said Nicole.

'Why? It's bad for the digestion to bolt food. Have you never heard that?'

'But we're going to Iona,' The Bat told him--'Nikky's finished now. Aunt Jane, may we go and get out The Worm?'

They rushed, colliding with Althea in the doorway.

'You take porridge?' Charles asked her as she came over to the sideboard.

'No, thanks--what's all the fuss about?'

Nicole put her head in at the window. 'Shall I say ten o'clock? It'll take us about two hours to get to the Ferry, so we won't be in Iona till nearly one.'

'What about luncheon?'

'There's a hotel there. I think we'll be sure to get something.' Nicole withdrew her head and Lady Jane said: 'I think she is too optimistic. It would be as well to take sandwiches and be independent.'

'Sandwiches make such a dull lunch,' Althea said.

'If you eat a large enough breakfast,' said Charles, 'you won't want any lunch.' He surveyed Althea's plate. 'A square inch of toast and a spoonful of marmalade won't take you far.'

'I hate breakfast,' said Althea, looking pettish. 'In fact, I'm not a morning person at all. Not like Nicole, who positively prances. She does so irritate me with her glorious morning face.'

Nicole's mother laughed sympathetically. 'I know,' she said. 'Some of us are never happy until the day gets properly aired, so to speak; we're only half alive in the morning, but Nicole...'

'Welcomes the unknown with a cheer,' said Charles poetically. 'Miss Althea, you should have lived in a French memoir, in a silken bed-chamber discreetly curtained from the light with scented beaux coming in to pay you compliments.'

Althea turned to John Dalrymple, remarking with a backward look at Charles, 'He's quite a wit, isn't he? But, Aunt Jane, are we really going to Iona? What is there to see?'

'A cathedral, I think, and--what is there at Iona, Charles?'

'Celtic crosses,' said Charles, 'and the graves of Scottish kings.'

'How cheerful!' said Althea. 'We'll have a long happy day, won't we?'

By ten o'clock they had started; Lady Jane in the first car with Althea and John Dalrymple: Nicole following with Charles and the boys and Spider.

It was a drive of great beauty, skirting the loch side for miles, running under great headlands, mounting winding roads, until they could look down and see far below them a panorama of little crofts, emerald green patches of pasture, shining waters with islands floating like a mirage in their misty blue. They ran through tiny clachans, each cottage with its stack of peat, across wide moors, along a rocky coast road, until they came to the village and the ferry. There they all got out and stamped about while they waited for the motor-boat to come across.

'Lucky it's so calm,' Nicole said. 'I just hope I won't disgrace myself.'

'Nikky, you couldn't be sick on a motor-boat, could you?'

'Barnabas, I'm capable of being sick on any craft, but I think I'll be all right to-day, for I can see the place I'm going to.'

'It seems the Oban steamer calls just now for two hours, so I'm told Iona will be overrun with people,' Lady Jane said calmly.

'Which means,' said Charles, 'that we won't get any lunch. First come, first served: they'll have eaten everything.'

'Oh,' said Alastair, 'and Spider so hungry'; while Barnabas produced some toffee from his pocket, remarking that it had got melted a bit with being sat on but was still very good.

'How did this boat know to come for us?' Alastair asked.

'The people telephoned across,' said Althea.

'*Did* they?' There was deep disappointment in his tone.

'Why, how did you think it came?'

'I thought it just came,' Alastair said.

'Like Lohengrin's swan?' suggested John Dalrymple.

When they landed at the jetty they found Lady Jane's information had been only too correct. The whole place swarmed with people, dogs and visitors staying on the island, tourists from the steamer. It was so unlike the peaceful isle of their imagination that the party stood and looked at each other in a dazed way.

159

'More like a Liberal Demonstration than anything else,' Charles said, surveying the swaying mass.

'Look at Spider,' said Barnabas proudly. 'He's made four friends already.'

'Put on his lead,' Althea advised, 'or he'll be off with them.'

'Hadn't we better find the hotel,' Lady Jane said, 'and see about luncheon. Ask some one, John.'

John went off and accosted an old man with a beard, returning with the information that the hotel was only a little distance away.

They straggled towards it, up the village street, past a grocer's shop, past booths with tempting displays of jewellery and beaten brass articles, and when they reached the hotel, which was gaily washed in colour, Nicole was sent forward to make enquiries. The harassed but still courteous landlady explained that the hotel was packed, the guests were even now sitting down to lunch, there was no room and nothing to spare for casual comers.

'There are seven of us and we're all hungry,' Nicole said, and the landlady so far relented as to say that if they came back about two o'clock there would be a ham-and-egg tea ready for them. Nicole thanked her with a chastened air and went back to her friends.

'Any hope?' her mother asked.

Nicole surveyed the group, remarking, 'What tramps you look! Something in your attitudes... a slouch: something vaguely supplicating. Even you, Mums... and of course Barnabas and The Bat and Spider----'

'Why these insults?' Althea asked; 'we want to know about luncheon. Can they take us in?'

Nicole shook her head. 'House full! They are busy eating now, you can hear them. But as a great concession, the landlady says that any time after two we may have a ham-and-egg tea.'

John Dalrymple emitted an awed ejaculation which made Nicole giggle.

'Don't you think,' said Lady Jane, 'that bananas and biscuits from that shop we passed would be nicer? And we could eat them outside. What a blessing the sun is shining!'

'Biscuits and bananas,' Nicole pointed out, 'would be all right if we were sure of a good tea, but we cross again at four and we won't be home till seven. This would be a portmanteau meal, lunch and tea in one--Come and let's look at the jewellery, they make lovely things.'

They all trailed away, and passed an hour looking at the handiwork displayed, and making various purchases which were to be kept until they called for them on their way back to the boat.

160

Shortly after two they again presented themselves at the hotel, and were admitted to the dining-room. It was a wooden annexe which smelt strongly of past meals, and was still hot and stuffy from the last, but they thankfully took their seats at the end of a long table and were each presented with a heaped plate of ham and eggs. Strong tea, new bread, and mixed biscuits completed the meal which was eaten with hilarity, though, towards the end, a note of almost too complete satiety crept in.

'Another biscuit, Barnabas?' Charles suggested.

'No, thank you,' said Barnabas, and added: 'I don't think I'll ever want anything to eat again.'

'D'you feel like that, too?' said Althea. 'Alastair, please don't begin chewing toffee. Let's go out and walk. Couldn't we get round to the other side of the island where there are fewer people?'

'We must see the cathedral,' Lady Jane said, and presently they went out and looked at it, and were much impressed by its dignified simplicity and beauty. Then they walked across wide downs, and climbing down to the shore, found a long stretch of pure white sand, such sand as they had never imagined, and marvellous green water shading into deep blue. Not a soul was visible, and with a whoop Spider and the boys dashed across the tempting whiteness followed by Althea and Charles, while Nicole skimmed like a sea-bird down to the water's edge.

'Why, John,' Lady Jane said, 'this is fairyland. Leave me to dream.'

John spread the coat he carried on a flat rock.

'Is that all right?' he asked.

'All right, thank you. Go with the others, John. This is the place and the weather to make us children again....'

Towards four o'clock, as they went reluctantly towards the jetty, it was found that Spider was lost. The boys went back to look for him, while the others waited. The crowds were gone now, and the village was sunk in afternoon peace.

'Just think,' said Nicole, 'how wonderful this must be in winter and early spring when there are no tourists, no tramp-like people wandering about demanding ham-and-egg teas, just the white-washed cottages with their little gardens, and the people who belong. Imagine that bay on a frosty afternoon with the sun going down behind the islands, and the green and rose sky meeting the blue-green water, and the shining white sand. Nothing could be too wonderful to happen.'

The boys came back, hot and dusty, dragging the recovered Spider.

'We found him in the nunnery,' Barnabas announced.

'Disgraceful fellow,' said Charles. 'How did he get in?'

'You don't need to get in,' The Bat explained. 'It was once a nunnery, now it's only

161

some grey stones and green grass and flowers.'

Chapter XXIX

'Still so cruel?'
'Still so constant, lord....'

TWELFTH NIGHT.

It was, on the whole, a good week of weather that Lady Jane's guests spent in the Isle of Mull, and she could not but feel that it had been a most successful one. The men had had some good sport, and the picnics to Calgary Sands and other places had been enjoyed by every one; indeed there had been no weary hours in the house or out.

On the last day of their stay they discussed at breakfast what they should do.

'What about fishing the top of the loch with Dugald?' Nicole suggested. 'Neither of you has got a salmon yet, you know. And we would meet you at the empty shepherd's cottage for tea.'

'Will the Empty Shepherd give us tea?' The Bat asked, and was advised by Barnabas not to be a young idiot.

'It is sad that you must go to-morrow,' Lady Jane said. 'We shall miss you both dreadfully. You're going home, Charles?'

'Yes. I've got to appear at the Langtoun Horticultural Show, worse luck! The sorrows of a candidate!'

'Have you much of a chance?' John asked.

'Not an earthly! Labour is very strong, as you can well imagine in what is largely a mining district.'

'You can't blame them,' Nicole said, 'if they vote for the man who promises most. The promises are heartening at the moment, and memories are wonderfully short.'

'I don't blame them,' Charles said, 'who could? It seems to me many a good man will take a toss at next election. In their hearts the people respect and trust Mr. Baldwin, but they've had this Government for a long time, and changes are lightsome. Labour will probably get its chance, then the wheel will come full circle again--Meantime, I suppose I must go on grinning at Horticultural Shows!'

'Good man,' said John, 'you're one of the props of the country.'

'It's all very well for you,' grumbled Charles.

The men did as they were bidden and went off with Dugald to the head of the loch, and at three o'clock the others followed them. Nicole went with the boys, who were anxious to row her in the boat, while Althea walked with Lady Jane along the shady path by the side of the loch and watched their progress.

'They don't row very steadily,' Lady Jane remarked, as she took a long step over a marshy bit.

'The Bat *will* stop and argue,' Althea said. 'Odd how damp this place always is. I expect it's the steepness of the hillsides. Dugald was telling us that in winter you can't see the loch for flying spindrift. Rather wonderful it must be. And the caretaker stays in Ardmore entirely alone! Just imagine that lonely house with its empty rooms, and the wind howling round it, and that one little old woman sitting in the kitchen. Can you understand any one being able to stand it?'

Lady Jane was picking her way on boulders over a wide shallow burn. When she reached the other side, she said: 'I don't think it should be allowed. Suppose she took ill, it might be days before any one knew.... I must say I love Ardmore. I shall always look back with pleasure on this time--And I think our visitors have been happy, don't you, Althea?... John doesn't say much, but----'

'He does not,' Althea laughed, 'he's just about as conversational as a post. I asked Charles if he spoke to him when they were out together, but he rather snubbed me; said it was so like a woman to expect people always to be talking, and had I never heard of a companionable silence and so forth.'

'John was a silent small boy,' Lady Jane said; 'I think because he was so much alone. He liked to come over and play with Nicole: he was like a kind old Nannie to her and obeyed her slightest command. Ronnie and Archie adored him, of course. He was a few years older than they were, and they looked up to him and admired him. They were so keen to get into his regiment when they were old enough to join up, but that couldn't be managed.'

She looked across the shining water at the black boat which was going neither straight nor steady.

'Now I'll sing,' they heard Nicole say, 'and you'll try to row in time.'

'Row, brothers, row, the night comes fast,
The rapids are near, and the daylight's past.'

The result of this effort was that the oarsmen became convulsed with laughter and lay helpless on their oars.

'Sillies!' came Nicole's voice across the water, and undeterred by failure she again broke into song. '*Oh Shenandoah...*'

'That's a lovely thing,' said Althea humming the words.

'Yes,' Lady Jane agreed, 'but not quite suitable for a West Highland loch. Ah, that's better,' as the strains of '*Speed, bonnie boat, like a bird on the wing*' came to them. 'They are speeding a little now.'

Althea leapt on to a boulder and waved her scarf in the air, shouting encouragement. She made an attractive picture in her tweed skirt and jumper, with her hair flying; a study in russet and orange that went well with the September hillside, and Lady Jane watching her realised what a change had come over the girl. The silent, listless Althea with the discontented little made-up face was gone. This was a joyful creature, young-eyed, with freckles on her nose and a healthy tan on her cheeks. It had come so gradually that she had not consciously noticed the change. But, looking back some months, and realising how unlikely then it would have seemed that Althea should ever be interested enough in anything to laugh and shout, made her see the magnitude of it.

They walked on and Althea said: 'Tell me more about Rutherfurd and your children--. Were you very happy?'

'Very happy. I think there could have been few happier. We were so contented to be together, so pleased with our home and with each other, we envied no man anything. Indeed, perhaps we were a little selfish in our happiness. I never could bear to have large house-parties. What would have been the use? Our simple ways would have bored people who needed a lot of amusing--But we had loads of relatives, who came and went--you know something of that large clan, and all our neighbours were our very good friends, people like Jean Douglas at Kingshouse, and Alison Lockhart, and the Langlands; and there were lots of small gaieties.... We would probably have had to smarten ourselves up and entertain in earnest as the boys grew up, but the War was waiting for them when they left school, and afterwards we never had the heart.'

'Then had Nicole no fun? Didn't she come out like other girls and go to balls?'

'Oh yes, she came out and was presented by one of my sisters and had a London season. Then she went out to another aunt in India for a cold weather. She said she enjoyed it all, but she was glad to get home. Her father's health began to fail about that time and she didn't leave home again. He seemed to cling to her.... You will hardly remember the War, child?'

Althea shook her head. 'Eight can't remember much about things that happened outside. Nicole would be sixteen when it stopped. Too young to have the fun, the glory, or whatever it was they got out of working in the War--nursing, driving a car or what not, but old enough to realise it. Hard luck!'

Lady Jane said nothing, and they walked in silence through the wood at the bend of the loch. When they got out into the open again they saw the two men, with Dugald, the gillie, watching the progress of the boat.

Charles came to meet them, loud in welcome, announcing that they had a fire made all ready for the kettle.

'We're eaten alive by midges and perishing for tea,' he added.

'Have you caught anything?' Althea asked sternly.

'Dalrymple got a salmon: I only caught a few trifles, but I've drunk everything drinkable. Why won't they hurry with that boat?'

'Here they are,' Lady Jane said soothingly. 'Be nice to them, for it must have been hard work for the little boys rowing in this heat.'

When the boat grounded the exhausted mariners threw themselves on the turf and examined with much self-pity their blistered palms, while Dugald put the kettle on the fire, and John Dalrymple helped Charles to lay out the cups and unpack the eatables.

'Listen to Spider panting!' said Nicole. 'You'd think he'd done all the work. Now I have a right to pant. I sang to cheer the rowers.'

'We heard you,' said Althea. 'We weren't particularly cheered.'

'You didn't need cheering, walking coolly and quietly along while we laboured----'

'Sandwiches, Lady Jane; tomato, cucumber, banana; which will you have?' Charles held out a selection on a paper plate and added: 'If the kettle doesn't boil soon I shall go mad. I'm frothing at the mouth now.'

Alastair studied him anxiously and said: 'You aren't really, but why don't you drink out of the burn? Tea'll only burn your mouth.'

'Besides,' John pointed out, 'one small kettle won't do much for you, it has to go round us all, remember.'

'No,' said Charles, looking scornfully at the kettle; 'six breakfast-cups of scalding tea is what I want.'

'Unrestrained creature!' Althea said, helping herself to a cucumber sandwich. 'It's odd how one's idea of people change as one gets to know them better. If you, Charles, had not paid this visit I dare say I'd have gone on thinking of you as an earnest young politician with his country's best interests at heart. Now it seems to me your ambition is to clown.'

Charles groaned in bitterness of spirit, while John Dalrymple remarked, 'You don't seem very popular, my lad,' but Nicole rushed to his defence.

'These young people,' she said, looking scornfully at Althea, 'so serious about things of no consequence, so fatally flippant about what really matters, they can't understand that even the greatest must unbend. The kettle's boiling now, Charles. Make the tea, and we'll fill it up again for the second cups....'

Tea was nectar, lying there on the flower-starred turf with the cool lap-lap of the loch at their feet. After every one had eaten their fill, Barnabas and The Bat finished what was left--even to the lumps of sugar.

They sat on afterwards in the scented warmth, loth to leave.

Barnabas, burrowing his nose into the turf, said: 'I wish I knew all the names of the things that grow here, like bog-myrtle and bog-asphodels and meadow-sweet and sundew and bracken and sweet-fern...'

'I'd rather know the names of the birds,' Alastair said. 'Look, Dugald, there's a heron-crane.'

'Are you sure it's not a "Scotish gull"?' Althea asked.

Alastair rolled his head in an abashed way and every one smiled, for the night before he had shown them with pride a poem he had composed, beginning:

'Would I were a Scotish gull
Flying o'er the Sound of Mull.'

'Never mind, sonnie,' Nicole said, comforting him, 'perhaps Althea can spell Scottish, but I'm pretty sure she couldn't make any sort of poem.'

Charles rowed Lady Jane and Althea home, the boys stayed to fish with Dugald until supper-time, and Nicole and John Dalrymple walked round by the loch side, Spider accompanying them. They walked almost in silence, and Nicole with some relief in her tone said as they came in sight of the jetty and the road leading through the little pine-wood to the house, 'How easy walking is, compared to toiling in a boat; and what a perfect evening to walk in.'

'Let's walk on,' said John, 'round the moor road to Loch-na-Keal. We've loads of time.'

Nicole hesitated for a second, then nodded agreement. Spider had been pursuing thankfully his homeward way--he had had an exhausting day--but when he saw his chief man friend going on, after one regretful look towards the good meal that he knew awaited him, he meekly turned and trotted after him.

'He wouldn't have come for me,' Nicole said, 'you were always the dog's idol, John.'

'It sounds a lofty destiny!'

'I think it's rather a nice thing to have said about one.... Listen to those buzzards--mewing like cats.'

John bent down to pat Spider, saying, 'Did the buzzards want a little black-and-white dog?'

They stood by the shore of the loch and Nicole made a feint of looking for tiny shells, yellow and white and blue.

'I thought of decorating the lid of a box,' she said, 'as they used to do long ago. Mother says...' Then she saw her companion's face and was silent.

'Nicole,' said John, 'I asked you to marry me years ago, nine to be exact, and you sent me away. I asked you again at Kingshouse in February and you told me to wait....'

Nicole stood very still, holding her hands tightly together. When she spoke her voice was so low that he had to stoop to hear it. 'John,' she said, 'you're more to me than almost anybody in the world, you're my oldest, dearest friend, so you must know how I hate to hurt you.... Oh, John, *don't look like that.*--I was weak that night at Kingshouse, the very fact that I didn't know might have shown me I never could; I was braver and more sincere when I was eighteen and sent you away--Putting my feelings out of it altogether it would be so unfair to you.'

John Dalrymple shook his head as he said with a wry smile. 'My dear, don't worry about that. I'd take you thankfully on any terms. Is there--I've no right to ask, but is there some one else?'

'No one, John, no one in this world.... D'you mind sitting down? I want to tell you something....'

They sat down looking into the sunset but seeing nothing of its beauty, John listening patiently while Nicole spoke, brokenly, with long and painful pauses.

'...you were away when we left Rutherfurd and went to Kirkmeikle. It was odd going to a strange place leaving all our friends, the people we had been brought up amongst, and becoming quite a different sort of person. Barbara hated it, naturally, and it must have been awful for Mother, so I had to pretend I liked it. And afterwards, when I got to know these people and the place, I did like it--without any pretence. There was a man who had taken rooms in Kirkmeikle to get peace to write a book, a climber and explorer--Simon Beckett. He had been in the first Everest Expedition. I think almost the first time we saw each other we knew--Love is like that, John; you just know without any doubt--but Simon was rather a speechless person and nothing was said until he was going away again. Then he told me.... We had only three days together, John, three days together as engaged people--that's all. But he's still my Simon.... Death is supposed to loose all ties; but if you don't want the ties loosened? You don't stop loving people when they die any more than you stop loving them when they cross the sea--If I thought there was no life but this, then I dare say I'd be glad to warm myself at a fire of affection--and yours, John, is so warm and kind--but I believe that some day I shall go to Simon. Yes, I believe he's waiting for me just on in front, not wearying, happy in the work he's been given to do, and when I'm fit I'll go to him.... Perhaps this sounds like fantastic nonsense... but it keeps me going, and--Oh, John, forgive me.'

'It's all right, my dear.... I've always loved you and always will, but there is nothing more to be said. We'd better be getting back.'

He helped her to her feet and they stood for a minute in silence. The light was beginning to leave the loch and the Greeban Rocks were dark. Close to the shore there stood a low thatched cottage before which a man was playing the pipes. A girl stood in the doorway with a baby in her arms, its tiny head pillowed on her cheek: she tapped her foot to the beat of the music----

It seemed to Nicole that she would remember every detail of that scene so long as life lasted.

Chapter XXX

'But, mistress, know yourself; down on your knees,
And thank Heaven, fasting, for a good man's love.'

AS YOU LIKE IT.

The two men left after breakfast the next morning to catch the steamer at Craignure.

'It's not much use,' Nicole told them, 'getting on at Salen and wriggling back and forwards. Better to get your breakfast in comfort, and you can keep your mind in perfect peace about catching the boat, for you will see it puffing along beside you most of the way.'

Barnabas said, 'I wonder how the boatmen know when to take out the ferry-boat to meet it. It's so neat the way they just hit it.'

'Or rather, don't hit it,' said Althea. 'A collision on the high seas would be tragic.'

'It's beastly that you're going away,' Barnabas went on, 'it spoils everything.'

'Indeed!' Lady Jane said, 'you will leave a great blank. We shall be quite glad to leave ourselves, in another week. You'll need a day or two at home before school begins, boys.'

Groans broke from Barnabas and The Bat, and Charles said: 'Why aren't we all "Scotish gulls"?'

'It's easy for you,' Barnabas told him, 'you haven't to go back to school.'

John was standing by the sideboard supping his porridge, and Althea, regarding him, said:

'I've wanted dreadfully to know, and this is my last opportunity to ask why do you eat your porridge standing? Does it taste better like that? Or is it perhaps some sort of rite?'

John laid down his plate and considered.

'I really don't know,' he said, 'I've always done it. Rather absurd when you come to think of it----' He helped himself to bacon and mushrooms and took his place at the table.

'Here's your napkin,' said Alastair. 'I used it to kill a wasp--d'you mind?'

168

'Disgusting child!' Nicole said, 'why didn't you take your own.... Don't use that, John. I'll ring for another.'

'No, don't trouble. A dead wasp's a harmless thing. Move along, Scotish Gull, and let me in.... Yes, it's a miserable business having to leave Ardmore this lovely morning.'

Again Barnabas raised his voice in protest. 'It's all right for you, you can go anywhere you jolly well please: not like Bat and me.'

'Don't pretend you're not quite happy at school,' Nicole said. 'You know you'd be very sorry if you heard you weren't going back to Evelyns----'

'Oh well,' Barnabas admitted, 'it's not bad perhaps, as schools go.'

'We all like to grumble,' Lady Jane said cheerfully, 'even if it's only about a crumpled roseleaf.'

'We'll all get a sight more than that to grumble about before life's done with us,' Charles prophesied gloomily.

'Yes,' said Barnabas, 'a revolution might come any moment and we'd be shot in batches.'

'How pleasing!' said Althea.

'I don't believe Aunt Jane'd be shot,' Barnabas went on, 'but you'd be about the first to go, Althea. You look so dashed condescending, they'd *enjoy* shooting you.'

'I wouldn't be shot,' Alastair boasted, "cos I'd be one of the revolters.'

'What will you do to-day, Barnabas?' Nicole asked.

'Dunno. Fish probably--can we have our lunch out and poached eggs for tea? Here's the car. Catch Spider, Bat----'

* * * * *

When the good-byes were said and the car had disappeared from view, Nicole left Althea outside wrestling with the boys and Spider, and followed her mother into the drawing-room.

Lady Jane sat down at her writing-table and at once began to write, while Nicole moved restlessly about the room. She lifted a book, read a sentence or two, and laid it down, she shifted the things on the mantelshelf, then she went to the window and stood for a long time looking out at the road across the field over which the departing car had gone.

At last she said, twisting the blind cord as she spoke: 'Mother, I'm not going to marry John.'

Lady Jane's hand paused, poised over her letter. She was surprised at the blank disappointment that swept over her like a wave. She thought that she had schooled herself to count on nothing; but the hope had been there, stronger than she had

169

realised. It would have been so perfect.... But it was not to be----

'You don't want to get rid of me, do you, Mother?'

The defiant note had gone out of the girl's voice, now it was pleading.

'Oh, my dear, is it likely? But I want you to remember that we can't always be together.... John could give you so much--and he's such a good fellow, Nikky.'

'John is everything that's dear, he's everything except--except the right man.'

'Then there's nothing more to be said.'

'But you understand, don't you, Mums?'

'I understand, darling,' and Lady Jane sighed as she said it.

Nicole laid her head on her mother's lap and sobbed:

'Oh, it's all such a *waste*.... And I feel such a selfish beast about you, Mother. I know what it would mean to you to have John as a son----'

After a few minutes she sat up and dried her eyes. 'Well, that being finished with we must just go on. I'm going for a walk, Mums, a long walk: don't be surprised if I don't turn up for any lunch. I'll take a biscuit in my pocket----'

Lady Jane sat on at her writing-table after Nicole left her, but she wrote no more letters that morning.

* * * * *

When the two girls went up to bed that night Althea followed Nicole into her room and stood looking out at the loch, and the stars above the dark shadowy mountains.

'I don't like windows opening out like this,' she said, 'aren't you afraid of kelpies coming in from the loch?'

Nicole laughed. 'I did think one had got me the other night. I woke to a perfect tempest; the wind had risen suddenly and that little window over there had burst open, making a tremendous draught. I couldn't get the candle to light, and that tall flower-glass on the dressing-table had been blown over and I heard the water dripping on to my best slippers. Something had to be done, so I lay under the bed and lit the candle, then I had to lean out and get hold of the window. I nearly overbalanced and something caught my arm and seemed to be trying to pull me out-- It was only a spray of honeysuckle, but at the moment it felt very queer and eerie.'

'Horrid!' said Althea. She was looking at some faded photographs in battered leather frames that were ranged along the mantelpiece, but she made no remark about them, and began to speak of Kirkmeikle and the people there.

Presently she said: 'Lady Walkinshaw will be glad to get Charles back. She must miss Belinda. It seems she's gone with some friends to the Dolomites.... How still it seems to-night without men's voices! Men make such a difference in a house.'

170

Nicole agreed. She had taken off her dress, wrapped herself in a pale-blue dressing-gown, and now began to brush her hair vigorously, and as she brushed she said:

'I'm very fond of Charles Walkinshaw: you're a lucky girl, Althea.'

The girl stared, and gave a short laugh. 'Oh, Charles,' she said airily, 'he's quite amusing to wile away the time with.'

Brush still in hand, Nicole sprang to her feet and faced the astonished Althea. Her face was white and her eyes blazing as she said: '*You little fool!* How dare you speak like that! Don't you know that you may be throwing away the best thing life has to offer you. Don't throw it away; you may never get the chance to pick it up again.' She turned and sat down again at the dressing-table. 'I beg your pardon, Althea, I don't know what made me break out like that.'

Althea moved to the door, looking somewhat shaken.

'Anyway,' she said, laughing rather uncertainly, 'I've seen you really angry and that's something.'

Chapter XXXI

'*...Some have greatness thrust upon them.*'

TWELFTH NIGHT.

October again in the Harbour House!

Nicole had taken the two boys back to school, and had spent a few days in London, seeing friends and plays, and buying clothes; and now she and her mother and Althea had settled down for another winter.

They were in the drawing-room late one afternoon, Lady Jane trying the embroidery, which she had just finished, on the seat of an old chair, and admiring the result.

'It does look rather nice, don't you think, Nikky? I almost think I'll do a piece for that other chair as well.'

'But it's such a big undertaking, Mums!'

Lady Jane smiled. 'It keeps my hands occupied, my dear--Where is Althea?'

'Golfing, I think. She's getting quite keen on the game.'

Nicole took up two letters which had come for her by the afternoon post from Mrs. Jackson and Barbara.

She opened first Mrs. Jackson's, which showed signs of having been written in haste; the writing ran about unevenly, and there was a breathless look about the undotted i's and the unstroked t's. She read aloud:

'MY DEAR MISS NICOLE,--What do you think, Father's to get his Knighthood after all! I was a wee bit afraid it wasn't coming off, and thankful I was I hadn't said a whisper to a soul except you. But we heard to-day that it's all right. It will be announced when the scheme Father has helped such a lot with is completed. I can hardly believe it. I've pictured it to myself so often you'd think I'd be used to the idea by this time, but now that it's come I'm fair knocked out. Sir Andrew and Lady Jackson, I get quite red in the face when I think of it. Father'll carry it off well, he has a lot of natural dignity, but I doubt I'll give myself away many a time. But what does it matter? There's many a queer ladyship going about in these days! Anyway it'll add a great interest to life--What a queer thing human nature is! No sooner do you reach what seemed an impossible goal than you look beyond it--I'm just thinking if it had been a baronetcy wee Andrew would have been Sir Andrew Jackson of Rutherfurd.'

Nicole stopped to remark, 'The gods will destroy Mrs. Jackson: to reach an almost impossible goal and to look beyond is impious....'

'Well, there it is. I want you and your dear mother to know the very first. It ought to be in the papers about the beginning of November. I just hope people won't laugh, but I expect they will. I sometimes feel like laughing myself when I think of it.... You might ask your mother if I should be presented at Court, and I would be much obliged for a few hints on behaviour. I can ask you what I can't ask any other body.'

'I'm very glad,' Lady Jane said, then, wonderingly, 'but imagine wanting to be a knight.'

'Oh, I don't know, there's a great thrill about it. It's really terribly nice for Mrs. Jackson--she will so thoroughly enjoy it all.... Have you any hints to give her?'

'I shouldn't think so, but I must send her my congratulations. I'll address an envelope now. My memory's so bad I'll forget otherwise.--Any other letters?'

'One from Barbara,' Nicole said, but she did not read this letter aloud. It was brisk and complacent.

'DEAREST NICOLE,--I've been meaning to write for ages, but really my life seems to get fuller every day. They have elected me President of the Nursing Association which, of course, means a lot of work, but I am glad to do it, for I feel it is most important. Lady Langlands, dear soul, was not very efficient, and it was high time new blood was introduced. I had some difficulty at first with the executive--several old members resigned--but now everything is working smoothly and they are all in my pocket. All except Jean Douglas and Alison Lockhart. I fear they will try and thwart me in my attempts to reconstruct. I do dislike Alison Lockhart with her twisted smile and caustic way of speaking! I thought her ageing fast the last time I saw her. I've got my friend Mrs. Brunton on to the executive. She is so practical and sensible, and, of course, she'll back me up always. I've also been put on the committee of the County Appeal for Cripple Children. I simply *had* to accept for, as they said, who was better fitted to plead for their cause than a young mother. My dear, the boy is *too* beautiful, *so* large and placid. He can stand by himself, but I don't encourage him to try to walk for he is a heavy fellow and we must keep his legs straight--Did I tell you that on his first birthday Andy gave me a second string of lovely pearls? It was *rather* sweet of him, wasn't it? And I liked the idea of giving it to me on the boy's birthday. Andy is, like me, very busy--County Councils and Education and things, indeed I was telling him the other night we saw very little of each other, for he has often to give up the evening and sit late over papers.

'We are looking forward to quite a cheery winter. Tilly Kilpatrick has a young cousin with her--such a pretty girl. We dined with them the other night to meet her. John Dalrymple was there and seemed, for him, quite impressed. I shouldn't wonder if that was Tilly's idea in having the girl here. It would be an excellent "down-setting" for her, and nice for the neighbourhood to have a mistress at Newby Place.'

Lady Jane looked up and asked if Barbara had any news.

'Oh, nothing much. She seems very well pleased with life. The boy continues to flourish, and she has been made President of the Nursing, and other blushing honours----'

Presently Lady Jane folded up her work and went out of the room, and Nicole sat on in the window-seat looking out. The days were drawing in, it was grey dusk now, and the lamps were lit outside; she could see them all along the coast. The ships in the Harbour looked ghostly, and the sea was a whispering shadow----

The door opened and Althea came in. She looked round the firelit room, and seeing Nicole in the window, crossed to her.

Her tight-fitting cap framed a face flushed with fresh air and exercise, her curls were beaded with mist.

'You smell of fresh air and sea-mist,' Nicole said. 'Have you been all this time on the links?'

'More or less.' She sat down in the arm-chair. 'Where's Aunt Jane?' she asked.

'Gone up to her room--did you want her?'

'No. It's you I want. I've got something to tell you, and I don't know how to say it--It's about Charles.'

'My dear--you needn't say it. I *am* glad. That's the best news I've heard for many a day. I'd hug you if I didn't know you hated that sort of thing.'

'Well,' Althea said soberly, 'I'm glad you're pleased, and if it turns out a failure you're largely to blame. Oh yes, you are. Don't you remember your winged words in the Isle of Mull when you thought I was treating Charles lightly?'

'As if you cared anything for my remarks!'

'As a matter of fact, I do.' Althea looked gravely at Nicole's amused, sceptical face as she sat half-turned towards her. 'It's a year now since I came to the Harbour House, and when I realise how I looked on things then and how I look on them now, well--I suppose it's partly the atmosphere of the place and partly Aunt Jane, but it's mostly you.'

The girl folded her lips together as if, looking back a year, she remembered bitter things.

Presently she went on: 'I must have seemed a little beast. I meant to be one so that you'd get rid of me at the first opportunity. You see--but of course you don't see, how could you? brought up in a real home with the sort of mother you've got, and a father and brothers, all of you loving each other frightfully, all happy together--I'm not saying it by way of excuse, but I never knew what a home meant until I came here.... I don't think I could have been an attractive child--I saw too much. I resented being caressed in public and neglected the rest of the time. It's awful to be the child of divorced people, something to be fought over, a nuisance to be got rid of. If they had sent me to a good school and let me remain there, but my parents kept quarrelling about that, and I was always being removed. Sometimes my mother would use me as a chaperon, and I stayed with her in Paris and Monte Carlo. I heartily disliked my mother.... It wasn't so bad being with my father, at least he was always good-natured and pleasant.... When they died, as you know, Blanchie took me, wept over me, introduced me to the world as "poor Sybil's child," and waited for me to develop evil tendencies. Naturally I did, at least I defied her and went my own way, and made friends with the wrong set, and was attracted by one of the least worthy of that set. I knew he was no good--though I was only eighteen life had taught me quite a few things--but he had endearing ways, and--Oh well, it doesn't matter now. Aunt Blanchie cried and said what was to be expected from my father's daughter, then she took to bed and thought of the brilliant plan of planting me on you, while she went to sun herself in Egypt. I was furious, not only because I hated being banished, but because I knew that no one, least of all the man I was silly enough to care about, would give a thought to me once I was gone. Also--I didn't like what I'd heard of you.'

'So,' said Nicole.

'Yes. Blanchie was always talking in her fulsome way about her dear sister-in-law Jane Rutherfurd--so sweet, so good, so unselfish. And she talked *at* me about her niece Nicole. "My dear, such a refreshing change from the girl of to-day: so full of charm; so *good* to her mother; so gay and yet so really *deep*, you know."'

Nicole laughed appreciatively as her aunt's tones were faithfully reproduced, and said, 'Well, and you found it all true, didn't you?'

Not heeding her Althea went on: 'I thought I knew exactly what you'd be like. Bright. I hate bright people, they take the life out of everything by their determination to find sparkle in dull things, and when I came here I thought you were like that. Your appreciation of Kirkmeikle, of the people--Mrs. Heggie and her like, seemed to me an affectation. And your sympathy and kindliness. Then we went to Rutherfurd, and Barbara talked, and I realised that your content had been hard won, that life hadn't been all fair going for you, that your tolerance, your tenderness, wasn't mere sentimentality. I found that you really were pitiful--*pity full*.... I'm telling you this by way of asking your pardon, of saying thank you. You and your mother have given me my chance. You took me in and behaved as if I were a welcome and desired guest, even my appalling behaviour didn't put you off, and now, well, it sounds a sloppy sort of thing to say, but I think I know what a ship feels when it reaches harbour, after just escaping being wrecked.'

The girl turned to the end window and stood looking out into the gathering darkness. In a minute or two she came back to Nicole.

'That's all about me,' she said, 'but what about poor old Charles? What sort of bargain is he getting?'

Nicole held out her hand and took Althea's. 'A very good bargain. Charles is a lucky man. He deserves a good wife and he's getting one. For goodness' sake, don't get an inferiority complex. You haven't had the life or the upbringing of the ordinary girl, but your experience will make you a much more interesting, understanding companion.'

'I wonder,' said Althea.

'Of course it will. You've learned to hate crookedness, so you care more about straightness than most people; you've seen the selfishness of sin and you value goodness; having known cruelty you prize kindness. And it's frightful luck for Lady Walkinshaw getting you for a daughter-in-law. You will make life altogether a different thing for her--Let's go and tell Mother.'

Chapter XXXII

'So they were married and lived happy ever after and never drank out of an empty cup.'

THE ENDING OF ALL TRUE FAIRY TALES.

The news of Althea's engagement made a loud splash in the quiet pool of Kirkmeikle society. It flung Mrs. Heggie into a tumult of sympathetic excitement, and she drove her daughter to the verge of distraction by her sentimental outpourings on the subject.

'But you never liked the girl,' Joan reminded her.

'No...' Mrs. Heggie admitted, 'she seemed distant and hard, but Love is the great softener.'

Joan closed her eyes in a sickened way. 'It sounds,' she said, 'like bath-salts! It amazes me how the average woman can gush to any time over engagements and babies.'

'Well, I'm sure, it's a harmless pleasure. And there is something very touching somehow about Love's Young Dream: the mutual trust and the confident happiness, when there's never really any saying what will happen.' She shook her head. 'I'm sure, Joan, as a poet, you shouldn't belittle love.'

Joan laughed in an unamused way. 'Goodness knows I've no desire to do such a thing. It's the old imperious "god of the fatal bow," even where it seems most placid and respectable. I dare say this Gort girl isn't bad at heart--how she'd hate to hear me say it!--and young Walkinshaw is quite a likeable creature. They'll have a jolly time together, if the girl has the sense to take an interest in what interests him.'

'I hope,' said Mrs. Heggie, 'that she'll take an interest in poor Lady Walkinshaw! She must be a great sufferer, and so uncomplaining.... It matters so much to her to have a sympathetic daughter-in-law.... I hope she'll be a sunbeam in the house.'

Althea refused utterly to listen to her aunt's advice about having the wedding in London, and read aloud with malicious pleasure that lady's outpourings on the subject.

'"Of course, darling, the wedding will have to be at St. Margaret's, and where would the reception be but in *this* house?--My dear sister's only child! The young man sounds all that is *suitable and nice*, and I am glad he is Scotch, for I always feel that there is something rather particularly steady about Scotchmen--perhaps because their manners aren't always very good. I think you should have at *least* six bridesmaids, and Betty's babies would make darling pages with their curls, in pale yellow satin Georgian suits, and perhaps two *tiny* girls in dresses to the ground and blue ribbon sashes. But we can discuss *all* that when you come. Do wire when I may expect you, there is *so* much we must talk over if the wedding has to be soon, and I hear the young man is most *suitably* impatient...."'

'Well,' said Nicole, 'is that how it is to be done?'

'It is not.' Althea's tone was very decided. 'Nothing would induce me to have a London wedding, and Charles hates the idea as much as I do. We've made up our minds to be married in Mr. Lambert's church without any fuss, at least as little as possible. Of course Aunt Blanchie must be invited, but I think you'll find she will be prevented at the last minute from coming. She loves a *tamasha* if she may arrange it all herself, but she wouldn't discompose herself so far as to come to Fife to see me married. But that won't matter, for all the people I care for will be there.'

What was perfectly obvious was that there was no point in delay: Charles wanted his wife, Lady Walkinshaw wanted her daughter-in-law, and it was decided that the wedding would take place in the second week of November.

'And where will you honeymoon?' Tibbie Erskine asked. 'It's too early for Switzerland, so I don't know what you could do. Vera said it was such a blessing to have something to do on a honeymoon. She went to the Lido, so that was all right; where you bathe and bask and watch people you can't be bored.'

'We're going to Paris,' Althea said, 'to be trippers. Charles is keen on French history, and we're going to spend a fortnight pyking about in old Paris. And we want to see some cathedrals that we're particularly fond of. Amiens and Rheims and Chartres-- above all, Chartres. Then we're coming back to Kinogle for the winter--also for the spring and the summer and the autumn, and so on for ever and ever. At least I hope so.'

'My dear,' said Tibbie solemnly, her eyes round with surprise. 'You *mustn't* give in to Charles like that. You'll be simply bored to death shut up at Kinogle with poor Lady Walkinshaw. Charles is a dear, but he's got a simply merciless sense of duty--he'll drag you round the district doing political things, if you're not careful.'

Althea laughed, and it was a happy little laugh, as she said: 'Does it sound so appalling to you, Tibbie? To me it sounds quite attractive.'

'Oh, well----' Tibbie shrugged her shoulders.

It was a busy, bustling time in the Harbour House, and a happy time, because no one was sad or sorry about the wedding; no one was being left behind. Charles would take his bride to Kinogle, where Lady Walkinshaw was looking forward eagerly to having a daughter.

'I want one for keeps,' she told Nicole. 'Belinda's a darling, but she belongs elsewhere.'

(As a matter of fact Belinda was taking her curls and her smile and her merry blue eyes to India. She was joining her parents there, after the wedding was over.)

'Althea and I shall get on well, I think. I may not always approve, but I shan't say a word. If a roast fowl is tough, I hope I'll be given grace to keep from saying "Don't you think it would have been better boiled?"--and that sort of thing. Althea is a capable young woman, and she will take charge. It'll be a tremendous interest to have her, and I shall be so grateful, not only for myself but for my old Jim who is far too much tied to an ailing wife. Of course I won't for a moment expect the child to shut herself up here with me. I don't want to build on it, but if Charles does get into Parliament they will be a lot in London, and that will make a full, busy life for both of them--How are the preparations going? Althea came over yesterday and described all her dresses. After she was gone I was thinking over things, and I wondered if I might suggest something. I expect you are having a show of the presents--could we have it here? We have lots of room, and it would be a way of entertaining all the people who can't be asked to the wedding.'

'But are you able for it? Wouldn't the fuss and arranging be a nuisance?'

'I'd enjoy it,' Lady Walkinshaw said with conviction. 'I can't go to the wedding very well, and this would make me feel less out of it. And then think what fun for me to meet all the people you've told me about--Mrs. Heggie, and the Lamberts, and Dr. Kilgour.'

'I think it's a lovely idea,' said Nicole. 'How pleased Mrs. Heggie will be!--Oh, and I'd like you to meet my friend Mrs. Jackson, I don't believe she'd think twice about motoring from Glasgow for such an occasion.... May I ask her?'

'Ask anybody and everybody. What fun to give a party again! I don't believe my day is quite done after all!'

* * * * *

The party at Kinogle came off two days before the wedding and was such a success that Althea said to Charles as they sat with Lady Walkinshaw after the guests had departed:

'Our little show the day after to-morrow will be a mere anti-climax!'

It was a real house-warming. Cars and charabancs blocked the drive, for the company was large and very varied, Charles having friends in every walk of life. There was a band and a sumptuous tea, and the display of wedding-presents was more interesting than such shows generally are, for the presents were as varied as the company.

Nicole took care that Mrs. Heggie was shown all over the house, and enjoyed a ten minutes' talk with her hostess. Her other friend, Mrs. Jackson, had accepted the invitation with alacrity, and arrived in her car at the Harbour House on the day of the party in time for luncheon.

Her first words were: 'Have you seen the papers? No? Well, *it's in it.*'

Nicole, after a moment's bewilderment, leapt to it. '*Lady* Jackson,' she cried, and kissed her old friend heartily.

Her new ladyship swallowed hard, and said: 'Oh, well--there it is. Let's hope we won't disgrace it.... Yes, Lady Jane, thanks, I'm very well. Uch no, it's nothing at all to motor from Glasgow, I enjoyed it fine. Yes, we've good news from Rutherfurd; Andy writes to me about every day. Wee Andrew's coming on well--I wonder what they're thinking to-day when they open the paper... *Sir Andrew Jackson.* Doesn't it sound well?--And here's the bride. I must say, Miss Gort, happiness becomes you, you look a different girl. Stouter, too. I remember thinking when I saw you at

178

Rutherfurd you were awful thin.'

'She's wearing one of her trousseau frocks,' Nicole pointed out. 'Don't you think it's very successful?'

'Lovely! So simple and yet such a style about it.'

Lady Jackson was so appreciative that Althea offered to take her upstairs after luncheon and show her the rest of her things.

'They're all lying ready to be packed,' she said. 'All the presents have gone to Kinogle, so an empty room could be spared for clothes. I think the wedding-dress is rather nice....'

'We must start punctually,' Lady Jane warned them, 'and be there not later than three. How are we going, Nikky?'

'Well, I wondered if Mrs. Jackson--let me call you that for to-day--would take us in her so large and comfortable car?'

'I should think so indeed,' was the hearty response. 'You just tell the chauffeur when you want him--and I'm not in any hurry home, for Father's had to run up to London to-night.'

At a quarter to three Effie came into the drawing-room and announced very distinctly in her demure voice:

'Lady Jackson's car.'

The visitor started, as if for the moment she had forgotten her elevation, then she looked round at her companions, and a broad gratified smile spread itself slowly over her face.

'Lady Jackson,' she said. 'Fancy!'

* * * * *

The wedding itself was quiet and very simple. Althea had wanted to be married in her going-away things, but at Lady Jane's special desire she wore a bridal dress of white, soft thick satin that fell in folds to her feet. Belinda followed her as bridesmaid in a dress as golden as her curls.

The little church was bright with chrysanthemums sent from Kinogle and Windywalls; Mrs. Lambert herself played the organ, and Mr. Lambert hardly stammered at all as he said a few wise simple words to the young couple.

After the ceremony they drove straight out to Kinogle to Lady Walkinshaw, and later in the afternoon set off for their honeymoon like two happy children.

* * * * *

There is always a flatness after excitement, like the dullness of the thaw after sparkling frost, and Nicole was conscious of a certain dreariness as she followed her mother to the drawing-room after dinner on the day of the wedding. But as she saw the bright fire Effie had put on, the chairs drawn invitingly up before it, and Spider on the rug with an absurd bow of ribbon fastened to his collar, her spirits lightened. The room was delicately gay with fresh chintzes, and filled with the spicy smell of chrysanthemums; new books and papers were everywhere; a 'woman's litter of significant souvenirs' lay about, relics that had memories.

Lady Jane gave a little thankful sigh as she settled down with her work.

They talked of the wedding--'Did you see Mrs. Brodie?' Nicole asked, 'sitting at the back, glowering? She is very suspicious of the ways of "the gentry," and only lent her countenance on this occasion because she believes in you--. We must take some bridescake for "the wee horse" and the others. Which reminds me, Alastair and Barnabas will be eagerly awaiting a large consignment! I'll pack it to-morrow--Don't you miss old Betsy at this time, Mums? She would have had something amusing to say.'

'Yes,' Lady Jane said, 'I miss Betsy greatly. When I pass the Watery Wynd there's always a pang at the thought of the shut door.... Nicole, I wish Blanchie had made an effort to come. I'm afraid the child was hurt, though she said it was what she had expected.'

Nicole shook her head. 'I don't think anything could really have hurt Althea to-day: she was wrapped round in happiness. As for Charles!--I rather think, Mother, that marriage will be one of the stars in your crown. It seems to me pretty well ideal, and it was you that made it. You brought Althea here--against my will, let it be remembered!--and as she says herself, you gave her a chance. I don't know what would have been the end of her if she'd been left to Blanchie.'

'It makes me happy that you think so. So often when one tries to help one only makes a mess of things. She did look charming to-day coming down the aisle of the little church to Charles.'

'Oh, *didn't* she? Mrs. Heggie was weeping with sentimental pleasure. What a thrill that decent woman gets out of a wedding!'

'Nikky, I'm afraid you will miss Althea dreadfully!'

Nicole was sitting on the fender-stool with a large box of chocolates in her lap. She picked out a hard one and bit it as she said cheerfully, 'Why, no, Mums. She's going to be so near. It will be fun having her come in and out--I was glad Joan Heggie came to the wedding. I'm going to try to be a lot nicer to her than I've been; there are heaps of things I could do to make life pleasanter for her. And Esmé Jameson, Mother. I think to-day brought things back to her. As Charles watched Althea come up the aisle I suddenly got a glimpse of her face.... Perhaps it's rather impertinent to want to be kind to people, but there are a lot of women in the world who need comforting--Why, Mums, you're beginning a new bit of work!'

'Yes,' Lady Jane said, looking at her array of bright-coloured silks and wools, 'and like Mrs. Heggie and a wedding, I get quite a thrill out of it.'

Nicole nodded. 'I know. I'm beginning to read right through Sir Walter, and I'm getting a thrill out of that--Why, Spider, my patient dear, are you still wearing that absurd bow! Althea insisted on tying it on--Did you ever see anything more incongruous than his little sober black-and-white face and that garish ribbon! Lend me your scissors, Mums; it's got knotted.'

Spider lay down again on the rug and fell asleep; the flames purred, licking at the logs; Nicole sat with the box of chocolates on her knee, thinking.

Presently she looked up at her mother and said with a little laugh: 'A new bit of work, old books to read--small things, Mother!'

Lady Jane smiled at her daughter.

'Small things, my Nikky, but certainly not to be despised.'

Chapter XXXIII

'A great while ago the world begun,
  With hey, ho, the wind and the rain,
But that's all one, our play is done,
  And we'll strive to please you every day.'

TWELFTH NIGHT.

Jean Douglas stood at a window in her boudoir and looked out at the November landscape.

'The leaves will soon all be down,' she said to her husband who was standing behind her filling his pipe.

'And a good thing too! A day or two of high wind after this frost, and there would be some use in tidying the place. It's labour lost just now.--I see an account in *The Scotsman* of Miss Gort's wedding. That's a sound stroke of business: clever of Lady Jane to bring it off!'

'Tom!' said his wife, 'you've a low common mind, and you know I don't like you to smoke a pipe in this room----'

'Oh, all right: I'm just going out----'

Jean Douglas stood twisting the cord of the blind.

'Funny that John Dalrymple has never been to see us. The last time he was here was in September, before he went to Mull to stay with the Rutherfurds. He was going to pay other visits after that, but he's sure to be back long ago.'

'Oh yes, he's back. I saw him yesterday. He sent a message to you, by the way. By Jove, I forgot that! He's going away again. You know he had some job, I never quite knew what, but he gave it up a year ago and meant to settle at home. Well, it seems they want him to come back, so he thinks he'll let Newby Place on a long lease.... I know. I told him it seemed a pity just when he'd got settled down and was taking an interest; but John's obstinate, always was.'

'This is Nicole's work,' Jean Douglas said.

'Eh? Did he want Nicole? That's a pity, now.'

'A pity! I'm *bitterly* disappointed.'

'Still,' Tom Douglas puffed his forbidden pipe, 'you can't expect people to marry to oblige you. I suppose Nicole had her reasons, didn't care for him or something.'

'If she'd any sense she would care for him. Men like John Dalrymple aren't to be picked up every day.'

'My dear Jean, I don't think you're quite fair to----'

His wife whirled round on him. 'Of course I'm not fair. I'm far too sorry for John to be fair to Nicole.'

Tom Douglas looked bewildered. 'I can't see that it matters as much as all that. I'm sorry John is leaving the neighbourhood, but, after all, we did without him before. He's going back to a job that interests him, and if he wants to marry there are girls in plenty. I like Nicole: it would have been pleasant to have had her at Newby, but seeing it's not to be, why worry?'

'Thomas!' said his wife, 'you're a philosopher, but don't stay out in the damp or you will get a bout of sciatica, and then there will be precious little philosophy in you. And I warn you that my temper is very brittle.--Bless me, is that the time! I must hurry and dress. I promised to go to tea at Rutherfurd....'

As the car was going through the Kingshouse gates Alison Lockhart appeared on foot, explaining that she was on her way to call at the house.

'And I'm on my way to Rutherfurd,' Jean Douglas told her, 'invited there at four-thirty; dressed, as you see, in my best.'

'I'd better go with you, uninvited and in a woollen scarf. I dare say Barbara will give me a cup of tea though I did help to thwart her the other day at the Nursing.'

'Jump in, then,' Jean said, and when they were comfortably settled under the fur rug, and the chauffeur had resumed his seat, she added, 'I'm really quite glad of your company, for my thoughts are no pleasure to me.'

Alison Lockhart looked at her friend enquiringly.

'Tom has just told me that John Dalrymple is going away, taking on his old job, and means to let Newby on a long lease. Of course you know what that means?'

'I suppose that Nicole has turned him down--Poor Jean! And you were so hopeful. These best-laid schemes... Well, I suppose that finishes it--the Rutherfurds will never be back now. You haven't seen John?'

'No. I think he might have come to see me instead of sending a message by Tom. After all, I've known him all his life.'

'And he knows you!' said Alison. 'I expect he didn't want to hear Nicole criticised even by you--I see the Gort girl is married.'

'Oh, that's come off all right. I might have known from Nicole's letters that this is what had happened, not that she has said anything, but there was an undernote of apology in them--No, the Rutherfurds will never be back now. And we must endure the sight of Barbara queening it--Here we are. Pray Heaven I hold on to my manners!'

They had tea in the hall (after Alison Lockhart had apologised for her presence and her woollen scarf), and even the most prejudiced person would have admitted that it was a charming setting for a most personable young couple. Andy said little, as was his wont, though when his wife laughed about the knighthood bestowed upon his father he spoke with some vigour, declaring he was proud of it. Barbara herself was in high spirits, and full of talk about what she meant to do.

'This hall now,' she said: 'don't you think it's tremendously improved? Mr. Hibbert-Whitson did it--such *wonderful* taste. I'm determined that some day he will do the drawing-room, but Andy is *so* obstinate--' She looked across at her husband, pouting a little, prettily.

Jean Douglas's blue eyes flashed. 'But it would be sheer sacrilege,' she said. 'Who is this Hibbert-Whitson that he should be allowed to lay hands on the Rutherfurd drawing-room?'

'It was always a place of enchantment,' Alison Lockhart remarked soothingly. 'I can remember how even as a child it laid its spell on me. You wouldn't change it, Barbara.'

'Oh,' said Barbara, 'it isn't that I don't appreciate the beauty of the room; it's because I do that I want it made quite perfect.'

'And I,' said Andy, 'want it to remain as it is.'

'So now we know,' his wife laughed. '...Won't anybody have something more to eat? No more tea?--The cigarettes, Andy.'

'Let's go into the drawing-room,' Andy suggested. 'We haven't been sitting there lately, I don't know why.'

'We use it when we've people staying,' Barbara said, as she led the way. 'There's something a little eerie about it unless it's well peopled.'

It seemed to Alison Lockhart that as she entered the allurement enfolded her. She noticed how, by some queer trick of perspective, the room seemed to slope down towards each end as if the roof were a shallow arch so that the fireplace became the centre and shrine of it. It was the picture framed in the panelling above it that gave the room its peculiar quality, the picture of Elizabeth of Bohemia, called the Queen of Hearts.

As if drawn by an unseen hand they all gathered round the picture, and the eyes of the Queen of Hearts looked down on them, not commanding, rather beguiling.

Jean Douglas said softly, half to herself: 'Do you remember how Nicole used to kneel on this stool and repeat Wotton's lines,

'"You meaner beauties of the night,
        That poorly satisfy our eyes...
You common people of the skies,
        What are you when the moon shall rise?"'

'Yes,' said Andy.

'Why,' said Barbara, 'you didn't know Nicole when she was a child, Andy, how could you remember?'

'I couldn't, of course.'

'Well,' said Barbara, looking round, 'you see what I mean about the room--. This would all remain as it is, of course (that picture looks as if it needed cleaning), but Mr. Hibbert-Whitson thinks...'

But what that gentleman thought was obviously of no interest to her companions in spite of the polite attention they gave her, and Barbara dropped the subject, and seating herself on one of the old settees covered with faded Mortlake brocade, began a sprightly conversation about the doings of her neighbours.

Several matters were touched on, then she said: 'And Tilly Kilpatrick's giving a dance in December. It's for her pretty young cousin, Betty Beauchamp, who has been so much with her. There's a rumour that she may remain in this countryside--at Newby Place.'

'Probably spread by Tilly herself,' said Jean Douglas dryly. 'Why, John Dalrymple has belonged to Nicole since they were children.'

'But when a man is given no encouragement,' Barbara insisted, 'you can't blame him if he goes elsewhere.... And Betty is *very* young and *very* pretty.'

'Well,' said Alison Lockhart, 'I for one don't believe it. Loving Nicole is a whole-time job; something to lose youth for, to occupy age--' She stopped suddenly, looking rather startled, and asked: 'Did I say that myself?'

184

'Not quite,' said Andy, smiling. 'At least Robert Browning once said something rather like it. But, anyway, I don't think there's any truth in the rumour, for Dalrymple tells me he's letting Newby Place on a long lease.'

'*Oh!*' said Barbara, evidently thinking rapidly. 'Well--that may be rather a good thing if pleasant people take it. We do need some fresh blood in the county, and I must say I welcome changes.... I had a letter to-day from Aunt Jane describing Althea Gort's wedding. It seems to have been quite charming, and Nicole had taken no end of trouble. She is so good at that sort of thing. It looks as if Providence had cast her for the rôle of maiden aunt.'

She laughed as she said it, and Jean Douglas moved quickly away to the fireplace, that no one might see the hurt, angry tears that sprang to her eyes.

A maiden aunt, Nicole--while meaner beauties...! Half-remembered words came to her mind.... *There was a lady once, 'tis an old story, who would not be a queen, that would she not, for all the mud in Egypt.*

Realising that some one was beside her, she turned and found herself looking into Andy Jackson's eyes. He understood, she saw that.

Together they looked up at the pictured face above them, and Jean said: 'I wonder what she thought of life! She suffered, you can see that from her mouth, but I dare say she found things to make up.'

Andy nodded.

'Life,' said Jean, 'is full of compensations.'

Just then the door opened, and the nurse came in carrying the heir of Rutherfurd.

Barbara ran forward, prettily eager, and came back with him in her arms.

'Isn't he a great fellow?' she cried with pride.

The child, seeing his favourite playmate, held out his arms, and when Andy had taken him, he laid his fat, pink cheek lovingly against his father's lean brown one.

'Good little chap,' said Andy. 'Kind little chap.'

To Jean's annoyance tears again forced themselves to her eyes, while Alison Lockhart, turning to Barbara, said with a bright, congratulatory smile:

'How *like* the child is to his grandmother!'

185

Printed in the USA
CPSIA information can be obtained
at www.ICGtesting.com
LVHW050859021223
765467LV00048B/865